The Power of the Eight

Suzanne Rho

First paperback edition November 2021

Cover design by Cover Dungeon Rabbit
(www.coverdungeon.com)

Edited by Nick Hodgson

ISBN 978-1-7399736-0-5 (paperback)
ISBN 978-1-7399736-1-2 (ebook)

www.suzanne-rho.co.uk

For A, R, & K

When the sky goes dark, you are my stars.

The
POWER
of The
Eight

Caerisle

Loreleith

Caeracre

Arrik

Sanguine Sea

Shimmering
Vale

Village of Lira

Forest
of
Ververos

Ch—
Brook

Shim—

Longwatch

Axilion

Hidden City

Glendale

Endermarch

Scorespike

Pointe Sea

Five Years Ago...

Maps littered the car. She didn't know why. It was always maps. Some had been printed, others ripped from books and atlases. Close to fifty in the past five years alone. Each was covered, vandalised in the same way: with hand-drawn lines. Some scored out, others different colours.

The girl had stopped asking what they meant a long time ago.

The road was almost empty, and they overtook each vehicle they came to with ease. Though a part of her wanted to, the girl didn't dare look at the gauge on the dashboard. She knew what it read was too fast.

Asking the woman to slow down would be fruitless. Instead, the girl studied the woman's face. Framed by the wild, auburn waves the girl hadn't been blessed with, the woman's face was too lined to be considered young, yet not lined enough to be called old. In many ways, the face was a mirror.

In many more, an unopened box of secrets and lies.

They flew past the sign. Less than five miles from Inverness.

The girl wished she were brave enough to ask why there. Why *then?* Why *any* of whatever the hell *this* was.

She said nothing as the woman indicated, not left, where the road led into Inverness, but right.

Culloden, the girl read. More questions.

The woman's grip tightened on the steering wheel. "Say it again."

"I–"

"Say it again," the woman repeated. The words were slow, but the tone was seething. Anger, or frustration, or something else the girl couldn't place, dripped from them. "You can't forget it."

The girl swallowed. She knew the woman wasn't aware of how hard the girl's heart was beating, or how much she was certain that, if she wasn't wearing a seatbelt, she would be frozen in place anyway.

The girl's words were a shaky whisper. "*Còmhla mar aon.*" She glanced to the side, hands clasped together, trembling in her lap. She dared herself to look at the speed gauge, then dared herself not to. They were no longer on the road they had been, the one used to such speeding. This one was darker, winding this way and that. The kind a crash would be less likely to be found on.

The woman nodded once and raised her eyebrows.

The girl blinked, taking a breath that did nothing to keep the shake from her voice. "It's how we'll always find each other."

The car skidded as it turned. The girl stifled a scream; the woman ignored it. Theirs was the only car in the car park.

For a few long seconds, neither moved, nor spoke.

The woman's hands hadn't left the steering wheel. "Say it again."

"*Còmhla mar aon.*"

Part One

1

The expression he wore was equal parts weariness and disappointment.

It would have bothered her once. She turned her head from him, wishing she could turn from everything he represented.

"Renée?"

Ren tore her gaze from the nearby window, yawning. Beyond it, a young rowan tree was bent almost double as an unforgiving gust battered against it.

"Hm?"

Dr. Michele steeled his face and regarded her in a way that was neither warm nor cool. As impassive as the room, a generic beige affair, that the two occupied. "We agreed applying would be a positive step."

Ren looked down, her eyes roaming the grey carpet tiles. "I know."

"You had a plan for each outcome."

Ren swallowed dryly.

"Both of which you could prepare for." A soft *beep beep beep* signalled the end of the session. Dr. Michele ignored it. "Perhaps we could try something different, something less... *monumental.*"

She looked up then. "Like what?"

Dr. Michele regarded her over his blue, oval-rimmed spectacles. "Something that invokes a, shall we say, *mild* level of unease."

"Do something terrifying? Got it."

"What if, this week, you did something...spontaneous?"

"Something terrifying *and* unplanned. Sure."

Dr. Michele stood, chuckling. "How did the appointment go with the–" his brow momentarily wrinkled "–pulmonologist?" Each syllable was trailed through the air, slow and unsure.

"Endocrinologist," Ren corrected, hissing as she rose through a bolt of pain down the backs of her thighs.

"Ah yes, that was it." Dr. Michele had reached the door.

"I was discharged." The *again* hung in the air like a cloud of dust particles, almost non-existent. Almost.

Dr. Michele's head bowed as he grasped the handle. "I am sorry."

Ren shrugged, crossing the threshold into an unassuming off-white corridor. "I'm not," she lied.

"Mild level of unease," the psychiatrist repeated. If eyes could twinkle like stars, the deep navy of Dr. Michele's would resemble the night sky.

Ren shot him a small half smile. "See you next week."

The hallway led her to a cold waiting area, as beige and unassuming as Dr. Michele's room, littered with plastic chairs and blank expressions. In the corner, a silent news report was being displayed on a tiny television. *The long-haired Caucasian man*, the subtitles read, *is still evading capture by West London police.* The same story from the radio last week. The man was seen brandishing what several startled onlookers had cited as a *sizable sword* at a number of cars.

Bloody weirdo, Ren thought, making her way towards a set of double doors.

It was a short walk to the car park. Ren made it as fast as possible, which wasn't all that fast.

A distant rumble of thunder met her ears, and she squinted against a blustery gust of wind as an alarm rang from somewhere behind. Fire alarm, no doubt. Not wanting to be stuck behind a bunch of doctors and nurses and patients congregating at some assembly point, no doubt in that very car park, Ren threw her bag in the passenger seat and jabbed the key in the ignition.

It shouldn't have been a long journey from the hospital back to Ainhill, but after being stuck first at every red light she came to and then behind two tractors, what should have been a twenty-minute drive took Ren over an hour.

A sharp flash of lightning illuminated a dark and angry sky as she entered the village. Ren blinked. In that moment, the sky had lit up...and, she was almost certain, purple.

She hadn't the luxury of time to ponder it. Shaking herself, Ren grabbed her bag, lamenting the fact she should have been able to go home and shower and eat. But not now. She would be lucky not to be late.

Her dad would call it *an utter waste of a day.*

The roll of thunder above seemed to agree.

Pulling out a notebook, a small purple one she kept in her bag's front pocket, Ren flipped through the pages. Through list after list. She had filled each, at one point, with words and hope, before scoring out each point, one by one, every page the same.

Only two bullet points remained on her most recent list:

- Endocrinology – Dr. Kumar

- Psychology – Dr. Michele

Ren scribbled through both lines so hard the pen burst through the page.

The Pentland Hill Hoose sat halfway along the main street of Ainhill. Though main streets were usually bustling and full of life, theirs was considered *bustling* approximately zero days of the year and *full of life* whenever two cars were stuck behind a combine harvester. The hotel was the biggest building for miles.

One glance in her mirror showed how beneficial that shower would have been. And she had at least eight hours to go before she would tell herself, yet again, that she would have one, but would be too tired to do so.

Ren sighed, either in frustration or with a vague sense of hopelessness, and made her way to the hotel's big, green front door. More gusts joined her. The unforgiving wind had been battering the wee village for the better part of a month now. She was accompanied by another roll of thunder and a pain in each of her calf muscles.

An unmanned reception desk greeted her, as did two empty corridors. She took the left-hand one, sidestepping around the cluttered surface of scratched and stained wood. Another yawn escaped her at the sight of her peg.

Ren readied herself to push the door to her left when it opened anyway.

Two figures stood. The first offered Ren an expression that hung somewhere between a smile and a smirk; Ren never knew which. She had seen several managers come and go in her time there, but Gill had lasted longer than the others. *Some people in life*, her father liked to say, *we just don't gel with.* For Ren, Gill was one such person. The jumble of ginger frizz Gill called her hair was piled high atop her head, fixed in place with a neon yellow band. It matched a sunflower brooch she had affixed to the front of a too big, black suit jacket. The second was a man. Ren eyed him, before she caught sight of, not *him*, exactly, but the space just above his head.

Ren gaped, then scolded herself for gaping.

Then gaped again.

"No need to look quite so alarmed, Ren," Gill said. "You've probably seen more new starts than anyone else here."

It wasn't the fact he was new that was causing Ren's shoulders to prickle. Situated half a foot above this man's head was – a cloud? A cluster? A gathering? Of what appeared to be specks of light.

Fireflies.

They looked like fireflies.

"This is Ren," Gill continued, as though there was nothing at all out of the ordinary about him. "She's been here since the Stone Age, haven't you, Ren?" Gill snorted at her own joke. "Anything you need, she'll sort you out." The manager turned her attention to Ren. "Oh," she began, "I have a surprise for you." Ren's heart hammered hard, harder than it should. "I've put you on the rota for tomorrow." Being robbed of a day off was a terrible surprise, even by Gill's standards. A tiny plume of panic rose deep in Ren's stomach, though less than it would have a year ago. Perhaps she didn't give Dr. Michele enough credit. "And you can have Sunday off." Gill beamed. Ren didn't. "This is Shae," she added, gesturing vaguely in the man's direction before heading towards her favourite haunt, the reception desk.

Ren took a breath, repeating a silent, *it's fine,* and turned towards Shae. And the fireflies.

Even without the luminous gathering above him, he would have looked somewhat out of place. She gathered he was around his early twenties, like her. And he was handsome, his long, dark face all cheekbones and angles; black hair cropped precise and symmetrical. What little facial hair he kept was just as meticulous. While Ren pulled her spare shirt, no longer black but a dull grey from too many washes, over her camisole, the newcomer donned a satin waistcoat.

She found herself blinking at him again and made herself speak. "Hi."

"Pleasure to meet you." He had an accent she couldn't quite place: English, better spoken than she was.

Again, Ren's mouth opened just before the door behind Shae did. A stocky figure emerged, taller than Ren only due to the chef's hat wobbling atop a mop of blond curls. Half a frozen cow was tucked under one arm, a string of sausages wrapped around the other.

Interrogating the newbie would have to wait.

"Hi," Ren said, feigning normalcy. She'd been holding onto the illusion that Gill really was that inattentive, and perhaps simply hadn't noticed the fireflies congregating above Shae's head. But Joe was a man who prided himself on paying the most meticulous detail to his dishes. He noticed everything.

"All right, gorgeous," Joe replied with a wink. "Weather's still barmy, eh?"

Ren nodded.

"Seen Gill anywhere?"

Ren inclined her head towards the reception desk.

Joe's eyebrows shot upwards. "Shocking," he muttered, shifting the cow as he headed through.

A clock nearby showed it was closing in on ten past four. Ren, and this Shae, she supposed, should have been behind the bar ten minutes ago.

"So," Ren began, determined to keep her voice somewhere in the vicinity of *normal*. Gill hadn't given her any instruction as to what she was supposed to train this mysterious newcomer in. Unsurprising. "Did Gill show you around?"

"Not entirely."

"Of course she bloody didn't," Ren replied. It earned her a soft smile. "Well, this is where we leave our coats, bags, that sort of thing. Through here," she said, leading the man through the nearby door, "as I imagine you'll have gathered, is the kitchen."

Pretending she had no more pressing matters on her hands than a lengthy shift ahead proved easy. Though they were permanently floating above him, she didn't pay the fireflies too much attention – except for the few times she caught herself staring at them, and a slight feeling of unease settled within her.

If it fazed Shae, he didn't let on. Each time he caught her staring, he gave her a soft, yet somehow knowing, smile. As though he knew the punchline of a joke she hadn't yet told him.

Yet, it was Shae himself who proved enough of a distraction from both the endocrinology appointment she had attended that morning, which had been over in far less time than she had spent waiting for it to begin, and the session with Dr. Michele. She didn't want to think of it, or the odd little homework assignment he'd set her. Each session ended the same, with a challenge. She had failed last week's: to fill in the application for the hospitality course that would have, were she accepted, seen Ren move away – a few hours, give or take traffic – to study at the nearby college.

She'd sat down with the application four times. Then she'd scrunched it up.

A crumpled ball, but still less of a mess than Ren.

Each time her mind wandered to that week's task, Ren – hellbent on ignoring Dr. Michele's *mild level of unease* that had etched itself into her mind and was, ironically, making her uneasy – pulled her attention back to Shae. If a tad aloof, he seemed pleased at any opportunity to discuss himself.

Four hours into the shift, Ren had learnt that Shae possessed an almost eidetic memory, had read over seven hundred books, and was ambidextrous. His last relationship had ended when his boyfriend, Doran, had upped and left in the middle of the night, and now Shae spent most of his time with his best friend whose name Ren couldn't remember.

He was, though, reluctant to disclose where he lived, where he had grown up, and how he had come to work in her tiny village.

She had been showing him the intricacies of placing a fresh bottle of vodka onto a rather stubborn optic when he halted, bottle poised between his palms, eyes fixed to the clock that hung above the long shelf of the older whiskies. It was shaped like a deer's head and painted a bright cobalt. Ren had always thought it a bit of an eyesore.

"That clock," Shae muttered, the ever-so-slight twitch in his brow Ren's only indication he was less than pleased, "is two and a half minutes slow."

"Oh." Ren blinked. "Is it?"

"Mm." He pulled his gaze from the timepiece. "I collect vintage clocks."

"Uh, do you?"

"Mm." His forehead was once again smooth. "Ones built between the fourteenth century and the seventeenth."

"That's very specific."

"I have over forty."

"Oh." Ren tried to imagine that many clocks covering her living room. "In your house?"

Shae turned his attention back to the vodka. "I have a room specifically for them."

A room solely for clocks. She tried to imagine having such a vast assemblage of anything.

All Ren managed to collect were ailments.

Shae, having deposited the vodka in its new, upside down position, paused, then asked, "Do you enjoy mushrooms?"

How random. "A-as in hallucinogenic, or go pretty well in an omelette?"

"Omelette," Shae repeated the word as though it were foreign. Which, Ren reasoned, it could be. Though it wasn't as if an omelette was classed as some exotic food. Once again, the slightest hint of a frown crossed his otherwise impassive features. "I...do not mean hallucinogenic."

"Then yes," Ren replied. "I like mushrooms."

Shae inclined his head. "That's good."

Ren opened her mouth to ask why, when it became suddenly dry at the appearance of one particular customer.

The hotel's clientele was composed almost entirely of the same regulars Ren served nearly every shift. Ren had known many of them her entire life and, on the whole, she liked them.

Most of them.

She cursed herself for seeking him out, the him in question being a geography teacher named Mike.

He didn't so much as glance in her direction, instead directing his custom towards Shae. It stung more than it should have.

"Ren?" Shae asked by the till, his eyes flickering between the various coins Mike had deposited in his hand. He held a silver hexagon aloft. "This one is worth fifty?" It wasn't the first time that evening he had struggled with money.

Ren nodded, too distracted to wonder again why currency seemed to confuse him.

Once finished, he positioned himself by her side. "Do you wish to speak about it?"

Ren had to work on her subtlety.

She sighed, and a pain rose in her chest. "His name is Mike." Ren wasn't sure why she was answering the question. Loneliness, possibly. Secrets, as fun as they often were, tended to be lonely things. Ren knew that now. "He...it...it's complicated."

It wasn't a lie.

Ren held out the keys. "And front door," she explained, her voice louder now they were outside. The wind always howled louder in the dark. "I'll just set the alarm, and that's us finish–" Ren's fist clamped to the centre of her chest, and she grimaced against the strange sensation.

"Are you okay?"

It was a simple question with a not-so-simple answer. Ren had no idea whether or not she was okay. Usually, the answer was *no*.

This, though…. Ren swallowed. It differed from any of her usual ailments; as though a wind tunnel had opened up and burrowed itself within her, *through* her. A fairly new symptom. Accompanied by a deep, almost *primal* confusion that Ren both couldn't explain and tried to ignore.

"Mm."

The sensation was dull. She looked up again. Shae's fireflies were vivid against the sharp, midnight backdrop. She watched them, lips pursed. The strange cloud remained there, bright against a starless night.

He was fastening some sort of cloak. Black, patterned with silvery dots. It billowed with his movements. Ren watched it, then realised he was watching her, his dark features impassive.

"I…" Really, she had to just come out with it. "I don't know why, but I can see these *things* above your head, and…" She trailed off.

She waited for a look not dissimilar from the one she regularly threw at Gill. She hadn't expected him to incline his head, a faraway smile dancing across his lips. Nor had she expected him to laugh. It was a brief chuckle, but it irked her. Who was he to laugh?

His gaze flickered upwards, mirroring hers. "Speak for

yourself." He turned on his heel. "Goodnight, Ren."

He didn't turn back.

Ren didn't follow. Instead, she remained there. The only parts of her not stock still were the hairs the wind whipped around her head.

She looked up.

Shae's fireflies were white, *so* white that it must hurt to stare at them for any length of time. And they were still, moving only when he did.

Ren's were also white.

Though hers were a different white. A *softer* white.

They were also moving.

Ren woke, as she so often did, unrefreshed. Having slept for eight and a half hours, she probably shouldn't still feel exhausted. Then again, at the ripe old age of twenty, her limbs probably shouldn't ache from such intense muscle spasms.

And yet they did. Every day.

With a good few hours before she was due at the hotel, Ren, wrapped in a dressing gown, once a duck egg blue, now a muted grey, deposited herself on her spot on the couch.

The front room smelt of furniture polish and sounded like a stadium. It was empty, save for Ren's father. John stood in the centre, still in his pyjamas – ones more aged than Ren's gown – singing into his half-drunk mug of tea. He shot her the same wink he always did. Ren smiled, trying to keep the obvious discomfort from her face.

She wasn't successful.

"Don't turn it down on my account," she said.

John didn't appear to be listening as he lowered the stereo's volume. "Your mum loved this song."

Ren swallowed hard and looked down. She didn't like to think of things her mum loved.

"You need to rest," John said.

"Can't." Ren pulled a cushion to her chest, hugging it. Her eyes flickered down to the aged grey carpet. "Working soon."

She knew his expression without looking. "You should phone in. That Gill will have to find cover."

Ren nearly laughed aloud. Gill wouldn't have the faintest idea how to arrange cover.

"Or she could cover you herself," John was saying.

At that, Ren did laugh. "I'm fine," she lied. "I'm training a new start anyway; he can do all the heavy lifting."

Deep frown lines ran across John's forehead. "Dare I ask how it went with the consultant?"

Ren shrugged. "Discharged."

"*Again?*"

"Yep." She wished it stung less.

"Maybe you're just an awful patient," a voice offered unhelpfully from the other doorway.

Ren's eyes snapped to Luke, the only one of the trio who was dressed. Ren's nose wrinkled at the sight of her brother's filthy rugby uniform.

"That must be it." She caught the pancake he flung at her. It was still warm.

She didn't miss the brief, shared glance between John and Luke. "And," her father began, "your psychiatrist?"

Ren shrugged. "He thinks I need to do more things that make me uncomfortable."

The sofa sagged beside her as Luke sat. "He's clearly never seen the state of some of the locals you need to serve."

Ren's fingertips tugged at a rogue thread. She might have been tempted to stay home and mope. It's what she might have done in the past. As much as she had asked Gill not to change her shifts at short notice, Gill continued to do so. Only Dr. Michele – and Gill – thought it a good thing. *Tolerable discomforts*, or *things Ren can't control but, ultimately, can deal with,* were, according to the psychiatrist, a good thing for Ren.

Ren disagreed.

But phoning in wasn't an option, not while the cloud of

whatever it was hovered above her head, visible only whenever she dared a glance upward.

Shae's fireflies didn't move, but Ren's did. They swayed, this way and that; dancing without music. That meant his were a different *type* to hers, didn't it?

She wondered for the umpteenth time what they were.

And what they meant.

John was waiting by the door, buttoning his trusty denim jacket. It was as faded as his pyjamas, and he wore it every week. While Saturday mornings were for impromptu, living room karaoke sessions, the evenings were for pints of lager, too expensive bags of peanuts, and sharing the same anecdotes with the same middle-aged men week in, week out. To another, it would no doubt sound a monotonous existence, but Ren knew John liked the humdrum of it.

Ren told herself she did, too.

Luke, though, craved more. He had let anyone willing to listen know almost from the moment he could talk. He had begun to craft the path to becoming the doctor he had envisioned himself as years ago.

Meanwhile, Ren remained a part-time barmaid.

One quick glance in the hall mirror and Ren wished she hadn't. The circles round her ocean blue eyes were so dark they looked like shadows. The fireflies didn't have a reflection.

She turned to John. "You ready?"

"Aye. You'd better take a coat, it's to be chilly tonight."

Ren gathered her keys. "Coats are for the weak."

Shaking his head, John stepped outside. "You'll be the one freezing to death at midnight." A practised statement they both knew held little weight. Ren was never too cold.

She spotted the familiar figure as they pulled onto the main road – as familiar as a figure can be when you've only known said figure for a day. His cloak was billowing again. Strange, considering there wasn't a whole lot of wind...for once.

His fireflies were a cloud of glitter in the late afternoon light. Ren passed off the sharp intake of air as a hasty need for a coughing fit.

"You're quiet tonight," her father observed.

He wasn't wrong. Anticipation had seeped into every part of her mind, leaving little room for conversation starters. Ren's foot twitched as the unknown conversation with Shae that awaited her gripped her with a tingly nervousness.

"What's that thing you say," Ren asked, "about turning the key?"

"You can examine the engine 'til you're blue in the face," John replied, chuckling, "but sometimes you just gotta get in an' turn the damn key."

"Yeah." Ren smiled softly as she turned her own, real, key backwards. The engine died. "Turn the damn key."

Inside, Gill was playing Solitaire on the reception computer. She didn't notice Ren, which was fine. Ren shimmied past, to the left.

John continued forward, to the bar's front entrance.

Shae's cloak was hanging next to Joe's parka. Ren stared at it – it was oddly bulky up close – and steeled herself.

She found him in the kitchen, leading Kirstin the pot washer in a rather enthusiastic Charleston-like dance. The corners of Ren's mouth rose despite herself. Shae had a natural affinity with people, especially for someone who seemed to possess no more than three expressions - indifference, mild knowing, and a small frown of confusion he had so far only reserved for when dealing with money.

Kirstin looked equal parts out of breath and disappointed when they stopped.

"Are you okay?" he asked as the pair headed to the bar.

"I've been better." She shot a look upwards, her gaze resting momentarily on the bright, brilliant white of his fireflies. One or two and she would have certainly overlooked them, they were that small, the size of toast crumbs; but there had to be at least a hundred of them. "I need..." What she needed, Ren wasn't sure. "Answers," she hissed.

He surveyed her face, his own face blank. "I know." *That* took her aback. "Later."

"Forgive me."

Ren blinked. Shae was watching her, eyebrows pulled ever so slightly inwards. How long had she been staring into the middle distance?

He continued, "You don't look well."

Nothing new there then.

"I never look well."

The door swung open, revealing two figures, Mike being one.

Ren sucked in a long breath, wishing her heartbeat hadn't increased. It was no longer his place to elicit any such reaction in her.

She was saved an interaction as Shae positioned himself to be the one to serve him. Most intuitive.

She should get used to seeing Mike, really. That would be the sensible thing to do. They lived in a tiny village, and Ren was present, several evenings a week when she was well enough, in the only pub within five miles. Of course she was going to see him. At least the bar was getting busier, which would make it easy to ignore him.

He didn't have to wear that same shirt, though, Ren thought. It was a petty complaint she ought to be above making.

The door opened again. A face appeared, the type that wasn't plagued by Ren's dark circles and blotchy complexion. The woman's hair fell in close-curled blonde ringlets. Katrina.

Ren's stomach lurched.

She was everything Ren wasn't and had everything Ren didn't. And she didn't usually bother joining Mike in the pub.

Ren shouldn't, and yet she still sought out Mike. He was watching her, his expression relaying one thing: *Act. Fucking. Normal.*

"Any reason," Shae asked lowly, "why he's staring at you like that?" The corners of his mouth were tugged upwards, only a little, at the round of applause he had received for pouring – and, possibly, creating – a violet-coloured cocktail.

"Oh, there's a big reason why."

Shae, now examining the till, clearly lost with what to charge for his newfound creation, muttered, "Are you okay?"

It was a dangerous conversation to have.

She had no right to be anything but okay. Punching in each of the many drinks Shae had utilised in his mixing, Ren replied, "Not really,"

The curly-haired woman, Katrina, walked towards the throng of punters, making a beeline for Mike as Ren and Shae turned to the front.

"Is he with *her* now?" Shae asked.

Not exactly.

Ren sighed, hoping Shae had it in him to be as non-judge-mental as she could hope for.

"He's been married to her for about ten years."

"Ah."

If this changed Shae's opinion of her, he didn't let it show.

He carried on, making sure he was the one to serve either Mike or Katrina, and spent the rest of his time asking Ren about Ren. Which was strange, though quite nice. She couldn't remember the last person who had.

She spent more time than she ought to watching Shae.

The man made pouring the same drinks Ren had been making for two years look like an art form. His smile, the few times he chose to showcase it, was catching. A natural sashay was present in each step he took. Yet, that aloofness remained in his demeanour. His expression was an almost constant blankness, unfazed by his continuing struggles when it came to counting money, or by a huge influx of orders. Ren, who knew the job well enough to do it in her sleep, still found herself flustered, her face growing hot as she fumbled in the busier moments. Yet Shae never fumbled. The man was as serene as a meditating monk.

"Night," *hic,* "Ren."

"Night, Bill." Ren replied as she waited for Bill, who had a rather dangerous sway in his step, to vacate the heavy front door she was holding open.

He stopped a step away from the threshold. "Your mum would've been proud."

A chilly gust blew, first through the hallway, then right through her. Ren turned to face Shae, fighting to keep her face as placid as his.

There it was again, that tiny hint of a frown.

"Everything all right?" she asked, hobbling to a nearby couch in front of the almost dead fire. It was easier to ignore pain, both physical and otherwise, when the place was busy and loud. The silence of the now empty pub rang through both her and her seizing muscles. So did Bill's words.

Shae claimed the shabby dark brown chair opposite. "Are you hurt?"

"I'm...always hurt, sort of."

"Oh?"

"I don't know why; no one does. I've been a medical anomaly for years." *Five years.* She paused. "It's not as exciting as it sounds."

Shae smiled his soft smile. "I am sorry."

Ren only shrugged as she ran a hand up and down her thigh. It didn't help. Not much did.

"What if you didn't have to?" he asked. She resisted the urge to scoff. Ren had spent a lot of the past half a decade wondering the same thing. He looked upwards, the same way she had several times since they'd sat down. "Deal with it, I mean."

Where he was going with this, Ren didn't know. She sought out his fireflies.

"Do you want a drink?" She began to rise with difficulty, though halted as Shae raised a hand.

"Allow me."

She shot him a grateful smile. "A beer, ta."

She heard various types of clinking before a glass bottle appeared in front of her nose. He had made himself what looked like a vodka martini.

"Thanks."

They drank in silence.

He gazed at nothing, whether waiting for her lead or not.

"Okay." Ren swallowed. "Do you feel like enlightening me on anything..." Her eyes were fixed on the cloud of fireflies above his head.

His own face gave nothing away except its usual reticence. "What, exactly, would you like to be enlightened about?"

Ren frowned. "There's more than one thing?"

"Yes."

A screech of wind passed the dark window. Three of the outdoor picnic-style tables were flung onto their sides.

"Woah." Ren squinted, but made out only their reflections. "This weather is crazy. There was a reporter here last week. It's been like this for weeks now."

"Twenty-eight days," Shae replied with a nod.

"That's...specific."

If Shae replied, Ren didn't hear him. Only a second before, the fireplace had been dark, the embers all but burnt out. Ren's head whirled around. The hearth was wreathed in darkness.

A lone cracking, so loud she flinched, rang out. A second spark, this one bigger, flew into the chimney with a soft *whoosh.*

Within seconds, the fire was re-lit. Ren's mouth fell open.

Another *whoosh*, though silent, and not within the hearth this time. Ren thrust a palm to her chest. She might have cried out as a red-hot inferno blazed through her like a dagger. Though daggers were supposed to hurt. Fire was, too.

This fire coursed and raged, right in the centre of her chest. A heat like no other barrelled against her, through her, all around. Flames licked her arms and chest and neck. Both Shae and the pub were thrust into a gloomy darkness, until Ren saw nothing but that coursing red eclipsing all else.

A struck match. A torrent of bonfire. The midday sun in the height of summer. The flicker of a single candle; the rage of a forest fire. Anger. Power. Red and gold and every shade of orange in between. The cracking of expanding wood and the following burst of red sparks and the glare from an enkindled log within a wrought iron fireplace.

It tore through her in an all-encompassing confusion.

And then it disappeared, snuffed out, leaving nothing but a lingering ghostly plume of smoke. Ren, all wide stare and hard breathing, stared into the flames in the hearth. They were roaring as though someone had stroked them. And yet no one had.

Until he cleared his throat, she had forgotten all about Shae. Breathing still laborious and awkward, she turned to him.

"Sh-shae?"

His face was set, once again, into a frown. "Yes?"

"Either I just experienced some *very* strong heartburn, or..."

He leant forward; impossible flames dancing in his dark eyes. "Ren?"

She didn't reply, determined to ignore both her heartbeat, pounding against her eardrums, and the scent of something charred she was certain hadn't been in the air a moment before.

"Look up," Shae instructed.

Any small part of her that wanted to look up in that moment was drowned out almost entirely by the many, many parts of her that didn't. The unknown wasn't something Ren relished, not anymore. She turned her face upwards.

If breathing wasn't already arduous, she would have gasped.

Her gaze darted back towards the strange man opposite, meeting his..

"This isn't the first time you've felt something similar." It wasn't a question.

Ren shook her head. "I felt...well, I don't know what I felt. It was like *wind*, a kind of gust of wind, here." Not for the first time that evening, Ren's fist met the centre of her chest. "It was a few weeks ago, I-I think, I'm not..."

"It was twenty-eight days ago."

A string of days and numbers whizzed around her mind. He was right. It had begun on her birthday.

A bush was still scraping against the window pane. Ren forced her gaze upwards again. The white fireflies were still there, moving back and forth, back and forth, in a rhythm. Almost as though they were...blowing. Like wind.

And then there were the other ones. The new ones. The *red* ones. They moved, too. Though their pattern was different. They sparked upwards.

Just like fire.

Shae had made her go home shortly after *the fire incident*, having explained nothing other than that she needed to rest.

He had stressed the point vehemently.

As much as she had wished to argue, an all-consuming tiredness came over her, eclipsing even the pain.

She had felt something similar only once. A month ago, Ren had taken nearly a week off work; she had slept like the dead for the majority of it.

This time was no different. She had arrived home eighteen hours prior, struggling to keep her eyes open to the point she definitely shouldn't have driven, and fallen into a sleep she suspected was akin to a coma.

Yet, with the weakness in her aching muscles and the fuzzy way her brain was jumbling any thoughts, she might as well have not slept at all.

Ren yawned. The view in the small crack in her curtains showed an already night-time sky. She had slept all day.

Thank goodness for days off.

Her nails dug into her palm as her thoughts turned to Shae.

How she was supposed to get in touch with him to obtain any answers was unclear. During the two shifts she had spent with him he hadn't so much as glanced at a phone and when asked where he was staying, his answer was a vague *around*.

She was beginning to make a mental list documenting the oddities of Shae's personality when a short rap on her door demanded her attention. Luke's knock.

The door opened and her brother's face appeared. "Dad wanted me to check you're still alive." He frowned. "*Christ*, have you put the heating on in here?"

Ren sat up with difficulty. The pains in her thighs were back. "What? No."

"It's like an oven."

"Is it?"

"You're so weird. Anyway, some guy came to the door for you a few hours ago." That got her attention. Ren hadn't exactly been spoilt for friends of late. "Weird-looking bloke, wearing a cape."

"What did he say?"

"It was covered in glitter or something."

"What did he *say*?"

"He'd be waiting for you in the cafe tomorrow morning, if you were up for it."

Ren swallowed hard. "Tomorrow." She could deal with that, as much as the familiar not-quite-sick feeling rose in her chest. She had to.

For answers, if nothing else.

She was filled with equal parts nervousness and relief.

"Yeah. Around nine, he said. I offered to wake you up but he said not to."

"Oh." Ren wondered why.

"You want something to eat?"

Who knew when she'd last eaten. "No, thanks."

Luke nodded, but the expression on his round face hardened. He momentarily vanished behind the still ajar door and reappeared no longer wearing the navy jumper he had been seconds ago. He threw the garment onto the bed and left.

The corners of Ren's mouth turned up at the gesture; the

never acknowledged pact between the two.

Pulling the jumper over her head, unaffected by the heat of the room, Ren sank her head back onto her pillow.

The wait was cut shorter still – in Ren's mind anyway. After her eighteen-hour snooze, she proceeded to pass out for another fourteen and a half.

Her father was staring at her, a half-eaten piece of toast hanging from his fingertips the following morning. "That's not normal."

She pulled her still-damp-from-the-shower hair into a ponytail. "I know."

"I really think you should see a doctor."

He was probably right.

"I will. I'll phone tomorrow."

John nodded. "Make sure you do. How are you feeling?"

Ren grabbed her keys. "Good, yeah...better." Lies. She probably felt worse. Standing, she offered him as large a smile as she could muster. "See you later."

"See you," he repeated, his attention once again on his toast.

Ainhill had only one cafe, named after a woman called Doris, who nobody alive in Ren's lifetime had ever known. Ren really should have walked, for the place wasn't half a mile from her house, but with each step to her car bursts of pain radiated from her thighs downwards. More stabbed her wrists and back. By the time she was sat in the sanctity of her front seat, door banged shut beside her, her palm was pressed to her mouth. The cuffs of Luke's jumper pulled down to cover most of her fingers. Silent tears tracked their way down her cheeks, dotting the blue fabric.

She looked up. Two sets of fireflies, one white and one red, danced in the space between her head and the ceiling. In her mirror lay nothing. Ren readied herself, one forced breath at a time, and turned on the engine.

Go meet Shae, she told herself. *At least something will make sense.*

She hoped.

He was waiting, full Scottish breakfast in front of him, spearing a mushroom with enthusiasm as she approached. Beside his plate lay several maps. Some local, others featuring various parts of Britain. Across each he had drawn several straight lines going in various directions. The sight of them jolted her for reasons far beyond the strange man in the familiar cafe.

Her mouth was dry as she sat.

She had always thought the tearoom was oddly decorated. The walls were a bright, azure blue that clashed rather spectacularly with the rest of the decor, primarily several black and white photographs of the village. A large stuffed stag's head was mounted above the counter. Shae kept glancing towards it.

"Is taxidermy not common where you come from?" Ren asked, keeping her voice light.

Not light enough, evidently, given the ever-knowing look he shot at her. *Subtlety, Ren.*

"Yes, actually. Probably more so. Though we don't tend to refer to it as *that.*"

"Taxidermy?"

"Bless you." He shot her a vague not quite smile.

Ren sat, her hands fumbling with the menu she had extraordinarily little desire to read.

Shae swallowed, inclining his head towards the short, laminated list. "Ah, you're eating. That's good."

Wrinkling her nose, noting for the first time the distinct scent of grease that hung in the air, Ren set down the menu. "I'm not, actually."

Shae's eyebrows shot upwards. "Yes, you are." In a movement that wouldn't have looked out of place were Shae a member of the royal family, he raised one arm in the air and clicked his fingers.

Ren narrowed her eyes.

"Hi, Ren." A waitress appeared by their side. "How's your dad?"

"He, uh...good, thanks. I-I'm not having anything, though–"

"Yes, she is; she'll have the same as me," Shae said.

Ren opened her mouth, twice, each time closing it. The smell was getting stronger.

Shae was watching her as the waitress walked away. "You need to eat."

"I'm not hungry."

"I know." His tone, while pointed, was kind. "That's why someone has to make you."

"Why?"

"You haven't eaten properly in days."

"And you know that how, exactly?"

He didn't reply. Instead, he smiled the same, soft smile she'd now seen at least a dozen times as a mug of tea was deposited in front of her. "You've rested? Your brother said..." he trailed off, munching on a piece of toast.

Ren was probably the most rested person in Scotland. "You could say that."

"Good." He nodded. "That's good."

Ren didn't know why that was good. "Right," she began, voice low, "I'm going to need you to tell me whatever the hell it is you know...about me...or these." She gestured upward.

Two words. "Not here."

If Ren had sat through a longer breakfast, she couldn't remember it. She spent the entirety of it looking anxiously between the door and Shae's maps, a prickling crossing her shoulders. As though danger somehow lingered, awaiting her outside Doris's yellowing net curtains.

She ate what she could despite her lack of appetite. The food tasted strange, *wrong*, somehow. It wasn't the only thing that felt that way. She didn't realise how much she was fidgeting until Shae told her to calm down.

He insisted she pay, though with his money. Ren couldn't deduce why money flummoxed him so much. He handed her a small wad of cash from a velvety drawstring purse. Ren eyed the purse. And the cash. There was a lot of it.

The man was an enigma.

An enigma wrapped in a velvet waistcoat with a penchant for vodka martinis.

Most people in the village were open books. Shae was a book that was bound closed, chained shut, and flung into the sea. He remained stoic, aloof. His face wore the same impassivity. Ren wondered if anyone truly knew the man who was folding each of his many maps with care and depositing them somewhere inside his cloak.

They headed to Ren's car...and hopefully towards something in the way of an answer.

An unspoken agreement passed between the pair inside the vehicle. Shae's *Not here* extended to Doris's small, cobbled car park. Ren's hands gripped the steering wheel tighter than they usually would. A small plume of smoke – so small it took her a second to notice it – rose from the black leather beneath her palm. Ren let go with a gasp. Where her hand had been only a moment before, there lay a tiny scorch mark in the leather. Her stomach flip-flopped at the sight.

It took Shae a good five times to click his seatbelt into place, his eyes betraying him for once. They were wide as they combed the dashboard. He then examined an ice scraper with such interest it might have been an artifact from another planet.

Perhaps it was. The possibility Shae was an alien seemed more likely the more she pondered it.

"What is this?"

Her words were dryer than intended. "An ice scraper."

She couldn't see his expression, but Shae's reply was full of amusement. "You *scrape* ice? With this?"

"If I want to see out of my windscreen on a freezing day, yeah."

"Fascinating."

Ren failed to see how.

She knew where to take them, where they wouldn't be disturbed.

It was a place that had seen a number of Ren's firsts: kiss... fight...taste of alcohol...time having sex – though she'd sworn soon after to lock *that* memory away forever.

Far enough from home for her and her friends' inhibitions to dampen more than they should have, yet still close enough to feel the safety of the place they would never admit to still needing. It was little more than a small copse, and not once had it changed in her twenty years.

Shae's knuckles paled as Ren drove.

The silence that fell the moment she stopped the car seemed to ring through her. Long seconds passed. Shae spoke first, though he looked lost in thought while Ren tried to ignore the way his knuckles were only then returning to their normal colouring. She didn't miss the relief in his voice.

"Are you sure?" he asked softly.

"No." Though she doubted she had a choice. "But there's a reason for all of this, you being here, and..." She gestured between them. The branches of a nearby tree were blowing wildly.

"Yes, there is."

"None of it is coincidence."

"It could be argued that nothing is ever coincidence."

"Right. But *these* things in particular."

Shae exhaled a long breath. "There are things that make you different here, aren't there?"

What? Ren blinked. "I don't think so."

"It's cold today," Shae said randomly, "especially with this wind."

"Uh...yeah, it is."

"You wear only that jumper."

Shrugging, Ren tracked a small skein of geese above a nearby hill, wondering vaguely how they managed to fly in such weather. "I don't really feel cold."

"Do you feel heat?"

"I suppose not." Her teeth were gritted together, and she bit down on her lip. Hard.

"Have you noticed how this wind is...*stronger*, wherever you are?"

"Don't be ridiculous." Ren scraped a hand through her hair. Her face tingled. Shae was talking nonsense, despite the fact the first night the wind appeared their whole fence had blown down.

"Ren?"

"Hmm?"

"You've gone very pale."

"I'm always pale," she said through a yawn.

"Are you okay?"

No. "I-I don't know what any of this is supposed to mean."

"I know, but I do."

The geese had disappeared. In their place, Ren turned her attention to a nearby sheep. "What are they?" she asked.

"Hm?"

"The fireflies."

"Fireflies?"

She pointed first to his, then her own, gaze still on the sheep.

"Ah," Shae began, "I know them by a different name."

For the first time, Ren turned her head, needing, somehow, to see his face. In the late morning light his eyes were the colour of tree bark, though flecked with other hues. Honey... acorns...freshly tilled earth. Ren swallowed as his mouth opened.

"*That* is your taio."

If he had expected something in the way of recognition, he was no doubt disappointed. Ren only stared at him in silence. It was broken after several long moments by a lowly *baa*.

"Tye-ohs," Ren said.

"Tai*o*, singular."

"Right. And *what*, exactly, is a *taio*?"

"A physical manifestation of one's magic," he replied.

For someone who never felt too hot, Ren was feeling the need to open a window. She searched, though, for what she didn't know. The only thing of note was the sheep. It continued to *baa* unhelpfully.

Magic. How ridiculous.

"A ph-physical manifest–"

"Magic, yes."

Ren closed her eyes. Perhaps when she opened them she would be back in her bed, the health issues of an eighty-year-old and the anxiety of a trauma-riddled veteran the only things setting her apart from everyone she knew. The new barman she was certain they hadn't even been looking for wouldn't be sitting in her passenger seat and instead be a figment of the fever dream this no doubt was.

A physical manifestation of one's magic.

The fever dream theory seemed the most plausible.

Or the alien one.

"And," Ren began, opening her eyes to reveal not her bedroom but her dashboard, "we're the only two people I've ever seen with one because…" She trailed off, ignoring the squeaky undertone now present in her voice.

"They're fairly common where I'm from. Well, *mine* is. Yours used to be."

"Mine?"

He nodded. "Mm. You're an elemental."

"A what?"

"Someone who can manipulate natural magic. Or, *NáDarra.*"

"Excuse you?" Ren scoffed. "Magic doesn't exist."

Shae cleared his throat. "Of course it exists."

"An elemental," Ren repeated, every fibre of her doubtful.

"A *weaver* elemental, at that. Powerful," he added. "I'm what's known as an arcanist."

"And where you're from, that's a sentence that makes sense, is it?"

"Yes."

"This is the part where you confess to being an alien, isn't it?"

He snorted. "I'm not quite an alien, no."

"That is precisely what an alien would say, Shae."

He wasn't listening, his hands digging in a number of different pockets concealed within his cloak. She imagined something akin to a magic wand and then wondered why she was indulging such a delusion. Instead, what he brought forth was less of a wand and more of a rock. How anticlimactic.

She inclined her head towards it. "What is that?" Perhaps it was a stress ball. Ren could use one of those. Or a vodka.

"It's called a *scrystone*."

Perhaps not.

"Oh, of course," Ren muttered. "A *scrystone*. I should have known."

Shae ignored her interruption. "There are different types. *This* type –" he held the stone in an upturned palm; it was covered in odd squiggles, "is part of a pair. You can only communicate with the other in that pair."

"A phone too high-tech?"

"Something like that."

Shae raised the rock to his mouth. And, as if it were a spherical, grey walky-talky, he spoke into it.

"Lance?"

Silence followed. Why was she surprised?

"Lance," Shae repeated, "stop being childish."

Who, or what, this Lance happened to be, did not relish being called childish.

The rock, the *scrystone*, glowed a light blue.

"I've been calling you for *days*," a voice, a sulky one at that, said.

Shae rolled his eyes. "I know."

"Stop rolling your eyes," the voice in the rock snapped.

In spite of herself and her current, far from normal, circumstance, Ren let out a small snort.

"I've had a terrible time of it, in case you were interested."

Whatever was going on, Ren understood none of it. She was supposedly a *weaver elemental*, whatever that was supposed to mean, who was now hearing voices from rocks.

Surely that was an elaborate way of stating she was mad.

Shae glanced at Ren, his eyebrows having shot upwards. He ignored Lance's words. "Do you know where you are?"

Lance, resentment seemingly gone, said, "I'm near a beach, on some grassy field or something. It's green, but *really* green. There's all these little flags on these strange posts. It's quite nice," he added, as though he were checking out a holiday park.

"We're coming to you."

They were *what*?

"We?"

"Yes."

Ren, who needed at least a week of planning to enter a supermarket, was not about to drive this man, who she barely knew, to meet whoever this other man was with no notice. Absolutely not. Shae would just have to hop on a bus. And yet...

Her gaze rose upwards.

A physical manifestation of one's magic.

The rock spoke again. "Is she *with* you now?"

Ren, frowning as her thoughts whizzed and raced, each conflicting with the last, rubbed her shoulders. A prickling had begun to spread over her entire body. No, not a pricking – a *buzzing* against her skin. It was somehow both slight and yet also so present, so *deliberate*.

Shae held the stone towards her. Ren glanced at it with a mixture of suspicion and intrigue. "Uh, hello."

"Hello." Lance's tone was less dry than it had been with Shae. "It's nice to meet you."

"I look better in person; less stone-like."

He let out a chuckle, a carefree noise that felt out of place. And yet didn't. "So do I."

Shooting Shae a sideways glance, Ren, still buzzing, reached for her keys. What the hell was she doing? A voice, neither Shae's nor Lance's, echoed in her mind.

Something that invokes a mild level of unease.

This would certainly fit that description.

Ren grasped the car key. A spark of something that looked an awful lot like fire flickered at the contact. In her peripheral vision a similar spark shot upwards.

Something spontaneous.

Ren swallowed. "Uh, Lance?"

He sounded almost cheerful now. "Yes?"

"Do you know where you are, at all?"

"I told Shae; I'm near some green field with–"

Generic golf course was one of the least helpful descriptors in the whole of Scotland.

"The flags, yes I *know* that, but there are hundreds of those." Provided, of course, he *was* in Scotland. "He is in Scotland, right?" she hissed at Shae.

"He's supposed to be," Shae muttered, "though he does have a tendency to...wander."

"I am *here*," Lance said, sounding somewhat di...

"And you're near a beach?" Ren asked.

"Now I'm *on* a beach."

"If you look up to where the flags are, is there a huge build-ing, with bigger flags, behind?"

"You know the place?"

"I think so. Does the beach you're on have a rocky bit over to the right if you're looking at the sea?"

"It does."

"Okay." Her mind was abuzz. "Lance?"

"Yes?"

Ren turned the ignition, heart racing. At least Dr Michele would be proud. Surely she was bypassing *spontaneous* and veering into *reckless*. Very un-Ren like. "We'll be about an hour."

in St. Andrews, she was fucked. But it
lace Ren knew that fit his, albeit not very
detailed,   :s.

She steered them north.

For the many, many questions she had, Ren found herself driving wordlessly for a good twenty-five minutes.

Magic. The word danced around her mind like its own brand of fireflies.

And then there was the buzzing.

As before, a small plume of smoke rose from beneath her palm. Ren loosened her grip. *Make a list,* she told herself, and mentally began to prepare a series of questions.

"So," Ren said, because it felt the least intense question she had, "are you and this, uh, Lance…together?"

Shae, in a most un-Shae-like fashion, burst out laughing. "No, we're work partners."

"Is he an alien wizard, too?"

"I'm an *arcanist.* And no, Lance isn't one."

"But I am?"

"No, you're a weaver." He said the words as though they ought to mean something. "An elemental."

"Elemental."

"You have power over natural magic, the elements. *NáDarra.*"

There was that word again. "*NáDarra*," Ren repeated, glancing upwards. "Like...wind? And fire?"

"Mm." He nodded. "There are eight. Once you're fully awakened, your taio will have four types of sparks in it, and you'll be able to manipulate those elements."

Ren doubted that very much. "Which ones?"

"Well," Shae began, "*usually* there are two groups. You've already had Air and Fire awaken, so I would personally bet you'll also end up with Ground and Water."

"Oh. What are the others?"

"There's Light and Dark, then Lightning and Aether."

Ren shot him a sideways glance. "And *what*, now?"

"Aether," Shae repeated. "Some call it spirit."

"Well, that sounds terrifying."

Shae chuckled softly as they whizzed past flashes of gorse-filled countryside.

"Which element is your magic?" she asked.

"None. You're gifted in what's known as natural magic, I'm gifted in unnatural. Or *NeòNach*."

"Right. And on the planet you're from, that's common?"

"Yes, and no. And I'm not an alien," he added.

"I'm afraid all evidence points to the contrary."

"But I *am* from another world."

"That sounds an awful lot like you saying you're an alien."

One glance showed his knuckles were, once again, paler than the rest of his hands. The sight irked her. "The world I'm from is linked to yours."

Ren fought a mad desire to laugh. Winding him up was proving rather therapeutic. "Through..." She elongated the word. "Space?"

She was certain he rolled his eyes again. "Through *scrylights*." Her own gaze darted to the now silent *scrystone* he was still holding. "It's a similar magic," Shae acknowledged.

"So, you came here using a skylight thingy?"

"*Scrylight*, and yes." When she didn't reply, he continued. "Travel through scrylights is possible where two, or more, lines of *NáDarra'n* charge meet. Scry*stones* work by creating a line of *NeòNach'n* charge."

He might as well have been speaking French. "Okay, let's pretend for a minute what you just said makes sense. Why?"

"Why?"

"Why come here?"

For the first time, he hesitated. "Would it come as a big surprise if I told you we were sent here to find you?"

"You mean to tell me your calling in life isn't pulling pints in a shitty little Scottish hotel?"

"Certainly not."

The sun, which had been bathing the land in a warm gold since they left Ainhill, went behind a cloud.

Ren, very aware of her own heartbeat, asked, "Why, then?"

"Hm?"

"Why were you sent to find me?"

"I'm not sure I'm the right–"

But *what*, exactly, Shae wasn't convinced he was right for, Ren didn't find out.

Seeing the outline of St. Andrews calmed Ren marginally, until something that sounded somewhere between a growl and a screech filled the air around them.

Through sheer will, she somehow kept the car moving in a straight line. "Uh, Shae?"

In contrast to his usual mask, he looked ill. "Yes?"

"Please tell me you heard that, too."

First he murmured something under his breath, ignoring her, before raising his scrystone. "Lance?!" he demanded.

For the second time, Lance ignored him.

The noise, whatever it was, came again, this time louder. Between the constant howling of wind came two more shrieks.

"Shae, what's–?"

"Keep going, and calm yourself. You're smoking." He wasn't wrong. Small bursts of smoke were rising upwards, no longer only from her palms. Shae's head was burling in every direction, wide-eyed and staring. "You need to relax your magic."

"*Relax my magic*?" She was shouting. "Oh yes, I'll get right on that."

Something was different: wrong. Ren tried, and failed, to ignore it. Every hair from her neck downwards was standing on end. Goosebumps coated her arms. There was a hollow in her chest, not full of wind, or fire.

But fear.

The smoke was thicker now, and starting to fill the car. Shae coughed, still fixated on the rear window.

Relax your magic.

Ren didn't know how to relax herself, let alone her magic.

"Shae, what's going on?" She wasn't shouting anymore.

But they were near the beach. A few streets to go and they'd find this Lance. And then what? There was no plan. Which, on its own, would have been reason enough for Ren to panic.

The Old Course loomed ahead.

"We're here."

Shae called for Lance again, to no avail. He turned to Ren. "You have to stay here."

Braking far more sharply than she'd intended, Ren whirled

around. "What? I can't–"

He was coughing again. "You have to."

Unbuckling her seatbelt, she was caught by the scent of burning rubber. It wasn't there a moment ago. Smoke was still rising from her, thicker than before. Ren had failed at many things in life but none more spectacularly than relaxing her magic. "No, we need to get out; the car is probably about to blow up."

"What?"

She tugged the handle. "Get out!"

It wasn't clear, until that moment, how much of the wind her car muffled. Outside it was a deafening, continuous roar. Shae followed as salt-tinged sea air hit her nostrils.

Nondescript figures, pulling hoods over their faces, arms wrapping around themselves, hurried past them. No one paid them any notice. If they had, they'd probably have called the fire brigade.

"Ren!" Shae shouted. He was barely audible. "We need to move!"

No, they needed to make a plan. Fat drops of rain began to fall, thudding against the car, and Ren. Maybe they'd suppress the smoke.

"To Lance?" she cried.

He was focused behind her. "Away from that."

Ren turned and wished she hadn't.

If she hadn't already believed he was from a world different to hers, that would have been the moment her belief shifted.

At first glance, she saw nothing but rain battering into the grey street, but then the silhouette of a man caught her. Watching and waiting, it was motionless. In a way that shouldn't be possible from anything living.

And then it rose.

Its form shifted before them into something new. Something awful. Its limbs stretched heinously, arachnid-like. It surpassed six, maybe seven, feet tall. Still humanoid, but so defiantly inhuman. A slender mass of the kind of pure darkness that rarely exists outside of midnight.

The thing had two pairs of eyes, glowing white and perfectly round, and were the only part of it that illustrated any semblance of life. They blinked in unison.

They were focused, all four of them, on Ren.

From somewhere came another drowned-out shout; Shae, no doubt, instructing her to run.

Ren turned, sole of her shoe crunching on gravel, and took off. Beside her, as their feet pounded the ground together, Shae's hand gripped her forearm. He was faster than Ren, which wouldn't take much. Wind whipped them, throwing her hair into a dark, tangled web around her. They pushed on, Shae just in front, and despite the burning in her lungs she dared not slow down.

Shae was shouting again, but Ren couldn't make the words out. Between the wind and the steady *thrum thrum* of her own heartbeat battering against her eardrums she was deaf to all else. They tore towards the beach.

The screech, the same part howl, part shriek, came again. This time it was far louder and closer as their feet met damp sand.

Shae had given up his scrystone. "Lance!"

The creature...thing...whatever it was, had legs far longer than either of them. Could they outrun it? The pain that held her chest answered a resounding *no*.

But then what would happen if it caught them...*when* it caught them?

Shae was shouting again, something about rocks. Ren swung them to the right, hoping she had caught at least the gist. Ahead, the North Sea was an angry mass of grey waves, loud and unforgiving, the scent of it strong.

The shriek rang out again, somehow not as loud. Had they outrun it? Ren doubted it, but couldn't afford to look back and find out. Shae's hand gripped hers as they dashed, sand spraying in every direction around them, towards the rocks.

"Keep going!" Shae urged through staggered breaths. "It won't hang back for long!"

The rocks were close. What Shae was planning on doing once they got there, Ren couldn't guess. They slowed just before. It would have been precarious enough if the weather was dry. In rain, which was only falling heavier, they would be lucky not to break their necks trying to navigate them.

They turned as one.

It should have been hard to see, between the rain and the backdrop of dark buildings, but she found it in seconds. It hadn't descended onto the beach. Yet.

Her stomach lurched at the sight.

"It's biding its time," Shae said.

"For?"

"Between the rain and the sea and *you*, I imagine, that's a *lot* of water. It can't contain it all."

"You just said a whole lot of things that made no sense."

"It needs a new plan."

It wasn't the only one.

Two people rushed past, heads bowed, missing it by what must have been mere inches.

"Can't they see it?"

Shae's head shook. "It's made of dead magic," he said, which made even less sense.

She sucked in a breath as it blinked at her. "What did you mean, it needs a new plan?"

"Well," Shae said, "it either wants your magic, or mine."

"Why?"

"To kill it."

"You can *kill* magic?"

Shae nodded. "And that's not something you want to experience."

Every part of her ached, but for once she barely felt it. "O-okay so...what do we do? How do we stop–?"

"*We* don't. We can't be touched by it." Once again, he pulled out his scrystone. "Lance?!"

She didn't expect a response.

Lance sounded rather cheerful. "Yes?"

This time, it was Ren who clutched Shae, who in turn nearly dropped the stone. "Where are you?" Shae demanded.

Whatever the thing was, it had dropped once more to a crouch. Shae led them around the rock, not quite out of sight.

"I was hungry," Lance replied. "Are you here?"

"Yes." Shae hissed out a breath. "And we've got a bodach for company."

"Wh–"

Ren, too scared to look away from the spindly magic thief, clutched Shae tighter. Whether through fear or something else, the strange buzzing had intensified.

"Hurry up," Shae was snapping.

"I'm about ten minutes away," Lance said.

Past Shae, a slender-shape rose in what would otherwise have been an elegant movement. Ren gasped.

"Make it two." Shae deposited the scrystone and turned. "You see how it's moving?"

Ren, whose eyes hadn't left the creature – the bodach – nodded. It was making its way quickly, weaving this way and that.

46

Every few steps it stopped to look at her, its lifeless eyes honing in before it continued. Shae hurried them further around the rock.

"It's tracking your fire magic."

Ren swallowed. It wasn't Shae's magic it wanted.

Shae continued. "It won't be able to see your air magic, not with all this wind." His words were hurried, blurring together. "And it's already confused." His hands gripped her shoulders. For the briefest of moments, her eyes met his. "Ren, can you swim?"

Blinking, Ren stared at him. At that moment she almost forgot the bodach. He absolutely did not mean what it sounded like he meant. "Can I–?"

"I know very little about bodachs. But I do know they will not enter water."

"And what if this one will?" It was closer now.

"It won't." Even with the lashing rain obscuring everything around her, she saw his desperation.

He was insane. Completely bonkers. As mad as everything else that had happened since she'd met him.

"B-but that's the *North Sea*," she cried, her voice a plea, "and those waves are–"

"Listen to me." Shae hauled her closer to the waterline. A wave rushed the sand to meet them. "It cannot touch someone Gifted. Instant death." Her breath hitched further at his words. "Get in the water and stay there until..." He trailed off, his face darting behind. The bodach was closer still, watching them in silence. "Your magic will protect you."

The wind made the tear tracks on her cheeks shrill and cold. A dark, featureless face poked around the rock. "What about you?"

Shae pushed her towards the water. "I'm going to try and distract it."

"Wha–?"

"Get into the sea!"

He backed away from her, towards it, while Ren, her chest gripped by some giant, invisible vice, snapped her eyes shut... and ran.

She didn't stop until the water was level with her midriff. She took a second to pant and wonder how long it would be before she was sectioned, before continuing, this time in a swim.

Her jeans were weighing her down but the sea itself wasn't too bracing or cold. Treading water, with the wind still whipping both her and the waves that surrounded her, wasn't too difficult. Further around her, the water was decidedly rougher. The scent and spray of the sea was overpowering, nauseating. It battered into her. Yet, the closest water, in a bizarre metre-sized circumference around her, was fairly calm.

Perhaps Shae was right.

Shae.

Ren was deeper now, up to her neck. She prepared to turn around when the buzzing, which had never really disappeared, rose. In the water it was a strange feeling. As if her entire body was being grazed, very gently, by tiny blades of grass. And yet it wasn't itchy in the way it could have been. It was strongest in her chest; anchored there somehow.

Between the wind and the waves, Ren could hear nothing save the raging elements.

Then the same, hollow shriek rang through the air, the one now imprinted on the edge of her brain. She'd have heard it through a hurricane.

It wasn't easy to get her bearings with the constant ebb of the water. She tracked them down just over from the rocks. And in that moment Ren felt terribly small.

Three figures, two human, one she knew, cloak billowing and with hands full of fireflies, and one she didn't. He brandished a sword and had hair longer than hers. Despite it being the first time she had seen him, he wasn't a stranger.

The third was not human.

Its movements were no longer tentative and curious, in the way they'd been when following Ren and Shae. Now they were stark and deliberate. It needed neither weapon nor magic. Long, spidery arms swept towards the pair. Lance was closer to it, and faster than Shae. Distant shouts, either from them or others, met her ears.

Shae was hanging back, throwing fistfuls of fireflies not at the bodach, but at Lance.

It cannot touch someone Gifted.

Lance himself was rolling and dodging and attempting to slice the creature's arms, but for all his twirling and manoeuvring, he kept missing.

Maybe she should leave while it was distracted. As soon as the thought left her sopping wet head, Ren was ashamed of it. The buzzing rose in her chest.

She couldn't leave. Too much in the middle of whatever this...whatever it was.

Lance caught it, nicking the end of where there would usually be a hand, or paw, and instead was a point.

That only seemed to anger it.

More shouting, which Ren realised was mostly coming from Shae, rang out. Once again, Lance, with his calculated swings that looked as though they were made with military precision, missed. The realisation hit her in a rush of sea spray. He was relying on Shae to instruct him on its whereabouts.

Ren's buzzing was no longer buzzing; it had turned to pain. Pain that roamed over her, uninvited and violating, still centred in her chest and worsening with each blow Lance managed to dodge.

He was fighting it blind.

As fast as Lance was, the bodach was faster. Its four eyes were fixated on him, an unforgiving stare, trailing every move he made and countering it.

The rain was falling heavier still, adding to the angry sea that surrounded her. Ren forced her weary limbs closer to the shore between exhaustion and the buzzing-turned-pain.

Three jabs from Lance's sword, so fast the blade was a blur, resulted in two misses.

But one hit.

The bodach howled. A different sound. *He's wounded it*, she thought. Hoped.

With what had to be the same thought process, a rock the size of a rugby ball flew through the air, thrown by a doubled-over Shae. It hit the bodach in the side of the head. Ren didn't dare breathe as the creature howled again. One monstrous, blank head turned, just for a moment.

It was enough. Lance spun as though choreographed to do so, jumped, taking the hilt of his sword in both hands. It arched overhead and met the figure in the side of the neck. And then there was no neck. Its head slumped to its side with not so much as another howl, before falling. Its useless body slumped against the rock.

Something she couldn't place lifted within her. The buzzing was no longer painful.

Shae was still bent double, his billowing robe the liveliest part of him, and Lance was shouting something inaudible while throwing his hands, and sword, up in celebration. Ren was contemplating both running away again and throwing a party. Not too far away, a roll of thunder met her ears.

She began to half walk, half swim towards them, barely tasting the bitter saltwater.

But something was wrong. Shae wasn't getting up. As she moved closer he fell forwards, his head only just missing a nearby rock. Ren hurried onward.

Lance, no longer celebrating, jumped from his own rock. Or tried to. Instead, as far as Ren could make out from her limited peripheral, he slipped, falling forwards, as Shae had, his torso landing atop a motionless bodach arm.

This time, the buzzing wasn't just painful. Ren's entire body erupted in waves of agony as her shaking body left the water. Coughing and spluttering, she held a fist to the centre of her chest before hers was the fourth body to fall to the sand.

R en met the ground in slow motion. Knees...palms...face. She felt none of them.

It was the kind of pain that obscured all else. Ren was used to pain; she felt it every day of her life. Shunning it was second nature.

Usually.

Rain was still battering overhead, hitting both her and the sand. To her left, Shae was stirring. He rose, his movements stilted and jerky. It was all Ren had to follow suit.

"Shae!" It took her three further shouts for him to hear. Another roll of thunder broke through the wind, closer than before. Grains of soggy sand wove through the gaps in her fingers as she gripped at nothing.

Somehow, she stood, the motions alien to her limbs.

Shae reached her in a gusty haze. Streams of rain cascaded down his forehead like a waterfall. He gripped her shoulders. "Where's Lance?"

Ren coughed, nodding ahead. Behind a smaller rock, jutting up from the sand, lay a pair of legs, alongside a bodach arm.

Shae took off. Ren followed, driven by some tiny shred of sheer will and not a lot else. By the time she reached them, Shae had hauled Lance free of the limb. Up close it was darker still: a void of lifelessness.

"Don't touch it!"

Ren had no intention of touching it. It was only the width of a mug, but she gave it a wide berth as she stepped over it, no easy feat with great waves of pain still coursing through her.

Shae was crouched over Lance. He had turned the unconscious man over. Ren caught sight of his face for the first time, what of it wasn't covered in stray strands of sopping wet dark hair. The rest was spread out, cascading up and outwards with the wind, framing his face like a wild mane.

It was his expression, though, that she fixated on. In the fierce rain and relentless wind, calm exuded from him. It was unsettling, an impossible serenity.

Unlike Shae, who was clean-shaven and presentable, Lance had a messier presence, from his unkempt facial hair to the tear in his oversized, black shirt.

She would never have perceived them as any kind of duo.

Several white specks, identical to his fireflies, were whizzing between Shae's fingertips and Lance's torso. Ren held her breath, and for a long moment nothing happened, during which her heart thumped louder than the wind.

A groan, coupled with a grimace far more fitting of their current circumstance, emanated from Lance. Ren *felt* Shae's sigh.

"We need to get out of the storm," Shae called, his words distorted by thunder. He was busying himself at Lance's side, throwing the latter's arm around his shoulder.

Lance didn't seem to notice.

Ren nodded, positioning herself on Lance's other side. At the point his arm, and then his side, made contact with her own, the buzzing, which was having trouble deciding whether to buzz or hurt, rose. It was like a static shock over and over. All that kept her able to hold him upright was the tiny speck of knowledge that he was unable to.

"Agh!"

"Are you okay?" Shae called as they began to manoeuvre, the two of them flanking a barely conscious Lance. He groaned again but made no other noise.

Ren swallowed, her arm tightening around Lance's back. His sword, which he had tied to his hip somehow, dug into her thigh through the soaking denim. "No idea!" she cried back.

Ren was not okay.

The way back from the beach took a lot longer than their sprint to get there. The town was more or less empty, except for a few folk, hoods pulled down tight, braving the worsening storm. They ended up, after what felt at least half an hour of aimless walking, on a street Ren didn't know – not that her knowledge of St. Andrews was particularly vast – lined with Bed and Breakfasts.

"There," Ren called, nodding across the road to a glowing *Vacancies* sign. How long had it been since their breakfast?

A kindly woman, most concerned at the sight of the three, greeted them.

"I can call...doctor or..."

"Oh," Ren replied, "no it's...he's fine." She feigned a smile as Lance's head lulled to the side, clunking against her own. He let out a soft grunt. "He had one too many at lunch."

"I see." The woman placed a key in Shae's outstretched hand. A small, silver *3* hung on a keyring beside it. "If there's anything else–"

"We're fine." Shae was already steering them towards the nearby door. "Thank you."

Inside room three was one double bed and one single, both made up in a matching, threadbare paisley. In the corner sat a small desk. A further door led presumably to a bathroom. The faintest hint of lavender hung in the air. In any other circumstance it would have been a peaceful place. Perhaps, for countless others, it had been.

It wouldn't be peaceful for them.

They deposited Lance on the double bed as Shae began to fumble in his many pockets.

Ren didn't see what he pulled out; her gaze too focused on Lance. "Is he...?"

Shae placed a small vial of something white and shimmery on the bed next to Lance. "Only he could dodge and kill a bodach he couldn't see, then fall off a rock and land on it anyway." Any signs of Shae's panic had vanished; his face was a passive mask once again. "He'll be okay."

Ren let out a shaky breath, the pain in her chest lifting a little.

"Can you help?" Shae asked. After removing Lance's shirt, he had begun to untie a lace from some kind of leather armour he wore underneath. "Loosen the other one," he instructed.

It was a tougher job than she had anticipated. The knot that held the laces together was complicated. Once undone, there were two large buckles at each side of his chest. The leather was thicker than any Ren had seen. "What kind of animal is this from, a rhino?" Ren asked, panting slightly with the effort.

Once unbuckled, the front of the armour separated from the back. Shae lifted it off, revealing a thin white undershirt. "Crodh-mara," Shae said, "toughest leather in Caerisle."

Ren didn't know where Caerisle was, nor what a *crodh-mara* happened to be, but she wasn't about to ask. As they lifted the leather from Lance's torso, a gasp escaped her.

The scar was unlike any she had seen. About the size of a large, closed fist, it looked as though a handful of soot had been thrust upon Lance's body, spreading sideways across his stomach like an angry, jagged vein.

"And it's a good thing he was wearing it," Shae continued, unfazed. "It probably saved at least a few of his organs."

He reached for the vial of white liquid and popped the tiniest cork Ren had ever seen. "Stand back."

"Wh-why?" Ren took a regretful glance at Lance before taking a few steps towards the door.

"*This*," Shae said, "contains a very concentrated amount of *NeòNach*, which is going to be hostile enough when it reaches the dead magic still lodged in him without it fighting with yours, too."

None of what he said made sense, but Ren nodded as if it did, backing up further.

"One drop would be enough to knock you out for several hours," Shae was saying.

The pain in her chest, though somewhat subsided, had made her wearier still. How long had it been since they had left Ainhill?

"That doesn't sound too unappealing right now."

"This amount," Shae held the bottle up, "would cause heart failure."

"Oh."

She watched him work from as far as she could get, massaging the death potion into the black mark on Lance's side with one hand. His other hand hovered around ten centimetres above. White specks that matched Shae's fireflies moved up and down the gap between his palm and Lance's side. The arcanist was still and silent as he helped Lance, but the exertion of it was clear on his brow, where a layer of sweat was glistening.

After what may have been ten minutes, or two, or fifty, Shae called over his shoulder, "Could you run a bath?"

"Uh, okay."

It felt better to have a task at hand.

"Should I put bubble bath in?" she called, examining the two small complimentary bottles they had been left.

"What?" Shae appeared at the door. He had taken his cloak off and was holding a second vial. He eyed the bottles in Ren's hands. "No, it needs to be this." He held the vial – this one full of clear liquid – up for Ren to see.

"Will that one also kill me?"

"Only if ingested."

He took the few steps needed to close the gap between the door and bath and dipped one hand below the surface of the water. With a hiss, he drew the hand back. "Were you planning on cooking him?"

"Oh." Ren didn't meet his eye. "I don't really notice when things are too hot."

"I suppose for you there is no *too hot*," Shae reasoned, turning the cold tap.

They walked back to the bedroom. Lance's face was still and serene. The black mark had faded into something patchy and grey.

"He'll have it for the rest of his life, I think."

"There are uglier scars to have, I suppose," Ren said.

Shae eyed her. "Can you help me get his clothes off?"

Ren blinked. "Uh."

"The potion in the bath needs to be absorbed by as much of him as possible," Shae explained. "Stripping him down to his underwear while he's unconscious isn't my idea of fun either. Stick to the parts of him furthest away from the scar."

The strange pain in her chest began to ebb and rise like a gentle tide as they, with difficulty, stripped Lance of his clothes. And possibly his dignity.

"This feels immoral," Ren said once Lance lay in only a pair of thin white shorts.

"Well, considering we're saving him, I'd say our morals can stay intact."

Shae carried him in a fireman's lift, grunting at the effort, towards the bathroom. The bath was much closer to the ground than the bed, and Lance entered the water with a large *sploosh*.

Shae turned to Ren, wrinkling his nose as his fingertips roamed across his still sopping clothes.

"I'm going to find the kitchen."

Ren's mouth fell open. "I'm not sure now is the time to ask for a beef Wellington."

"There are herbs I can use. I have very few ingredients on me, but I need more. I won't be long."

"And what the bloody hell do I do if he wakes up?" Ren hissed. "*Oh, hello, we've never met – except for the two minutes I spoke to you through a rock. Anyway, you nearly died but now you're fixed and almost naked. I'm Ren, by the way.*"

"Something like that," Shae replied, "though don't use the words 'nearly died;' he'd enjoy that far too much. And he already knows your name, so you probably won't need too much of an introduction."

Ren gaped at him as he turned to leave.

"Oh, don't put your hands in the water; it wouldn't do too much damage, but it probably won't feel pleasant."

"Funnily enough, I wasn't planning on putting my hands *in* the water, thanks, Shae."

He had already gone.

Shae had left her in a strange silence, and Ren had very little to do except wait and watch over Lance. It wouldn't do much good for him to drown due to her negligence.

She hovered, throat dry, stomach tying itself in knots. Still buzzing.

At least obtaining the room, then running the bath, had given her a focus. With nothing but worry and pain and confusion, and an unconscious, bathing man to fixate on, the last shred of whatever she had managed to summon to keep herself together finally dissolved.

It was then she broke down.

Grabbing a nearby towel, Ren buried her face, sobbing against the white fuzz. Then a quiet splash broke her jumble of thoughts.

"What the–?"

Well, Ren sniffed, *this is about to get awkward.* She cleared her throat.

Lance, almost twisting himself into a knot at the noise, sent a wave of water splashing onto the floor at the sight of her.

"Hello," she said, her voice oddly squeaky.

"Hello." Bemusement wasn't an accurate enough descriptor for his tone.

Ren didn't move. "You're awake."

"Apparently so."

"Good. That's good."

"Are you Renée, by any chance?"

"No, well...yes, but no one calls me that. I'm Ren."

"Well, it's, ah, nice to meet you in person, Ren."

"And you."

"Is there a reason I'm naked, or...?"

Ren took a breath, and sidestepped into view, taking great care to look only at his face. "You're not entirely naked," she pointed out.

His gaze held hers, and then he smiled. The sides of his eyes – a deep, mahogany brown – crinkled.

Ren, struggling to recall a stranger meeting, let out a sigh, and offered him a soft smile in return.

From outside, their room door opened.

Ren bowed her head, only to breathe in the smell that accompanied Shae's muffled greeting.

"Ren," Shae said, stepping into view, "you *bathed* him? How odd."

Blinking at him, Ren whacked Shae's arm. "I'd really appreciate me *not* being made to look like *quite* as much of a weirdo, thanks."

"You're really running that risk either way," Lance stated. "Hi," he added, looking at Shae, "I won, then?"

"Oh, yes." Shae's tone was dry. "You killed a bodach."

"Single-handedly."

"You were then bested by a rock."

"You win some," Lance said with a shrug. "Where's my sword?"

"Thank you, Shae, greatest arcanist I've ever met, for bringing me here and healing me with such limited supplies. You are the best friend I could ask for."

Lance sat forward, positioning his folded arms to rest on the side of the bath, and raised one eyebrow. "You forgot to mention how modest you are."

It might have been the least humour-filled day of her life, but Ren had to clamp her lips together to keep a small laugh from escaping them.

Shae shook his head and raised a plastic bag as he walked towards the beds. "I bought food."

Ren, after casting a look at Lance that probably lingered on him for a touch too long, followed. "You actually *bought* food. With money?"

He regarded her coolly. "It was a positively awful experience I never want to repeat."

From behind, she could hear a number of sounds that indicated Lance was getting out of his bath.

"Uh." He grunted, obviously examining his new scar. "What an eyesore."

Ren, halting mid-step, raised a hand to meet the centre of her chest. The pain was gone.

"Are you all right?" It was Shae. He was pulling his cloak off. The rest of his clothes, much like Ren's, were somehow dry.

"More than all right." For the first time that evening, Ren's face broke into a full smile. "The pain is gone. I'm just buzzing again."

Shae only blinked. "Buzzing?"

"So am I," a voice said from behind her. She smiled further at the sight of him, his long hair wet and tousled. It suited him, framed his face nicely...or something. He wore a big, fluffy, white dressing gown and the same smile as before. "I'm buzzing, too. All over, but mostly..." He trailed off, but his fingertips brushed his chest.

Shae mumbled something under his breath that Ren had little desire to investigate further.

She nodded in response, telling herself the reason the inside of her mouth had dried up when Lance had pointed to his chest was due to thirst. "Yeah," she said, mimicking the action, "right there."

Shae could have bought them a mouldy sausage each and Ren would have thanked him. As it happened, despite admitting he had made his choices based on which of the menu numbers he deemed powerful, he'd chosen well.

Lance, in his fluffy dressing gown and, she realised with a snort, matching hotel slippers, was demolishing a duck pancake.

"Your world has the *best* food," he said between bites.

And there it was. Though nothing more than a passing comment, it jolted her. A huge part of her wished to run from their room and never speak of it again. Not from her world. But instead, a world of magic and where people carried swords and wore armour. A world they had apparently been sent from, to find her.

She continued to eat but no longer tasted anything, looking down to the dull, blue paisley, the view distorted by her own tears.

In time, Shae began to pull out several small bags he'd filled with indistinguishable herbs and spices and a few more vials of coloured liquids from his array of hidden pockets. Arranging them neatly on one side of the double bed he and Lance were sitting on, he placed them in an order that made sense only to himself, and took them, a few at a time, over to the small desk.

Ren watched him silently, placing her now empty food container at her side. He pulled out his many maps, unfolding them with care, and began to pore over them. After a few seconds, her gaze moved to Lance.

He was already watching her. "Are you okay?"

No. She shrugged. "It's been a weird day."

"It has." He nodded. "You probably have a lot of questions."

"One," she admitted, her stare flitting between him and the back of Shae's head, it was still as a statue. "You weren't just sent here to find me, were you?"

Shae turned then, and a glance passed between them. "No," Shae replied. "We were sent to Collect you."

The words hit her like a slap.

"Why?"

Shae surveyed her. "You have a gift in *NáDarra*, the elements."

Ren nodded.

"In Caerisle, where we're from, that's technically not an uncommon thing. But the *type* of gift you have is." He had lost her already. "There are two types of elementals. *Bearers*, those gifted in one element, and *weavers*, who are gifted in four, like you - or how you will be once you're fully awakened," he added. "There used to be at least fifty weavers born into every generation," Shae said, "but two decades ago one was born and sent away."

"Me?" Shae nodded. Ren's mouth was dry. "Sent–"

"Here."

"Wh-why?"

It was Lance who answered, his tone soft. "All we know is that we had to find you...and take you back."

Silence followed his words.

His *lies.*

Somewhere above, a roll of thunder growled. Her chest, still buzzing, began to tingle. *Absolute lies.* Ren had travelled no further than the Costa del Sol. She had lived in Ainhill her *entire life.*

It had been mad, Ren decided in that moment, to trust them at all. A barmaid with zero prospects? No wonder she had been so eager to believe in magic. Who wouldn't in her position? But it had to end. She was probably going to end up the subject of a shocking news story people wouldn't know whether to believe. *Woman, 20, killed and eaten in St. Andrews hotel room.* They were mad, and Ren arguably was too for going along with them. Shae must have drugged her and the bodach was probably an escaped Labrador she had hallucinated into a monster.

She had done the same with Mike and *his* set of false promises. Believed him. And believed them.

She needed to stop. Right then.

She stood. "I have to go."

"What? Agh!" It was Lance. At his words the buzzing intensified – a side effect, Ren decided, from whatever it was Shae had slipped her. Not quite pain, certainly not pleasure. His fist was balled at his chest. Was he experiencing the same?

She wondered fleetingly, *madly*, whether he was also experiencing the deep knotting sensation that had developed in the pit of her stomach.

Lance looked suddenly scared. "You can't."

A second voice, Shae's, said her name.

She whirled around, eyes widening as she realised he was now standing beside her. She hadn't heard him get up. Shae's gaze was focused elsewhere, at a point above Ren's head as he gently patted her arm.

"Look up," he said.

Ren shook her head. Once again, tears blurring her vision.

"There's a reason why you're in pain every day; why you sleep for hours but never feel rested." She no longer cared about stopping the tears. "There's a reason your body shuts down, and you collapse." A shifting, of something on her other side, as Shae's grip left her arm, and another altogether encased her shoulders.

Ren sobbed harder. She had never told him about the fainting.

"And a reason you cannot be healthy, not here. You don't belong here." Lance held her against him as Shae spoke, *into* him. Her face pressed into the ridiculous, towelled robe. "You told me you were an anomaly."

"So?" She sniffed against Lance.

"If you stay here, you will deteriorate further." Shae spoke not with his usual indifference, but with something else. Something almost...pained. She dared herself to look at him. "You will die."

Silence, bar Ren's racked crying, followed his words. She didn't stop for a long time. Lance's hold on her never faltered, not when he led her back a step and gently prompted her back onto the bed. She sat, allowing her body to lean almost entirely against him. The buzzing prickled against her, strongest at the parts of her he was touching. It dissipated only a little as they broke apart.

"In case it had escaped your notice," Lance whispered, "Shae has a tendency to be dramatic."

Ren let out the smallest of laughs.

"He can't help himself."

"I suppose I wasn't meant to hear that," Shae remarked tartly, having returned once more to his vials and maps.

Lance's arm was bent, as was hers, their elbows a mere centimetre apart. Whatever the buzzing was, it was strong there.

"What is it?" she asked, yawning.

"A...connection. I think."

She yawned again, too tired to question him further. "That makes about as much sense as everything else that's happened to me over the last few days."

He barked a small laugh. "You should get some sleep," he said through his own yawn.

She allowed herself another small laugh in response. "You should take your own advice."

He looked, for the shortest of moments, as though he wanted to say something. Instead, he reached for the heap of wet clothes, and pulled out several knives, and a piece of thick and crumpled yellow parchment.

Ren eyed it. The word *dossier* was printed along the top.

In a second, he had grabbed it and stuffed it into the pocket of his robe. His mouth opened, and then closed. And then opened again, "I didn't thank you for helping Shae heal me."

"I didn't do much."

"Get some sleep," he repeated, "we'll talk more tomorrow." The words calmed her somewhat. It sounded, a little at least, like a plan. A part of her, a lonely part that wasn't wreathed in a numb confusion, clung to that. He smiled again, the sides of his eyes crinkling.

6

"REN!"

Utter confusion greeted her semi-conscious state. Someone, a man, shouted her name again.

"Ugh!" Blinking in the dim sight of the unfamiliar room, Ren sat with difficulty. Every part of her body ached in protest.

St. Andrews. Ren blinked again as an unfamiliar sensation rose up in her chest. Hazy details of the previous day became clearer, more distinct. She groaned again, realising the sensation was a buzz. It was still dark beyond the curtains. She turned to face the two others.

Lance was standing, sword raised, topless and bedraggled.

Shae stood at the bottom of her bed, holding a small corner of curtain aside, attention fixed out the sliver of window.

"Ren get behind me, *now!*" Lance shouted. There was no smile, no crinkles by his eyes. Instead, they were flickering between the window and Ren.

She rose and closed the distance between them in a second.

A monumental bang ricocheted off the window, and Ren let out a small scream. Lance's free arm wrapped itself around her front, ushering her further behind him.

Another assault on the window pane. She doubted it would hold much longer.

"It's another bodach," Shae said. "I don't know how it's tracked you in here, but..."

A deafening crash. A sickening howl.

She braced herself to see it, to see and do nothing, because what could she do?

Run. The voice in her mind was small. *Run.*

She readied herself to do exactly that, when Lance took two steps forward and, balancing one knee on the single bed where Ren had slept only a few moments before, thrust his sword forwards through the gap in the curtains.

A second howl followed, one she'd heard once before the previous day.

"You got it," Shae said.

Lance stepped backwards, wiping a black goo that coated his sword onto the bed covers.

Ren felt nauseous at the sight. One look at him told her Shae did, too.

"All right," Shae was saying, once more peering outside. "We need to move. I'm positive more will come. They're tracking Ren. Maybe me, too. You won't be safe anywhere near here. None of us will."

"But...my home, my family–"

Shae searched out the window again. "You can't go back there."

"What do you–?"

"Bodachs are hunters." He had the grace to sound apologetic. "And these ones have been sent after you."

What the hell could they possibly want with her? "Wh-why?"

Shae breathed a long sigh. "I have no idea."

Lance's stance was still poised, waiting. "Do you know where–?"

Shae bowed his head. "From what I can gather, the points don't match up as exactly as Gideon said they would, but I know roughly where it is." He began to gather up his various vials and maps. "Ren," he added, "we need to reach just south of somewhere called Innerness."

Ren didn't move. Her chest was suddenly very hollow. "I–"

"Do you know it?"

"Inverness, yes, but..." She trailed off. St. Andrews had been one thing. Ren could hardly drive them all over Scotland. Though both Shae and Lance clearly thought otherwise, as they got ready, with haste, to leave. She felt strange. If he had *just* said Inverness – or *Innerness* – it would be one thing.

But he'd said *just south.*

Ren, say it again. The memory washed over her the same way it always did. An unwanted wave. *You can't forget it.*

She hadn't.

Ren was very aware of her own heartbeat.

Shae finished folding his maps. "We need to get back to your car."

"I don't know, this is.... It's *hours* away, and we don't have a plan, and–" Would her car even start, after she'd almost set the interior of it on fire?

"Hang on." It was Lance. "You don't mean those mad, metal carriages."

"Mm." Shae, finished with his packing, placed his cloak over his shoulders in a sweeping dark semi-circle. "Ren has a red one."

Lance threw his arms in the air. "Absolutely not."

Reservations temporarily forgotten, Ren rounded on him. "What?"

"I value my life, thanks."

Shae, already marching his way to the door, shot, "Then I suggest you make peace with the fact you're entrusting it to Ren."

By the time they had navigated the darkened, almost empty, streets, and found Ren's car keys still inside, Ren was ready to leave Lance and his whining in St. Andrews.

"I," she said, turning on her heel to glare at him, ignoring the way the strange buzzing had taken on something of a prickling, "am perfectly capable of getting us to Inver-bloody-ness in one piece." Even if it was all she was currently capable of doing.

He looked between her and the car. The strange buzzing was rising and falling with each breath she took. So, she suspected, was his.

At first, he said nothing. Inclining his head, he lifted his hands in mock surrender. "All right."

Shae spent the journey in her back seat poring over his maps and mumbling. Lance shifted between two default settings: absolute terror and intense enthusiasm, and Ren pondered what it was, exactly, her life had become in the past few days. Not that she could think of any part of it in any great detail, every time she did, her chest began to seize. *If you stay here you will deteriorate further.* She could go home, only an hour away. If only that meant she wouldn't lead more bodachs there. She wondered, rather madly, whether Dr. Michele would consider Ren's past day and a half to be *spontaneous* enough.

You will die.

It had to be a fever dream.

Behind her, Shae's papers rustled.

"Your maps," Ren said, "what are they?" The lines he had drawn all over them, some covering the entire length of Britain, others smaller, snaking sideways across the country. She was lost when she saw them, and yet they were achingly familiar.

"Most of them show this country."

She stared at him in her mirror. His face showed no trace of humour. "I'd gathered that much."

"Ah, that's good."

"I meant the lines."

"They're called wey lines."

"*Ley* lines?" Those she had heard of.

"No. *Wey*."

"Oh. And they are?"

Shae took a second to reply, seemingly very interested in something out the window Ren doubted he could see out of. "Each one represents a line of *NáDarra'n* charge."

"Oh, right." Ren blinked. He had said something similar the previous day, she was sure. "Sure." If anything, she had far less idea what he meant. Beside her, Lance was concealing a snicker with a hasty cough. She ignored him.

"And we're trying to find one of these lines?"

"No." Shae sounded, if anything, rather bored. "We're searching for a mirror point."

Again, he offered no more explanation. "Right. And *that* is?"

"A point at which one of each type of line meets."

"Mhmm." She didn't press him further, driving in silence, ignoring both the way her heart hammered and her desire to find her notebook and start making a list. She could write *Go mad*, and strike it through. And then follow it up with *Go more mad.*

Once again, a tiny plume of smoke was rising from the steering wheel. Ren let out a shaky breath. She hadn't travelled this road since *that night.* It seemed unlikely this had nothing to do with that.

The night Ren had learnt not to think about.

"Hey." It was Lance. Ren shot him a sideways glance but said nothing. "Are you okay?"

Lying would be pointless, because really, who *would* be okay? Ren brushed a few rogue strands of hair from her face. She was with an alien wizard and his sword-wielding companion, driving over a hundred miles from the town where she had witnessed one nearly die by the hand of a...what? Monster? Whose monster friends would continue to hunt her. Unless she...they...? Her brain hurt with the bizarreness of it all.

There's a reason your body shuts down, and you collapse.

"No." Ren swallowed hard. *You will die.* "Not really."

The buzzing swelled a little as he smiled.

It took her a few minutes to gather the courage to address the rather large elephant in the car. "Shae?"

The rustling of maps stopped. "Yes?"

"Wh-why will I die? I don't...don't understand." Many, many things....

"*NáDarra*, natural magic, exists here, certainly. At the same time, it does not exist." Ren's nostrils flared. The man was a walking riddle. "It has a tendency to be, ah, rather temperamental. On our world, Faren, it is acknowledged. Celebrated."

Faren. The word turned itself over in Ren's mind.

"Magic...er...*NáDarra*?"

"Yes. And here it is not. *NáDarra*, in a sense, *likes* being acknowledged. And it *needs* to be acknowledged to sustain your taio, to allow itself to be manipulated."

The idea that magic could be sentient enough to *like* anything was unnerving.

"So, it's killing me because it's desperate for attention?"

Beside her, Lance snorted.

"In a sense...yes," Shae said.

"Well, that's ridiculous."

"I quite agree."

She didn't press him further.

71

"Ren?" Shae said, close to ten minutes later.

Her gaze was poised on the road. She was tired; they had only had a few hours' sleep. "Mm?"

"I believe we must turn northeast before we reach the city."

Ren nodded. "I know." A lump had embedded itself in her throat, making it hard to swallow. There were so few people she had told the sparse details to...and she was going to have to add these two almost strangers to that list.

"A place called–" She saw his head dip down in her mirror.

"Culloden," Ren finished for him. She felt both their frowns. "I-I've been there before. Once." She sighed, wishing she could imprint the awful, and impossible to explain, night into their minds, if only to save her from needing to tell it. "With my mother." Neither spoke. "It...I...." Ren bit down on her bottom lip, in the way she always did when she had had to speak of it, whether to the psychiatrist, or the police officers, or the doctors. Or her father.

Ren's grip was tighter still, though she forced her breathing to slow, certain she was close to either a panic attack or creating yet more smoke plumes. "She wasn't well. She hadn't been for a few years. She had maps like yours," Ren said, "with the same lines that you've drawn. And she took me there, but–" She steered them right, onto a smaller road at the instruction of a nearby sign. "I...I don't really know what happened," Ren admitted.

"You don't know?" Lance's voice was soft.

She shook her head. "They said I repressed it, or something. I remember bits and pieces, but none of it makes sense. We were in the woods, and it was dark. Then I'm screaming but I don't know why. And there's this big flash of light, and another scream." The buzzing gathered near her elbow, as Lance placed his hand there, just for a second. "The next thing I'm in hospital." She swallowed. "I was found by a couple walking their dog. Unconscious." Ren dragged a hand through her hair. Her pony tail had long since abandoned her and it hung, messy and limp. "The place had been burned."

Shae's maps rustled. "And your mother?"

"I don't know." Ren shrugged. There had been theories, whispered ones Ren wasn't meant to hear. But they didn't seem to matter. "No one does."

Ren pulled into the parking beside the woods. They had travelled the remainder in silence. It became absolute without the rumbling of the engine.

Her phone informed her it was not long after two. The sight made part of her groan, and another wish she could drive as fast as her car's 1.6l engine would allow, leaving them here. This was how people ended up murdered. Ren took a long breath, then turned first to Lance, then to Shae.

"I don't know what you're expecting of me."

She didn't know if what they were about to reveal to her was as bad as sitting there waiting to hear it.

Lance's gaze didn't move from her face. "Ren, we need to leave. *All* of us."

From somewhere out in the dark, there was a long, deep *creak*. Then a louder thud. Ren spun her head but saw nothing but her own reflection. "Wh-you mean *now*?!"

Lance nodded.

From the window, Shae said something in a language Ren didn't speak. And then she heard it. The same growl that wasn't a growl, but a screech, like metal against metal.

Lance's fingers had wrapped themselves gently around her forearm. She buzzed against him. "I know it's huge," he said, "but–" The remainder of his words were drowned out by the same sound.

Another crash.

Ren's heart fluttered uncomfortably, missing a beat. "I-I *can't* go. My family...I..."

You don't belong here.

There was still so much she didn't know, still so much she

73

should know *before* making any decision to go with them. A decision that was less a decision and more a stark and set path.

A path no part of her was sure she should take.

You will die.

The buzzing hurtled around her chest. She wanted to retch and scream and run. But she did nothing.

Shae's voice rang through her jumbled thoughts. "They'll be here in a minute. Come on."

Ren barely heard him, but she registered the click of her car door as Shae climbed out. Legs numb and weak, she followed suit.

The rush hit her more than either the night air or the thick rain. She had often felt things, oddities no one else seemed to. But nothing like *this*. And yet it was familiar.

Then she saw the specks. Far more than in the clouds above her or Shae's head. There had to be thousands simply *existing* in the air around them. Some were white, like her own, others blue and green. Most were a shimmery black.

A distant memory, a dream from long ago, where the details evaporated like water the more her mind tried to grasp them. It was nothing she understood, yet ought to.

A knowledge.

Of something greater than she.

"Is this the place?" It was Lance.

Ren shot him a disbelieving look. Wasn't he experiencing what she was? Seeing what she saw? She didn't know what *the place* meant but was certain they were there.

Beside her, Shae was walking and circling, looking this way and that, predator-like. "I think so." He pulled something from one of his many pockets, holding it aloft. It looked like the *scrystone* they'd spoken to Lance through, only bigger.

Another growl. Far too close. They whirled as one.

Shae's fingers were travelling across the surface of the new stone. "I need to set it."

She didn't remember having the thought to do it, yet she was. Ren prayed her phone – almost out of battery, would work long enough.

"Hello?" His voice was sleepy and concerned all at once and she replied with a sob. "Ren? What's wrong?"

"I have t-to go."

Several scratchy noises emanated from a nearby tree line. Beside her, Lance's sword rose.

"Go where? Ren, you aren't making any sense."

Shae stepped back, the *scrylight* complete.

Ren swallowed. A *doorway*, of sorts, stood, wreathed in a dense, purple light. Ready for them. Beyond it, *in* it, she saw countless fireflies.

"I love you," she stammered, "please know I love–"

"She told me to be ready." Her father sighed. "I'm not." She heard the wobble in his words, knew the sob that escaped her father as he spoke. "You're going to the *other* world, aren't you?"

She was dimly aware of Lance's arm pressing into hers. "Wh-wh–"

Shae's voice cried out, sounding far further away than she knew he was. "We have to go!"

"Dad, I–"

"Find your mother." He swallowed. She both heard, and felt, the pain there. "Oh God. I'm not...it was...it's been...an honour."

"Wha–"

"I love you."

"I love *you*!"

Shae was standing by the hovering *scrylight.* Through it a thousand specks danced across a backdrop of darkness.

Lance was watching her. He remained by her side, his hand on her arm. "We need to go."

She allowed herself to be steered by him, her breath somewhere around her throat, her father's words ringing in her ears.

Find your mother.

Lance brought her to the *scrylight* as a howl echoed somewhere too near, and his hand left her arm. Ren's eyes moved to his, long enough to see him nod. His hand, finding hers, squeezed; their fingers laced together.

You don't belong here, Ren.

One last screech.

Find your mother.

One last howl.

Go.

And she did...

End of Part One

Part Two

7

Darkness.

Falling, but somehow not moving at all.

More darkness.

A hundred thousand sensations at once, and yet...nothing. Until the abyss was shattered by something so bright it should have blinded her. Ren didn't know whether she was hurtling towards it, or whether she was *in* it.

Ren didn't know very much of anything.

Grass met the soles of her feet, which were covered only in a thin pair of socks. Though there hadn't been an impact, her knees still buckled, forcing her to all fours. She was panting as a burning sensation rose from her stomach. It reached her throat before it was sprayed across the grass in front of her in a series of splashes.

"Gah."

Hands, on her shoulder and on her back, patted her gently.

"You're okay," a voice said.

Ren shivered and watched the world – not hers – spin.

The hands left their previous position and caught her only an inch or two from the ground. It wasn't the world that had spun.

Ren attempted to realign herself, but the air was strange, thinner somehow, as though they had emerged on top of a mountain.

"You're okay," Lance repeated. "The air here, it's different. It messes with your head. I felt the same when I first arrived in your world." His hands gripped her tighter as she let out an involuntary sob.

"It's okay." She barely heard him; the last words her father had spoken rang through her mind, over and over.

Find your mother.

She wished to both turn it off and replay it forever. Had he known where her mother was, all this time? It seemed as impossible as everything else. And yet, everything else had come to fruition now.

I love you.

Throwing herself into the only solace she had, as small and unfamiliar as it was, she allowed her body to slump against his as he held her for the second time in the only day she had known him.

Her heartbeats became fuzzy. Then she couldn't breathe.

"Take a breath, as slowly as you can, through your mouth."

No matter how she tried, she couldn't. And so, she clung to him and his repeated comforts, which weren't all that comforting.

She didn't know how long they stayed there, on the ground.

What had she done?

Regaining her composure was slow and painful. Neither Lance nor Shae rushed her. In time, her breathing slowed, palpitations subsiding, heartbeat returning to close to normal.

One by one, her senses came alive again.

It was indeed different, though not unbearably so. Gone was the heady scent of the forest after the rain they had left behind. Instead, the slightest hint of peppermint hovered in the air. Ren blinked.

For the shortest of moments, everything that had transpired over the previous evening was pushed from her mind.

Using Lance as a support, Ren rose to her feet, legs shaking. One gasp and then another escaped her. Not at the grass, or the stark silhouette of a nearby tree line, past which she saw mountains.

At the sky.

Stars were scattered in every direction, each a diamond placed on black silk. Between them and the moon – larger than it ever was on Earth – hanging up to her right like a silvery beacon, she would have been enraptured enough. But Ren barely saw them.

Instead, she saw fireflies.

When not confined to one's taio, fireflies were able to *move. Really* move. Ren let out a breath, her gaze fixed on the sky. Goosebumps spread over her shoulders as she watched them dance across the night. They were mainly white, though there were blue specks over to their right. Those lay lower down, moving from right to left and back again. Some were grey; they stayed higher, barely moving at all. Closer to her, only visible thanks to soft shifts in the night, black specks were hovering, almost still and glimmering in the moonlight.

"I can *see* it," Ren said to both, or neither, of them. "And *feel* it." She didn't know what *it* was, but it resided in her, something endless, and ancient.

Something greater.

From behind her, Shae cleared his throat. "Welcome home."

Ren didn't know whether he was only talking to Lance.

"Wh-where are we?" Ren asked; the realisation that she didn't know was a jarring one.

"Caeracre," Lance said, "just outside Loreleith, to be specific." He pointed over to the left, where Ren realised several great silhouettes signified buildings of some kind. They lay in front of the mountains. "It's more impressive during the day."

Ren doubted that. "Caeracre," she repeated.

"It is, I suppose, our Scotland," Shae said. "Caer*isle* is our Britain."

"That's not confusing at all."

Both Shae and Lance snorted.

"Is it similar," Ren asked, "the land, I mean. To my world?"

"If you were looking at a map, Caerisle is a mirror image of Britain. Where those woods were in your world, we're at the same point, but in Caerisle."

That, she wasn't expecting.

Shae began to walk, not towards the place Lance had mentioned, which Ren had already forgotten the name of, but forwards, to a small cluster of lights some way off. A campsite, perhaps.

Lance was watching her. He hadn't moved. Ren looked between him and the back of Shae's head, which was becoming difficult to see, and the sky.

You okay? Lance mouthed.

Ren shrugged. Was she okay? *No,* she thought, *absolutely not.*

But also.... She tracked a dark firefly. *Yes.*

She turned, readying herself to follow Shae, when a bright, white, and also purple, light struck into the ground ahead of them, mere feet away from Shae. This was followed by a *boom* of what could only be thunder, only much, *much,* louder than

Ren had ever heard before.

She backed up, her own scream ringing in the air, and grabbed Lance's arm. As soon as it had come, it disappeared, leaving a faint tinge of smoke.

"What the–?"

Ren was clutching her other hand to her chest. Ahead, Shae was grumbling as he stood, having fallen over, and Lance, for some inexplicable reason, was chuckling.

She rounded on him. "That was *funny* to you?"

He only laughed more. "We probably should have mentioned that."

"Mention–" Ren gaped at him. "Yes, you probably should have."

"Do you remember," Shae began, "how I said the last weaver was sent away twenty years ago?"

"Vaguely."

"Well, that made *NáDarra*," he gestured to nothing, "a little unhinged."

Ren stared at him. "Unhinged?"

"Mm."

"So, this...is common?" Ren asked, her thoughts drifting to the unrelenting wind that had followed her for a month.

Shae was already turning away. "It is now."

She didn't know what that meant.

A second bolt of lightning, purple and forked and angry, charged downwards. This one didn't strike beside Shae.

Ren clutched her chest, but where there should have been pain – the kind of electrifying agony one expects when struck by lightning – there was something else.

Something...not awful. And it was ignited within her like a second heartbeat, one that rang not with a pulse, but with thunder. A deep rumbling of pure and static energy coursed through her, in no direction, and then in every direction. It sparked from deep in her gut to the tips of her fingers and each and every strand of her hair.

It disappeared as quickly as it arrived, quicker than the others had, leaving her panting and empty. But also, as several specks of purple leapt from her fingertips, zig-zagging into the air and vanishing somewhere out of sight, not empty at all.

"Uh," it was Lance, "are you...okay?"

"Your third element," Shae said, his words hushed.

Ren only nodded as Shae's eyes flickered upwards. Ren's followed. There, next to the white and red, was purple. Purple specks that neither sparked nor blew, but darted in no discernible direction like a crazed, caged animal.

For the first time since arriving, a small and unassuming smile crossed Ren's lips, meant only for her taio and its new violet, zig-zagging inhabitants.

She liked those ones best.

The *campsite* turned out to be a village, though with distinct differences to Ainhill.

Ainhill. Her breath caught thinking of the word.

"Everything okay?" Lance asked. Ren sucked in a breath, and nodded, once. They followed Shae, who was striding ahead, cloak billowing behind him as though Lance and Ren were his subjects.

Lance scoffed. "He does this a lot; lets his self-importance go to his head. Usually I'm carrying a huge bag, too, because he can't possibly worry himself with such menial tasks. People always think I'm some kind of hired bodyguard."

"So you're *not* just a hired bodyguard? Good to know."

"I was once. It didn't end well."

"Oh?"

"The man who hired me found me in a...compromising position."

"You can't just say *that*."

"The compromising position involved his wife."

The buzzing by her elbow shifted momentarily, once again prickling. "On second thoughts, I require no more details."

"It wasn't *my* fault; she set the whole thing up. I think she wanted his house, and goats. Nothing happened. He didn't believe me, though–"

"He's not the only one."

"Well, that's insulting."

She shot him a brief half-smile, and the buzzing returned to what Ren supposed was its regular state as they entered the village.

The streets were cobbled roughly and lined with wooden lanterns, though instead of a bulb, a small gathering of yellow specks hovered in place, to-ing and fro-ing. A few days ago she'd have believed them to be fireflies.

They came to a square, lined with various buildings, each one built using wooden panelling on a grey foundation. It was like stepping through the page in a textbook. The peppermint scent was fainter, and joined by something earthier, like the farms that surrounded Ainhill.

Shae halted in front of the largest building, digging in his pockets.

Lance was doing the same.

"Anything?"

Lance revealed a handful of what looked like peanuts, and one of his knives.

Ren eyed the small silver dagger. Its handle was black and carved into roses.

"Nothing," he replied, though with a cheerier disposition. He shot Shae a wink.

Shae sighed through his nose. "Tomorrow you're going hunting."

"Offer two sets so we can get breakfast," Lance replied, now grinning.

"I have some money," Ren offered, digging in her own pocket and producing a twenty-pound note. Despite its impromptu wash in the North Sea, it was in good condition. It probably wouldn't pay for a room, but it might buy them some food.

Lance shot her a soft smile. "That won't do us much good here."

"Oh." Ren's cheeks burned. "Right, your money will be different to mine."

"That's one way of putting it," Lance replied. "Money isn't a thing here at all."

What? Ren frowned. "How?"

"We trade for everything."

"Oh."

That did not seem feasible, though it did explain Shae's monetary incompetence.

Pausing again as they approached, Shae turned to her. "Your taio is probably going to attract some attention, as will your clothes."

"Probably my lack of shoes, too."

"A weaver is a very rare sight now. Stay with one of us and try not to answer any questions."

"*Definitely* don't say you're from a different world," Lance interjected.

"I'm not a complete idiot."

He only smiled further as Shae pushed the door.

Inside, it wasn't dissimilar from any other bar – if patrons of other bars were armed with a myriad medieval-looking weapons and spoke to each other under the light of magical fireflies. Taios, some similar to Shae's, others more colourful, hovered overhead. Ren was the only one with more than one type of speck. She tracked the zig-zagging within a purple Lightning taio nearby, only half a foot above her own head; similar specks were darting in the same haphazard way this man's were. The man wore a cloak like Shae and had a shaggy mane of long hair like Lance, though his was bright ginger. A scar on his cheek struck across his face like his own Lightning. He appeared to be snoozing in his seat, head drooped forwards, his chin clunked against his chest.

Shae pushed onward, through the throng of customers towards the bar. It wasn't like any Ren had seen. There were no beer pumps; instead, they kept the kegs against the back wall. There were only a few bottles dotted on a small shelf above them.

Lance nudged her, nodding to a free table on the far side. She led them, his hand brushing against her elbow every few steps as they navigated a mishmash of too many squashed-in tables, chairs, and people.

Weariness befell her as she sat, seeping into her limbs and making her thoughts fuzzy. How long had she slept for in St. Andrews? Not long enough. How much time had passed since she had seen her phone clock read 2am? Did they tell time here?

Shae had reached the front of the bar.

"What's *the usual*?" she asked.

Lance was smirking. "You'll see."

Ren shifted uneasily. From every direction, people were staring. Some brazen, unblinking as they stared at both her and her taio, others looked away once she had clocked them.

"Everyone is staring at me." Ren scanned the place. There appeared to be only one exit, the way they had come in.

"No, they're not."

"I have eyes, *look*," she hissed, trying to nod as subtly as possible towards a table of two women, both openly looking in their direction. "They aren't even trying to hide it."

"They're quite clearly staring at me, probably because I'm so ruggedly handsome."

He *was*, in fact, ruggedly handsome, but Ren doubted he needed the ego boost.

"See, you can't bring yourself to disagree."

She couldn't, but she wasn't going to tell him that. Luckily, Shae's arrival meant she was spared the need to. He placed three pints of what Ren soon deciphered was a kind of ale on the rough wood of their table.

"We're in room four," he said.

Lance reached for his drink. "And?"

Shae regarded him. "Why, thank you, Shae, for securing us a safe place to sleep and for trading your underutilised talents for the good of our cause."

Lance blinked at him, then took a sip. "And?"

Shae plonked himself down beside Ren. "The kitchen will open again in a few hours; we can have a meal any time tomorrow."

The corners of Lance's eyes crinkled again. "When do you start?" he asked.

Shae groaned. "In about fifteen minutes."

What, exactly, Shae had traded to ensure their room and board soon became clear. Standing with another groan, Shae made his way to a small, raised platform at the other side of the room. He stepped up to a scattering of applause and began, with neither introduction nor accompaniment, to sing.

Ren watched, mesmerised, as he crooned, somewhere

between a folk song and a show tune, of lost life and love.

From the window, the beginning of a sunrise was casting a soft glow through the nearby treetops. Soft yellow specks, similar to the ones they used in lanterns, were replacing the black ones. Ren wondered where the dark specks went during the day, making a mental note to ask Shae later.

Despite the late – or early – hour, Shae had roused the crowd and tables were being piled up. His next tune was jauntier, and the makeshift dance floor was soon filled.

Ren and Lance were two of the few still seated.

"He's good," she noted over Shae's applause.

As entertaining as Shae was, Ren was struggling. Muscles she probably hadn't used her entire life had been exhausted, from the calamity on the beach and her unplanned swim, to the transcending of worlds and yet another *awakening* without nearly enough rest.

"Lance," she said through a yawn, "I want to go to bed."

He looked relieved, and as tired as her. They left Shae to his adoring crowd and headed towards a door Ren hadn't noticed past the bar.

Two beds, one single and one double, greeted them. The exact same layout as the room in St. Andrews. It even smelled of lavender. Ren swallowed.

"You can have the bigger one."

Ren wrinkled her nose. "It's okay; you can share with Shae."

"Didn't you see the man closest to the stage? In the red?"

"No."

"Well, I did. And I've seen plenty of men – and women – give him that same look. We won't be seeing him tonight."

She swallowed, mouth dry. "You'll have plenty of room to stretch out then, won't you?"

"Plenty of room," Lance repeated. He looked as if he wanted

to say something further, and Ren didn't know whether it was the ale or the buzzing that made her wish he would. In the end, after undoing his armour, and extinguishing the one candle their room had, he simply offered her a plain, "Goodnight," leaving Ren to wonder, into the darkness, what the hell her life was now.

Not that of a lowly barmaid with the immune system of a gnat, apparently.

"Goodnight, Lance," she whispered into the darkness, the buzzing humming in her chest.

He answered her with a snore.

She slept like the dead, a blissful nothing, until it was broken by a loud *boom*. Four eyes, set in a featureless mass of black, blinked in time with a second bang, moving closer and closer.

She woke with a gasp, certain the same, advancing nightmare was mere inches away. A clatter of metal on wood jolted her further.

What greeted her was another bang, caused less by a *bodach* and more by a rap on the door. Lance strode across the room, his long hair wild. His sword lay in the gap between their beds, clearly responsible for the clattering.

Never in her life had Ren been so on edge.

Shae, dishevelled and sleepy, stood on the other side of the now open door.

"If it isn't any trouble," Lance said, seeking out Ren, "I'd really appreciate it if you knocked at a regular volume, instead of making us think we're under attack again."

"I *did*; it's hardly my fault you didn't hear it."

Ren sunk back against her headboard, heart still racing.

Lance rounded back to Shae. "She's been through enough without you terrifying her half to death for no reason."

At his words there was a minute rise in the buzzing.

Shae sighed. "You're right." He looked at Ren. "I apologise, Ren."

"It's okay." Ren looked down at her duvet, willing her hands to stop shaking. "I'm okay."

Shae's robes were sitting oddly, crumpled in a most un-Shae-like fashion. His eyes were bloodshot and puffy. The slightest hint of a smile was present as he kicked his shoes off.

"Good night?" she asked.

"*Very* good night." He sat on the bed. "And you two?"

"*We*," Lance said, "came here and fell asleep, because we aren't into debauchery, unlike you."

"I've saved you from debauchery more times than I care to count."

Ren was hardly listening, her attention drawn to Lance's bare torso. The scar from the *bodach* arm was stark and angry against his skin. It joined a collection of smaller scars and various tattoos littering his frame.

It took her a second to realise he was staring right back at her, eyebrows raised, half his mouth a little upturned. He beckoned to her as Shae, without so much as taking his cloak off, laid down and closed his eyes. With a satisfied groan he turned onto his side. "If you two wouldn't mind keeping the noise down, I'd be most appreciative."

Ren's mouth fell open at the bloody cheek of him.

Lance picked up a nearby cup, launching it at the already unconscious arcanist. It earned him no more than a soft grunt as the cup bounced off Shae's head.

Ren felt disgusting. Her body badly needed a wash. Her clothes, too, having remained on her person after being submerged in the sea, had developed an unpleasant odour. She didn't want to think about her hair.

"Are you okay?" Lance said as she reached him.

She looked down again, sucking in a breath. "I already said I–"

"I know what you said, but I also know that when *he* tried to break the door down to get in, *this* was..." He gestured back and forth in the space that separated them. The place where the buzzing centred itself. "Sore."

Ren swallowed. "I'm okay," she repeated.

He didn't look as though he believed her. "I have a plan, or, the beginnings of a plan, anyway." A part of her soared at his words. "We go get something to eat, and then find a store, figure out what we can do, or trade, to get you some clothes and shoes. In the meantime, wear his." He motioned towards a pair of pointy brogues by the bottom of the double bed. "There's soap and stuff in there, at least." He nodded towards the bathroom.

"You can smell me, can't you?" Ren grimaced as she touched her own hair. It wasn't pleasant.

"I can," Lance said, "but I'm a generous man. I'll put up with it for now, given the circumstances."

"Most appreciated."

They made their way out of the room, Ren walking rather penguin-like, due to Shae's shoe size being about five times her own.

Lance shot her a half smile. "You don't smell."

Ren, who had woken up with one arm raised above her head, knew that was not the case.

They were seated by a woman with an axe strapped to her back and a taio of red specks above her head.

"Everything we have available is on the board up *there*." She pointed at what looked like a blackboard above Lance's head. "Your companion is very talented."

Ren didn't miss the brief roll of Lance's eyes and resisted the urge to laugh.

"Oh, I know," Lance said.

"We can't wait to see him sing again tonight," she said, beaming. "I'll get you both a drink." She shuffled off to the bar.

"You've heard that before, haven't you?"

"Far too many times."

Their options for food were lamb stew or lamb soup. Odd breakfast choices. Ren read the board at least ten times over before she looked to the bar. The waitress was pouring something green and fizzy into two glasses. She would be the one to bring them their lamb, as Ren would have.

There was only one other occupied table, a woman with a little girl. She looked around five and was squealing at something the woman had said.

Ren turned her attention back to Lance, not all that surprised to find he was watching her.

"I can't imagine where your head's at."

"Somewhere pretty close to insanity. You know, my dad always told me never to go with a guy somewhere I wasn't familiar with. And now I'm with two, whose last names I don't know, in a *world* I'm not familiar with."

Lance let out his bark-like laugh. "If it helps, at all, Shae's last name is Ambroise, and mine is Allardyce." He probably already knew hers.

She regarded him. "Any middle names?"

"Two of them. Neither of which I have any interest in telling you."

"You can't say that and *not* tell me."

"I absolutely can."

She vowed silently to learn both. "How old are you?" she continued.

"Twenty-six."

The waitress appeared again, placing the two drinks in front of them, and took their order – two lamb stews – before disappearing. Ren watched her fire specks shoot upwards.

"*Her* taio only has fire magic."

Lance nodded. "She's a Fire bearer."

"A Fire *bearer*. And I'm a *weaver*?"

He looked momentarily up. "Indeed, you are."

"Then," Ren said, choosing her words, "why can't I, well, *weave* anything?"

"Pardon?"

"I can't *do* anything magical."

"You're still awakening."

She swallowed, then sighed. "I just wish I knew why."

She buzzed at the touch as he patted her arm. "Don't worry. Once we get you to Gideon, he'll know more."

"Who?"

"Senior Councillor, the one that–"

"Told you to *Collect* me?"

He nodded. "We were as surprised as you."

"I doubt that," Ren replied, hugging her arms around herself. "Do you and Shae always get sent together to *Collect* whatever it is you usually, ah, *Collect*?"

He nodded again once as the waitress returned, two piled plates in hand.

They took a few minutes to eat before Lance said, "Collectors always work in pairs."

"Why?"

"It can be dangerous."

"Huh." Ren regarded him. "You know, *delivery boy* isn't all that dangerous a career path where I'm from."

Spearing a chunk of lamb, which he jabbed towards her face, Lance narrowed his eyes. "I am *not* a delivery boy." His facade lasted approximately three seconds before a grin broke across his face. "What did you do? For a job, I mean."

Her own smile faltered at his use of the word *did*, inclining her head towards the waitress.

"*That* was my job." She took a bite. "I didn't carry an axe, though."

He laughed again. Ren liked the noise. "Enjoy it?"

When she was well enough to. "I suppose I did."

Outside, they were greeted by an angry sky and several rolls of thunder. The village, a tiny collection of around twenty or so buildings, was cast in shadow. There were only a few people, all of whom eyed Ren with looks ranging from alarm to confusion. She took a half step closer to Lance as they made their way down the only real street.

Ren, frowning as she grazed the front of her thighs gently, swallowed. "I'm not sore," she said, voice low, more to herself than him.

Lance only smiled. "I'm glad."

There was one store, which sold or traded for an assortment of random and general goods, some food, and even a sparse array of clothing.

Ren eyed them. On Earth they'd be outdated by at least a hundred years.

The shopkeeper, a woman with red eyes that made each of the hairs on Ren's neck stand to attention, had a shimmery taio. The specks were constantly shifting and changing colour. She claimed far more of Ren's personal space than was necessary, pulling and prodding at her jumper and jeans.

"New outfit," the woman said, her voice a throaty whisper, "for old outfit." A bony pair of hands ran up the seams of the denim.

Ren jumped away, ignoring Lance, who was slowly turning purple in his dismal attempts to conceal his laughter. "Agh! Yes, *fine*. I want *that* top, and *those* trousers, and *this* pair of boots."

"Ooh." The woman frog-marched Ren to a nearby changing area. It was concealed through a curtain so meagre and flimsy

Ren was certain it hid nothing. "Change now."

Giving the rather crispy jeans away was no hardship; nor was it a loss to part with an old, black T-shirt. Her jumper, though. Ren sighed as she handed the bundle over.

Lance, having composed himself, appeared around a display of purple pumpkins. "What's wrong?"

The jumper was being squished rather enthusiastically by its new owner. "It was Luke's."

"Luke?"

"My brother. It-it's fine," she lied, turning away. "Do you like my boots?"

"I do."

They left in haste as the woman, after thrusting a small woven tote into Ren's hands, took a sizable sniff of the jeans.

In room four, Shae was still unconscious. Ren deposited his shoes in their former position and entered the bathroom, never so keen to clean herself.

A deep tub, wooden and circular, stood in the corner. She approached it, taking stock of the few complimentary toiletries.

Lance knocked on the door, shouting something about hunting – a plan to obtain more they could trade with.

Ren had never given trade much thought before. It was something countries did, she supposed, in certain circumstances she couldn't fathom.

A world without money. Ren climbed into her bath. The bar of soap she had run under the tap had infused the water with some bubbles that smelled vaguely of vanilla. What did you *do* when you had nothing to trade? Lance had been no help on the matter. *What would you do when you had no money?* The logic had been hard to argue with.

She wondered, running her hands back and forth through the water, what, and, indeed, how, people were paid, and made a mental note to ask one of them. It seemed implausible, a world without any set currency. Somehow more implausible than a world where magic roamed like citizens and moved like dancers.

Blue specks were hovering above her bath; Water magic, Ren reasoned, while both white and yellow ones – Air and Light – hung in the air above.

Air was everywhere – which made sense, of course. So was Ground, to an extent – outside, anyway. Light was replaced by Dark when the sun set, and vice versa. She still needed to ask Shae where each disappeared to every day, or night. Water, and Fire, and Lightning appeared when they needed to. She didn't know what the other one, Aether, did. Ren watched them. Water had its own pattern. While Fire sparked upwards, and Lightning crashed around like a caged drunk, Water moved back and forth, wave-like and lazy.

For what had to be the hundredth time, the words *right thing*, along with many soundless question marks, crossed her mind. Ren dunked her head under the water, praying for answers no bathtub could provide her with.

Magic. It would be absurd to not want *that*, wouldn't it? In front of her, head now above water, a splash appeared, as though someone had plunged a closed fist through the surface.

"Helpful, thanks," she said to a blue speck travelling rather close to her right eye.

She finished washing, and found a few terrible quality towels, though really, by the time she'd combed her dark locks using her fingers, which took at least six months, she was already dry.

In the tote bag, she had found new underwear and socks and threw up a silent *thank you* to the thoughtful, if strange, shopkeeper.

Finishing pulling her new clothes on, Ren examined herself as best she could with no mirror. The trousers were an plain brown cotton, but they fit well at least, if a little long. The boots she had chosen because they looked like they belonged to a pirate. Her top was dark, cherry red. It had long sleeves, flared at the ends, and a square neckline she trailed her fingertips across, stopping near the centre of her chest. If the buzzing was a physical, tangible thing, that was where it would be visible.

Shae woke as she re-entered the bedroom, mumbling something about not enough sleep. Considering it was possibly late morning at the latest, he was right.

"Have you and Lance had a *pleasant* morning?"

She ignored his pointed tone. "We have, actually. What do you think of my new clothes?"

Shae looked her up and down. "Dull, and unassuming."

"Boring. Got it. Thanks, Shae."

"Yes," he replied, with no trace of humour, "but you suit boring."

"You really know how to make a girl feel good."

Shae arched an eyebrow. "As it happens, I do." He began digging into his many pockets. "But you don't want *me* to make you feel good."

"And that's supposed to mean what, exactly?" Ren busied herself with making her bed, because it needed to be done, and not so she had an excuse to hide the heat pooling in her cheeks.

"It means," Shae replied, "that I am neither blind nor stupid."

She opened her mouth to retort, but none came as Lance returned.

"Who missed me?" he asked. He was leaning against the far wall, the curls of his long hair unkempt and messy. The buzzing lurched at the sight. Ren ignored it.

Shae was pulling various vials from his many pockets. "Certainly not me, though I can't imagine that bothers you too much." He stopped looking at a handful of what looked like wheatgrass to linger on Ren.

"You imagine correctly." Lance took a step forward, his gaze also on Ren. "You look...nice."

"Thanks." If Ren could have learnt to control anything in that moment, it wouldn't have been Fire or Air, but the dopey smile she couldn't seem to stop. "Shae thinks I look boring."

"I *also* said you *suit* boring."

Lance snorted. For a moment so quick she would have missed it had she blinked, he looked downwards; down *her*. "Not the word I'd use." Ren's mouth dried as his gaze returned to her face. "Since you were both too rude to ask, I'll tell you what I managed to hunt then, shall I?"

"It's a trick question, Ren," Shae replied dryly. "He'll tell us regardless. Then he'll have a pint and tell us again–"

"A *stag*!"

"And again–"

"*And* four," he held four fingers up excitedly, ignoring Shae, "rabbits!"

"Then, for reasons neither of us will fathom, he'll tell us again in two days' time."

"I secured us the room for another night, *and*," he pulled something soft and blue from the satchel he wore at his hip and passed it to her, "turns out that batty faedra from the store loves a bit of rabbit stew."

Somewhere between her chest and throat, Ren's breath caught as her fingers stroked the fabric of Luke's jumper. "Lance, I..."

"Don't mention it."

She wouldn't, but she'd never forget it.

"Tomorrow, we need to start heading south," Lance was saying, tone still ringing with satisfaction.

"We do," Shae replied, "and–"

A short rap on the door halted his words. With the hint of a frown, Shae crossed the room.

The waitress who had served Ren and Lance their breakfast stood, holding a piece of what looked like parchment outwards. "This was left at the bar for *the Arcanist, the Swordsman and the Weaver*. You're the only guests who fit the description." She retreated without a further word as Shae unfolded the note.

His expression darkened.

"Lance."

"Mm?"

"Get that window open."

"What?"

"We need to run."

Less than a heartbeat passed, and Lance was positioned in front of a now open window, one hand outstretched behind him. She eyed it, then him. Her first instinct was to object, but it was quelled – just – by the unspoken plea in his stare.

And so, she relented to the madness that was sneaking out of the window of the room Lance had secured them for another night, and running goodness only knew where, or how, for that matter. Ren was many things, but a long-distance runner was not among them. And she had seen nothing that resembled a car since arriving.

His hand was both warm and rough against hers. Cradling Luke's jumper into her chest, she squatted beside him on the windowsill.

"Ready?" he asked.

It looked further than it should have. "No."

His hand squeezed hers.

They dropped. The air whizzed upwards a fraction of a second longer than Ren was comfortable with. Landing in a crouch, they shuffled, waiting for Shae. As he landed with a soft crunch of leaves, a fork of lightning, clear as day, crashed into a nearby tree. A scream escaped her. At the tree, specks that hadn't been there a moment before, both purple and red, were darting. The reds sparked upwards, like the fire that was beginning to absorb the tree, while the purples zig-zagged in every direction. Seconds later they had dissipated, leaving only the reds, the fire itself, and the soon-to-be-charred remains of a small oak.

Without paying it the slightest attention, Lance led them

past the fire, out of the village. The village Ren didn't even know the name of, but that had provided her with...what? A sliver of calm. Snatched from her in as swift a moment as Earth had been.

Beyond the last few buildings lay a forest. They entered the tree line at a jog, skirting around huge pines. It didn't take long for Ren's chest to seize, and by the time Lance and Shae slowed down, Ren's face was blazing and soaked.

Her muscles ached, her thoughts as scrambled as a long-forgotten ball of yarn.

The forest grew thicker and darker with each step they took. Figures loomed from all angles, each one turning out to be no more than an oddly shaped shrub or a fallen tree trunk. With each trick her eyes played, Ren's unease grew. Despite the layer of sweat between their palms, she clutched Lance's hand as her legs threatened to buckle beneath her. More than once, plumes of smoke rose from her. They were extinguished by a fierce and sporadic wind. It rivalled the one she had caused for weeks back in Scotland, blustering between trees like rapids through reeds.

Lance, shouting to make himself heard over yet another gust, cried, "What's going on?"

Shae only shook his head. "Not yet."

They walked for hours. As the sun set, Dark magic replaced Light. Around them, scuffles and hoots echoed. The wind, at least, had dampened.

Ren wished she could say the same for her heart rate.

They emerged in front of a large boulder, the size of a small house, and Shae stopped.

On one side, halfway up, the rock jutted out, making something of a small cave. They sat, Ren between them, like a trio of pigeons.

Despite having moved more than she had her entire life, her legs, though still aching, were only marginally seizing up.

Having let go of his hand as they sat, Lance pressed against her. Perhaps for her warmth: Ren's body temperature ran around two degrees warmer than the average person's.

She buzzed against the contact.

Perhaps not.

Shae pulled something small and crumpled from a pocket. He passed it to Lance.

"Fuck."

He passed the note to Ren. Her heartbeat, not long returned to regular, increased. A hollowness opened in her stomach.

Bring the weaver to the bar or all three of you die tonight.

"*Fuck*, indeed," Shae said.

It wasn't signed.

"Who the...?" Lance didn't finish.

She watched a nearby speck of Dark float lazily past her. "So, neither of you have *any* idea who it is that wants me, dead or alive, apparently?"

"There are...groups." Shae's voice was far too calm given their circumstance.

"*Groups?*"

"Mm," Shae replied. "Rebels. Tired of *NáDarra* destroying everything."

Ren bristled at his words, though didn't fully understand why.

"Others have grown to fear it. And those who wield it."

It wasn't hard to see why.

"But there are others who have wh-what I do; those who have only one element."

"Bearers." Shae nodded. "It's dangerous to be one now. Bearer murders are far more common than they were."

"Oh." In her mind's eye, she saw the Lightning bearer from the previous night. He was both heavily scarred and armed. So was the waitress, the Fire bearer.

"Before," Shae said, "*NáDarra* and *NeòNach* existed in harmony. There was balance. But that balance was thrown off, as less and less *NáDarra* entered the world, as there were no new weavers, and far fewer bearers."

"Why?"

"The Council have been trying to figure out exactly that for nearly two decades while the land, and people, suffered. Still suffer," he added. "What *NáDarra* is left now is very unstable. And that frightens people now more than it ever has."

Ren bit down hard on her bottom lip. So little made sense. "So, someone wants me dead because they're either scared of, or angry at, my magic?" Her voice was higher than it should have been. "They want to *kill* me because I have *Ná-NáDarra*?" The note was crumpled in a fist she couldn't remember making. A single spark, accompanied by at least ten red specks, erupted from her closed fingertips.

"We cannot know for sure." She didn't miss the glance Shae shot at Lance. "But we do know for the past few years, almost every weaver...has gone missing."

"*Missing*?"

"Yes."

"Why?"

"I do not know."

Ren barely heard him, her mind a world away. She had held it in disdain for so long, but now her heart ached for the mundane life that she had led in Ainhill. Ached for her brother and father. For a lack of death threats. She swallowed, musing over what information she had that made any sense. Ren didn't know much of being a weaver, despite the fact she was one. But she hated, with an intensity stemming from a deep part of her, a hidden part, that something was threatening them.

Shae shifted on the ground beside her. On her other side, Lance's leg pressed closer against hers.

The buzzing surged.

The rest of her throbbed.

Her body leaned into his. He didn't move as their breathing synchronised and the conversation stilled. Then Lance drew his arm up, settling it across her shoulders. Fingertips grazed the fabric covering the top of her arm.

His breath was warm against her forehead. "I imagine that was a lot to take in."

"Nothing new there then."

His words were hurried and whispered against the top of her head. "We'll protect you."

It was all she had to believe him.

She must have lost consciousness. It was darker, the air cooler. The scent of peppermint was back. Her head had lulled to the side and was resting gently on Lance's chest as she woke.

He whispered a soft, "Hi."

Shae was asleep on her other side, his breathing rhythmic, heavy. From somewhere to their right, several hoots sounded. She wondered if they were owls or something else.

On Earth, during the nights she would walk home, it was always still, as though she were the only organic thing for miles. On Caerisle, nights looked vastly different.

Alive.

Specks of *NáDarra* hovered in every direction. Green closest to the ground; they had a steady back-and-forth pattern. Above them were the white ones – the *wild* ones. They weren't dancing as wildly now, but they were still different from those within her taio; guided by a silent music only they could hear.

She sought out the Dark ones easier this time. They moved the slowest, a gradual mooch through the air.

She might like those ones the best.

"Hi," she replied, lifting her head, somewhat reluctantly, studying what she could see of his face. "Why aren't you asleep?"

"Shae and I never sleep at the same time when we're outside."

"Do you sleep outside a lot?"

"More than you'd think. I'll wake him up in a bit, though. I'm pretty tired."

"I can keep watch," Ren offered, "you should sleep."

He looked as though he wanted to decline, and she steeled herself to argue. It was almost a relief when he replied, "Are you sure? You need to rest, too."

Ren shrugged, despite the exhaustion that gripped her limbs and fuzzed her brain. "We all do, but I've had some. You haven't. I like watching them anyway."

"Who?"

"No." In spite of everything, a soft smile escaped her. "I mean the magic."

"Ah, of course; you'll see it really easily."

"Don't you?"

"Nah, only if I really concentrate, and even then, it's all pretty blurry."

Ren watched the dots of light burst through the sky, wishing she could share the sight with him, wondering what growing up in a world with magic was like when you didn't have any. Though, she reasoned, probably no different to growing up poor in a world with money.

Lance was shivering.

She handed him Luke's jumper.

"It's okay," he said.

Ren smiled. "Don't be stubborn; put it on. I don't ever get too cold, and you obviously do."

He didn't argue further. "Okay, this does feel good," he admitted.

"That's because it was my idea."

He let out one of his laughs that sounded like a bark. "And look how modest you are about it."

She didn't answer, once again looking skywards.

"Can you tell the difference," Lance asked, "between the types?"

Her mouth dropped open. "Yes! They're all *so* different." She pointed out each type, relaying its pattern to him. She told him, more and more animatedly, how vibrant they were and how, in her mind, each type was beginning to develop its own personality.

"Shae's fireflies are smaller, and they don't move like mine."

Another laugh. "Spoken like a true elemental."

"What do you mean?"

"That smugness you've got going on."

She opened her mouth to protest.

"Don't worry, from the few arcanists I know – Shae being one of them – they're just as smug about *NeòNach*."

Ren failed to see how. Not that she had seen much *NeòNach* in action, but *her* type was in each and every part of the world around them. That had to be far more impressive than wherever *NeòNach* happened to spend its time. A detail Ren, like most things in her life now, did not know.

Lance was watching her as she traced several swirling specks of Air magic just above them. "Do you feel better now?" he asked.

Ren swallowed. She knew how she *wanted* to respond: bravely. Though what that entailed, exactly... The buzzing began to hum in a steady pulse, as though excited. "Do I have to say no for you to put your arm around me again?"

He chuckled. "Not at all."

"Then yes, despite us being on the run from some mad rebels that want me dead, I do."

His arm wound its way around her shoulders once more. "Good."

"Sleep," she ordered.

His reply was encased within a yawn. "Yes ma'am."

Before long, though, the magic couldn't entertain her. Once Lance's breathing slowed, a quiet snore began to emanate from his every exhale. Ren settled herself leaning against his chest, the steady *thump thump* of his heart serving the soundtrack to her thoughts – jumbled at best, downright terrified at worst.

She watched the white ones, and then the green, and then the black. In that order. A wondrous thing, but even flecks of pure magic couldn't curb her hunger-and-exhaustion-fuelled nausea.

Ren was used to pain, and though it was somehow less than it might have been a few days ago, she wasn't used to the wobbliness that had settled in her legs. She attributed it to the sheer amount of cardio. They must have walked miles, more than Ren had ever done any one day – or week – her entire life. And it had been nothing to Lance or Shae.

Ren shuffled. What few parts of her weren't sore were numb. When Shae woke, a long breath escaped her. "I'm so glad you're awake."

"I imagine I do make better company when conscious. How long has Lance been asleep?"

"Long enough for me to regret saying I'd stay up."

"You haven't seen anything of note, I assume?"

Ren stretched her legs out in front of her. "I've seen nothing at all, either of note or not."

"Good. Get some more sleep," he said, "we have a long walk in the morning."

The muscles behind Ren's shins let out a burst of pain in protest. She groaned. "Where are we going?"

"South. We should be able to reach Ververos in a few days."

Ren blinked into the dark. "Reach *what* now?"

"Ververos," Shae repeated. "Forest. Huge, very magical. It takes up over half of Caerisle. We have to go through it to reach Glendale."

"You say these words as if you expect me to know what a *Glendale* is and why we need to reach it."

"It's our England, I suppose. And it's where we have to take you."

Deliver me, you mean, she wanted to say. "So, here Scotland and England are separated by a giant forest?"

"Yes."

"What about Wales? Is it *in* the forest?"

"*Our* Wales is called Axilion."

"Gesundheit."

"And no," Shae continued, "but, again, you have to go through Ververos to reach it."

"So, this forest is the only way to get anywhere?"

"Anywhere else in Caerisle, yes."

"I don't suppose we could just rent a car to get through it?"

"I hadn't *seen* a car until I went to Earth."

At least his paled knuckles hadn't been a slight on her driving. Sighing, Ren lay her head on Lance's chest again. Her car was possibly still sitting in the car park beside Culloden wood, abandoned. Who knew what would become of it...or her...

Resigning herself to questioning them further the following day, Ren yawned. "This world is bizarre."

Shae mumbled something she didn't quite make out, though it sounded sarcastic.

Ren closed her eyes, feeling aware of so very little, and then of only the way Lance's heart thumped in time with hers.

Ren woke to hunger, stiffness, and something tickling her face – something she quickly realised was Lance's hair. Her head, while still against his chest, was closer to his face. His chin rested against her forehead, arms enveloping her.

He smelt of leather and firewood.

If she hadn't needed to pee quite as badly she'd have feigned more sleep.

"Morning." He breathed the word against the top of her head. The buzzing rose at the sound.

Ren's voice was more frog-like than his. "Hi," she croaked, and instantly regretted it. She stood, sore and sluggish. Not close to rested enough. "I'm going to pee."

There wasn't a shelter on the other side of their boulder.

Ren sighed, toeing the dry dirt with her new boots.

"You look delightful," Lance noted as she emerged.

"Leaves do not make for good toilet roll."

"Ah," he replied, pulling her jumper off in one swoop and tossing it towards her. "I don't have that problem." He dodged past, winking.

They gave Shae, who had dozed off almost the very second after they had woken up, a while before rousing him to begin on what seemed to be shaping up to be a walk that would apparently take *at least ten days, probably more.* Lance didn't seem bothered by the prospect.

Ren could not say the same. She sat cross-legged, picking at the grass. "Do you people not ride horses or...?"

Lance, who was sharpening a dagger on what looked like a pumice stone, replied, "We don't have anything to trade for to feed ourselves, let alone at least two horses. And do you even know how to ride?"

"Well, no," Ren admitted, "but–"

"And you think you'd manage to ride five hundred miles?"

She didn't answer. The last – and only – time she was within any close vicinity of a horse occurred when she was seven and plopped on top of a bored-looking piebald at the Ainhill Highland show. Lance didn't need to know that.

It was still more appealing than walking what was essentially over two-thirds of the British mainland.

She stood as he pulled out another dagger, identical to the first, and watched a few nearby specks of Light magic. It moved differently to Dark; quicker and livelier. She barely saw them, her mind elsewhere.

Bring the weaver to the bar or all three of you die tonight.

Well, Ren reasoned, *they were wrong.* It was one of the few comforts she had: all three of them were alive. This time at least.

It seemed futile to hope there wouldn't be a next.

"What's wrong?" Lance asked. The buzzing swelled as their eyes met.

"How harshly would you judge me if I said I was marginally uncomfortable at the fact we had to flee for our lives last night?"

He stopped sharpening the knife and beckoned. "Come here."

Ren slumped down beside him as the first fat droplets of rain began to fall, bringing with it flecks of blue. She watched them, then watched him.

"I'd consider you incredibly stupid if you *weren't* scared after last night."

"Oh, okay. Well, that's good because I'm pretty scared." The words tumbled out, along with a sound that wasn't quite a laugh, and wasn't quite not.

His gaze bored into her own.

Lance's eyes, unlike Shae's, held only one shade. Rich mahogany: warm and yet cool, the moment summer met autumn.

"I meant what I said." He swallowed, the space between their elbows closed. *Buzz buzz buzz.* "About protecting you."

"Because it's your job?"

She hoped for many things, but none more so than for Lance to answer no.

"No."

"Because of this?" Her elbow nudged into his, resisting the urge to add *connection.* That wasn't right somehow, though she didn't know why.

"I..." She watched a speck of Light magic reflected in those mahogany eyes as he paused, bringing his hand upwards. His fingertips – and the buzzing, stopped by the side of her jaw. "I don't know."

The mingling scents of leather and rain hung in the air between them. He leant closer, his fingers finally meeting her jawline. The ends were rough, yet like velvet. Despite the chill in the air, as they trailed to the back of her neck, they were warm. So was his breath.

"Look at this rain! When did that start?" Shae's voice rang right through her.

Lance's eyes shot open. "I swear to–"

"I'm famished. Have you had a chance to go hunting?"

Ren didn't know whether to laugh or shout.

Lance looked livid.

"Should forage at least," Shae continued obliviously, "should be able to find some mushrooms." He began to rummage in his vast array of pockets. "I'll make my broth," he added, his tone far brighter than it ever was. For the first time, he turned to them. "You both look dreadful. Didn't you sleep well?"

Shae remained enthusiastic about his mushroom broth, which he informed Ren was famous.

Lance, gathering his collection of knives, scoffed. "For being the worst-smelling food in the world, maybe." He stood, mumbled a brief *see you* before walking into the surrounding trees, his footsteps soundless.

She turned to Shae. "Does he hunt with those?"

"He does."

When Ren envisioned hunting, a rifle, or at least a bow, came to mind. She had served plenty of hunting parties at the hotel and none had ever, to her knowledge, used knives. "That seems impractical."

Shae was building the beginnings of a fire. "I quite agree."

Ren failed to see how he would light the few dry leaves and bark scattered around their cave that wasn't quite a cave, let alone keep it lit long enough to cook either any kind of meat, or broth. Once satisfied with his rather paltry stone circle, he stood and ventured out into the rain, muttering about fungi.

It took him only a few minutes to return, hands bursting with mushrooms. They were deposited, along with rainwater and a few of Shae's various herbs, into a large metal mug he had plucked from yet another pocket.

Placing the mug carefully, Shae put his palms together, as though praying. A number of tiny white specks, identical to the ones in his taio, surrounded his hands. It had taken him less than a second to summon them. Next, he swirled each hand in two large, sweeping circles. At the silent command, each speck began to mimic the motion, around a foot above the still

113

unlit fire. A further gesture and they closed together, forming a bright white disk. He placed the mug on top where it sat, spinning on its makeshift, magical turnstile.

"I can't imagine," she said, "being able to..." She gestured towards his *NeòNach*.

"You will."

Ren snorted. "When? How?"

"Your magic is unstable now, and it will be until you're fully awakened, maybe longer," he replied.

"How long will that take?"

Shae's focus didn't leave his specks. "I have no idea."

Oh.

"You're very focused," Ren observed. The man barely blinked. A calm was present there, greater than it was in his usual demeanour. As still as the rock they perched beneath.

"Mm. It is a must."

She supposed that made sense. "Focus?"

"It is what gives my power strength."

Ren ran a fingertip through the dirt by her side. "I suppose I should work on being calmer."

Shae, statuesque, didn't even snort. "I quite agree. Though it will do nothing for your powers."

"Oh."

"*NeòNach* is intrinsically linked to the logical – or, I suppose, the part of an arcanist's brain attuned to logic. It is more powerful when one has learnt to separate oneself from one's emotions."

Ren bit her lip, trying to imagine having such stringent control over any of her emotions.

"I'm too emotional a being for that, I think." For the first time, Shae looked as though he wanted to say something, though he remained as silent as a shadow.

"So, what is *NáDarra* linked to?"

"The elements." He had the grace to not sound sarcastic.

Ren blinked. *Oh.*

"But in the way you mean, emotion. *NáDarra* is more powerful when a weaver – or a bearer – has *less* control of their emotions."

"Oh," Ren said again, watching a nearby Air speck.

His words, though still laced with mystery, made some kind of sense, in a way. The elements were wild, uncaged things that often defied logic. So were emotions. She looked again at Shae's disk of light.

"Where do they come from?" Ren asked. They moved as one, each an intrinsic part of something bigger than itself. But, though they were beautiful, and quite incredible, their presence irked a part of her. A part she didn't understand.

"Me," Shae said simply.

"How does it *feel* to use them?"

"It is an overwhelming calm."

Lance returned then, a rabbit and a fat wood pigeon in tow, both of which were slung at Shae.

Once prepared, various cuts of meat hovered and rotated, rotisserie style, in flames Shae had created by causing two rocks, each encased by his specks, to slam together at such a speed that they sparked, setting the meagre twigs alight. He then directed the specks to remain there, cocooning almost all the small fire.

"How does that keep it lit?" Ren asked, sceptical. Ren had lit many fires, and none would stay alight with nowhere near enough kindling.

"Wielding *NeòNach*," Shae explained, "consists of utilising both precise control, and the strength of the magic itself." He gave his broth a quick stir. "Right now, it has created a covering so strong it can keep heat over a hundred degrees hotter than itself within."

Ren watched the structure closer.

There were tiny openings, set in a kind of honeycomb pattern around its perimeter, providing the fire with oxygen. And below, within the flames themselves, lay yet more of the tiny white specks.

"Your specks," she said, frowning. It didn't seem like a possible thing. "Are they kindling?"

"Yes," Shae said. "And no. *NeòNach* itself cannot burn, but it can add its strength into any object."

"Like leaves and twigs?"

He nodded. "It mimics them, really, or their structure, at least, *while* strengthening them. It can also mimic NáDarra, in a sense, but it's weak, and can be overpowered by its natural form very easily. I don't like to do that if I can help it."

It seemed the most unnatural way to burn anything. "For how long?"

"As long as I wish."

The rain had stopped by the time they headed south, each full of rabbit, and pigeon, and mushroom-flavoured water Ren had struggled to swallow without shuddering. Exiting the sanctity of the forest, they emerged to miles and miles of dry, brown earth. Her gaze trailed the barren landscape. It looked as dry as a desert. Far across to her left, above a cluster of low-lying peaks, she could make out a thunderstorm, purple lightning forking downwards, accompanied by distant growls of thunder.

Ren tied Luke's jumper around her waist as they joined a nearby dirt track that wasn't all that separate from the earth that surrounded it. From behind, a lowly *coo* of what sounded like a wood pigeon rang out. Hopefully not a relation of the chap they had shared for breakfast.

To their right, a sea glittered in a mass of blue and white specks. What she could see of the water was grey and angry. Ren wondered what lay beyond it. Did this world have a Denmark? A France?

"Did you know," Ren began, "about my world, before?"

"No," Shae said, "we were given somewhat vague information and told to locate an elemental that was most likely partially awakened."

"We were shoved through a *scrystone* portal," Lance said, "and we slammed into a brick wall because your world, apparently, sees no problem with putting up buildings on top of wey lines. *Then*, we were almost run down by one of those awful car things. Bigger than yours."

"Gunter," Ren said, "I miss him."

Lance eyed her. "Gunter?"

"Yes." The hint of peppermint was back, though fainter, along with an earthy after-rain muskiness that was apparently universal. "How long did it take you to find me?"

"Three weeks." Shae replied.

That only raised more questions than it answered. "Three *weeks*? But what did you *do*? Actually, how did you get money? You had loads."

"We found a shop that had a sign saying *You got gold? We pay cash*," Lance said, "and by this point it was day three and we had worked out whatever this cash was, we needed some. We were hungry," he added. "And Shae had gold."

"What, on you?"

"I like gold."

"We rented a room in this dingy little hotel," Lance continued, "and we were feeling pretty defeated. We'd been there nearly four days and we had wandered from place to place, and not much else. People kept calling me a *geezer* and telling me to have a wash, and I had to keep my sword down my trouser leg after a mad old man tried to arrest me for nothing. *And* once we'd got away from him some woman laughed at my armour, so I covered *that,* too." He sounded glum. "Then we saw, by complete chance, some man on one of those picture box things talking about the weather."

"A freak occurrence," Shae interjected, "that's what he called it. Fierce wind, only in two places; they couldn't explain it."

"Two places?"

"Mm, one was you, of course, and the other was in England, some place called Marchester."

"Manchester?"

"That's what I said. Anyway, we had wasted so much time already that we split up."

"By the time I got there, no wind," Lance said. "No anything at all; think he might have made it up. So, I headed north but, well, couldn't remember where you said you were going." He shot Shae a glance. "So, I just–"

"Wandered?" The ghost of a smile crossed her lips. The prospect of someone simply *wandering* from Manchester to St. Andrews was absurd.

"Well, I wasn't going to get in one of those *things*," Lance replied, "if I could avoid it. Which I did."

She shot him a sideways glance. "You survived being in mine."

"Just." He winked.

Ren scoffed. "I'm an excellent driver."

It was comforting in its own way, having the unbridled opportunity to question the pair of them.

"So we're heading to your Council?"

"Sort of," Lance replied. "We're going to Endermarch, which is about fifty miles away from the Council headquarters."

Ren wrinkled her nose. *Endermarch.* The word turned itself

over and over in her mind. "Why?"

He shrugged. "That's what the dossier says."

"Oh." *Of course.* "What is Endermarch?"

"It used to be a prison."

Ren stopped walking. Goosebumps crept over her shoulders. "What?"

"It hasn't been functioning as one in years," Shae offered. He and Lance paused beside her. His words didn't offer much comfort.

"Why have you to take me there?"

Shae turned, cloak swirling, and continued on. "You'll have to ask when we get there."

Ren didn't move. Neither did Lance.

"Hey," her elbow buzzed against his, "everything's going to be okay."

Ren wasn't so sure. "A prison?" She swallowed dryly.

"Not–" It only took a split second for Lance's demeanour to shift. He looked past Ren, his body stiff, still, one hand poised close to his sword's hilt. "Shae," he said, voice low.

Shae, at least five metres ahead of them, paused. "Hm?"

For the shortest of moments, he turned his gaze back to hers. "We're being followed. Over *there.*"

Both Shae and Ren turned.

Ren saw nothing, until her eyes attuned to the base of a nearby hill. Several small black blobs appeared. They didn't look all that threatening.

"Are you–?"

"They've been following us for three miles," Lance said.

"Oh."

Shae was squinting. "Cù-sìth?"

"No." Lance shook his head, gripping his sword.

It happened quickly. The collection of whatever animals were across the arid landscape decided they had had enough of stalking.

They didn't run so much as glide. An effortless descent, and soon the three of them were surrounded.

At least ten sets of identical yellow eyes stared at them, unblinking, from every direction.

Wherever Ren's breath was, it wasn't anywhere in her body. She was dimly aware of Lance pulling her to him. The creature closest to her emitted a sound that was neither growl nor hiss.

Each of them would have dwarfed an Alsatian. She had thought them dogs at first, but they were distinctly feline, all with pure, black fur save for a white mark in the centre of their chests.

Panthers?

No, not panthers. Imagine a normal house cat, but much, much bigger.

Cool!

Where, only a few minutes before, she had heard bird calls and the occasional wave crashing from the sea to their right and a far flung roar of thunder, now she heard nothing but her own rapid pulse, and a sort of strangled snarling from every direction.

One of the creatures, in front, was stomping the ground. With each pat, green Ground specks flew from the creature's paw. Another, to its left, had flames licking up its front legs. Red flecks sparked upwards every few seconds. When it opened its mouth, there were flames there too.

And sometimes, they have magic in their paws.

Around them, specks of *NáDarra* exuded from the creatures, surrounding their claws and sparking from their jaws.

Wow!

One by one they lowered their heads. More snarls. Ren surveyed the first. The one doused in Ground magic. Yellow eyes bored into hers.

Something passed between them, resonating deep in Ren's stomach. A knowledge. This giant cat, with its white patch and tufted ears, wouldn't harm her. Ren drew a breath as something else, something new, coursed through her. A wobble, not in her but in the very earth they stood on.

And then the same wobble crashed through her chest.

It was dirt under fingernails and leaves crunching underfoot and sun-warmed grass. A solitary flower surviving a hurricane. In the centre of the situation that was anything but beautiful, she knew the beauty of nature and the harshness of survival.

It rumbled and cracked deep within her, centring her to each distant peak, each nearby gorse and grove and blade of grass.

Shae called it Ground. But it was so much more.

In that moment *she* was so much more.

Moving a half step from Lance, Ren watched the cat. Its head lifted a fraction, so slight the rest missed it. Its head dropped again.

It flooded through the tips of her fingers as her fear began to be replaced.

Ren hadn't travelled, leaving her life and family, to be mauled by a bunch of overgrown house cats.

We say 'cat shee,' but the words look like 'cat-sith.'

She thought the words three times. Cat-sith...*Cat-shee.* Cat-sith...*Cat-shee.* Cat-sith...

In her peripheral vision, one of the creatures had sunk, readying itself to pounce. Ren flexed her fingers. It was aimless, and at any other time would have been an experiment at best.

The ground wobbled again, larger than before. A rumble,

louder than thunder, more vicious than the snarls, threatened to break the world in two.

She heard Lance cry, "Woah!" while each of the cat-sìth emitted a low, continuous hiss.

Once more was all it took. The tiniest flick. The ground growled and moved beneath them. The cats scampered, taking off across the grass, silent as the night sky. All but one. It hovered for the shortest of moments. A thousand unspoken truths passed between them, none of which she could hope to understand.

Then it too was gone.

They're called cat-sìth.

For a long moment, they neither moved nor spoke. Ren's fingers flexed again as though of their own volition. Nothing happened.

Can we get one?

Ren brought her hands upwards, intent on examining them, when a body collided against hers. His arms wrapped around her and for a second all she knew was buzzing and sweat and leather. Next, he grabbed Shae, who didn't seem to notice, his gaze fixed on Ren.

"Ren," his eyes, more chestnut than any other shade in the high sun, were wide, "that was...uh, something."

Lance, replacing his sword, let out a low whistle. "Yes, Shae; Ren, who has never so much as lit a candle, caused an earthquake." He snorted at his own words. He looked at her, then at the point above her head. His mouth fell open.

Ren followed his gaze.

Emeralds.

They looked like flecks of pure emerald. And they joined her white, red, and purple ones.

They don't exist here, honey.

Oh.

Lance called them trading points, and they had taken advantage of several over the past few days. They were a combination of campsite and marketplace, sprawled over a plain that Ren knew ought to be lush and grassy, but instead was cracked and bare.

They had walked the last hours it took to reach this one in silence.

She hadn't missed the pointed looks passed between them at her refusal to acknowledge either their encounter with the felines, or her Ground magic awakening. Or anything at all.

Eventually they stopped engaging her.

Lance shot her a wary look. "You hungry?"

Ren nodded, mind far away.

They gathered anything they might trade with. Lance speared two rabbits while Shae foraged. Ren, glum and silent, followed his lead, picking wild garlic and mint, blackberries, even acorns.

Their wares earned them some bread, pork and three bowlfuls of soup. Vegetable soup, regardless of the world it was made in, smelled the same. Like winter, and home.

It was neither winter, nor home.

They ate cross-legged on the ground, surrounded by green, yellow, and white specks, as the sun set beyond the sea.

"Um, Ren?" It was Lance, his tone uncertain.

Black specks had begun to join the green, replacing the disappearing, yellow-tinged ones. Ren bit her bottom lip as the buzzing rushed through her chest, urging her to answer him.

"You know," she gestured to herself, and then to him, "this makes it far harder to ignore you than it should be." Shooting him as much of a smile as she could muster, Ren put down her now empty bowl beside his. "Sorry," she added.

His elbow nudged and buzzed, against hers. "No need."

Whether due to her imagination, or the buzzing, or something else, it passed between them like a current: understanding.

"Apology accepted," Shae interjected pompously from Lance's other side. "What?" he demanded as both Ren and Lance erupted into a kind of breathless laughter that made sense – or didn't – to only them.

By the time they were composed enough to do anything more than grasp onto each other, both Shae and the sunset had vanished. The latter had gone entirely and the former some ten metres away, cocooned in his cloak like a large fajita.

Lance, his hand resting against her forearm, said, "Are you okay?" He asked that a lot.

All trace of humour vanished as quickly as it had arrived. "No." His hand reached down, taking hers. The buzzing rose, a static energy coursing from her palm to his. "I–" Their fingers laced together. "I need to tell you something."

He listened in silence.

"I told you about that night," Ren said, "with my mum, in the woods."

He nodded, brow furrowed. The pad of his thumb traced imaginary lines up and down the back of her hand.

"That's not all." Nearby, a wave crashed, louder than the others as a gust of ferocious wind coursed past them. "The cats, the ones that surrounded us," Ren continued, "they're called cat-sìth." She said it as her mum had taught her to. *Cat-shee.*

Lance nodded.

"We don't have them on Earth, but..." She dragged her spare hand through her hair. "I haven't even *thought* about what he said, how awful is that?"

"Who?"

There was a harsh squeak to her tone she wished would vanish. "But it must be, mustn't it? She told me about them. I *knew* about them. Sometimes I-I don't remember much, less than I should, but I remember that. And that night...I knew, the second Shae said about Inverness, maybe before then, but–"

It came with its own specific brand of pain, one that Ren hadn't allowed herself to suffer in a long time. It resided in a metaphorical box, shut tight in the furthest depths of her mind, and that had taken five years to close. Five years of therapy and nightmares and the pills she learnt how to lie to doctors to obtain.

Until then. A flash of purple erupted just beyond Lance.

The lock was smashed to pieces and the box was unguarded and vulnerable.

The box was open.

"Ren?"

A roll of thunder sounded nearby, loud and imposing.

She gripped him tighter, with everything she had. "Before we came here, before we left Earth, I phoned my dad."

He inclined his head. "I remember." His voice was low and soft, a stark contrast to her own.

"H-he said he loved me." There was a coolness on her cheeks that hadn't been there a second before. "And then he told me to find her."

"Your mother?"

The wind whipped against them, stinging a chill into the tear tracks that lined her cheeks. Ren nodded. "Lance, I...what do I do?"

He gave her hand a small squeeze, before letting it go, only to snake his arm across her shoulders.

A further gust of wind streaked through the night air, battering against them.

His voice was muffled against her hair. "*We*," he corrected, tightening his hold, "do exactly that." Her own arms reached around, anchoring herself to him. Her fingertips grazed a curve of leather beneath his shirt. "We find her."

Ren didn't know how long they stayed, clutching each other.

Lance shifted, manoeuvring the pair of them.

Her head remained on his chest as they lay down together, his arms wrapped around her. Tighter than they needed to, as though he would never let go.

A part of her didn't want him to.

They hadn't had enough to trade for one of the already pitched tents, so they had to make do with the dirt and the backdrop of a soundless, magic-encrusted sky.

And each other. Whatever that meant. No person had affected her as he did. He had the power to undo her with a look, calm her with a touch. And she had certainly never experienced anything as tangible that connected her to another.

Perhaps it should frighten her. And perhaps it did, for it was neither normal nor rational. Through his armour, his torso buzzed against hers. So did his arms around her back. A part of her wanted to ask what it was, what it meant.

A part of her didn't want the answers.

"Lance?"

"Yeah?"

Ren placed one balled fist over the centre of his chest. "Does this scare you?"

He swallowed, weaving deft fingers through her hair. "Terrifies me." His lips met her forehead.

Her mouth opened, and she yawned before she could reply, and before she felt him smile against her. "Get some sleep."

Ren didn't argue. The last thing she knew, as her eyes closed and her breathing slowed, was his hold on her, a heart beating in time with hers, and the intertwining scents of sea air and peppermint and leather.

She woke through a fog in her mind, broken only by words she didn't quite understand.

"Don't want to."

"You have to."

"I'm providing a service."

An exaggerated sigh. "Here." Something soft and heavy flumped on top of her. Ren hadn't the energy to groan. "Go kill something."

"What if she—?"

"She'll be fine."

"I—"

"Lance," the voice said firmly, "she'll be fine."

It took several attempts to open her eyes. They were met with a dusky light, broken by several dry stones by her head. She yawned, pulling whatever had been placed over her further up to her chin. It smelled vaguely like cinnamon.

Not leather.

She didn't hear him approach. "Hey," Lance said, settling at her side.

"Oh good," came another voice, this one a tad further away and far droller. "I can get my cloak back."

Ren pushed the weighty black fabric off. It weighed about as much as a person. Though for all its many pockets and trinkets she knew it held, she had felt nothing but squashy material. Shae, appearing above, picked it up with ease.

"I don't give this up for just anyone," he informed her.

Ren eyed him. "Most appreciated."

"How do you feel?" It was Lance. In the dim light his irises were almost black.

Ren blinked. It looked like dusk, though it couldn't be, surely. "H-how long was I asleep?"

She didn't miss the glance he shot Shae. "Twenty hours, give or take."

"Oh." An entire day. Ren should probably feel more rested than she did. "Sorry," she added, voice small.

Shae, cloak back in place, replied, "It's understandable; you've had two awakenings and not very much sleep."

"What have you two been doing?"

Lance shrugged. "I went hunting, got enough to trade for these." He handed her a small paper bag. Inside she found several pieces of bread and meat, two apples, some cheese, and a few small cakes.

Ren's mouth dropped open.

"That's your share."

"My *share*?"

"I got another stag." His eyes crinkled at the sides as he smiled. The buzzing settled in the pit of her stomach at the sight. "Save some for the morning."

They set off early. After her mammoth twenty-hour slumber the night – and day – before, Ren still managed to fall asleep with Lance and Shae. One cocooned a little way off; one cocooned around her.

There was no build-up, no Ren having a breakdown to prompt them. It just...was. As though his arms surrounding her was as natural as the earth beneath them.

Which it was. Of that, and not a whole lot else, she was certain.

Their trading point had few facilities. The toilets, each surrounded by a six-foot-high wooden fence, were little more than bottomless buckets placed upon holes that ran deep into the ground. A sink stood opposite, offering a measly bar of white soap with the kind of floral scent Ren associated with fussy, old women.

She was glad to be shot of the place.

Each munching an apple, they headed south through a scattering of trees, accompanied by a rain that continuously shifted between a drizzle and a downpour, and the collective cooing of wood pigeons. Far off, on the horizon laced with snowy peaks, another lightning storm was taking place. Deep but distant booms met her ears every few seconds.

"How are you feeling?" Shae asked, cloak somehow billowing behind him even when no wind was present.

"Okay." Ren offered him a half-smile. "I think."

"You don't feel any...different?"

She felt exhausted. "Not really."

His brow held that familiar hint of a frown. He didn't reply.

They had only been walking for what Ren deduced to be around an hour, Lance's sword bouncing as he walked, when a low hiss broke through the babble of pigeon-song.

They stopped as one.

Ren was holding her breath when she saw it, a flicker of shamrock in the undergrowth. And then another. A slinking mass of green fur.

A wolf.

Absolutely not. Giant cats were one thing; giant wolves were quite another.

Shrieking, Ren leapt backwards as a gust of wind blew through the trees, so strong both Shae and Lance steadied themselves against nearby trunks.

"Agh! Ren, pull yourself together!" Shae shouted above the wind's howl.

The wolf, the only one appearing unfazed by Ren's impromptu cyclone, came further into view. Up close, it was around the size of a small cow, but its shaggy fur, deep emerald in colour, made it appear bigger still. Through a dip in the high-pitched howl of wind came a contrasting low growl.

Ren shrieked again, though it was cut short by Lance's hand on her arm.

"It's okay!" he cried. "Honestly, it's okay." The wind, despite the thumping in her chest, died, leaving them in a shower of hail.

Letting go of her, Lance, to Ren's astonishment, held his arms out to the creature as though it were a lost Labrador. "Hey, boy! You found me!"

Her mouth fell open. He'd been aware this wolf had been searching for him?

The wolf padded closer and emitted a long whine.

"Now," Lance began, "don't be like that. I told you I was

coming back, and I was."

Ren had never seen a wolf outside of pictures, and even then, never one as unnaturally coloured as this. It stared up at Lance with a crease in its snout, which gave it a rather disgruntled expression.

Lance, wearing a look similar to the creature's own, crossed his arms. "Well, you be like that, then."

If his words were meant to guilt the wolf into gracing him with a friendlier welcome, they failed. Instead, with the softest of howls, it turned, making its way towards Shae, who offered it a quick pat.

Ren, still fighting the urge to run as fast as she could back north, peered at it.

Beside her, Lance threw his arms into the air. "Are you… Brogan! You're being childish now."

If anything would have made her laugh in that moment, it was Lance proclaiming the newcomer was acting childishly. The wolf itself, at the sound of her laughter, made its way past Shae, towards her.

It appeared larger up close.

Blinking, the wolf, Brogan, flared his nostrils as he let out another soft whine.

"Uh, hello," Ren said. She reached a hand towards it. In spite of her alarm, the corners of her mouth tugged upwards as it cocked its head at her voice. "I'm Ren." Taking a single step towards her, the wolf bowed his head, allowing Ren's fingers to brush the soft hair atop his head. "You're lovely, aren't you?"

Lance snorted.

"Is he, ah, your wolf?"

"He's *supposed* to be. And he's not a wolf, he's a cù-sìth." *Sith,* like before, pronounced like *shee.*

Brogan turned. His paws, which would easily outsize a man's hand, were silent, and shaggier still. A huge tail wafted to and fro as he made his way through the shrubbery.

Both Shae and Ren followed suit. Lance, muttering something that contained the words *unbelievable* and *stubborn,* brought up the rear.

The journey would have taken days had Lance, using far more charm than Ren deemed necessary, not persuaded a woman, Lis, to allow them passage on the back of her cart. Raven ringlets cascaded over the shawls Lis pulled across her shoulders. Yet more of the garments were draped across the cart. Ren eyed it, and the horses that pulled it, with a wary eye. Then with a sour annoyance after the third time Lis looked up and down Lance's frame.

Ren spent the entire journey tucked in the corner of the cart, one hand resting on the back of Brogan's neck, feigning sleep to the soundtrack of Lance and Lis's exchange of pleasantries.

The cù-sìth, at least, wasn't taken with the woman. A low, throaty groan escaped him whenever Lis spoke to or about him. Ren wished it didn't give her quite as much satisfaction.

They bade Lis goodbye a few hours away from sundown, giving them a short opportunity to obtain wares to trade with to secure them a night's stay at a nearby inn.

With the addition of Brogan, whose hunting skills vastly eclipsed Lance's, the task was shortened. They settled into their room as Dark specks once again replaced Light, and Shae proclaimed he *absolutely needed* to find someone willing to trade him some rowan berries. They lay side by side on what Lance insisted was a bed but felt like an oblong hay bale covered in burlap.

"Are you buzzing or prickling?" he asked. "Because I'm prickling."

Ren didn't reply, but turned her head, to find his was already pointed towards her. His smile irked her, though not as much as the fact she didn't seem able to help herself return it.

"You know I was being nice to her because she agreed to

give us a ride for free?"

The *most* irksome part was that Ren *did* know that, and the guilt over the full extent of her bitterness was eating away at her.

She nodded, her gaze dropping to his chest. Devoid of both his shirt and armour, a scattering of tattoos and scars littered his torso. Two green paw prints were stamped across his left bicep. "Are they Brogan's?"

Lance nodded. "Not true to size, though; his wouldn't fit," he added with a soft laugh.

Ren smiled, and began to trace one.

He let out a soft hiss and Ren wrenched her hand back. "No," he said. "It's...intense." He wasn't wrong. "Don't stop."

Ren swallowed, placing her fingertip once more to his arm. She could scarcely more than whisper. "Are you still prickling?"

His throat bobbed as he swallowed. "I think you know I'm not."

She did know. From her fingertip, down her entire fist, was coated in an invisible static. "I want..." What did she want? Him? Assuredly. But there had to be more than *that*. "I want to know about you, Lance Allardyce."

"All right." The sides of his eyes crinkled. "What would you like to know?"

Ren finished the second paw print, and moved her hand diagonally downwards, to his chest, where a *B* was encased in a Jack of Hearts. His heartbeat, pulsing beneath her touch, quickened. "Everything."

Lance blinked. "Everything?" He looked both bemused and amused.

"Everything."

Lance surveyed her, before, much to Ren's dismay, he rose and crossed their small room, gathering the small tote of what remained from their trade with the innkeeper. Ren watched him silently. The plain of his back rippled as he moved. She clocked several more tattoos, including a crudely drawn skull, a poker chip, and what looked like a pirate ship. "I've got a plan." He turned, shooting Ren a wink as he pulled his shirt on, before heading for the door. "Don't move."

He returned five minutes later, wearing an easy smile and clutching a bottle of what looked like whisky in one hand. In the other he clinked two shot glasses together. "One condition."

Ren sat up, trying and failing to raise only one eyebrow. Leaning back against their pitiful bed's pitiful excuse for a headboard, the corners of her mouth tugged upwards. "And what's that?"

"You tell me everything, as well."

"Deal."

Lance, taking more care not to spill his whisky than Ren had seen him take doing anything, perched himself beside her before pouring two measures. He handed hers over. "You ask a question," he said, placing the bottle between his now crossed legs, "you drink."

Ren nodded.

"You can go first," he added, trailing his free hand through his long curls.

"All right." Ren sat up a little straighter, curling her legs beneath her. "Do you like your job?" she asked, taking a large sip, grimacing as the liquid burned her tongue.

"It's all right." He shrugged. "Good and bad. I like travelling, and the fact that Shae insists on doing ninety percent of the paperwork, but I miss..." Pausing, Lance stared into his glass. "I used to work for myself. I miss that sometimes." His eyes rose. "Was your childhood good?"

"It was good. I was lucky." Ren smiled softly. "Apart from Shae's *famous* broth, what's your favourite food?"

"Hooter."

Ren barely managed to stop choking on her whisky. "I beg

your pardon?"

"Don't tell me your world doesn't have hooters?"

A generically attractive woman, scantily clad in a gaudy orange, came to her mind. "I don't think so."

"Wait 'til we're in Ververos." Lance swallowed the remainder of his shot. "Weirdest place you've ever fallen asleep?"

"Inside a bush," Ren said, holding her own newly emptied glass outright and ignoring Lance's snort. "Do you have a big family?"

"Mm." Lance inclined his head. "Three sisters. Two brothers."

"*Six?*"

"There wasn't much peace and quiet." He laughed softly. "What's one statement you live by?"

Ren swallowed. The words had emerged, easily and freely, at the forefront of her mind. "You can examine the engine 'til you're blue in the face." She took an extra, unprecedented sip. "But sometimes you just gotta get in and turn the damn key." Lance's look of utter confusion helped, a little, to curb her sudden urge to break down. "It won't make much sense to you."

"No, it...makes perfect sense."

Though she was tinged with a sadness that had caught her so off guard, Ren found herself laughing. "Do you believe in second chances?"

"I didn't used to." Lance let a long breath escape him. "Now...I'm not sure." He drank slowly, more than a sip. "What was the last promise somebody made you?"

Ren groaned. "Pass."

"Oh, now that's not fair."

"You really want to know?"

"That's sort of the whole point of a question, Ren."

She shot him as much of a scowl as she could muster and

sighed. "It was: *I'll leave my wife.*"

"Ah."

"More alcohol, please."

Lance chuckled, obliging her request.

"What's your favourite thing about yourself?"

"I assume you mean besides my ruggedly handsome features, flawless hair, and impeccable charm?"

"Yeah." Ren rolled her eyes, though couldn't quite bring herself to refute his words. "Besides those."

"I survive," he said simply. "What's something that scares you?"

Her mind, a little fuzzier than it had been, went blank, save for one, solitary statement: *how I feel about you.* Her mouth was dry. The whisky was no help in the matter, only succeeding in making her dry mouth hot. "I-I guess my magic…" she lied. In truth, while her powers pulled her conscience in many different directions, *fear* wasn't one. "Mountains or beach?"

"You know, I think that *bodach* might have ruined beaches for me." He laughed again. So did she. "Mountains." He spoke slower, his words slurring slightly. More than they should have been. The bottle was half empty. Perhaps they had been taking more than sips. "Something you've never told anyone?"

Her head slumped sideways, clunking against his shoulder. "After my mum left…"

Lance's hand reached for hers.

"I took pills. A *lot* of pills."

Lance's grip tightened.

"I don't now." She raised the glass to her lips, the scent of the stuff so potent it burned against her nostrils. "But sometimes I miss them. A little."

Lance shimmied around, beside her, and rested his head against hers.

"Has..." She couldn't continue, despite the words being *right there.*

"Has?"

"Has anyone made y-you buzz before...before I did?"

She both heard and felt him swallow. "No."

Several minutes of silence followed. Their soft, collective breathing was the only sound. "What does it take," Lance said eventually, his voice hoarse, words all jumbling together, "to earn your trust?"

Ren hadn't the chance to open her mouth, not that she had any notion of a reasonable response, when their door opened, and in strode a haughty-looking arcanist, cape billowing despite there being no hint of a draft. He looked first at Lance, then Ren, eyebrows raising higher with each glance he took, before frowning at their whisky.

"I've been gone an hour," Shae informed them, though Ren couldn't quite fathom why, or what about his words she found terribly funny. Only that she did, and so, apparently, did Lance.

Shae, shaking his head as he deposited handfuls of small, red berries on a small desk, marched across the room, opting not to join them on the only bed, and instead positioned himself on a small lumpy red couch, ignoring the continued gasping hysterics coming from a helpless Ren, and an equally helpless Lance.

"N-night, Shae."

Shae grunted something unintelligible as Lance, still snickering, blew out the candle, their only real source of light. He and Ren shimmied downwards, until they lay side by side.

Ren smiled into the dark, her tipsy laughter for now under control, and rolled, her head finding its place on his chest as his arm found *its* place encircling her shoulders.

It took a while, long enough for a quiet, rhythmic snore to emanate from Shae's couch, for Ren to speak. When she did, it was no more than a whisper, one to which Lance said nothing, but shifted, holding her closer still. "It takes this."

Other than a few fleeting glances at the half empty bottle, Shae didn't mention their spontaneous drinking session. Although he did insist they leave far earlier than either Ren or Lance deemed necessary. It was, apparently, important. Though he wouldn't say why.

To Ren, sluggish and bleary-eyed, it was a mild inconvenience.

Lance, however, felt otherwise.

Ren was used to hungover people. She had seen enough hotel guests eating breakfast with haunted looks and green-tinged cheeks. Plenty of punters had unloaded their next day woes and regrets onto her and she had seen her father hunched over a toilet bowl on more occasions than Ren cared to count.

None came close to how badly Lance Allardyce handled a hangover.

He spent most of the morning ambling behind the others, one hand clutched to his temple, groaning vaguely about dying. It didn't take more than fifteen minutes for even Brogan to grow tired of his moaning, and instead opted to trot beside Ren.

Shae regarded him in a lofty silence as he led the group away from any tracks and into some thick undergrowth. Once at least half an hour away from the inn and the village, he started to speak, keeping his voice low.

"Last night, I witnessed something of what I believe to be some kind of hunting party."

Lance groaned. "So?"

Shae's tone was grave, even for him. "It wasn't hooter they were hunting. It was anyone gifted in *NáDarra*."

Ren's hangover disappeared. In its stead, a muted sense of panic.

Lance was suddenly beside her, his form stiff, as though he

expected to see the perpetrators pop out of the ground in front of them.

"No more tracks." Shae said. "Until we're inside Ververos."

Lance's voice was low, dangerous. His elbow bumped Ren's arm. "Agreed."

A few hours of near silent walking later, they passed another small village. "Are there no cities here?" Ren asked.

"The biggest is Steerpike, in Glendale," Shae replied. "And there are two in Caeracre," he added, "they're further north. We were outside of Loreleith the first night, then there's Arrik."

"Otherwise known as the worst place in the world, and the best, respectively," Lance said, his voice gravelly.

Shae's dark eyebrows raised skywards. "No prizes for guessing where he's from."

"Arrik," Ren repeated. "What's it like?"

Lance appeared at Ren's side. "Full of character."

"Full of criminals," Shae muttered. "Loreleith is bigger, known for being the Home of Magic."

"Why?"

"It's where most with a gift go to study. There are two main Academies there, one for those gifted in *NáDarra*-"

"Like me?"

Shae nodded. "And one for those gifted in *NeòNach*."

"Like you?"

"Mm."

Ren wondered what such an academy might be like. She hadn't considered the possibility of controlling her magic, like Shae could. "What's it like?" Ren stepped over a hole that must have been made by a rabbit the size of a large cat. "At magic school?"

"My time at the *Academy of NeòNach*," Shae said, "was the finest of my life."

Lance coughed. "Thank you very much."

Led by Brogan, the group emerged from the concealed woodland onto one of Caeracre's dirt tracks, this one on an incline. Lance closed the small distance between him and Ren, walking so close her arm permanently buzzed. The sun was high overhead as they climbed. Though the hilly land surrounding them reminded her of Pentland Hills around Ainhill, these were decidedly less enticing. That same dry, cracked earth coated the ground. She wondered whether the earth was ever luscious and green like Scotland was. As they climbed, she was certain she smelled something burning.

A wooden signpost was set into the ground at the top of the hill, informing them they were leaving Caeracre. As they reached it, Shae handed Ren a small vial. It housed an unappealing, grey substance

"*Eileamaid lag*," he said.

"Uh, thanks."

"You'll need to take it before we enter."

"If you think I'm drinking this sea sludge, you're mistaken."

"If you want to get through Ververos alive you will."

Her eyes snapped from the vial of sludge to Shae. "What do you mean *alive*? Did you forget to mention this forest could kill me?"

Shae took a bite of one of the peaches he alone had pilfered from the breakfast buffet, in no apparent rush to continue their conversation.

By the time he finished, Ren was glaring.

"I didn't *forget*, no."

Ren examined the sludge. It looked like tar. "How can a forest kill someone?"

"It doesn't have the effect on everyone. Only those with a

gift."

"Why?"

"Ververos isn't like any other past of Caerisle," Shae said, "it is entirely magical. That potion dampens your magic temporarily so Ververos can't."

The place didn't sound very appealing.

"Everything is different," Shae continued, "while everywhere relies on *NáDarra*, Ververos also utilises *NeòNach*. And *feeds* on both. Almost everyone born there is a faedra."

"A what now?"

"Faedra. Someone Gifted in both *NáDarra* and *NeòNach*."

"Oh."

It was unnerving, the idea of a forest, of all things, draining her magic for the benefit of its own ecosystem. They reached the bottom of the steep incline.

"So if I don't take this," she held the vial out, "this Ver-ve-thingy will steal my magic?"

Shae nodded. He looked, if anything, bored.

"And this would kill me?"

"Your magic is as much a necessary part of you as your organs and blood are. Without it, you'd cease to function."

"Oh," she repeated, glancing upwards. "I didn't know that."

"You told me when we met you always hurt."

"I did." There had been a lot less of that of late. "It was... there was more. My lungs and...it was bad." She couldn't continue.

As she trailed off, Lance's hand met her shoulder. He gave it a small squeeze.

"That's what that was," Shae said. "Without such close proximity to *NáDarra*, your own was being suppressed. That's why you were always ill, and why you didn't start awakening until much later than normal."

Ren frowned. "But Earth *does* have the elements."

"But they aren't acknowledged, and they aren't balanced with *NeòNach*," Shae said, which made very little sense. "Imagine the symptoms you experienced, but each developing much, much faster, and all at once. That's Ververos."

Even less appealing.

They had almost reached the top of the hill, Ren slightly behind the others and feeling rather unfit, if her panting was anything to go by. The tips of what had to be several dozen trees came into view, and then more as they hiked higher, until the only view ahead was down.

Ren's mouth dropped open at the sight as it came into focus, tracking one giant pine to another. Each was easily a few hundred feet tall.

The treeline stood, roughly fifty or so metres from them. The beginning of Ververos. The trees were neat and packed and ran as far as she could see in either direction. They weren't like any pines Ren had seen, not with their magnitude. There was a red tinge to both their enormous trunks and dense leaves.

The place only grew bigger still as they made their way down the other side of the hill. Ren stayed as close to Lance as physically possible as they approached. Ververos loomed, each footstep making the hollow sensation that had settled in her chest intensify. It wasn't just a forest.

Ververos was a juggernaut.

Ren took the elixir in one. There was less liquid than any measure of whisky she had taken the previous night and yet her whole mouth filled with the stuff.

And it was vile.

Ren clamped one hand over her mouth as she coughed and spluttered. It was akin to what she imagined drinking tar might actually be like: thick and bubbling on her tongue, hot enough to burn even her. That she could have excused.

The taste she could not.

It brought to her mind all at once sulphur, cigarette ash and white spirit and its journey down her throat wasn't a quick one. Ren swallowed, then immediately gagged.

Shae's voice rang from behind. "It's not pleasant, I know."

The entire elixir was threatening to charge right back up her oesophagus. She watched as an identically filled vial appeared in Shae's hand. He downed the potion with little difficulty.

A white noise, whether from somewhere nearby or all around them, rang in the air.

Ren failed to pinpoint it. "What is that?" she said, her words muffled against the palm of her hand.

Lance was frowning. "What's what?"

"That noise." It was louder now.

His words sounded like a whisper. "There's no noise."

There was, but she didn't press the matter. Instead, she turned to Shae.

"No, it's not *pleasant*."

He had the audacity to shrug, placing both their now empty vials in a pocket. "It is done now."

Her ears were ringing as a small whoosh of nausea rose within her. "Easy for you to say."

The downward incline came to an end as they approached a raised platform, set three metres or so high, stood beside a fence far taller than she. Running as far as she could see in either direction, the fence had been erected in front of the treeline. Far off to the left, Ren made out a second platform. The one they were approaching was carved against a single trunk, hand and footholds cut crudely into the bark. It wouldn't pass any health and safety inspections on Earth, yet the man climbing down did so at remarkable speed.

Ren had to crane her neck; a ringing loud in her ears. His skin was similar to Lance's, a weather-beaten tan, though his hair was light instead of dark. It hung loose around his face. A pair of icy blue eyes scrutinised them, hand raised to his brow against the springtime sun.

"Aha! Haven't seen you two in a while." Before, she would have called his accent northern.

Stretching out his arms, he embraced first Shae, then Lance.

"Tell us about it," Lance said, as the man bent to pet Brogan's shaggy head. "This is Ren."

The man nodded to her as he rose.

"Ren, this is Tobias."

"Hi," she said, legs wobbling. The ringing was louder than ever.

"Nice to meet you, Ren." His eyes were fixed above hers. Her taio barely reached his shoulders. "Have you taken an *Eilee*?"

Had she what?

"She has," Shae said, "hence the green tinge to her face."

Tobias snorted. "Didn't want to be presumptuous." He clapped his hands. "Stick with these two, Ren, and you won't go far wrong." He led them towards the fence.

Ren only nodded. The use of her voice seemed risky with the nausea roaming her body.

The fence was larger up close. A thin, rectangular outline had been carved into it, the same size as an average door. Locating a spot in the upper left corner, Tobias pounded three times.

It swung open soundlessly.

"Safe travels," Tobias offered as the four crossed the threshold and entered the forest of Ververos.

The darkness was expected, as was the air's tinge, more pink than red up close. Shae had explained briefly that no one really understood why. What she hadn't banked on was the way her body succumbed to the effects of the place.

It made the *eileamaid lag* an enjoyable experience.

Her head was buzzing, but not in the way Lance made her feel. *This* buzzing was loud and disorientating, all around, yet caged within her mind and accompanied by the same white noise as before. Only this time much, much louder.

Her hands snapped first to her ears, which made no difference, and then to her face. Pain, the kind that ought to belong to the end of a knife, struck behind her eyes.

Pressure, on each of her arms, steadied her. It took her longer than it should have to realise it was caused by Lance gripping her.

"Ren?" He sounded at least twenty metres away.

Ren blinked, wrinkling her nose against an aromatic assault. The peppermint she had grown accustomed to had been replaced by some giant, invisible spice rack.

Lance's face came slowly into view, all apprehension and frown lines. His mouth opened and Ren supposed words emerged, but she heard only more white noise.

"Nnrgh!"

She half walked; half stumbled into his front.

"-t's -kay."

At least she could hear him again. Sort of. He led her, one arm tight around her waist. In any other circumstance she would be buzzing like a beehive, relishing the contact. Ren relished nothing as Lance stopped in front of a fallen log and lowered her down.

She promptly toppled off; logs don't have backs.

What felt like hundreds of tiny twigs met her back. It wasn't comfortable. Ren groaned and Lance's face, contorted, still frowning, appeared above her.

"Oh." A shift, which in any other scenario would have been subtle, befell her. Everything that had been blurry and misshapen mere seconds before was clearer. Colours brighter. She made out every strand of his dark curls. "I can see your face again." A giggle, very un-Ren-like, burst from her mouth. "Good," she added, "I like looking at it."

She then started to hum some jaunty, irregular tune as the pain began to dissipate.

"All right." Lance's arms surrounded her. "Let's get you up." He pulled her upwards in a swift whoosh, accompanied, thanks to Ren, by a loud, *Whee.*

He deposited her back onto the log. "Think you can stay upright?"

"Hm," Ren replied, admiring the bark of a nearby pine. There were deep grooves in it, as though something had hacked at it. How odd. "Maybe." She wasn't opposed to him picking her up again. "You look best like that," Ren informed him. Standing, she grabbed at his shirt to curb the swaying. Both her arms and legs felt weightless. Maybe, without him, she would float away.

"Like what?" Behind him, Shae was observing the pair of them in silence. He was surrounded by magic.

Her fingertips grazed the top of Lance's right arm. "Worried about me."

He looked, if anything, alarmed. Which was rather funny.

"Ren, look, if the magic here is too strong, there's another way; we *could* sail to Glendale, it would..."

He must have gathered that she had stopped listening.

Instead, having turned her back on him, Ren watched the steady to and fro of Brogan's tail. "Oh," Ren said, "look how pretty he is."

The path beside Brogan was littered with leaves, each one at least half a size larger than average.

"Yeah," Lance replied dryly, "he's gorgeous."

"Don't worry." Ren let out a hoot of laughter. "So is his owner."

She spent the next hour in a similar euphoria. They followed what seemed to be the biggest path through the forest. Others intersected theirs, none she could see more than a few metres of.

Of the few people they came across, only one acknowledged them, despite Ren's wide smile that Lance kept telling her to put away. The woman was aged and shaped like an isosceles triangle, all broad shoulders and long, skinny legs. She was barefoot, wearing what looked little more than an oversized pillowcase, arm and head holes torn roughly into the linen.

"You, girl." A bony finger jabbed the centre of Ren's chest. Eyes, with irises as red as maple leaves, bored into Ren's. "Will be taken." Her accent was unplaceable. "By one who was betrayed." In a flash, her gaze shifted to Lance.

If the leaves on the shrub behind the woman's head were

not quite so spiky, and purple, and the air wasn't as warm or scented quite so much like Christmas, Ren might have been bothered by her words.

"Right," Lance mumbled, pushing past the woman, his fingertips digging into Ren's side; any deeper and it would be painful. "Goodbye."

The woman offered them no such farewell. She grabbed Ren's other arm. Ren barely noticed, wondering what kind of bird a nearby chirp was from. "It's a dangerous time to be what you are, girl." It was somewhere between a squawk and a hoot. "Now, he wants–"

Between Lance hurrying her away and the steady din of what sounded like running water, Ren didn't hear what some mystical *he* wanted.

Nor did she care.

It was the smallest of sensations, no more than a pinprick. Ren's hand shot to her left eye.

"Oh." The red hue surrounding them wasn't the bright scarlet wonder it had been a second or two previous; it was dulling. The pain was increasing. "Oh, no." Her stomach lurched as the rushing water sounded louder. "Lance!" Heat was pooling in her cheeks.

He pulled her closer. "You're okay."

Nausea rolled in her belly. She wanted to believe him. The heat in her face rose with every step they took. A layer of what could only be sweat was forming in her palms. Her fingertips ran over her eyebrow, willing the pain away. There was more sweat on her forehead. She groaned against Lance. Never had she felt so hot.

It wasn't a pleasant sensation.

Below the neck, the opposite. For maybe the first time in her life, Ren shivered.

"Whassawater?"

Somewhere over to her right, Shae said, "It's called the

Shimmering Vale."

"That's nice." Unlike everything else.

"There are five rivers," Shae said. He sounded far away; his voice distorted as though they were *in* one of the rivers. "We need to cross them."

Except for her head, Ren's entire body felt sheathed in a cloak of ice. A gust of wind, from nowhere, whipped her hair. It was followed by a roll of distant thunder.

"Less nice now."

A whisper, from neither Lance nor Shae, called what sounded like her name.

Ren trembled. "No swimming."

Lance chuckled gently. "Even if we had to, you'd only have to hang on."

If only her head would stop hurting long enough for her to appreciate that mental image. Ren hummed, braving a brief look upwards. Not too far ahead, through tree trunks thicker than an average dining table, was a long grey blur, the first of the five rivers they had to somehow navigate.

The noise from it was far louder up close.

Ren swallowed, willing herself not to vomit when a second whisper echoed in her mind, clearer than the first.

Be careful, Ren.

She wanted to ask how the hell they were meant to cross not one, but five separate rivers, but didn't trust that only words would spill from her mouth. She was saved from the mystery, though; the *how* in question appearing in the form of a man. *Where* he had emerged from, Ren didn't know. Only that he had a short mop of blond hair and far too wide a grin.

Lance introduced the newcomer as Ronin.

"'Lo," Ren mumbled.

If he thought her rude, Ronin didn't let on. "I see it some-times," he said, "remember feeling funny myself the first time I came through."

A taio, composed of blue Water specks, hovered above Ronin's head. He was an elemental, like Ren: a water bearer.

He led them to a raft that, were Ren more together, she might have questioned. It didn't look all that safe.

The raft, little more than a large rectangle, edged with a raised bench of sorts, smelled damp. Lance settled himself and Ren, whose eyes were closing despite her best efforts, in a corner, Shae placed himself in the one opposite and was joined, rather comically, in his lap, by Brogan. The cù-sìth's whines were barely audible over the sound of the water. Ronin took a seat at the rear.

"Ren," Ronin said, "do not lean out of the raft."

She didn't bother to answer.

"All right," he cried, his voice cheery, "everybody ready?"

A voice answered him. *Ready, yes.* It belonged to none of them. *A long time.*

Ronin propelled them from the shore.

Something rose within her, caused not by the numb iciness of the wave that crashed against their backs, nor the several lurches the raft took as Ronin worked to steady them. A sense of wrongness.

A delighted hiss. *Ready.*

More water splashed her. It was a biting cold Ren had never felt.

Every part of her was shivering. Except her face, still burn-ing despite the cold.

Lance's grip on her tightened. "I've got you," he cried, somewhere close to her ear.

She hoped he was right.

The first river was rough, but not wide. Ronin jumped first, guiding the raft against the bank. Shae followed suit, staggering. Brogan clearly had no desire to set his paws down, even on dry land. Lance followed him, holding Ren.

"Don't...feel good." Her legs were throbbing and weak, growing more useless by the second.

His free arm flew down and snaked behind her knees. "I know."

The second river made the first resemble a meandering stream. The raft rocked perilously against the current, hitting off what had to be rocks. Big rocks. Though for the unpleasant sensations, of which there were many, she had the smallest comfort in the way Lance's arms pressed into her. She buzzed against him. If only that was all she felt.

Ren. The voice echoed her name, louder than the current. Ren tried to reply. The words would not come.

The second voice was different, the one that hissed, *Yes.*

The throbbing in her limbs was spreading, first to her stomach. Then her chest.

Again, she tried to speak. "La–"

The raft took its hardest battering, throwing Ren and Lance from the bench. Ren landed on the soaked wooden base, Lance on top of her, with a painful smack down her entire side.

"Hang on!" Ronin yelled, "we're almost–"

It happened in a second and tore the words from him. A mass of grey and white. It appeared behind the blurry figure she knew was Ronin. A wall of water.

Through half-lidded eyes, she watched it descend on the raft. Had it happened any slower she might have had time to scream.

If having several waves splash up her back from the first crossing had made her cold, it was nothing at all to being plunged into the depths of it.

Ren's thoughts froze with the water. Her limbs pulled and pushed. Her body, powerless to anything except the writhing current, whirled in every direction.

There was only darkness. And nothing.

Instinct had made her mouth clamp closed.

Her eyes opened, first to more nothing, then to a ripple of light.

The surface.

Breathe, the voice said.

With everything she had, which wasn't much, she did the only thing she could. She swam up.

Or tried to.

It was an impossible thing. Already weakened, Ren's arms barely lifted. Even turning herself around was laborious; the tiniest movements and the time they took caused her lungs to burn.

It came again. *Breathe.* Louder. *Breathe.*

And then it changed.

To a hiss.

Ours.

An ironclad grip settled itself around Ren's ankle.

Breathe.

Everything around her, the current and the thrashing, even the pain, ceased. The light was less, too.

Breathe.

Maybe she should. She did feel, in that heartbeat, lighter somehow. Maybe...she should.

Her mouth opened just as she was gripped, this time around her back, and dragged in the opposite direction.

A scream, a sound both hard and hollow, hit her a mere moment before the surface of the water did.

Aware of little except the faint din of a rushing current, Ren dimly felt some ground meet her back, and then as quickly leave as her body convulsed of its own accord, retching and spluttering. The water she expelled splashed on a grassy bank.

"Ren!"

Throat burning, Ren lay back, panting. Her head didn't hit the ground, instead it landed on something softer. The back of her head buzzed against it.

Exhaustion gnawed at her as she attempted to open her eyes. If only to see his. All she saw was fog.

"She's burning up."

"Send for–"

"No." Their words were fainter than they should have been and meant very little.

"Send for her."

"Ren." A caress swept her cheek. "Please, wake up."

She buzzed at the touch.

"Lance." Shae's face swam in her mind's eye, only to be swept away by more fog.

"Send f–"

End of Part Two

Part Three

14

A hoot, and a soft scurrying. A muffled din of footsteps and indecipherable voices. It sounded busy and smelled like firewood.

Both the pain and nausea were gone.

She'd been placed upon a surface, soft, but not quite mattress-soft. Ren rubbed her fingertips across the fabric beneath her, then across the side of her thighs, which were bare.

A concerning realisation.

Squinting against the light, Ren began to study her surroundings.

It was far from both the river bank and Ronin's raft. The room was smallish and cylindrical, walls crafted from what looked like stalks of bamboo. Across from where she lay, a paneless window was covered in a blind of yet more bamboo. Below it lay two figures.

All else, from the walls, to the blanket she'd been placed under, to the breath in her lungs, vanished.

Brogan's sheer size took up the majority of the floor. The cù-sìth lay on his side, legs, and tail sprawled outwards, his head resting on Lance's chest.

Ren smiled, the buzzing rising and falling in time with each exhale.

He lay on his back, one arm slung over Brogan's neck, the other curved upwards, his forearm lying between the floor and a lump of navy.

He had slept on Luke's jumper.

Both Ren's heart rate and the buzzing swelled, and Lance, with a few sharp intakes of breath, woke, grimacing as he shifted his limbs.

His gaze swept the room, honing in on the one bed. His dark gaze widened at the sight of her own.

Ren barely mustered a smile. The buzzing, now whirring and catapulting, her body a sky on Bonfire Night, was spinning and merging in her mind, with flashes from the raft. The Shimmering Vale, that's what Shae had called it. Ren swallowed, remembering. It had looked like water but felt like ice, and it had thrown her, suffocated her. Something. A voice she still didn't know had spoken. Tried to...what? Take her? *Drown* her?

Lance rose, soundlessly, save for a soft grunt from Brogan, and took the few steps it took to close the space between them.

A hollow opened within her chest. Her heartbeats, all she heard, echoed within it as she sat up, hoisting the threadbare blanket into a ball by her throat.

The mattress must have dipped as he dropped to her side, but Ren felt nothing but buzzing. It erupted over every inch of her, sparking outwards like hot coals and hailstones and static.

His eyes hadn't left hers and didn't until the second before his arms engulfed her.

Ren saw nothing but black, her face pressed against his bare chest.

She felt everything.

For a long moment, there was silence, broken only by their ragged breaths. The commotion outside the window had died.

He smelled of earth and sweat, his skin cool, then warm.

The world might have disappeared.

Her fingertips shimmied back and forth in tiny lines across the small of his back, and three words, muffled against her shoulder, cut through the quiet.

"You made it." He spoke through a sob.

The bamboo blinds flickered inwards as a gust blew through wherever the hell they were.

"Wh-what do you mean?"

Lance placed a hand on Ren's shoulder and squeezed gently. With the other, he found hers. Pulling it upwards, he pressed his lips to her knuckles. "I think it'd be better if Shae told you. He understands it better."

But Ren was blinking back tears. "I don't want Shae to tell me."

"Alright." He placed their intertwined hands to his own chest. "The magic was too strong, or I think it means that your magic is actually too strong. The potion should have been enough, but it didn't dampen your powers enough, which meant Ververos could drain them more, or something."

"That doesn't make sense."

"I know. Anyway, you were weakened. And the fuath in the second river sensed that."

"The what?"

"Fuath," he repeated. "Trapped water spirit. Only Light magic can free them."

"Oh." Ren blinked at him. "But I don't have Light magic."

"No, but..." His words were cut short by the clearing of a throat. Across the room, the flimsy fabric of the curtain covering the doorway was pulled aside.

A woman appeared.

"I hoped you'd be awake." Her voice held a sing-song quality. It matched her smile. Two sets of dimples framed her features, all delicate save her eyes. Hardened and fierce. They drifted over Ren, their colour that of fresh strawberries. "I'm Brielle." She carried a familiar bundle in her arms. Ren breathed a sigh at the sight of her clothes. They, along with Ren's boots that Brielle had slung over one arm, looked clean and dry.

Wobbling atop the soft pile Brielle carried was a small tray, which held several small vials.

"Your clothes were soaked through." Brielle smiled again and placed the items on a bedside table and busied herself examining each vial in turn. "We had to take them off."

"Right," Ren mumbled, hoping the *we* wasn't a particularly large number of individuals. She dressed awkwardly beneath the blanket.

Lance rose with a final squeeze of Ren's shoulder. "I said I'd let Shae know when you were awake."

Ren nodded numbly as Lance took a few steps back to the window he had slept under. How long had he stayed?

After wrestling his crumpled undershirt from beneath Brogan's cumbersome size, he chucked his makeshift pillow to her. Ren swallowed, hugging Luke's jumper, wishing Lance wasn't going anywhere.

He left then.

"And these," Brielle continued, forcing Ren's attention from the stilling curtain covering the door. She gestured to her vials. "You need to take them to keep your magic stable, or it'll go haywire again. We've had to inject them for the past three days, which I hate doing, but you can drink them now."

"Three *days*?"

Brielle offered a sympathetic smile.

There were eight. Each one appeared clear but on further inspection the specks in each were obvious.

"One for each element," Ren said, more to herself than Brielle.

"That's right."

Taking a breath, Ren looked at the vials, then Brielle. "Shouldn't I only need four?"

Brielle handed her the first, infused with Fire, and cleared her throat. "Look up."

Ren knew the specks in her taio well enough. Knew where they hovered, which moved this way and that. From white Air, to red Fire, purple Lightning to green ground.

To blue.

Water.

"Wha–"

"We believe," Brielle began, "it's what saved your life."

Was it possible? "I didn't even feel it."

Handing over the Lightning-infused liquid, Brielle replied, "Not consciously, no."

"But I thought weavers can only control four elements." She downed the potion in one.

"Four." Brielle's shimmery taio twinkled. "Or eight." She said no more. Ren took the remainder of her potions in silence.

"Where are we?" Ren peeled the blanket from her now dressed form and swung her legs over the side of the bed. Brogan, now on all fours, stretched with a yawn that sounded more like a moo.

"The Village of Lira," Brielle replied, "close to the very centre of Ververos. I live here."

"That's a nice name."

Across the room, the curtain was once again pulled to the side. Two figures appeared.

Shae's usually impassive face was lined, brown eyes worried. He was the first to cross the room. Lance hovered by the door, his expression unreadable.

"It's good to see you up."

"It's good to be up."

Shae swallowed. "I had no idea one *eileamaid* wouldn't be strong enough. I am terribly sorry, Ren."

"You have nothing to be sorry about," Ren replied, "I promise." In unison, they both looked above Ren's head. "I should have known." There was a croak to his words. "It's so rare."

"Is it bad?"

He didn't look at her. "Just very rare."

"So, Ren," Brielle began, breaking Ren's train of wonder, "want a tour around the most beautiful place in Ververos?"

Ren followed Brielle and Shae from the funny little room she had unknowingly spent the last three days in.

Brogan trotted beside her, Lance behind.

The red hue of the air was more obvious outside. Ren drank in the sight. They had to be at least fifty metres off the ground. Tinges of light from a setting sun streamed through the gaps in the trees, bathing everything in various tones of pink.

The trees themselves were dense. Her room had been built against a giant oak, each of its leaves larger than Ren's head.

They followed a nearby pathway. Her room wasn't the only treehouse. There were many, each built against trunks and separated by walkways, lined by lanterns lit by swirling specks of Light magic and floored by lines of identical rungs. Ren looked down and wished she hadn't. The gaps between each plank were larger than she'd have liked. Below it was nothing but leaves, and a long drop.

"There's a circle starting," Brielle said.

Further up ahead there was a hubbub. A din of voices, and notes of what sounded like a violin, loudened with each step they took.

On account of Brogan, who, despite being incredibly competent at padding across miles of countryside, was struggling to navigate such terrain, Ren and Lance fell into a slower stride than Shae and Brielle. Ren shot him a few sideways glances. His face was still hardened, almost expressionless. A flutter of nervousness rose within her gut.

As with most experiences Ren had had since Shae had flounced his way into her life, she hadn't had the chance to dwell on it, the shared *moment* on the bed. He had felt it, too. He had to have. And though she still didn't know what it was they shared, she knew one thing.

It was stronger.

Since the moment he had thrown his arms around her frame, the buzzing had skyrocketed. A sensation she couldn't have explained were she to try. It hummed through her, *all* of her, so strong it should hurt, yet didn't. Reverberating so wildly it should make her itch, and claw at herself, but didn't.

It was comfort and frenzy, adventure and contentment all at once. Much like her taio, though her understanding of it was dismal at best, she craved its presence.

And right then its presence was erratic.

She glanced again. This time he mirrored her. The corner of his mouth tugged upwards.

"You okay?" he asked.

Her right elbow bumped his left. A rush of buzzing. "I was going to ask you the same thing."

"I–" Lance closed his mouth, then sighed, pushing a hand through his hair. "I'm sorry."

That, she wasn't expecting. Sorry for what? For holding her while the intangible and enigmatic whatever it was that connected them went haywire?

Ren bit her lip. She'd done that too much lately; a dull pain pulsed from the contact. She almost didn't want to ask. Didn't want to hear his answer. Wondering, anxiously, was more appealing than the words she now feared she was about to hear. "For?"

"Do you remember being in the water?"

Ren shrugged. "Barely." Their elbows touched again, just. Enough to make her skin hum against his.

"You were under for so long," Lance said, "I couldn't find you for ages. I–" His voice cracked. "I'm so sorry."

Understanding dawned. It wasn't regret he felt, not for that, anyway. It was guilt.

"There's nothing–"

"I let you go." His hand rubbed one eye, then another. "When the wave came."

Ren was flooded, an acute sadness replacing her short-lived relief.

"I let you go and couldn't find you."

She didn't remember halting, yet they were stationary. She placed one hand on his forearm and raised the other, her thumb rubbing gentle circles on the side of his neck.

"Lance." In Ververos his irises were almost maroon. A floating lantern was reflected in the glassiness. "You have nothing to be sorry for."

"Yes, I do." His arms had found their way around her, and Ren must have taken a step, or maybe he did, for they were closer now, their fronts flush. Buzzing, and what might have been both their hearts beating. And not a lot else.

"That wasn't even a wave. It was a *wall* of water. You couldn't have...y-you did everything."

"I thought I could protect you."

"Lance." Ren drew back, only a little. In Lance's eyes, more tears had gathered. "You *saved* me."

She watched him swallow, then saw nothing as she pulled him, closer still, holding him tighter than she had ever held anyone. "C'mon." His voice was muffled, buried somewhere within her hair. "You need to eat."

They broke apart.

"Annoying logic," Ren muttered as they began to walk.

Brogan, having waited patiently, padded as best he could beside them.

Lance slung an arm over her shoulder, guiding her forwards. They were close to the circle now. They passed several others, each offering them a wide smile, and stepped onto a flat, circular platform, larger than the ground floor of Ren's house.

Shae and Brielle sat within a group of ten or so others. Lance, though, led them in the opposite direction, towards several wooden crates. A slew of breads and meats, fruits and cheese, were laid within them, buffet style. Several large kegs stood to their side.

They loaded a plate each.

There were no chairs, instead squashy bean bags.

Ren snorted, poking one with the toe of her boot. "This place is bizarre."

Lance, laughing for the first time since he'd awoken, sunk down into it. The other side puffed up. "Care to join me?"

There was very little Ren cared to do more. She sat cross-legged as she munched what she would have called a chicken leg were it not almost a foot long.

They ate in silence, Ren finding herself so hungry it was a wonder her food wasn't inhaled.

Across the circle, Shae and Brielle's group were chatting

animatedly.

"Don't you want to sit with them?"

Lance took a long drink of something purple and fizzy. "Nah." His demeanour was calmer, his frame relaxed. Anyone else would assume he was happy.

So would Ren, had the buzzing not become weird and irregular again. Raising both eyebrows, she turned to him.

He sighed. "You know, to everyone else I'm a pretty good liar."

"So am I."

Lance took another drink. "I don't suppose *I don't want to talk about it* will do?" He looked across the circle.

Shae was off to the side slightly, talking quietly, *intimately*, with a woman.

Ren wondered who she was. They looked close, comfortable. The cloak he had begrudgingly thrown over Ren however many nights previously was wrapped around her shoulders.

Brielle sat a few metres over, one arm wound around a woman's neck, while her legs, long and bare, were intertwined with those of a man beside her. Brielle spoke, and each of the three burst out laughing.

Beside her, Lance sighed again.

It was an instinctual thing, a truth she knew deep down in that moment.

"It's Brielle, isn't it?"

The spaces between Ren's fingers were filled then, with his.

"Want to go for a walk?"

Ren nodded, and, grabbing them a flat bread each, allowed him to lead her, away from the circle, and Shae, and Brielle.

"Until recently, I thought I'd been in love two times." His hand squeezed hers. "Brielle was one of those times."

"Oh."

The buzzing that circled their hands was so strong it was a wonder it wasn't a visible, tangible thing.

"You have nothing to worry about," Lance said hurriedly.

She believed him. "How recent is recently?" Did she want to know? Probably not.

"The last time we were here was when we got the message from Gideon, the brief to Collect you."

They were passing a line of small tree houses. Each looked only a little larger than the room Ren had woken up in.

"Oh," Ren said again, voice small. Very recently.

"That was when I realised it was over." He paused.

Ren counted their steps. One. Two.

"The way she made me feel, I didn't want to feel like that anymore."

Five.

"I'd come here and try, and it was like it was for nothing."

Nine. Ten. Eleven. Twelve.

"She wouldn't, or couldn't, stop..." he trailed off.

Sixteen.

"I used to love the place but now that's all I feel here. Not good enough."

A pair of eyes, not dark brown, but blue stared at her from her mind's eye. *Months.* Ren swallowed. *Months of trying.* Twenty-three.

"I get it." She studied a nearby lantern before turning to Lance, his free hand raking through his long curls. They weren't sleek, nor well kept, but wild and disorderly. A notched scar was etched across his left eyebrow, barely visible from anything other than how close Ren was. She bit her lip again, wishing it was his. His stubble had grown. Perhaps to some he would look unkempt; to Ren he looked beautiful. She stopped counting. "I had...I felt that way."

"Well." He paused to push a stray strand of hair behind her ear. "He was an idiot."

His words broke something between them. Cracked the tension down the middle, dissipating it.

"So was she," Ren said, "an idiot, I mean."

Lance chuckled. "Doesn't matter now. Hasn't since I heard your voice through the scrystone."

"Because of our buzzing...connection...thing I don't understand at all?"

"No." His laugh was soft, meant only for her. He paused again, though this time he pulled a nearby curtain aside. He led them inside. "Well, maybe initially." She smiled, remembering the way the buzzing had crept upon her at nothing more than his voice. "But then, because you couldn't bear to leave your brother's jumper behind, and the way you look when you talk about *NáDarra.*"

They were standing in a room similarly sized to the one Ren had woken up in. At the end of the bed sat a trunk and a familiar sword. Beside it, eyeing them through one half-open yellow eye, lay a green cù-sìth. Ren hadn't noticed him leave their side.

"And the fact you came here, to another world. Because we asked you to."

They were closer again. She wouldn't be able to take a step without him taking one back. Her words emerged as no more than a breathy whisper. "I didn't have much choice in that, in the end."

"Then I thought I'd lost you," Lance continued, "and I finally got it. What *being* bound means." Had she held any desire to, she could have counted his eyelashes. "To be *bound.*"

"Bound?" His breath was warm against her forehead, and that might have been that, or perhaps the way his fingers were weaving through her hair, that made the sigh escape her. "Is that what it's called?"

"Mm. *Anam*," he whispered. His hold, both on the back of her head, and her waist, tightened. "Soul."

She understood little to none of what he was saying, and yet, to some deep-down part of her, it made all the sense in the world.

"I fought it, in my head. Didn't want to tell you because it still sounded mad and impossible. But I...I want you to know now." A sharp intake of breath as Ren's hands gripped his waist. "With you, I feel..." He trailed off, his breathing heavy and laboured.

So was hers.

She had scarcely needed anything more than to kiss him. Instead, she prompted him, her own fingertips dancing across the back of his neck. "You feel what?"

"Like...a part of me...is home."

Then, she kissed him.

A thunderclap in her heart and a rainstorm in her veins; the moment summer met autumn. The buzzing, no longer hers but *theirs*, and no longer buzzing but a wild reverberation, pulsating and rushing through every part of her being.

And he was everything; *they* were everything.

Everything she'd needed since his voice had rung through Shae's scrystone.

There were barely any moments over the next hour or so where Lance wasn't kissing her. Gently at first, and then not so. She neither knew nor cared which of them began the manoeuvre towards the bed, only that her thighs were suddenly pressed against the edge of the mattress. And then her entire back was as she lay, her fingertips pressed into the back of Lance's neck, imploring him to join her.

He relented to her touch, his movements hurried, yet smooth as silk as he positioned herself on top of her, over her, his lips leaving her own only to meet her neck, her throat, her chest.

"Lance." She encased his name within a soft sigh as she tangled her fingers through his hair. His only response was a throaty groan. Ren arched her back, a silent instruction, or perhaps a plea, to feel far more of his skin against her own.

It was a wonder her clothing didn't rip with the veracity in which Lance wrenched it from her body. A moan she failed to stifle escaped her as several long, teasing kisses were trailed down her stomach. His own shirt was removed with a similar enthusiasm.

He stared down at her then, for the first time unmoving save the gasping breaths erupting from both. Ren was bare from the waist up. So was he. He swept a hungry gaze down her chest, her stomach. Realising she was watching him, he shot her a grin, then a wink that alone was enough for another strangled moan to escape her.

Still grinning, Lance dipped his head to hers, his long curls surrounding her like a mane, peppering her jaw with kisses. Her fingers explored his chest, his torso, then his back as she pulled him closer still. The buzzing was a series of micro explosions encased in static, an indecipherable and unstoppable force clawing its way from her, to him, and back again.

At some point, Lance had lowered himself onto his side, one arm acting as her pillow, the other hand busying itself exploring her waistband.

In what might have been less than a few seconds, or several minutes, Ren's hips rose.

Lance's mouth contorted into a smile against her own as, together, they shimmied her trousers down her legs. With her boots, they hit the ground with a soft *flump,* followed by Lance's own.

And then all there was between them was bare skin and two pairs of thin underwear, his far less revealing than her own. A hungry look was present in his mahogany eyes as they roamed her form.

"You," he said, his tone holding a slight croak, "are unreal." One soft nip to the side of her neck. "Don't you dare argue," he snapped, his lips suddenly against hers, her mouth, poised open, ready to retort his words, closed with a soft smile as Lance moved his attention to kissing her neck. "And I've wanted you," his words were muffled against her, "from the moment I met you." His hand dipped then, the lowest yet, lower than her hips, his fingertips grazing the curve of her thigh.

"When you met me, you woke up in -" She tried to point out, her words whispered and breathy and snatched from her as his touch swept across the thin fabric of her underwear.

He chuckled darkly. "A part of me, even then, wanted you to join me."

She might have laughed, too, had his fingers not began to stroke, slow and deliberately, up and down. Instead, all she managed was a gravelly moan. And then, as her underwear was tugged ungraciously aside, several more.

And she knew nothing, except him. And buzzing, in and around every part of them. Joining them, in more ways than one. Far more than any physical act could.

Anam, he had called it. *Soul.*

Hers, and his. Theirs.

A blissful ecstasy.

That she never wanted to leave.

"What are you doing?"

The charcoal words were blurry. Almost every line, and all her fingers, were smudged. While many things intrigued her about this world, none had irked her thus far more than its pitiful excuse for office supplies.

"Making a list."

"Of?"

"I found these on your table." Ren held the parchment and charcoal aloft. "I hope it's okay. Ugh!" Her thumb distorted yet another word. "Ridiculous," she muttered darkly.

The mattress contorted as Lance sat up. "Of course." Shimmying around her, stopping only to place a quick kiss to the top of her head, he headed towards the bathroom.

Lance's room – which was apparently some trade deal with the Council; a refuge for resources – was homier than the one Ren had woken up in.

They had fallen asleep, in a happy, buzzing ecstasy, wrapped up in blankets and each other.

"So, this list of yours," Lance said, appearing in the doorway opposite, "does it document all your favourite things about yours truly?"

She shot him a look of what she intended to be disdain, though it turned into something very different upon the realisation he was still naked.

Scoffing, Lance made his way towards her. "My eyes are up here."

Her gaze flickered upwards, before immediately returning to his torso, and then not at all his torso. "I'm perfectly aware of where your eyes are located, thank you. Wh-no!" The charcoal crumbled, coating the pads of her thumb and index finger in a soft grey. "No!" Ren cried. Happiness at the sight of him vanished, and something inside of her, something she had managed, through too many almost deaths, to keep dormant.

"Ren?"

She didn't turn. "I needed that!"

The floor creaked beneath Lance as he took a step towards the bed. "Why?"

"I need–" Ren gasped between what few words she managed to speak. "A list. I need–"

"It's okay," Lance said.

A flash of anger gripped her. It wasn't okay. "No, it's not."

A gust of air rolled through the small, circular room, scattering each of the blank papers.

Tightness crushed behind her ribs. His hand lightly brushed the centre of his own chest. Had he felt her anger?

He took a step towards her. "You've been through a lot. I understand."

"No, you don't."

For a long moment, he neither moved nor spoke. "You're right, I don't." He ran a hand through his dark curls. His fingers tangled in what looked like several grimy knots. After a second or two he took a single step, his movements tentative, careful. He spoke with a softness. "Help me to."

The anger dissipated almost as fast as it had appeared, leaving a deep well of emptiness in its stead. "It-it's what I do. Or it's what I did."

"Make lists?"

Ren nodded. "And...plans. It helps; it helps to plan."

Several lines crossed his forehead. His jaw was tight, mouth pursed. His eyes, though, were soft. "You can't plan for everything."

In another circumstance, she might have laughed. She had been able to plan for exactly nothing that had transpired since Shae had entered her life. Not to mention the fact Dr. Michele had bored the same sentiment into her almost every week for the last year.

She'd had no say in coming here, in being chased and hunted and almost drowned. She didn't know what the powers she possessed would do or strike next. Her understanding of what lay, buzzing and dormant, between the two of them, despite the previous evening, was still laughable. The magnitude of the chaos that had warped so many parts of her life into something Ren couldn't hope to grasp was so great it left her gasping and breathless when she thought of it for too long. It wasn't only a world without money, without decent law enforcement, or sausage rolls. It was a world without the way Ren had learnt to navigate life, with her lists and carefully constructed plans that, despite usually depicting nothing, had been what her existence had centred around.

Lance took another step, closer still, almost to the bed. Close enough now she wouldn't need to extend her arm much at all to touch him. Ren's fingers flexed and, for a few silent moments, her breathing stilled. In the wake of her panic-stricken outburst, the room was quiet enough to hear him swallow.

He sank into the mattress beside her. Leaning back, he settled himself against the headboard, arms raised, elbows bent, hands tucked behind his neck, and jerked his head to the bed's vacant side. "Come here."

Ren did, slotting herself beside him, legs curled beneath her. Without meaning it to, her knee came to rest against the side of his thigh. Whether because of the buzzing that centred there, or just *him*, or both, Ren's heart began to slow.

She stared ahead, across the modest room. Opposite, Brogan was snoozing, his body wound in a spiral.

"I didn't used to be like this," Ren said. "Obsessive about lists and writing down plans. I didn't used to care."

Lance said nothing as he brought the arm closest to her down, placing his palm on the back of Ren's hand. For a few seconds, neither moved, until Ren turned her hand upside down, palm upwards, flush with his. Their fingers interlaced.

"And then my mum disappeared." The pad of his thumb brushed back and forth across the side of her finger. "I didn't remember anything for eighteen months," Ren recalled. "And I did...things to myself. Hurt myself." Her voice had dropped to scarcely more than a whisper. "A year or so after, I did something. Something stupid. My leg was broken in three places and I'd done something to my back and I got prescribed these painkillers. My back was better pretty quickly, but I kept telling them it wasn't. And I got more pills." She was gripping Lance's hand so tight it had to hurt, but he said nothing. "I finally told some therapist, then immediately regretted it," she added with a laugh, neither warm nor reciprocated. "I didn't get prescribed any more pills. And then I remembered something."

"From the night your mum...?"

"Yeah. Her. Just her. We were driving and it was dark. And she said, *I should have made a plan.* Again, and again. I never knew what difference a plan would have made. I still don't," she added. "But it stuck in some part of me, I suppose."

Lance's hand left hers, only for his arm to curl over her shoulders.

Ren leant against him. He was warm; his hair tickled her cheek. "I know," Ren began, "that you were sent to find me by your Council, but I don't think that's *why* I'm here."

Lance placed a gentle kiss on the top of her head.

"Lance?"

"Mm?"

"I'm not going to the prison."

His face turned towards her, as hers had turned to his. "Okay," he said simply. "So, where *are* we going?"

She took a long breath. "Is there somewhere–?" Ren paused to sigh, not sure what she was asking. No such place that she knew of existed in Scotland. "Where, I don't know, we could find anything, *information,* or..."

She expected a *no,* or a snort of derision. "It's a long shot." Lance's voice was distant. "I used to have tons of contacts there, but..." He trailed off. "I think, if we're going to find out anything, we'd better start in the Hidden City."

"How is a city *hidden?*"

"It's underground."

"Oh."

"And hard to find. Full of bad shit. Criminals, black markets, that kind of thing."

"Sounds lovely."

"If there's information about your mum somewhere, and the Council doesn't know about it, someone there probably does."

Ren, biting her lip to keep her newfound smile from widening further, pulled herself from his side, enough to face him. "We could find her?"

"Look, it won't be easy." Lance's expression was hard, sharing none of her optimism. "People don't give information away for nothing, and then there's finding who might have any in the first place. Ren, I don't want you to get your hopes up."

Too late, thought Ren.

"It might not work."

"But it *might...*"

"Yeah," he conceded. "It might."

Lance's pessimism aside, he had given her what she'd yearned for since arriving. It wasn't much, and who knew if anything of value would transpire from it, or if Shae would be willing to go along with it, but Ren had, if nothing else, a plan.

She didn't even feel the need to write it down.

Ren shuffled, manoeuvring herself back, away from him

a little. The dark, lightning-like scar from the bodach jagged across his torso like an oil slick. It covered most of some script she hadn't noticed before.

She nodded at it and gathered both her lists. "What did that say?"

He twisted, examining the remains of it. Only a few letters were visible now. "No informers, no disorder...no surrender. It was my gang's old mantra." He snorted at the distorted tattoo. "That's almost ironic," he mumbled.

She blinked at him. "You had a *gang*?"

"Mm."

"But now you don't?"

He shook his head as her fingertips grazed over one of the lines of the scar. Lance flinched, hissing.

Ren wrenched her hand back. "Oh, I'm sorry. Is it sore?"

"No." Laughter. "I'm a little ticklish, and–" He didn't get the chance to finish.

Ren, grin far more wicked than his, discovered Lance's definition of *a little* varied greatly from her own.

"S-stop!" He was panting.

She relented, wrapping her arms around his neck.

He manoeuvred them back, leaning against his headboard, Ren's head against his chest.

She reached for her lists.

"What are they?" he asked.

"These," she said, showing him the first page, "are symptoms." There were numerous ailments listed, from joint and muscle pain, to breathlessness, to heart palpitations. Kidney failure was at the bottom, underlined and circled. She had given each a number between one and three.

"These things," Lance said, frowning, "are what you suffer with?"

"Mm." Ren took her first list back. "Well, suffer*ed*. And not all at once. Most of them haven't bothered me since leaving..." She flexed an arm. A week ago it would have hurt. It wasn't the first time she had realised the pain had lessened, gone, even, but it felt poignant, somehow, then.. Ren swallowed. "Since leaving Earth."

"But you had all of them, at some point?"

"Yeah." Her eyes scanned her second list. "Why?"

His hold on her tightened. "I'm sorry." He placed another kiss on the top of her head. "But why write them all down now?"

"I don't want to forget any." Ren handed him the next page. "When I *eventually* confront your Council about why I was sent away as a baby."

"That's fair. What do people get for working?" he read aloud. "Are there weather reports?" He sounded confused. "Do they have pizza?" He pronounced it to rhyme with *fizz*, which didn't bode well for the answer. "What do these mean?"

She shrugged. "They're things I want to know."

"Well," he replied, "people get paid in lots of different ways. After every five years of service to the Council, for example, you can opt for some land, or a small property. Some have livestock. I have a room back at the Council chambers, and you get enough food. There's also a workers' store, where you can get things to trade, for clothes, or anything else."

"Oh," Ren said, "that's interesting."

"There are elementals that study the skies, and the weather is a part of that," Lance said, "and I don't know what pizza is, so I don't know." He kept reading. "Yes, there are other countries; you have to sail to them. I've never been to any."

Did they all mirror her world? Was there a backwards Italy, or Mexico somewhere?

"What's contraception?"

She wished she were surprised. Bloody primitives. "It stops a woman from getting pregnant."

"Oh, you mean like alderbark?"

"Do I?"

He reached over to his bedside cabinet and pulled a small vial from the drawer. He had at least a dozen. A sort of off-yellow colour. "It's infused with *NeòNach*. It halts the absorption of, you know, *impurities* for a few hours."

What a way to put it. Ren arched an eyebrow. "Impurities?"

"Mm. That's what they say anyway."

Handing the potion back, Ren asked, "Do both have to take it?"

"Yes." He placed the vial back in its drawer.

"Could...*I* take it?" One of the only things she knew of *NeòNach* was that it can fight, in a way, with *NáDarra*, which she seemed to have in spades.

"I don't know," Lance admitted. "That's why I didn't suggest it last night."

A flush crept up her neck at the memory. "Last night was still amazing," she said, sighing contentedly. "Even if we didn't..."

"Hm." Another kiss, this one longer. "Yes, it was."

They fell into a comfortable silence. Lance's fingers played absentmindedly with her hair; Ren's brushed up and down his stomach.

"What does this one mean?" she asked, tracing around another tattoo, the playing card on the side of his chest. A *B* was drawn into the centre of it.

Lance sighed through his nose. "I got that a long time ago."

"When you were still in your gang?"

"Before."

"What's the *B* mean?"

He paused. The buzzing quelled slightly. "Brother."

They made their way back to the huge, raised platform from the previous night. It was busy. New foods had been placed in the crates.

"Don't we need to pay, or, ah, trade, for this?"

"Nah," Lance said, taking three rolls, "the folk here are too community-minded for that."

Shae was sitting over to one side, cross-legged on a large purple beanbag, poring over parchment. He was next to the woman he had been speaking to the previous evening. Her black hair was cropped close, a shimmery taio hovering above it. She was surrounded by a myriad coloured specks as she bent over the fabric draped between her hands. She looked up as they approached, her red eyes hovering over Ren's own taio.

Shae's didn't move. "Afternoon."

"Hi, Lance," the woman said.

"Hi." Lance's reply was muffled thanks to the mouthful of rib. "Ren, this is Astrid."

Shae's eyebrows narrowed at the sight. "Must you do that?"

"What?"

Shae didn't reply.

"How are you, Ren?" the woman, Astrid, asked.

"Uh."

Well, I'm still not sure how, or why, but I've been taken from my home to a whole different world I only found out existed a week and a half ago, despite the fact I was apparently born here. On top of that I've been nearly killed three times, have magic I know exactly nothing about nor how to use . Oh, and the mere thought of this bloke next to me, who I know probably five things about, not being next to me anymore makes me sick with dread.

But I also have a father and a brother and a home that's far too far away. But at least I'm not going to a prison, of all places. Instead, I'm going to some mad gang-filled underground city. If I can avoid the mad rebels and giant cats and fucking river ghosts enough to get there.

"I'm fine, thanks. How are you?"

"Good, thank you."

The specks around her were swirling and looping and sparking.

"What are you doing?" Ren asked.

Astrid's eyes, red like Brielle's, and reflecting all the various flecks around her, lit up. "I'll show you." She rose like a ballerina, all long legs and sharp edges.

The specks followed.

Depositing herself next to Ren, Astrid held the parchment out. On it was what looked like watercolour. A coastline, behind a sandy beach. To one side there was a grassy bank with a white building. It had a balcony looking out to sea. Ren narrowed her own eyes. The sea was shimmering in a way that looked real, and the clouds, after closer inspection, seemed to move across the sky.

Astrid was an impeccable artist. But it was her medium that caused Ren's breath to hitch somewhere near her throat.

"You painted this...with magic?"

Astrid smiled. "I'm a faedra."

Still not entirely sure what a faedra was, Ren studied the picture more.

Using nothing but a tiny flick of her index finger, Astrid sent a single blue water speck into the sea of her painting. The place it hit glittered and shone. A gentle wave splashed onto the shore.

"It's beautiful."So enraptured by the painting, Ren hadn't noticed another figure plonk herself in their group. A vial of clear liquid, though laced with red specks, appeared half a foot from her face. Ren blinked at it.

"Hello," Brielle offered brightly, sinking into a beanbag. Without waiting for a response from any of them, she continued, "Ren?"

"Hm?" Ren placed the now empty vial in front of her.

She handed Ren's next potion over. Air. "We *must* get you something new to wear."

"Oh." That, she hadn't expected. "That's really nice of you, and–"

"Ren." Brielle said again, raising one hand and one eyebrow. "You simply cannot *not* have a change of clothes."

Ren picked at the sides of Lance's shirt she was wearing. It wasn't as appealing as her red top was. "I do have a change."

Brielle didn't bother to keep the disdain from her face. "Those shapeless sacks *he* wears for reasons I cannot fathom don't count. They're ugly, for one, and do nothing for you for another."

It was a harsh statement.

It was also hard to argue with.

Lance's expression darkened. "I like these shirts, and I happen to think Ren looks good in them."

"You'd think Ren looks good in a potato sack," Shae pointed out.

Lance blinked. "Well, that's hardly the point." He turned to Ren. "You don't think my shirts are ugly, do you?"

"Of course, she does," Brielle interjected. "She has eyes."

"I..." All but Lance, who was glaring at Brielle, faced her. "I happen to look very good in a potato sack."

Astrid and Brielle burst out laughing.

Shae let out a soft snicker.

Lance muttered something under his breath, and Ren

wondered whether to feel guilty.

She decided she didn't.

Brielle, her long legs crossed at the ankle, handed the remaining few potions to Ren. Her flawless features held a knowing smirk. "You know I'm right."

"I can say no, and hate her, if you really want me to."

They had reached the outside of Brielle's room, where Ren had been summoned.

Lance had been forbidden, which had been fine with him. He exhaled a snort. "No, I don't want you to hate her. The thing is," he looked down, avoiding her gaze, "she never did anything wrong. Well, until she insulted my shirts."

Ren stifled a laugh.

On a walkway over from theirs stood a woman and two men, embracing in a group hug. The sight wasn't an uncommon one.

"They do seem very, ah...open here."

"That's one way of putting it." He stepped back. "I'm going to hunt.

"Have fun," she said brightly.

He turned to leave, fiddling with the leather pouch on his waistband that housed his knives. "Likewise."

The inside of Brielle's room was separated from the outside world by a thin curtain, pale green and dotted with holes.

Ren stepped inside.

Three faces greeted her, along with a pile of fabric so large it took up the entirety of what Ren assumed was a fairly sizable bed.

"Oh, good," Brielle exclaimed, "now we can have some

fun."

Astrid nodded, matching Brielle's enthusiasm.

Shae, leaning against the wall opposite, cloak swaying slightly, inclined his head.

A delicate, fluttery something rose in Ren's stomach.

Fun.

She hadn't had much of that lately.

Brielle owned exactly zero shoes, two pairs of trousers, and around three hundred of her long scarf-like wraps.

The following few hours were spent with Ren in various stages of undress, with Brielle and some brightly coloured fabric circling her. Astrid and Shae, having spent the entire first hour critiquing Brielle's choices – something Shae was most enthusiastic about – opted to leave after what must have been Ren's thirtieth change.

"I think this is the one," the blonde exclaimed, expertly tying the navy material by Ren's waist. "It would look much better without the trousers, but–"

"The trousers are staying."

Brielle ushered Ren towards a floor-length mirror. Her room was bigger than Lance's. More lengths of fabric had been hung like tapestries, covering almost every inch of the circular wall. On the far side stood a large desk covered in vials upon vials of ingredients. Beside it stood the mirror.

She had never spent much time examining her own reflection, but there had been less call for it of late. Ren stepped into view as Brielle busied herself with some of her vials. They clinked against each other in her hands.

Ren swallowed, smoothing her hands over the fabric covering her abdomen. The deep blue was threaded with silver constellations. They sparkled with every movement. Brielle had cinched the material at Ren's waist, yet loosened it over her shoulders. The effect should have been odd, yet wasn't.

"Right." Brielle appeared at her side. "Now take it off."

Oh.

"I–" Ren frowned as the other woman handed her a towel.

"I'll fix it back the same way," Brielle said. "After you've washed."

The sound of running water met her ears. "Oh, a-are you sure?"

Brielle turned to face the reflection, her gaze roaming over Ren's hair. It was, admittedly, not in its finest condition. "Yes, Ren," she said dryly, making no efforts to hide the wrinkling of her nose. "I'm sure."

B rielle, swinging a picnic basket as she walked, led them to somewhere called *the Spire*. Ren didn't know where, or what, the Spire was, only that Lance would apparently find them there.

They walked down not quite back streets, but back walkways. The air was quiet, save for the occasional hoot and distant din of chatter which dissipated more the further from the circle they travelled. Ren's boots clacked on the wooden slats, though Brielle's bare feet were soundless. Ren sucked in a breath. The air smelled like cinnamon and something else, something herby. Oregano, maybe.

Brielle had plied Ren with more of her elixirs before marching her to the bathroom, where Ren experimented with an array of soaps, shampoos, scrubs, and a highly effective hair-removal cream.

Combined with the scarf-top Brielle had once again expertly tied, Ren felt better – physically, at least – than she had since leaving Earth. And for several years before then.

"You didn't have to do all this." Ren gestured down, over herself.

"I know I didn't."

Ren ran a hand over the long braid – more of Brielle's handiwork. It stopped above the middle of her back. "Thank you."

They took several turns Ren couldn't hope to remember.

"Are you excited for Lance to see you?"

Ren took a second to search for the buzzing. Having grown so used to the sensation, she had stopped noticing it. It hovered there, in the centre of her chest like a large, expectant bee.

"Yes."

"I'm glad that he has you," Brielle said.

The words caught her. "You are?"

"I love him."

Ren fought to keep her expression nonplussed at the statement.

One glance and several snorts of laughter from Brielle later, the blonde continued. "Not like *that*, Ren, calm yourself – you'll give yourself heart failure, and I've already had to save you once this week. I've never loved him in that way; I've wanted him to find someone who would." Linking her arm through Ren's, she steered them round yet another bend. "I've never seen him like that before. Scared, I mean. When they arrived with you. Terrified," she added. "And rightly so because you were almost dead. I didn't know if I could save you, and he told me if I didn't, he'd kill me."

Ren's eyebrows rose. "Bit rude."

They were further now; all chatter from the circle had vanished.

"I thought so, too, and then later I saw it." She paused. "How long have you known?"

"Known what?"

"That you're bound to him?"

There they were again. Those five letters. By all counts, it was a simple adjective.

Bound. Bound *to* him.

That didn't sound simple, yet it did. It made lots of sense and also none.

"It's rare," Brielle said. "Finding your *co-anam*."

Her *what*? "Bless you?"

"The one with whom your soul is shared."

During her and Lance's dizzying exchange the previous evening, it had sounded an awful lot like a soulmate. *Felt* an awful lot like a soulmate. Ren's fingertips sought out the same spot on her chest. Was it a possible thing, that souls could be shared, hers by him?

Yes, her consciousness informed her.

Could it be that his soul was meant to be found by hers, across not just miles, but worlds?

A thousand times, yes.

"Can I ask you something?" Ren said. If she didn't now, she never would.

"Of course."

"You know, er, alderbark?"

Brielle did nothing to hide her widening smile. "I do."

"Is it safe...for me, I mean?"

"Yes." Brielle squeezed Ren's arm. "Perfectly safe. The *NeòNach* is so diluted it doesn't even affect weavers. Except, of course, in the way it's supposed to."

"Good to know."

Brielle shot her a grin that was far wider than necessary. "I'm sure it is."

The Spire turned out to be not the church steeple its name suggested, but a gathering of ponds.

Brielle led them down a ladder, carved and smoothed into the trunk of a large oak.

Ren landed on the forest floor with a dull crunch.

Up close, the pools appeared purple. Below the surface of each was a scattering of Light magic. Each speck gently to'd and fro'd, casting a violet glow above the water. They loomed oddly, like large, flat lamps across the moss.

They were separated by what Ren had assumed were trees. Up close, they were mushrooms – if mushrooms were over four feet high, with tops as large as dining tables.

Three people, two men and one woman, sat on one nearby.

Ren prodded the side of the one closest, expecting a smooth surface.

It wasn't smooth.

"It's hairy," Ren said, not quite knowing whether she felt intrigued or repelled.

Brielle didn't appear to be listening. The picnic basket was launched on top of the nearest shroom before Brielle hoisted herself upwards. She offered her hand down to Ren, whose climb up was far less graceful.

Opening her basket, Brielle withdrew two peaches. She handed one to Ren. "Why do you have a tattoo of a sheep on your leg?"

Ren fought the urge to roll her eyes. She did not have a tattoo of a sheep on her leg. "It's a cloud," she replied dryly.

"It looks like a sheep."

"I know." She took a bite. Peaches tasted different than they did on Earth, more bitter, but not unpleasant. Ren chewed slowly as she looked at the other woman.

Brielle's legs were stretched before her; they appeared longer up close. Half a foot above her head, her taio lay, sparkling in the late afternoon air. Neither attuned to *NáDarra* or *NeòNach*, Brielle's specks hovered somewhere between the two.

This marked her as a faedra.

It had been almost two weeks since she had met Shae. Almost one since he had first uttered the word *faedra* in her direction.

She had thought him mad.

186

She looked around the Spire. More people had arrived, and pairings and small groups alike were selecting their own mushrooms. Most waved at Brielle and, by extension, Ren. She offered each a half smile.

Then a surge in the buzzing forced her attention from her mostly eaten peach. For the first time, she didn't question what it meant. Casting the peach stone over the side of their mushroom, she sought him out.

Joined by Shae and Astrid, he wore the same easy smile, the one that made his eyes crinkle. Ren drank in the sight of him. His armour sat half open, his long tresses slick with sweat. Flecks of dirt littered his arms. He definitely hadn't washed after his hunt.

It ought to disgust her, the sheer griminess of him.

Instead, each of her pulse points came alive.

Jumping the last few rungs with ease, his gaze swept the scene, landing on her. The rise in the buzzing was no longer confined to her chest.

Lance led the trio towards Ren and Brielle's mushroom, face steady with a set determination.

Each of the three hoisted themselves up with no apparent difficulty, unlike Ren. It might have irked her were a dirty and bedraggled Lance Allardyce not pressing his lips to hers.

"You look–" He smelt like sweat and leather.

"So do you," she whispered against his mouth.

His fingertips grazed the small of her back. "Pretty sure I look filthy."

Ren cocked her head. "You do."

He arched one eyebrow but said nothing, before shimmying himself beside her, facing the others. Ren half wished they'd vanish into thin air.

"Kill anything big?" she asked as his arm slunk across her shoulders. The buzzing pulsed alongside her heartbeat, and his.

"Mm." He swallowed, eyes glazed. "Really big. Big hooters."

Ren still didn't know, or care, what a hooter was.

"Oh, I hope they roast them," Astrid said.

Lance nodded. "My mum does the best roasted hooter." His look shifted, as though he was suddenly somewhere else, far from their mushroom. "She does this thing with the gravy..."

Only Ren and, she suspected, Shae, saw the sag in his shoulders.

Only Ren felt the momentary dip in the buzzing.

Astrid ran a hand through her cropped locks. "You'll have to go home soon and have some."

Lance didn't reply.

"You know what goes best with hooter?" Looking expectantly at each of them in turn, Shae continued, "Mushrooms."

The word was met with a general air of disagreement, despite Shae's insistence that the others pay no attention to *Lance's slanderous claims* about his cooking.

They feasted, not quite on roasted hooter, from Brielle's basket: peaches and crackers with a rubbery cheese, followed by fruitcake and washed down with wine.

Lance and Shae, more the latter than the former, had spun a tale upon their arrival to the village, about Ren having been confined to some island off the north coast of Caeracre, her powers denied and suppressed.

It wasn't really a lie.

"Then," Brielle was saying, "once you've gathered them, like *this*." A small collection of white Air specks hovered above her outstretched palm. "You can direct them." The specks whizzed into the gap separating Astrid and Shae's faces. An impressive feat, given there was barely an inch between them. Neither of them batted an eyelid at the magical intrusion.

It was the most at ease she had seen Shae. He used his elbows to prop himself up. In the darkening air, Astrid's eyes were reflected in his own and his cloak covered the pair of them.

"Now," Brielle said, "you try."

Ren placed her palm upwards, as Brielle had.

"Concentrate."

She searched for a speck to hone in on.

"No." Brielle's hand grabbed Ren's forearm. "You're a weaver. Search *inside* you."

"What do you mean, *inside* me?"

"Close your eyes."

Ren did as instructed.

"Now," Brielle's voice instructed, "find them."

Ren didn't know how.

"I don't see–"

"Don't *look* for them. Feel for them."

At first there was nothing, neither sight nor feeling, only a red-tinged darkness. Ren frowned, feeling nothing except Lance's fingertips trailing across the centre of her back.

And then, so brief it was a miracle she didn't miss it, came the smallest of flashes. A single speck.

Ren dared not breathe. "I found one," she whispered as more came into view. Hovering, blowing back and forth.

Air.

"Steady your hand," Brielle said. "And visualise them there."

Ren did. At first, she saw each of the specks individually. Then as a whole. They were stronger that way. *My hand,* she told them. "I-I think–"Refusing to let the soft gasp from beside her break her concentration, Ren thought the words again, repeating them. *My hand.*

"Open your eyes." Lance's voice was hushed.

There, hovering above Ren's palm, were at least twenty specks of pure Air magic. "I did it!"

Brielle squeezed her arm. "Well done, Ren."

Across the mushroom, both Shae and Astrid, and Lance, offered her a brief round of applause.

"I," Ren began, but she was having trouble forming words. Her heart and head were soaring, as though she had jumped from the top of one of the giant pines and hit the ground unhurt. As though she had flown or driven ninety miles per hour down an empty M1. The colours of the darkening evening were brighter. Sounds sharper. "What do I do with them now?"

"You have only a few seconds before they'll leave, but until then, you can direct them wherever you want."

She looked first ahead, and then to either side; they landed on Lance, who was beaming.

Sending them onward, towards him, Ren broke into a laugh as they hurtled by him, blowing his long hair in a hundred directions. "Where will they go?" she asked.

"*NáDarra* seeks out its own kind," Brielle explained. "Since that was Air, it'll join the Air around us. Were it Water, it would have gone to that pond." Brielle nodded at the nearest pond, over to their right. "And the Air magic within you will begin to replenish." A breeze, gentle and unassuming, passed over the small group. She already missed them.

"It will?"

"Of course."

"You will need to be aware of how much you can bring forth," Brielle was saying, "Magic is like a drug, and you don't want to overdose, Ren. You'd experience a *lag*, and believe me, it would make the effects of this forest feel like nothing."

Ren took a drink of wine, her mind far from Brielle's warnings and rife with the wonder of it, of what she had done...of what she could do. *Would* do.

"Brie." The voice cut through her awe. A woman stood beside their mushroom, her eyes narrowed at the small group. They were red, like Brielle and Astrid's, though held none of the same warmth. Her taio matched theirs, too. "Lance." The greeting wasn't friendly.

The buzzing prickled. "Clara."

The woman, Clara, ignored Shae, Astrid, and Ren, turning her attention back to Brielle.

Across the mushroom, Astrid was feigning a cough.

"We had plans tonight."

"Did we?"

"Yes," Clara said curtly. "Unless you're having a better time here." A cold gaze swept over them.

Brielle wrinkled her nose. "I'm having a lovely time here." She took a long gulp of wine. "But I'll come." Shooting them all a smile, she climbed over Ren and Lance, caring not to do so carefully. "We can practise more tomorrow," she added, before squeezing Ren's arm.

The four watched them leave in silence.

Shae sat up. "She's as friendly as ever."

Astrid followed suit.

Lance was chuckling.

"I," Shae began, "am starving." He was watching Astrid's face. "Want to get some food?"

Nodding, and still giggling, Astrid allowed Shae to lead her over the edge of the mushroom. "See you both tomorrow."

Ren offered them a brief wave.

Lance's eyebrows rose skywards.

"Enjoy your...*food*."

The daytime had been cast aside, replaced by a mask of darkness. Both Shae and Astrid's forms disappeared almost as soon as they stepped away from the mushroom. A speck of Dark magic drifted lazily by Ren's face. She blinked at it; she hadn't even noticed the Dark specks replacing the Light ones.

Lance's hand met the back of her neck, and Ren flopped her body against his. "What is my life?" she asked no one.

Lance held her, planting a single kiss to the top of her head.

A sense of something rose in her chest. The same something from the Culloden woods and the island on the loch, the one she and Luke had spent summers chasing each other over, learning each inch of the grassy land. That she felt every time she had passed the graveyard that lay off the road to Edinburgh. Some knowledge, far greater than she. She hadn't understood it then.

She still didn't.

"I used magic." Her words were muffled against the thin fabric of his shirt. They didn't sound real. She still felt the rush of it.

They buzzed together as he held her, tighter still. "Yeah, you did."

Ren didn't reply.

His fingers fiddled with her braid. "That's a good thing, isn't it?"

Before uttering them, her words sounded rather silly. "I sort of…thought it was a mistake or something."

"What was?"

"Me and magic…even with my taio."

It was quieter now. In time, most others had left the Spire. The din of chatter surrounding them had been replaced by hoots and scurries. Somewhere further than they, a quiet howl pierced through the night.

"Understandable."

"But it wasn't a mistake."

"Definitely not." The pad of his thumb stroked up and down her cheek.

It should have made things simpler, and yet...Ren held the sides of Lance's waist so tightly it probably hurt.

"What's wrong?" he whispered into her hair.

Ren swallowed. Her worries sounded odd even to her own mind. Pulling back from him, she took a breath. "I'm apparently from here, but I only know somewhere else." She chewed on her lip. "I don't know if I'm Ren, the barmaid, who was always sore and tired and whose lungs didn't work properly. Or if I'm Ren th-the weaver, who doesn't hurt all the time but is hunted by mad rebels and mad cats and who causes earthquakes and lightning and makes wind appear from nothing." She took a breath. "Which am I?"

His words were as soft as down feathers. "I think you know."

Her thoughts were erratic, yet numb. Gripping his hand, Ren shook her head. "If that's true, and I'm the second Ren, the Ren from Caerisle, the one with magic..." Taking another breath, this one bigger, Ren looked down, the fingertips of the hand not clutching Lance's stroking the strange fibres of the stranger mushroom. "Then my dad isn't my dad and my brother...is he my brother? What if being the second Ren means never..." She couldn't continue.

"Tell me about them, your family."

It took her a long moment to compose herself. "There's only really my dad and Luke. Both my mum and dad were only children – or my dad is." Ren paused as the realisation washed over her. "I don't know if I know anything about my mum. Except that she's supposedly..." Her voice quieted, "here, somewhere." Ren's eyes darted this way and that in the dark. Had her mother ever visited the Spire, or the Village of Lira? Maybe she should be asking. But then, was her name even Murryn?

And what does it mean?

Together, as one.

Ren looked at Lance.

That's right...and that's how we'll always find each other....

"It was the four of us, until it was the three of us."

"Tell me about them," Lance repeated, "your dad and Luke."

And she did.

She told him about her dad's garage and his love of elephants and his hellbent determination to embarrass his children by whatever means necessary. Of what they only referred to as *the hair dye incident.* When the dye had got everywhere, including his legs and the ceiling, except the top of his head. Of the time he had fallen into a pond after one too many gin and tonics, hoping to befriend a koi carp. And then of Luke's dreams of becoming a doctor, the way his first word was *rugby*, much to their mother's annoyance. How, at twelve years old, he once ate an entire bar of soap as a dare and was convinced he was going to die for three weeks after and the way, a few summers ago, he started writing rap songs. Increasingly bad ones.

She must have talked for at least half an hour.

"I can't lose that; them. Lance, I can't." Above, a single roll of thunder roared.

"I know." The buzzing was erratic between them, surging and dipping in no discernible pattern. "I know."

She didn't know how long they remained there.

"Lance?"

"Yeah?"

They manoeuvred down, her head settled on his chest.

"Tell me about yours."

"My family?"

"Mm."

He sighed deeply through his nose, then spoke of his siblings with a kind of quiet pride she had scarcely heard. He said little of his father. The man had upped and left when Lance was ten, mistress and ready-made secondary family in tow. "She had land, and a big house, and horses, tons to trade with," he said bitterly, as though each word stung, "and we...didn't have much."

"She sounds like a bitch."

He barked a laugh. "She is."

"So does he."

"He is."

"What about your mum?"

"The greatest woman I've ever known."

Ren smiled softly as she pressed herself against him. The buzzing quelled slightly.

"She hates me, though."

"Oh, I'm sure she doesn't–"

"The last words she ever said to me were her telling me exactly that."

"Why?" Ren asked, and then caught herself. "You don't have to... Sorry, that was rude."

"No, it wasn't. I don't want to keep anything from you, but there's a lot about me you don't know."

"That sounds ominous."

"The thought of you knowing certain things...scares me."

Somewhere nearby, the coo of what sounded like a pigeon rang through the night. The air had cooled.

Lance pulled Ren closer still, though she suspected it was for her natural warmth. The darkness cloaked them like a blanket. The ponds, with their small supply of Light magic, lit very little outside of their own water.

She dragged her fingers through his messy curls. "Why?"

"My own mother didn't disown me for nothing."

"Is this because of your old gang?"

"Yeah." He paused, stroking the side of Ren's arm. "Where I'm from, Arrik, it isn't how it is here, or Loreleith, where the Academies are. It isn't on any major trade routes – not that much is produced there that can be traded with. If you have a gift, you get out; you go to one of the Academies and you get a future and make something of yourself. But Arrik has the highest number of those born without a gift in the whole of Caerisle. The only real way to make anything of yourself is to become a criminal. Or a victim," he added.

"I'm guessing you chose the former."

"I chose the former," he confirmed. "We were...we started out as everyone does: petty stuff. And when others we knew got complacent, we got better – or worse, depending on how you look at it." His voice cracked; it didn't suit him. "I wasn't a good person, Ren. And my mother saw it more than anyone. She begged me to get out. To leave the Hull – that was where we operated from – behind."

"But you did?"

He sighed. "Yeah, I did."

"Isn't that good?"

"Yes and no. The fact I did, yes. The reason I did it, not so much. I didn't do it for my mother."

He said no more, and she didn't press him; his thoughts in a painful place far from their mushroom.

Minutes passed. "Do you miss them?"

He shifted beside her, holding her as though scared she'd disappear."My family or my gang?"

"Either?"

"I miss both." He hummed as Ren continued to roam her hands through his hair. "In some ways, they were the same thing. Family is something that can be forged from the darkest of places."

She smiled at that. "Would you go back to it? Your gang? The Hull place?" she asked. "If-if you could?"

Lance looked away. "If I said I didn't know, would any part of you see me differently? Worse?"

Ren moved, laying her body on his, their fronts flush together. "To be honest, it's so dark I can't see any of you at all."

He barked a laugh again.

"I don't care about your past." She pressed her lips to his. "I care who you are now and I care that despite the fact I've been taken to a different world I don't understand, it was you who was sent to bring me here." He tried to kiss her again then, but Ren pulled back with a smirk he couldn't see. "And I care that the only thing about my life, across two separate worlds, that doesn't confuse me is how I feel when you kiss me."

The next time he tilted his face upwards, she didn't stop him. He tasted like wine and reason; peaches and sense, for he was the only thing in her life that made any.

Lance kissed her in a way nobody ever had. A way that fractured every breath her lungs possessed into a million pieces.

She could have kissed him all night.

Would have.

Ren opened her mouth, enough to whisper his name when the word was snatched by a scream, piercing the air around them like an arrow in the dark.

"Wait here."

Ren was already manoeuvring herself off the mushroom in time with Lance. "Absolutely not."

His head spun towards her. "Ren."

"You're not leaving me here while you go."

What little she could see of his face in the darkness was set, determined. "Yes, I am."

Another scream rang out, longer than the first, followed by several bangs. They sounded like gunshots.

Ren, ignoring him, was already shimmying herself over the edge of the mushroom when his hands gripped her upper arms.

"Ren, you can't go up there."

"But you can?"

Lance swung himself over the edge, landing on the forest floor with a soft crunch. "I know how to fight."

"You don't have your sword." Her voice sounded alien, high and hysterical. The distant din of commotion was louder.

"Look, Ren. No. Please, *please* stay here and wait for me. Jump down," he instructed.

She did.

"Stay low, by the ponds."

Her chest was hard and heavy. "What if something happens to you?"

A series of bangs, and more screams, echoed around them.

"Nothing is going to happen to me." He lifted one leg of his trousers up and took a knife Ren hadn't known was strapped there and handed it to her. "Just in case."

"Lance, I–"

"Please," he repeated, "for me?" He turned. "Keep your head down." His footsteps, barely audible to begin with, vanished after a second or two.

And Ren was alone, clutching the handle of the knife she was certain she would be useless with in any type of combat situation, the roses carved into its handle digging into her palm. She dared not loosen her grip.

Her fear became palpable.

Further banging, and a faraway shout, inaudible and unsettling, and the buzzing – currently an irregular pulse – caged within her ribcage, all she had for company.

Those, and her thoughts, on edge at best, downright panicked at worst, made time stand still. Eternity might have passed, and she would have believed it so were it not for the far-off continuous noise in the treetops. She did as he had instructed, keeping her head as far down as possible. In the dark, her taio shone as bright as the ponds.

Small sounds surrounded her: slithers and coos, twig snaps and ominous rustling in the undergrowth. Had she not more pressing matters, each might have been alarming.

More eternity passed.

Were her ears not so attuned to the night around her, she might have missed the steps.

A mass of blonde hair. "Ren?"

Ren rose.

The shimmer of Brielle's taio was almost invisible against the expanse of night air. Up close, her face, usually wearing an easy smile, was set, frowning, her mouth a straight line. She held an arrow poised in a long wooden bow.

"Where's Lance?"

Brielle surveyed her. "Lance is fine. Shae isn't, but he will be. We need to head south."

"Wh–"

Brielle had already begun to walk away, in the exact opposite direction of both the Village of Lira and Lance. "Come on."

"We can't."

"Yes, we can." Ren didn't miss the snap in her tone. "Lance told me to get you to the Brook."

"The what?"

"Ranger station, next to the Axilion border. *Please*, Ren."

"But Shae, and...shouldn't we help?"

"Shae will be okay, but you won't if you go up there. Your taio is too recognisable."

"What does my taio have to do with anything? What happened?"

Brielle's face, barely lit by the light of a nearby pond, looked haunted. "Ambush. *Please*, Ren."

Ren chewed on her bottom lip as she gave a small glance in the direction of the village. She saw nothing but heard another scream. The buzzing hummed in time with her own pulse. *He's okay.* She took a few shaky steps towards Brielle.

"Keep your head down."

Ren's heart thumped so hard it was surely threatening to escape. The villagers, from what she had seen, were a peaceful people. Kept to themselves high in the trees. "Ambushed? Why?"

They left the clearing and the ponds, into the thick of the forest. Trunks as thick as armchairs surrounded them. It was even darker without the illuminating glow from the ponds.

Brielle's voice was low. "They were looking for you."

The attackers had waited until darkness before taking down the village's guards. Guards Ren had never known existed. By the time any kind of alarm had been raised, a whole group had infiltrated the place, grabbing and asking anyone they could the same question: *Where is the weaver?*

A sinking, queasy feeling dropped from Ren's chest to her stomach. "This is because of me," she said flatly.

She didn't miss the wobble in Brielle's voice. "Don't blame yourself."

The forest air was thick, the darkness all-consuming. Her taio, though bright, offered no guiding light, and Ren cursed it for its uselessness. Navigating was nigh on impossible, even with Brielle's whispered warnings. Ren tripped multiple times. Several times more she stopped, not daring to breathe, as a noise met her ears. It might have been a whisper, or a laboured breath, or nothing.

Each time, Brielle pressed her onward.

Were the ambushers the same group that had sought her out at the first village? Who wanted Ren, and everything she was, destroyed?

A freezing panic gripped her chest at the wondering. What if they didn't stop hunting her?

Eventually, after a dense, grey mist surrounded them, making the already dismal visibility worse, Brielle suggested they stop. In a feat that would have been impossible for Ren, she found them a patch of soft moss.

"Brielle?"

Beside her, Brielle shuffled. "Yes?"

"Thank you."

"For?"

Ren chewed her lower lip. "Saving me...again."

"Thank me when we get to Aria's."

"Whose?"

"She runs the Brook."

"Okay, I will."

Their voices were low, almost whispers. All around them various croaks and chirps rang through the night, joined by the gentle trickle of running water. The temperature had dipped, and though it didn't bother Ren, Brielle's legs and arms were ice against hers.

"You're s-so warm," Brielle said, teeth chattering.

"Here." Ren placed her legs over Brielle's. "Bit weird, I know." It was an awkward manoeuvre, more so as Ren's arms wrapped around Brielle's torso.

"It's not weird." Brielle yawned. "We're friends."

"I don't tend to make a habit of spooning my friends." As she spoke, a not-too-distant howl met her ears.

"Spooning." Brielle let out the smallest of laughs. "Well, I do."

The buzzing lay low and constant. Almost in time with Brielle's deepening breaths. Ren leant her head back, tuning into it as best she could. It meant he was okay; physically at least.

It had to.

It seemed an impossibility, but she must have dozed off. Groaning, and blinking against the pinkish morning light, Brielle stopped patting Ren's arm. "I think we should get going."

Ren nodded, bringing a hand to her chest. "Okay." The buzzing was pulsing in time with her heartbeat.

They stood, sore and groggy. A deep grumble echoed from Ren's stomach. She should have eaten more than a peach and a few crackers.

Brielle located the nearby stream with ease, and after a meagre breakfast of raw mushrooms and berries, they continued, Brielle ahead, her bow relaxed but ready. Ren held Lance's knife by her side.

Their journey was far easier in the daylight, the way serenaded by birdsong and scurrying, less eerie than it had been the previous night.

According to Brielle, they would reach the Brook ranger station that same day. There, everything would right itself.

There Lance would join her.

A short, sharp breath sounded to Ren's right. Brielle threw her arm outwards, walloping Ren in the stomach. Whirling her head around in time to see Brielle drop to a crouch, Ren followed suit.

In a breathy whisper, Brielle said, "We can get there quicker." She nodded off to the right.

At first, she saw nothing but trees. Then a flash, white against red-tinged shrubbery.

A horse. Or something at least the size of a horse. They watched it in silence. At first it didn't move, but then a slender neck rose.

Ren stifled a gasp. "You have *unicorns* here?" A whole new buzzing spread within her.

Brielle shot her a sideways glance. "You don't have them up north?"

"I..." Ren began. *Up north.* Bit of an understatement. "I've never seen one before."

Brielle probably thought her mad. Unicorns were probably as common in Caerisle as horses were in Britain.

"Wait here." Brielle rose, her movements as smooth as a dancer's.Before Ren could blink, Brielle's bow was raised, an arrow taut against the string. The unicorn patted the ground nervously.

Ren was suddenly aware the birdsong had stopped.

A thick silence befell them.

Ren didn't dare breathe.

Brielle's arrow pointed one way, before jerking another. Somewhere behind them, a twig snapped. Brielle whirled around.

It was Ren who saw him first.

He was crouched like she was, barely visible in the undergrowth. The bolt from his own bow, an entirely different contraption to Brielle's, pointed towards them.

With no time to think or speak, acting on something between fear and adrenaline, Ren balled the hem of Brielle's dress in her fist, and yanked. A knife whistled overhead. It stuck in a nearby tree trunk with a dull *thunk*.

Wasting no seconds, Brielle was once again standing, the point of her arrow now level with his chest.

The stranger rose, then laughed.

"I wouldn't do that if I were you."

"Luckily for me," Brielle said, voice steady, "you aren't. Who are you?"

He spoke with an accent similar to Lance's – almost Inverness-like, and he possessed no taio above his dark crop of messy hair. Raising his hands in mock surrender, bow dangling, he took a step towards them. Brielle's hold tightened.

"All right, it's up to you, but know the moment you do you'll have a knife in your neck."

At least seven others, from all around them, stood at his words, rising around them like plumes of smoke. Brielle pointed her arrow towards one, then another.

They were hopelessly outnumbered.

"You two aren't easy to track," the stranger said, as Ren rose, now side by side with Brielle. "Well, *you* aren't. *You*, on the other hand," he continued, his gaze flitting between Ren and her taio, "a wounded bear would be harder."

Her arm pressed into Brielle's as she fought her desire to scream. Brielle pressed back. Whatever this was, or meant, all they had was each other.

"Take them," he said, focussing behind them.

She fought against the hand that grabbed her, though it was futile. Something sharp and intrusive was thrust into the small of her back and Ren succumbed to her desperation to scream.

To her right, Brielle was enduring a similar capture. Though she watched, determined that her eyes remain on Brielle and Brielle alone, the other woman's outline was growing fuzzy. It wavered, distorting the pained expression Brielle wore as she floundered and squirmed against the two men holding her. Then all Ren saw were lines and shapes, none of which made sense. They began to darken.

Then she saw nothing at all. In the darkness, a sound – the same cold, soulless laugh – rang out once more.

18

Ren awoke, for what was probably less than a minute, twice.

The first time offered her a white-hot pain. It encircled her right wrist and radiated up her arm in nauseating waves. Ren's mouth opened, no doubt to scream.

Whether she did or not, Ren didn't know.

The second time, a cold unlike any other pierced through her. The stone floor she lay upon, so freezing it felt damp, was ice against her. It seeped into every part of her shaking body as rolls of agony spread down her arm, then spread further. Ren heard herself hiss, then cough. It was then she realised it was missing.

Where was her magic?

The third time she woke granted her the smallest glance of whatever slice of Hell she had been taken to. Blinking, her face a stark grimace in the dark, Ren took several shaky breaths.

She had been placed in a small room, its only light source a single lit torch on the far wall. It sat within a sconce and belonged to the past. She was lying on her side, limbs sprawled awkwardly, her right arm cast along the floor above her head. Her taio, barely a light in the dark, flickered dully above. A short-lived jolt of relief filled her at the sight.

Something, no doubt the reason for the pain, was attached to her wrist. Ren squinted in the dim light. Groaning, she raised her head as much as she was able, which wasn't much. From what she could see, it was a kind of metal cuff. Ren groaned again at the sight. That and her own heartbeat were the only sounds to meet her ears.

Her eyes, sore and bleary, scanned the room. What strength she had possessed had vanished along with her freedom and dignity.

The door stood to her left, visible only by the teasing rectangular thread of light signifying something that wasn't the dank darkness.

To her right stood a bucket. Ren swallowed. A dark stain loomed on the ground beside it.

The room reeked of damp and mould and something else: something sour. The hint of cinnamon, so faint, overpowered by the other smells, was her only clue that she was still within Ververos.

Nothing else. Wherever Brielle was, it wasn't here.

With no indication of time passing, and after what could have been two minutes or fifty, her eyes closed again, Brielle's pained expression burning into the darkness of her mind.

A cry, possibly her own, and a scraping, cut through the dark. A vaguely familiar voice asked, "She's alive?" It was followed by a grunt of agreement. "Cuff her. Zed wants her alive."

Another, this one Ren didn't recognise, no doubt the grunter, barked a laugh, somehow both very much, and not at all, like Lance's. "Probably so he can kill her himself."

Ren neither knew, nor cared, who Zed was. Instead, her mind focused on another.

He would be waiting for her at the Brook for a reunion that wouldn't come. Then again, Ren let out a hiss as her uncuffed arm was yanked. Her chest buzzed, the sensation sad and faint; he would know something was wrong.

Wrong being a vast oversimplification.

The grip on her wrist was rough, the grunter's movements jerky. "I doubt she'll–"

"Cuff her," the first voice – the man from the woods – repeated, his tone harsher.

The grunter was doing something behind her, something

involving metal being dragged across the stone floor – the elusive cuffs, no doubt. He panted with the effort, and squeezed her wrist tighter and, with force far beyond necessary to drag her weakened frame, yanked not only her free arm upwards, but both.

Her screams bounced off the stone walls as the second cuff was placed not only over her left wrist, but her right, over the one already in place. The pain, already the greatest she had ever endured, lurched. Metal clamped around metal and, as her head hit the cold stone, Ren, unaware of much except a white hot desperation, vomited. The grunter laughed.

Ren coughed, spitting pale, hot bile in front of her. Her whole body shuddered.

Through laboured breaths and the kind of shaking that rendered most movements futile, Ren turned her head as best she could to the first man as she tried, and failed, to rise to her knees. Her face hit the floor. She shimmied, which took a long time, and raised her head to meet his again. Even in the dim torchlight, she made out the sneer that crept over his mouth. It matched a very specific madness present in his eyes. They flickered between the grunter, whose boots had thumped in place somewhere close by, and Ren.

"Finding you hasn't been easy."

Ren didn't know what she was supposed to do with that information. Saying nothing, she attempted, once again, to position herself upright. This time she was successful, just.

She glared.

"I've wasted *days* tracking you."

"I…" Her voice cracked, throat raw. "I-I'm…terribly sorry…" Fresh waves of pain radiated up her arm. All there was, both keeping her upright and enabling her to speak, was gritted teeth and the tiniest sliver of determination. Despite her shaking, she didn't allow herself to look away from him. "To have caused you so much…trouble."

"Do you know who I am?"

Her throat burned. "Is there a reason I should?"

"My name is Brennett Graves." He searched her face.

Ren blinked at him. "Good for you."

That got his attention. His eyebrows, very slightly, twitched towards each other."You don't know who I am?"

It wasn't a question, but she answered it anyway. "Why would I?"

The grunter let out a low whistle that both Brennett and Ren ignored. In the dingy light, Brennett's eyes looked black. Black and, for the first time, glaring. In spite of her bleak situation, it sparked a curiosity within her. This man had literally drugged, kidnapped and locked her up and yet...a paradigm shift had occurred in that twitch of his eyebrows and the blink-and-miss-it change in his expression. His animosity had shifted.

He was either a psychopath, or held some kind of connection to her.

Or both.

A long pause. "You will."

Her heart pounded hard and fast. Beside it, the buzzing surged, in a way it never had, its pattern sharp and staccato. Ren blinked. Were it something solid and were her hands not bound in iron, she'd have clutched it, for it was all she had left. Instead, she gripped it with something else. Something more. And glared right back at Brennett Graves.

"Where's my friend?"

"Alive." Brennett cocked his head, his face once again fixed in a sneer. "For now."

Breaking the stare between them, he began to walk towards the door. Ren's sharp intake of breath was like ice in her lungs as the realisation of what was about to happen washed over her in an unforgiving wave. "Wait! You can't leave me here again."

He turned. "You're hardly in a position to tell me what I can and can't do."

She wasn't. Once again, Ren's empty stomach lurched; she

fell forwards. Her arms, too sore and weighed down with the chains, abandoned her. Stone met face with a crunch and flash of white. For the second time, bile splattered the stone, this time tinged with red.

Brennett had turned back towards the door; he was joined by the grunter, who strode to join his superior, crossing the small room with a limp. His bad foot – his left – scraped the ground with each step.

"What do you want with me?"

Brennett tutted. "Such self-importance. *I* don't want anything from you other than to settle an old score." He paused. "Some people want you, though, and if you think this is bad...." He didn't continue.

A cold numbness spread through her at his words.

"Who? Who wants me? Why?"

He drawled, as though she were boring him. "I have no idea." For a second, as Ren twisted her body enough to see his face and the way he looked, for a second, at her taio.

Turning again, he opened the door. Light flooded in. In any other circumstance it would be gloomy, yet for the few short seconds it was blinding.

"C'mon," Brennett instructed the grunter. He followed. Both tightness and ice held her chest. She was going to be left alone again.

"Wait!"

Brennett's eyebrows shifted upwards. "What?"

"Wh-what old score?"

The grunter laughed, the sound as hollow as before. Brennett didn't. Instead, he turned and led them from the room, leaving Ren with the darkness broken only by the solitary torch and the small light her taio offered.

Neither Brennett nor the grunter returned. Every so often, what she assumed was twice a day, a plate of food was pushed through a letterbox-sized slot at the bottom of the door. Ren was just able to reach it, thanks to her shackles. So far, she hadn't been conscious when any of the three were pushed through.

A day and a half, Ren mused. Not that it mattered. Time meant next to nothing when held captive.

Her thoughts danced a sad merry-go-round between Lance, and Shae, her father and Luke. Even Dr Michele with his *mild discomforts.* He would be thrilled, no doubt, to see how much *discomfort* Ren had thrust herself into lately. The last day she had seen him, unless her hazy and exhausted brain was mistaken, was also the day she'd met Shae.

The day it all changed, irrevocably.

Her go-to lifeline was fruitless, because what would any list she could make even say, other than, '*1. Survive?*'

She had tried shouting until her voice grew hoarse, hoping to hear Brielle reply. If they were held close together, perhaps they could escape. Somehow. None of her shouts were ever returned.

It was turning out to be a miserable existence. She held a balled fist to the centre of her chest where the buzzing was, at best, erratic and at worse, barely there. Sometimes it would rise, the sensation of it growing stronger within her, only to dampen down again. What that meant, Ren could only guess at. It held no discernible pattern or reason and yet it was the only part of him she had.

The thing attached to her wrist remained, snug beneath its secondary cuff of the shackle. The pain from it no longer rolled in waves, but was continuous, an unceasing river of agony, her entire arm suffering with the intensity of it. The cuffs were tighter than they needed to be, no position offering any relief.

The extinguished torch sat in its sconce, remaining the same no matter how long Ren stared at it. Her magic, not all that impressive to begin with, save the earthquake she couldn't hope to emulate, was impossible to feel for in the way Brielle had taught her. Her gaze tracked upwards, to each individual speck of magic hovering above her.

They were there, each one of them. Five elements and each one had deserted her. A single tear rolled down her cheek. Ren made no effort to wipe it away.

She was panting as she came to.

Little time had passed for no more plates of food had been pushed through. She was weaker now. Weaker than she had felt on Earth with her wracked body and broken health. Weaker than she had been upon entering Ververos. At least her spirit had still been intact then.

From some indecipherable place, a single clang rang out, echoing through the silent darkness.

Breathless from the shock of it, Ren climbed, with difficulty, to her feet. There had been little need to do so over the last few days, other than to close the short distance between the patch of cold stone she had been sleeping on and the bucket, which held only one, grim function.

Silence followed the clang, and Ren was debating sitting back down when a small voice met her ears, so faint it was barely there,

"Ren?"

Her heart stopped on the spot as a wobble passed over her body. Pressing her palm to her stomach, Ren sent a silent, *Thank you* to any deity willing to listen and crossed her room, just short of the door.

"Brielle?"

"I-I can hear you. What room are you in?" Brielle's tone lightened. "Say something else."

"This one," Ren called. She was motionless, but shaking, and flooded with something almost foreign, something she'd almost abandoned: hope.

Brielle's voice was louder. "Ren?" Just beyond the door.

"Yes!"

"Stand back."

Ren did. Scurrying across her cell, her hand touched the wall opposite, not eight feet from the other. There was a click, followed by a long creak as the door opened inwards. Ren turned to a swirl of tiny white specks, breathing light into the cold, dark room. *NeòNach*. Behind them, a familiar figure came into view. Ren's breathing hitched somewhere close to her throat.

There were dark red patches streaked through her pale hair, and bruising, dark purple and nasty, coated an entire shoulder. Otherwise, she looked unharmed.

The embodiment of hope itself.

"Ren!" Brielle rushed forwards, tears tracing delicate tracks in the patches of dirt that covered her pale features. There, surrounded by humiliation and hopelessness and the scent of vomit that had hung in the air for almost the entirety of her capture, the two women clutched each other. Or, as well as Ren could, given her chains.

"I hate them," Brielle exclaimed. "*Hate* them."

"I know," Ren said as they drew apart. "I hate them, too."

Up close, more of Brielle's scantily clad body was bruised. Still, she moved with relative ease.

"I can free you," she said, "then I'll get that shikkane off."

Brielle pulled a small silver key from a fold in the front of her dress with one hand and beckoned with the other. A flurry of *NeòNach* crossed the room and hovered beside Brielle in a glittering cloud.

Brielle held the key outright. "Hold your wrists out."

In the light of the flurry of specks, Ren got a proper look at her wrists. The left was bruised. Brielle placed the key in the lock and the first cuff came apart in her hands. Beneath the metal, Ren's skin was red raw and angry. She hissed as the cool air hit it. The second cuff – the first on her right wrist – burst open next. The metal chain clanged to the floor as Brielle placed the key back inside her dress.

"Where did you get that?" Ren asked with a hiss as Brielle gently brought the last cuff closer to her face.

"They didn't attach mine right," Brielle began, calling a few of the specks to her with a flex of her index finger. "There's hardly any *NeòNach* here at all." She was muttering, her brows drawn together as she examined the cuff. Protruding from it, Ren realised, were thin strands of black, tattooed into her skin, snaking from the metal in each direction. "It's easiest to attach them to a weaver," Brielle was saying, "because your magic runs *through* you, and that's what they need." She sent first one speck, then another, onto the instrument. Ren couldn't hope to guess what she was doing. She surveyed each speck and commanded it forward. "A man came into feed and, I suspect, question me. He didn't get the chance to. I'd loosened my own *shikkane*, then I threw it at his head. They didn't cuff over mine; I suppose because they believed you were more dangerous."

Ren scoffed at that.

"Anyway, I strangled him," she added nonchalantly. "The key was in his pocket."

Ren, suddenly very glad she and Brielle were on the same side in whatever this nightmare was, yelped as something sharp pricked at her wrist, beneath the *shikkane*.

"It's sensing the *NeòNach*," Brielle informed her.

"Oh," Ren said, swallowing.

"Okay." Brielle took a long breath. "Ren, this isn't going to be pleasant." Without any further warning, Brielle removed the shikkane, and with it, several centimetre-long needles, each coated in blood. That was nothing to the streams of red liquid pouring from her wrist, splashing the stone floor.

Ren threw her left hand to her mouth, stifling a scream as best she could into her palm. The *shikkane* hit the ground with a louder crash than the chain had. Ren looked down at it, appalled such a thing existed. A whoosh. Ren gasped. Her wrist, which had been bleeding steadily onto the ground, was suddenly surrounded by specks. Ren blinked at them. Red Fire specks had gathered at each of the needle sites, halting the flow of blood, cauterising each wound. It should have hurt, and yet flecks of blue magic, Water, were coating the area, cooling and soothing and numbing the skin as her own white Air specks circled round and round, creating a gust.

The relief was palpable; so was her anger. It roved around her like its own cloud, pulsating and waiting. And then it was met with something different entirely. And so was Ren.

Darkness. From a night sky to the very depths of the ocean to unseen caves cut from deep, craggy rocks. Deep underground, from the black of midnight to the glint in the eye of a stalking panther. A watching raven and the fluttering of unseen, leathery wings. It poured through her, dripped from her. Calm, and power. She didn't *feel* it; no one could. And yet she did. Felt the depths and gloom of it surround her.

Dark.

Ren's eyes met Brielle's, then shifted upwards. Black specks, barely visible against the dimness of the place, lay, still and low, nestled within her taio.

Brielle sucked in a breath. "Your sixth element."

A crushing sensation settled in her chest. "Thank you," she whispered.

Brielle offered her the smallest hint of a smile, which then faltered.

Ren heard it, too.

Unintelligible voices, from where she couldn't tell.

They spoke in unison. "We need to go."

The corridor outside the cell was a longer version of the cell itself: grey and windowless. The voices, louder now and more distinct, were coming from their right. They swung a hasty left and padded down another stone hallway.

At the end they faced a further choice: another hallway, or an ajar door, through which light snoring could be heard. Hardly daring to breathe, they began down the second corridor. It led to a stairwell.

Without a word of discussion, the pair headed downwards.

Down a floor, the place looked no different. Yet more grey stone and distant sounds.

Ren held her breath through each clatter.

The air was mustier. Ren sucked in deep breath after deep breath. Having had the *shikkane* removed, the full force of Ververos's heady aroma was, again, nauseating.

They walked with neither clue nor conscience. Once a door was flung open a few metres ahead of them, forcing them into what turned out to be some kind of cleaning cupboard. Voices, one male, one female, neither friendly, passed by the door behind which Ren and Brielle held their breaths, praying the two would keep walking. They did.

They waited longer than necessary before risking a peek. The corridor was empty.

And on they continued.

The buzzing, which had been pulsing on and off since Brielle had appeared, gave a sudden surge. The hand that wasn't clutching Brielle's rose to her chest. *I'll find you*, Ren thought, her fingertips brushing the spot where the sensation lay.

At the end of their last corridor stood a door. It was open a crack yet contained no noise.

"I'm not sure–" Ren began in a rushed whisper, until footsteps from somewhere behind made the decision for them. Pushing the door in unison, Ren and Brielle stepped through the doorway.

At first glance, the room – far grander than any other she had seen in the place – was empty. And then, with a collective gasp, they clocked the only inhabitant.

He was standing beside a fireplace, eyes widening more with each passing second. Running a hand through a chin-length mop of brown hair, he stared at them. He made no sound or movement, and while his appearance no doubt alerted Brielle, almost everything about him stunned Ren to her core.

His clothing was so familiar, yet already strange and foreign. The garments did not belong here, no more than Ren's had. He wore one of the only two pairs of jeans she had seen since arriving, and the others were now in the possession of the woman from the store in the first village. In the same vein, the only jumper Ren knew here was faded and blue and slung over the bottom of Lance's bed in the Village of Lira. And still, it wasn't his clothes, as much as a ghost from the past as they were, that jolted her; it was the moving cloud of colour hovering around a foot above his head.

White, grey, yellow, and blue.

Air. Aether. Light. Water.

He wasn't just from Earth.

He was also a weaver.

The footsteps were closer now, much closer, and headed in their direction.

"Please," Brielle whispered, "*don't* say anything." Pulling on Ren's arm, Brielle steered them towards a large cupboard Ren hadn't noticed. "Please." The door shut with a quiet *click*, and plunged them into almost complete darkness, save several small slats, through which the room was just visible.

The door to the room was pushed open. Brennett Graves waltzed in, flanked by two others, one being the grunter, and wearing the same sneer Ren recognised from upstairs. Ren swallowed, clutching Brielle's arm close to her.

"Take him back to Clayton and Hess," Brennett instructed. The third of them, a woman Ren hadn't seen before, gestured to the other – the one from Earth. To his credit, whoever he was, he didn't so much as glance at their cupboard.

Swallowing again, Ren wished she could get to him, free him somehow.

But her situation in the cupboard was far more pressing. Brennett had taken a seat opposite, framed by a large window. Beyond it, the tops of great pines were silhouetted against a dark, red-tinged sky. Specks of magic were scattered across it.

The grunter grunted. He was a large man whose neck dissolved into his shoulders. His nose looked as though it had seen several breaks. He lifted one beefy hand to scratch it, moonlight bouncing off the top of his hairless head. "He might not come."

Brennett snorted and retrieved something shiny and familiar from an inside pocket. "And miss the chance to play hero? He'll come." He twirled the knife – the one Lance had given her – between his fingers before replacing it.

"And we're to just let him walk in, armed? He'll have the arcanist with–?"

It took all Ren had not to gasp as Brielle's nails dug harder into her forearm.

"That's what I said, wasn't it?"

"Yes, but–"

"Then that's what I meant," Brennett replied.

The grunter didn't reply, instead slouching into another chair by Brennett's side, though Ren didn't see him, either of them. Her attention was directed at the fireplace. Dark would have been easier, for it was all around, but Fire would do more damage.

The buzzing surged again, but this time Ren ignored it. She focused on the flames. A task made harder by the nausea. It was more difficult to isolate them than it would be were she using the ones within her, and it took her longer but, eventually, she had them. A small sphere of red specks, pure Fire, hovered in the corner of the fireplace, awaiting direction.

Brielle was shimmying, and in the corner of Ren's peripheral vision was a glint of silver: the key she had used to unlock

Ren's cuffs.

Brielle's words were quieter than Ren's heartbeat. "I'll take left." Brennett. It made sense: he was facing them more than the other.

Ren nodded, steadying her Fire, then the grunter's stupid bald head.

Only a smidgen louder than before, Brielle said, "Now." The door opened, revealing them.

"Wha–?" Brennett began, but the word was cut short and transformed to a howl as Brielle's key lodged into his left eye. The other man was letting out short, sharp screams as he hopped, having launched himself upwards from his chair, head wreathed in flame and smoke. The ball of Fire had zoomed forward at Ren's instruction. A second later he collapsed, as Brielle crossed the room in a flash and placed one hand around Brennett's throat. His howl became a strained gurgle.

The commotion hadn't gone unnoticed. Before Ren could register what it, or anything, meant, more footsteps were thundering down the corridor. All within her was led by one thing: sheer will to survive. Her stomach lurched as the door was flung open.

She turned to it with only adrenaline and a newfound focus on freedom, to come face to face with a ball of bright white and a silver sword...and a rise in the buzzing so great it nearly knocked her flat.

Only Shae looked anywhere close to calm. Lance was a wild-eyed statue. His hair, the only part of him moving, was a dark hurricane. He gripped his sword, blade more red than silver. Ren didn't dare look away for fear he wasn't real. Further splashes of blood covered his hands, his arms. Even his face. A gouge ran across his left cheek. It oozed a dark burgundy down his face.

He surveyed the room, his gaze landing first on Brennett, who was screaming on the floor below Brielle, clutching his face, then Brielle herself, whose hold on Brennett's throat had tightened. Brennett's screaming became a croaky moan. Then to Ren.

Every part of Lance softened.

Closing the gap between them in a few strides, he reached his free hand for her shoulder. It didn't feel real, not his touch nor the hint of his breath on her forehead. The buzzing surged, not only in her chest but the top of her head and the soles of her feet, to the mess of dried blood that no doubt made up her face, running rampant over her as it attuned itself to him.

Ren let out a long breath, then slammed her body against his, not caring that the throbbing from her nose worsened with each second it was pressed into the blood-streaked armour. She heard her own faint groan as his arms enclosed her.

Then, he felt real.

Brielle was saying something Ren couldn't hear.

Brennett, having apparently calmed down enough to stop screaming, was muttering a string of expletives.

"Shut up," Brielle said.

He did.

"I thought I'd never see you again." They were Lance's words, spoken in a cracked whisper, but the sentiment wove between them. "I shouldn't have left you."

For the first time since she and Brielle entered the room, Ren spoke. "Y-you couldn't have known."

"I'm so sorry."

From somewhere to Ren's left, she heard Brielle. "It isn't you who should be saying sorry, Lance, it's this piece of *squantet*."

Ren and Lance turned to her. Ren didn't know what a *squantet* was, but judging from the expression Brielle wore it wasn't an endearing title.

Lance's arms left Ren. His movements were stiff, his demeanour dark. Brennett's eye widened. Lance's sword twitched. He took several slow and controlled steps towards Brennett. The head of the key protruded from between that latter's fingers.

"Hello, brother," Brennett said, teeth clenched. He swallowed as Lance reached him. His eye blinked several times as the tip of Lance's sword met his throat.

"Give me one reason why I shouldn't."

Brennett appeared to be having difficulty keeping his breathing normal. "You...wouldn't," he puffed. "Lance–"

"I would."

"You *owe* m–"

"I don't owe you shit." His sword was stiller than the air at midnight, yet Lance's words shook with an unadulterated rage. "I didn't then and I don't now."

Brennett's chest rose and fell with shallow breaths. "I didn't *do* anything to her."

Brielle let out a sharp laugh, devoid of any warmth. "Except locking her in a dark cell for two days with a *shikkane* attached to her wrist."

It happened quicker than it took Ren to blink.

Lance's sword clanged against a nearby chair leg, the sound reverberating around the room. Lance lunged forward, bearing down.

Brennett had no time to gasp before a fist crashed into his nose. The accompanying sound was a mix of a crunch and a squelch, repeated over and over, until Lance's arm was covered in yet more red stains and Brennett's face was a bloodied, unrecognisable mess.

Neither Ren, nor Shae, nor Brielle attempted to intervene. They stood in silence, flanking the attack.

Brennett groaned and spat yet more blood onto the floor beside him. "You done?" he gasped.

Lance, not done, brought a boot crashing onto Brennett's shoulder. "A *shikkane*?" he demanded.

"I had...to subdue...her...somehow." Brennett was panting through his words. "She's got...about fifty...types of magic...in her taio."

"You didn't have to *subdue* her at all, you piece of shit." Lance loomed over him like a storm cloud ready to burst. "Because you didn't have to kidnap her."

"I was told to."

Lance snorted. "You expect me to believe that?"

"No...but that doesn't...make it...not true."

"You've never done what you were *told* in your life."

Brennett, wincing as he brought one hand to gently touch the key still embedded in his eye, replied, "I've never been... indebted...to anyone...before."

As Brennett's words grew quiet, another sound, this one more alarming, met Ren's ears. Shae had turned to the door as the footsteps grew closer, his hands raised as he drew more specks of *NeòNach* to him, joining them to the sphere hovering between his palms.

Ren swallowed. *The fireplace*, she told herself. She had done it before. The body lay forgotten, its head charred and blackened, grunting no more.

Had she killed him?

Her mouth was dry.

Did she care?

She turned away as Lance leant down for his sword. "Shae, seal that door for as long as you can. "You," he spat at Brennett, "are going to tell them to fuck right off."

With what looked like a great degree of difficulty, Brennett's only working eye blinked. "I–"

"Brennett, I *swear*–"

The footsteps were close enough to isolate at least three individuals. Just outside the door, they stopped. The door handle began to shake, though thanks to a congregation of Shae's specks, it did no more.

A muffled voice called out, "Brennett?"

They all turned to face him.

Ren held her breath.

Beneath the extensive injuries Lance had inflicted to his face, Brennett was looking rather ill. "Go back to the other side!" he called. "Wait for me there."

There was a pause. "Uh, okay, but Rees is here for the weaver girl."

Brennett's mouth fell open. "Shit."

His good eye, which was puffy and bruised and wouldn't be classed as *good* in any other circumstance, was fixed on Lance. "K-keep him talking, tell him...I'm coming...to meet him out front...with the girl."

The man on the other side of the door didn't reply. Instead, they heard his footsteps once more, this time heading in the opposite direction...to inform someone called Rees that Ren was being brought to him.

Something heavy dropped in her stomach.

"Who the *fuck* is Rees?" Lance demanded.

"He wants her." Brennett inclined his head towards Ren.

Lance's sword once again touched Brennett's throat. "I'd gathered that much, genius. Why?"

"I don't know. I was just...told to take her."

"And what did you get out of it?"

"What does...that matter?"

"It *matters*, because I want to know how much Ren's life is worth."

Brennett steadied himself, breathing slowly in through his nose. "No more...than Priya's life...was worth...to you." He said the words as though they tasted bitter.

Lance's frame stiffened. "This is nothing like that."

"Not to you."

From the door, Shae's voice cut, albeit unsuccessfully, through the tension. "Uh, can you finish this later, Lance, or... not. We need to go."

He wasn't wrong, but how were they supposed to leave?

Lance bowed his head, before jabbing the sword, enough to elicit a hiss from Brennett. "Tell us how to get out of here."

"I-Lance I'm...dead if I...do that–"

"You're dead if you don't."

Letting out a long sigh, Brennett's eye darted between each of the others, until eventually, stopping on Brielle, he said, "Fine. But *she* gets this fucking key out of my eye."

Brennett, with a high level of reluctance, led them. The tip of Lance's sword remained dangerously close to the centre of his back as they walked down the corridor Ren and Brielle had followed less than an hour before. Ren walked behind Lance. Shae and Brielle, side by side, brought up the rear.

They passed several doors, none of which Brennett paid any attention to and none of which Ren remembered from their previous journey. Stopping at one door, wooden and unassuming, Brennett hissed as the sword made contact; he pushed it ajar. "Is that really necessary?"

"Yes," Lance replied.

"How many of my men did you kill to get here, by the way?"

"Why?"

"Just wondering..."

"A few." Lance's free hand flexed backwards, touching Ren's arm. "None I knew."

"Fantastic," Brennett muttered as he stepped through the door.

It led to a gloomy stairwell. One small torch, long since extinguished, hung on the wall in a dusty sconce. There was a window, through which a dark silhouette of giant pines across a red-tinged magic-strewn sky was visible.

They were swaying, or Ren was. She took a long breath she instantly regretted, and reached for Lance's hand, clinging to him like an anchor in her sea of wooziness.

Lance's fingers closed around hers as they began to descend the staircase.

The walls of the place were castle-like: thick and grey and old. The place was vast, and Ren suspected she had seen very little of the building...fortress...whatever it was. They started down yet another identical hallway.

Who knew when she and Brielle had last eaten, not to mention the effect the forest had on her. No doubt the *shikkane* had dampened the symptoms, but Ren was unprotected, and grew weaker with each step. A sharp pain was settling behind her eyes. How she missed Brielle's potions.

Just as she was beginning to question how long she would be able to keep going, Brennett stopped. He stood in front of a door so small only Ren was shorter than it. It looked older than all of them put together, and what had to be knife marks were cut across the dark wood.

"This is a side entrance," Brennett said, turning. "You'll be able to find cover quickly if you head to the right, but if anyone spots her taio I won't be able to stop them chasing you." He turned his head, to Ren, boring into her eyes with his only working one. It was, Ren realised, not the black she had first believed, but blue. "But I'll try to give you enough time to get away." Ren suspected it wasn't for her. "Some very dangerous people want you."

Lance's hand tightened over Ren's. For the first time, he lowered his sword. "Brennett, I..."

Brennett's face was an unreadable mask.

"Priya isn't dead."

At the mention of whomever Priya was, Brennett's breathing shifted, his jaw twitching. "Don't–"

"She wasn't in the Hull."

The only part of Brennett that moved was a further twitch in his jaw. "Lance, if this–"

"She was at the docks, already on a boat."

Brennett's brows met. "How the fuck–?"

Lance was looking as if he would rather confess to anything else. "I arranged it for u...her."

Brennett's nostrils flared. "You were about to say *us*. You were going to fuck off with her, weren't you?"

"Was," Lance admitted quietly, as Ren pressed her head against the side of his arm. The door behind Brennett, and indeed Brennett himself, was spinning. "Then she left me too."

"Good." The ghost of a smirk that trailed across Brennett's mouth didn't meet his eye. "How long?"

"Does it matter?"

Brennett's eye momentarily darted to Ren. "It would to you."

"Six months, maybe eight."

Though his breathing was somewhat laboured, Brennett kept himself composed. "Did you love her?"

"I thought I did."

"Did she love you?"

"If she did, she'd probably have waited on me."

"If this is a lie–"

"It's not."

It took Brennett a few moments of silence to speak. "She fucked us both."

Lance nodded, but didn't reply.

"After you both fucked me...or each other."

"For what it's worth, I regret it. Or I *did*, until you kidnapped Ren."

Brennett let out a long sigh, then laughed, though it was a hollow, joyless sound, shaking his head. "I've mourned that bitch for years." His shoulders visibly dropped as his head turned up to face the ceiling. "How the fuck did we get here, Allardyce?"

Lance gently shook his head. "No idea."

Nodding, though Ren suspected it was more to himself than to Lance, or anyone, Brennett reached for the door handle. "Keep to the right, stay close to the wall until you come to a path. As long as you stay on it, it'll lead you back into the thick of Ververos. *Don't* head left, whatever you do."

Lance inclined his head.

Brennett let out another long breath as he ran a hand over the top of his head. His eye fell to Ren. "You two are bound, aren't you?"

Ren squeezed Lance's hand in hers before nodding.

"Priya could sense bonds," Brennett relayed. "I..." Whatever he had wished to say, he changed his mind, his good eye once again fixed on Lance, then Shae. He swallowed. "Don't take her to the Council."

"What—"

From somewhere far off, a bang, followed by a shout.

"No time." Brennett nodded through the small door and began rifling through his pockets – he had many, not unlike Shae. "Go to the Hidden City."

Ren's heart thumped so loud it would be a miracle none of the others could hear it. Lance had spoken of the Hidden City. It was a sign. It had to be.

Brennett cast a hasty glance behind and ushered them onward, outside. "Casino, by the Shell," he was saying to Lance, "you'll know the place. There's an *abairt*, but I don't know it. Find it; someone will know."

They began to file out of the castle, past Lance, who didn't move.

"Brennett—"

"If you take her to the Council, you'll never see her again. Find out the *abairt*," he added. "Others there know about you." His eye hovered this time on Ren as he rummaged in his pockets. "Here."

She took the knife in silence.

Brennett took a breath. "The Hull," he said, daring the shortest pause. "That's what I was offered."

Lance's grip on Ren tightened, but he allowed himself to be herded from the building. "I—"

But Brennett was already closing the door. "Hidden City,"

he all but whispered.

The door closed with a deep thud. Commotion of some sort, the sounds dulled through the door, met their ears.

"We have to go," Shae said, taking the lead and heading right, beside the thick stone wall.

Only Lance did so with any reluctance.

Ren squeezed his hand in hers again, as much to steady herself as encourage him."Lance?" she asked, voice small.

He sent a last glance at the door, nodded once, his face a set grimace, before following.

Only Ren knew of the tremble in his hands as he did.

They followed Brennett's instructions in silence, skirting the huge, grey walls of the fortress-like building until a dirt track led them forwards, away from the most miserable days of Ren's life.

It led them for a good few hours before widening enough that they didn't have to travel single file. Ren was half supported and half hauled along by Lance.

An illuminated ball of light, hovering in place above Shae's outstretched palm, provided them enough light to navigate their way through the thickening trees. At night, Ververos held an entirely different kind of beauty. Ren would no doubt have appreciated it more were she not struggling to both remain conscious and not vomit.

Lance blew a low whistle three times. After a minute or two, or ten for all Ren knew, they were joined by a soft rustling in the undergrowth. In the night-time, encased within the red hue of the air, Brogan appeared a deep chestnut brown.

They stopped at a clearing. Ren plonked herself on the ground. So did Brielle. Specks of *NáDarra* zoomed towards Brielle's twirling hands. She sent them to Ren's taio.

A *faedra*. Ren turned the word over and over in her mind. Attuned to both *NáDarra* and *NeòNach*. And currently the only reason Ren had survived, not only the forest, but capture. *Torture.*

Around them, Lance and Shae made something that didn't really resemble a camp. By the time Brielle had finished, Ren felt marginally more human, though Brielle's strength was sapped from the effort. For the first time, the bow-wielding, bare-footed pillar of strength looked frail.

Somewhere above them, an owl-like hoot echoed through the quiet night.

"Lie down," Ren said, full of guilt and sadness.

Brielle didn't argue, laying her head against a patch of moss, her expression pained. Shae placed his cloak over her weak frame.

Lance's back was resting against a nearby tree, his own expression a blank, unreadable stare. He was stock still, except for the one hand he used to rub back and forth across the back of Brogan's neck. The buzzing was low and erratic, and Ren couldn't hope to guess at what seeing Brennett had meant.

The air was thick with its mixed spice aroma, the beginning crackles of Shae's fire and Brielle's deep breathing. Brennett's words hung silently, the heaviest of all.

If you take her to the Council, you'll never see her again.

For a long time, no one spoke.

It was Shae who broke the silence by a short clearing of his throat. "Do you remember what Gideon said at the briefing?"

Lance barked a single, empty laugh. "It sounds complicated but it's a simple enough job, all things considered."

Shae let out a small chuckle.

"Turned out to be our most complicated." He shot Ren a slight half smile.

She didn't return it. Ren didn't care about Gideon or his briefing. Nor the fact that she was ever some job.

"Just a bit." Shae was sitting, cross-legged, trailing a line of *NeòNach* between his fingers. "Although the *incident* with the troll on the Isle of Gee could have gone similarly for you." Though his face remained impassive, Ren didn't miss the spark his eyes held as he spoke. "You know she wanted–"

"I beg you not to finish that sentence."

Ren was only half listening. She looked at the fire, then her own wrist, where the black marks from the *shikkane* were still visible, stark against her pale skin.

A simple enough job. Ren swallowed.

She still didn't know why this Gideon at their Council had sent for her.

Or why she had been taken away in the first place.

Some very dangerous people want you.

Before Brennett, she had felt in the dark. Ren blinked several times as she hugged her knees and stared into the flames, contemplating everything she knew.

Each small thing she did know was surrounded by much larger numbers of things she didn't.

The existence of magic alone had been almost too much, let alone the fact she held as much of it as she did. Then there was the soulmate thing. That would have been enough to overwhelm the most level-headed.

Level-headedness had never been a quality Ren possessed.

Her wrist ached, and so did her stomach. Her mouth was dry and she forced herself to focus on the scent of woodsmoke rather than the growing desire to scream, or cry, or punch something.

And yet.... She looked at each of them in turn.

Shae, who had run with her from the bodach on St. Andrews beach, who had faced giant cats and madmen to get her this far. He had been there from the very beginning of whatever this was, and there he was still.

Brielle, who had saved her not once but twice, left an attack on her people to ensure Ren got to safety but instead had entered, and escaped, Hell with her. And done so not because of a job, or contract.

And then there was Lance.

Leaving his tree, he scooted sideways towards her, his arm finding its way across her shoulders. His lips met the top of her head. "I won't ask if you're okay."

"I'm not," she said simply. And then something lodged itself into her consciousness. A niggling. And a pair of blue eyes, wide and confused. How had she forgotten him? "Wait – you were told to retrieve the *last* weaver?"

He stroked the top of her arm. "Yeah."

"But I'm *not* the last weaver."

Shae was frowning. "What do you mean?"

Ren relayed seeing the boy, clearly also from Earth, in the room before Lance and Shae had arrived.

"Something does seem…" Shae began. He wore a frown that didn't suit him.

"Off." Ren nodded again. "I don't like it. I mean, I never did. And I wasn't going to some stupid prison anyway. But now…" She trailed off.

Lance squeezed her shoulder. "What can we do?"

Ren turned to face him, and then Shae. "Tell me everything."

Lance looked momentarily confused. "About?"

"This Council of yours, which apparently might mean I'll never see you again if I go there. Who runs it? Where is it? And this prison? Everything you know. And everything you know about *NáDarra*."

Lance didn't speak as he squeezed her shoulder again.

Shae regarded Ren with something that might have been tinged with admiration.

"Okay," he said, his voice low and steady, "we'll tell you everything we know."

"Thank you."

And they did.

They sat, the three of them, with the unconscious Brielle and the dozing Brogan, until the fire died and the night was replaced by streams of daylight, penetrating the gaps between the trees with a pinkish glow.

When it came to *NáDarra*, Lance knew next to nothing.

Shae knew more, but not all that much. "It didn't used to be this volatile," he said. "But now it is."

"Until when? What happened to make it volatile?"

Shae, examining the nails on his right hand, replied, "I haven't the faintest idea." His tone was as aloof as his expression. "But I have an inkling it involves you."

"But how? Why?"

He only shrugged. Ren sighed. She hadn't thought about the internet, or technology at all really, but deeply missed it in that moment.

"Right."

The Council, at least, they knew something about.

Shae had worked for the Council for nine years – a baffling realisation in itself, to learn Shae was pushing thirty when he looked a decade younger. Lance for just over three. They had been partnered upon Lance's first mission and had remained so ever since.

"Collectors always work in pairs."

"And," Ren said, "you can get sent to Collect anything?"

"Yes," Shae said as they nodded in unison. "Sometimes documents, sometimes animals, sometimes the love and affection of rogue trolls–"

"Will you stop bringing that up?"

"No," Shae replied. "Sometimes we have to transport Council officials through Ververos.

"How many Council officials are there?"

"Around thirty, though we only really deal with three of them."

Specks of Ground magic were dancing by Ren's hands.

When touched, they bounced off her palm. Ren felt it, not on her hand, but in her mind. "What do they do?" she asked, focusing on the flecks of green.

"The three?"

"All of them."

"The main departments are creatures, the magicks, societal upkeep, and acquisitions – where we work. Then there's the Dragon Corps."

"What's that?"

"Our law enforcement."

There was law enforcement here? Ren let out a hollow laugh as, beside her, Brielle began to stir. "Well, they're pretty shit at their job, aren't they?"

"They have no power in Ververos."

Ren blinked. "The massive forest that takes up, what did you say, over half the landmass of Caerisle? That's really bloody useful."

"They're shit at their job in the places they *can* operate." Lance stood, flexing his knees a few times, before declaring he was going to hunt them something at least mostly edible.

"The fire is dying," Ren pointed out. The few remaining specks of Fire magic sparked upwards in a pitiful display.

Shae raised an eyebrow. "You're telling me you managed to set a man's head on fire, but can't keep a campfire going?"

"I'd forgotten about that," Ren admitted. Perhaps she ought to feel guiltier than she did. "It needs more wood," she observed.

Beside her, Brielle sat up with a yawn.

Shae reached to the side and deposited a large log on top of the dying embers. The fire all but went out.

"Oh, no!" Ren flapped her arms at him. "Not like *that.*"

Both Shae and Brielle were laughing for some reason.

Ren ignored them, closing her eyes. She found them easier this time. Dark, oddly enough, she found the easiest, and Ground. Fire appeared next. Ren honed in on them as she held her palm out.

And there they were, nestled above her hand. She began, then, to guide them towards the fire, and Shae's ridiculous log.

Lance returned with three large pheasant-like birds slung over his shoulder. Shae and Brielle busied themselves preparing the meat as he plopped himself down beside Ren, shooting her the kind of smile she liked best.

They spent the remainder of the day dozing and attempting to forge something that vaguely resembled a plan, which led into what was turning out to be one of the least pleasant conversations Ren had had since arriving in Caerisle.

No one wanted to trust Brennett's words, none more so than Brielle.

"I can't ignore what he said," Lance said darkly.

Brielle's head snapped to Lance, eyes livid. "He *kidnapped* Ren and me–"

"I *know* that." His hand was resting on the small of Ren's back; his fingers flexed at Brielle's words. "But I also know him."

Brielle's mouth was a straight line. "He doesn't strike me as a trustworthy man."

"I know." He said no more. They were sitting in a circle. Their clearing was bordered by a loop of smaller pines and giant bushes with purple leaves. The undergrowth was dotted with toadstools and wildflowers. Some had petal spans the size of dinner plates; others were barely larger than drawing pins, with tiny, intricate plumes in every colour.

Brielle pressed, "If you *know* that, why are you even thinking about listening to him?"

"Leave it, Brielle."

"You haven't even thought it could be a trap?"

Lance clenched both his fists and jaw. "Of course I have."

"Then why–?"

He answered in a shout that made each of them flinch. "Will you *please*, for once in your life, leave it?"

A silence fell on their clearing. The birdsong halted.

Lance stood, breathing heavily.

"Where are you going?" Brielle demanded, also standing.

"Anywhere *you* aren't."

She stared daggers into the back of his head. "You *need* to decide what you're doing, and if keeping Ren safe isn't–"

Lance turned, murderous look matching hers. "Keeping Ren safe is *all* I care about!"

Shae was the third to stand, and he did so raising both arms, pointing one palm towards Lance, the other towards Brielle. "You both need to calm down."

"What I need," Lance said, his voice a steady and low growl, "is for *her* to either say what she *actually* means, or shut up."

His words struck the air like a whip. Brielle's stare bored into him. "What I *actually* mean?"

"Yes, what you *actually* mean."

This time, her eyes shone with something else entirely: tears. "Why don't you *hate* him?" she demanded. "He hurt Ren. He hurt *me*, and my *home*. And. You. Don't. Care!"

"When the *fuck* did I say I didn't care?"

"Please! You basically *made up* with him, we all saw." Her tears flowed freely, cascading over her cheeks and bare shoulders. She made no effort to wipe them.

"Brie," Shae placed a hand on Brielle's arm. "He does care."

She turned away. "Not enough."

"Now just hang on a minute," Lance said. He looked just as angry.

Ren, watching the scene unfold, had had enough. Her exhaustion, hunger, and sense of being utterly fed up with both Ververos and having her every move dictated for her already grating on her enough.

Her knees wobbled as she stood, and three pairs of eyes, two livid and one desperate, faced her.

"Enough!" Ren cried, louder than she had intended. "I can't listen to you two fight anymore."

Shae nodded. "I quite agree."

Lance opened his mouth, then clearly decided otherwise, as did Brielle.

Ren turned first to Lance. "Brielle has a right to hate him as much as she does."

"I never said–"

She held up a hand to silence him. "I *know* you haven't said otherwise outright, but all Brielle is seeing is this guy who attacked her village, and then drugged us, fitted us with those *shikkane* things, and left us alone in separate cells, in the dark, for two days. And that's understandable. I'm having trouble seeing anything other than that, but," Ren turned, this time to Brielle, "I *also* know there's more to Lance and Brennett's past than any of us know, and he has a right to feel conflicted. He did seem to change – a little, anyway, after he learnt Lance didn't kill – or whatever – whoever that Priya person was. The one he thought he was in love with," she added unnecessarily, and with an equally unnecessary bitter undertone.

She was met with silence, and turned to Lance, ushering him away. "Go and hunt."

He stared at her blankly. "We just ate."

"Well," Ren snapped, "I'm still hungry. Go take your anger out on whatever poor creature you decide will be my second breakfast, and then when you come back, if it's okay, you could tell us more about you and Brennett...and Priya if you must," she added bitterly. "And then *I'm* going to decide where we're going next."

Lance's eyebrows were halfway to his hairline, though his face was mostly unreadable. She half expected him to argue. Instead, he took a deep breath, and nodded as he turned to leave. Looking back, he sought out Brielle. "Brielle?"

She swallowed, and nodded also. "Ren's right," she said shakily, "go and hunt. I would, but I never got my bow back."

Inclining his head, Lance turned back to face Ren, offering a small smile. "You should be assertive more often."

When he returned, it was to a sullen Ren, a subdued Brielle and a most enthusiastic Shae. The latter had spent the past quarter of an hour gathering an array of mushrooms, which their clearing had in abundance, and was boiling them in his trusty pan with a selection of his herbs and spices. He whistled a jaunty folk tune as he stirred the pungent mixture with a stick.

"What..." Lance began, wrinkling his nose, before his gaze fell upon Shae's pan. "Oh no. That's not what I think it is. Shae, that's not funny." He sank into the moss beside Ren with a soft *flump*, dumping two hares in front of them. "You do this on purpose. No, don't pretend you don't."

Shae's tone was droll. "I have no idea what you're talking about."

"You bloody do."

Shae ignored him. "My broth," he began smugly, "is known all over, has won several awards, and it will accompany those hares beautifully." Lance's *ha* was so loud it echoed around the clearing. Shae ignored him, his attention focused on his pot.

They ate in silence.

"All right," Lance began, finishing his meal, "what do you want to know?"

For several seconds none of them replied.

"I hear the beginning," Shae said eventually, attention upon an intricately patterned pocket watch he had pulled from inside his cloak, "is often an optimal starting point." His voice was somehow bereft of sarcasm.

Lance took a long breath.

"Brennett and I…" He paused. "Started before we were born, in a way. Our mums were best friends. We even have the same birthday. "We shared everything." Lance paused again and ran a hand through his long hair. "Toys, then transgressions." He snorted. "Nothing too bad, not in the beginning. Pickpocketing, graffiti, those kinds of things. But then, of course, those things lead to worse things. We earned protection. Everyone needs protection in Arrik."

Lance balled a fist of Brogan's thick neck fur. "When you have nothing, you have two choices: live with it, or do damn well anything you can to change it. And once you do, you begin to prove yourself to those around you who are also working their way up the fucked-up ladder we were. You start to gain respect you never had before, and once you have respect from enough of them, it isn't you who needs the protection you once did. The tables turn. The hand of cards shifts."

The three sat in silence.

"And once you're willing to take that, that power, you have to hold onto it, or else you lose it. We held on really fucking hard. *Too* hard," he added bitterly. "We had the Hull, this small pub we operated out of, and maybe thirty or so people willing to do whatever, and we had all of Upper, and most of Downtown Cinnook. A word of advice: if any of you are ever in Arrik, don't go there. But, like anything, it got…messy.

"Brennett – and me to begin with, if I'm being honest – wanted more. *Needed* more. He's always been that way. Nothing was ever enough. Give him a sword, he wants a mace. Give him a boat, he wants a ship. Give him two parts of a district hellbent on destroying itself, he wants the whole city. He agreed something – something *I* never would have. He called a meeting with us, and the Merricks, our main rivals. His plan was to blow up the Hull, with them and half our men inside.

'He asked me one thing, get Priya out, which, as you heard, I'd unknowingly done, and get myself out." Lance's fingers were running lines up and down the sides of his face. "The moment he was willing to endanger not just the Merricks, and not just our men – our *friends*, but the families that lived nearby, was when I turned my back on him, and the moment I made my decision to leave with Priya.

'He was responsible for three kids dying that night."

Ren could see a twitch in his jaw, not dissimilar to Brennett's, and a slight shake in his balled fists.

"But Priya fucked off alone. And there I was, with no one, and thanks to the man I'd considered a brother for my whole life, what felt like the blood of nearly a hundred people on my hands because I was the one stupid enough to not see through his *meeting*, and a warrant for my arrest plastered all over Caerisle.

"I tracked him down only a minute or two before the Dragon Corps surrounded us. Brennett tried to fight, the stupid fuck, and begged me to tell him I had managed to save Priya. I didn't.

"We were hauled to the Iron Valley," he turned to Ren to explain, "a prison, not too far from here actually. First, they locked me up. Then they offered me a job...in exchange for anything I could give them on Brennett Graves, and anyone we'd associated with.

"It was us – both of us – but he was the face, always had been. Which had always paid off for him. Until then. Until I accepted and became the very thing our own mantra forbade. *No informers, no disorder...no surrender.* "He sat, as quiet as the moss beneath him, a look on his face suggesting the words he had spoken tasted sour, and examined his own fingernails.

It was Shae who spoke. "You don't appear quite as louche as you believe you do from that tale."

Lance snorted. "I don't come across as very good either."

"No," Shae agreed, "you won't win any awards for humanitarianism."

Brielle offered a soft smile as Ren took Lance's hand in her own, their fingers gently lacing together.

"I'm not looking for sympathy, or–"

"Well, that's good," Brielle began, "because you weren't getting any."

Her words seemed to slice through the invisible barrier of tension that had fallen around them, and the sides of Lance's mouth twitched. "Thanks," he said eventually, "for not hating me."

"You're welcome," Brielle said.

Shae, now examining a mushroom he had plucked from the ground, shrugged. "Over the last five years I have kept, rather tediously, needing you to save my life. Hating you would be counterproductive to my welfare. And I'm rather fond of my welfare."

Ren squeezed his hand in her own. "And I don't think I'm capable, or allowed, to hate you," she said with a soft smile, gesturing with her free hand towards her own chest, and then his, and at their ever-present buzzing.

"A bonding wouldn't stop you from hating him," Brielle stated. "I imagine it might be a bit awkward, but your true feelings aren't taken away; you'd still feel it."

"Well, then," Ren said, throwing Lance a sideways glance, "I guess I don't hate you either."

Their words seemed to cheer him up a little, though it was with a slightly more subdued air that he joined the rest of the conversation, his hand still clasped within Ren's.

"I can't trust him," Ren said. "I don't trust him, but..." She looked down and swallowed. "I saw the way he looked when..." She didn't continue, her mind on Brennett's last words. "What's an *abairt*?"

"A phrase," Lance explained, "like a password. I don't know how we'd go about finding it. I suppose we could try the casino Brennett mentioned..."

But Ren had stopped listening. "A-a phrase?"

"Mm." Lance sighed, running a hand through his blood-stained hair. "Could be anything."

Say it again.

Ren chewed her lower lip. She looked at Brogan but saw another. One decidedly more human. And more absent.

You can't forget it.

"I know what it is." She felt three frowns. "*Còmhla mar aon.*" Her gaze lifted to each of them in turn. Both Brielle and Lance looked baffled. A flicker of something Ren couldn't place crossed Shae's impassive expression.

"Together, as one," he translated, "I think."

...and that's how we'll always find each other.

Ren nodded, though it wasn't Shae's words she heard; it was her father's.

Find your mother.

End of Part Three

Part Four

21

If she had looked forward to anything more than leaving Ververos, Ren couldn't remember it. As the gigantic pines around them began to thin, and the bright sky beyond the perimeter of the mighty forest filled the spaces between them more, her pace quickened.

Adios, Ververos.

They were once again a trio – a quartet with the addition of Brogan. Brielle had bid them farewell the previous evening as they reached the Brook, the infamous ranger station Ren had finally seen. The outpost was run by a tall and somewhat scrawny woman called Aria, who, upon their arrival, hurled a large silver axe whistling past Ren's left ear into a nearby tree. Ren had stopped thinking of the woman as scrawny then.

They had dined on meat that wasn't rabbit or hooter, and on vegetables that weren't mushrooms, before Shae acquainted himself with a pitcher of red wine and a ranger called Joel, while Ren and Lance did the same in a private tent, where a concoction of memories of the past few days, and a little too much alcohol had ended in Ren fighting with too short, panic-stricken breaths, finding solace in arms she had feared would never enfold her again.

Setting off early, each of them had a light step and air of ease they had so far been denied. With each step, relief filled her more and more.

It wasn't much to go on, the phrase. The one that had consumed her thoughts since she was fifteen. The one written in what they called the *old tongue*, and what Ren knew as Gaelic, though not speaking any of the language, she didn't know how accurate the translation was. She wondered then why she had never bothered to learn.

Còmhla mar aon. Her mother had taught it to her first when Ren was around eight, and proceeded to repeat the lesson on an almost monthly basis, offering little information other than how it was imperative that Ren memorise the words.

Ren watched the red-tinged sky. *Find your mother.* That was a simple enough instruction, on its own. The reality struck Ren hard. Both the enormity of the task, and the part of her, buried not all that deep, that held nothing but reluctance to carry it out. But it was all they had.

Well, that or the prison.

"It was bad," Ren told them, wishing she had the means to make a list. "Not always, but, for a few years anyway. She was obsessed with maps, and..." A few small pieces of a much larger puzzle made sense. Her mother had spent years working out where Britain's wey lines lay, as Shae had, though without the skeleton map Shae had been given by this Gideon before he and Lance had left Caerisle. Ren's mother had had the task of finding them from nothing. A feat that wouldn't have been possible, according to Shae, without a gift.

But then, Ren thought for the hundredth, infuriating time, *where was her taio?*

"And what?" It was Lance.

Ren's mouth opened and closed several times. "My health,"

she said eventually. Another unknown that now made sense. "We all thought she was paranoid, because I was never ill, not really. Not until *after* she'd left, which is kind of ironic." Ren thought over every appointment, every disappointment, every ailment and hospital visit. Each existed not because of unknown, chronic illness, but magic. Unawakened magic forced in a world where it was, as Shae stated, *unacknowledged*.

Or something.

Maybe one day she would understand.

Her fingernails were digging deep grooves into her palms. And then there was the plan itself, full of holes and what ifs.

And yet, for all the uncertainty, for the first time, their journey, and the lax strategy they had developed, felt like hers.

The path beneath narrowed as they approached the fence.

Ren eased out a breath as they approached, turning her head.

The darkened forest, with its strange, red hue, which now held many of Ren's most bizarre, and frightening, but also wonderful, experiences, stared right back.

A sign informed them they had crossed the border into Axilion. It was, according to Shae, Caerisle's equivalent to Wales. And while Wales is generally comparable in appearance to Scotland, Axilion was already proving quite dissimilar from Caeracre.

While Caeracre had little in the way of roads – that Ren had seen, anyway – they emerged through the fence and stepped onto paved, grey stone. In time, the side of the path became littered with streetlights, lit via magic instead of electricity. But they were metal instead of wooden, and rather more modern than ye olde type from Caeracre.

Along with Ververos, they also left behind the overpowering, heady spiced aroma. The air in Axilion wasn't spicy; nor was it minty, like Caeracre. It held the faintest hint of citrus. Clean. Like lemongrass and dew.

Ren sucked in a deep breath. "I can't say I'm sad to see the back of Ververos." Her words were met with general agreement.

They arrived, quicker than she'd expected, to civilisation. Gone were the sparsely dotted villages. The buildings in the town of Fern were almost all crafted from a similar grey stone to the road and, unless Ren paid close attention to the magic, the place could almost have been Earth. Minus the lack of transportation.

They traded what they could for wares more edible, and carried on, veering due south. Eventually, as the sun rose to its highest point in the sky, they arrived in another town, this one called Shin.

"Wait," Lance instructed, pointing to a nearby cluster of oak trees.

Brogan blinked, and trotted his way across the road, his large tail sweeping from side to side.

And then they entered Shin.

The place was as grey as Fern, but far crumblier. It felt older somehow, and not from the decrepit state of the buildings. An ancient something Ren couldn't hope to pinpoint was present in the air.

Shae led them, turning this way and that through darkened back streets, past cobweb-strewn doorways and deep-set windows so dark she couldn't see what lay behind. They passed several others, the majority of whom held fistfuls of grey cloaks to their throats, making them little more than hooded, faceless figures. What *NáDarra* was in the air was sparse. It made Ren nervous for reasons she couldn't understand. True to Shae's instruction, Ren looked directly at no one. But it didn't stop their gaze seeking her out. Of those she glanced at, each one was staring, not quite at her, she was certain, but her taio.

None of the inhabitants spoke, and neither did they. Their footsteps were the only real noise to the place.

The same damp, mouldy scent that seemed to emanate from every street they descended grew stronger, and Ren shivered. Not because of the temperature. She focused, as best she could, on the back of Shae's head and the way Lance's arm gently bumped against hers every few steps. Each of their easy strides from the morning had been replaced: Shae's with an assured glide of bravado, his cloak billowing more than usual; Ren's with a hesitance to each step she took, which she tried, and failed, to dampen, and Lance's with an expectant stiffness. His hand twitched sporadically in the corner of her vision.

Concealed down the side of her left boot sat the knife he had insisted Ren kept. For the first time since she had been left alone on one of the Spire's giant mushrooms, did Ren wonder, as they passed the entrance to yet another dingy alleyway, down which another silent somebody watched her and her taio from the shadows, what it would mean to use it.

Shae's pace slowed as he brought them to a black door. It was in two parts, separated horizontally across the middle as though it led to a stable. A faded silver symbol glinted from the centre of the top half: a snake wrapped around what looked like a goblet. Shae raised his right hand and rapped three times on the snake's head.

For a long moment, there was silence, before the sound of several bolts being drawn across several locks met their ears. The top half of the door swung inwards.

They were greeted by a man. His head was smooth and hairless and his skin so sallow he looked jaundiced. Above him, barely visible, hung a cluster of pale grey specks. They moved so slowly they appeared as still as Shae's. He looked Shae up and down through a pair of small, beady eyes, pure black.

"Yes?" he spat. The word was a hiss.

Shae cleared his throat. "We've come to offer tr–"

But his words were drowned out as the man spotted Ren, or rather what hovered some half a foot above Ren's head. "Oh ho," he offered, the malice in his tone gone. His mouth, a cracked and sad affair, twisted into something Ren assumed was supposed to resemble a smile. Several teeth, each shaved into a point, and hopelessly yellow, were visible.

Ren looked away.

"What do we have here?"

"As I was saying," Shae said pointedly. "We've come to offer trade." He placed an arm to Ren's shoulder, steering her a step forward. She wished he wouldn't. "Trade," Shae said, "in *NáDarra*."

The man disappeared, only to reappear seconds later having opened the bottom half of his door. He beckoned Shae, and then Ren, forwards. At the sight of Lance, he narrowed his eyes, which considering they were so small, made them look closed, and shook his head. "He waits outside," he hissed.

Lance pressed a hand to Ren's lower back. "No."

A low grunt sounded from somewhere near the man's throat. "The ungifted waits outside."

Lance blinked at the man. "If you think I'm—"

But Ren had placed a palm to his chest. "It's okay," she said. "Wait here, I'll—"

His mahogany eyes bored into hers. No crinkles surrounded them. "Ren, I—"

She didn't want to say the words any more than she wanted to enter whatever lay beyond the man's split door. "I'll be fine; I'll have Shae."

"What? No. This is ridiculous." Lance turned back to the man. "You don't even have a gift," he snapped.

"He does," Ren and Shae replied in unison.

The strange man hissed at Lance like an alley cat. "The ungifted waits outside," he repeated.

"I don't like this," Lance mumbled. "Is there nowhere else you can get one?"

"Nowhere close," Shae replied. "Nowhere I know of."

Lance turned his head, looking this way and that across the dull street. His hand left her back, only to grasp her own. "Be careful," he whispered, squeezing her fingers in his. His gaze flickered downwards, to where they both knew the knife lay, nestled against the side of her calf.

Ren inclined her head just enough, and turned, following the man, and Shae, across the threshold.

Shae had informed her they had been heading to an apothecary and Ren– rather foolishly she soon realised – had expected an outdated pharmacy.

Where they stood was no pharmacy. It was a single, meagre, dimly lit room. Shelves, so packed in they could barely walk, and so coated in dust each breath she took felt heavy, stood floor to ceiling. A second door sat into the back wall, splintered and strewn with mould. A deep red stain was splattered across the aged wood. The shelves held jars in every size, featuring various ingredients, though how one used what looked like human eyeballs, and bat wings, Ren wasn't sure she wanted to know.

Nothing was labelled, and each vial, or pot, or jar, looked as though it had sat in the same position for a decade. They followed the man to the very back of the room. He disappeared behind a desk, as rickety and covered in as much dust as everything else in the place. Upon the surface was a grimy fish bowl filled with live maggots. It took all Ren had not to heave. But then the smell - pure rot - hit her, and she heaved anyway.

Shae shuffled on the balls of his feet but remained composed. The man grunted, pushing the bowl to one side.

He regarded them one by one, before settling on Ren. "You come to trade *NáDarra*, yes?"

Ren glanced at Shae, who gave her a curt nod. "Yes. For coordinates," she relayed the information Shae had prepped her with that morning, "to the Southern pass."

The man was examining her taio. Ren wished he wouldn't. Reaching under his desk, he placed six empty (save for more dust) small glass pots on the surface of the wood.

"Fill," he instructed.

Ren bit her lip.

...and that's how we'll always find each other.

"And you'll give us the coordinates?"

He reached beneath again, and after several seconds of rustling, produced a piece of yellowish parchment, and a fountain pen. "Fill," he repeated, touching the nib to the page.

Letting out a breath, Ren held out her hand, closing her eyes.

Locating them was easier each time she tried, though doing so to relight a campfire was one thing. Placing her specks in the care of this man was something she approached with far greater reluctance. Swallowing dryly, Ren opened her eyes, and guided the green specks of Ground into the nearest pot. The man, smiling again, clamped a lid on top with such haste Ren was half surprised the pot didn't shatter.

Once again she closed her eyes, this time seeking out Fire.

By the time four of the pots were filled, it was far harder to concentrate on the specks. She was panting as she blinked. "I don't know if I can," she said, puffing, seeking out Shae, "it's hard."

"I know," he replied, before turning to the man. "Four is more than fair."

"Six," the man said, defiant and unsympathetic. But Ren was only half listening as something, unrelated to the unease in entering the apothecary without him, rose within her. It *buzzed* within her. "Six was–" But what six was, they didn't find out. A series of shouts from only a few metres away outside rang through the air. "Wha–"

They turned as one as another shout, this one muffled but recognisable, and louder than before, called, "No!"

Ren reached the door first, ignoring whatever Shae yelled behind her as she dodged his attempts to grab her arm. She wrenched it open. Her mind, and any rationale it ought to possess, was eclipsed by the fact the buzzing was no longer buzzing, but pain.

Ren surveyed the scene. She saw his sword first, abandoned

on the drab stone. The sight made her stomach drop and her heart miss several beats.

At least twenty people stood, their attention turned to fix on her. She recognised only one, and he was being detained by three others. They wore identical scarlet, military-like uniforms.

Ren didn't move.

"Ah," a man by Lance said. He clapped his hands together, stepping forward. "That only leaves the arcanist." His words were accompanied by a roll of thunder overhead.

Lance, struggling against three sets of burly hands, snarled, "I *told* you, he's not here."

It wasn't a lie. Ren swallowed as she glanced back into the room. Shae was gone.

Ignoring Lance, the man turned to three others behind him. He examined the door with a sneer. "Search the place. And him," he added, nodding at Lance. He turned to her as several of his men rushed past. "Hello, Renée."

The buzzing, low and painful, had settled both deep in her chest and on her arms, mimicking the spots Lance was being held at. As though of their own accord, her wrist flexed and Lance, who she could see behind the biggest of his captors, stopped struggling. The pain in her arms somewhat dipped.

In her chest it worsened.

The man, their presumed leader, turned his attention back to Ren.

"Renée." Across the street, a bin burst into flames. His eyes flickered to the side, but he otherwise showed no signs of alarm. "We've found you." He spoke the words as though they ought to offer comfort. They did the opposite. Behind him, Lance was watching her in silence. Her hands shook. She wished they were clutching his.

Her voice was timid, quiet. "Who are you?" She scolded herself for sounding so weak.

Before he could answer, the apothecary door was pulled ajar and the men re-emerged.

"Empty," one said.

Ren let out a breath.

Their leader nodded once. "My name is Umber," he informed her. "I've come to bring you to the Council."

Ren looked to Lance. He was silent, though she saw it in his eyes: fear. *If you take her to the Council, you'll never see her again.* A gust of wind, so strong it forced Umber's own eyes to squeeze themselves shut, blew through the street. It was darker now, and colder. Where a few specks of Light magic had been floating when they arrived, they were being replaced with Dark.

Perhaps.... Ren turned to Umber.

His eyes were a pale blue, his nose a bit too large for his face. Ren longed to punch it.

Her whole mouth was dry, her limbs tingling. The buzzing rose and fell in time with her breathing, and in time with Lance's.

Ren looked into Umber's punchable face and barely saw it.

She had to locate them, and she couldn't let him know. She couldn't let any of them know. Until it would be too late...for them.

Umber was talking. Ren wasn't listening; she was searching.

Dark, she told herself. *Dark first.*

She knew without looking that the specks appeared, one by one, in a painfully slow fashion, in her not quite closed fist. It was harder than it should have been, and harder than it would have been had she not filled four of the strange man's jars. She *felt*, rather than saw, the stores of them within her. They were depleted, and with little hope of being filled again given the empty state of Shin. Ren looked at each man in turn. Umber would be first, then those surrounding Lance. Dark first, and then–

Whatever caused it was a mystery. It left the side of her neck stinging, then numb. At some point someone – Lance maybe, shouted something broken and confusing. A blurry, grey mishmash of nothing, which was strange, followed by the realisation the numbness was no longer centred in her neck, but spreading to each of her extremities at once.

It probably should have bothered her, and to some, distant, closed-off part, it did. She thought it did anyway. *Tricky things,* Ren deliberated, *thoughts.*

Someone, whose name she really should know – shouldn't she? – had placed one arm behind her shoulders and another behind her knees. Ren felt the arms there, holding her in place, and then felt nothing at all. That was strange, too.

It was then, or perhaps it was before, or maybe after, through far-off shouts and a nearby banging Ren didn't understand, everything went white, and then black.

22

Something wasn't right.

Ren was lying upon something too hard, in a place that was too bright behind her closed lids. There was a distant din of what might have been voices, dull and distorted and confusing. Like everything else.

There was something else, a sensation that wasn't quite a sensation at all. A numbness. Her body was both present, pressing against the too hard surface, and not there at all.

Snippets of information, truths, memories, rose within her. Giant pines and giant cats; the scent of mushrooms fried in a pan hovering above a campfire. A unicorn. A village hidden high within the trees. Then, a sense. Wrongness. It sensed it too, the unicorn. Ren longed to join it as it turned, stiff and alert, and ran. Ran from a crossbow wielded by a man she knew but couldn't see. From a wall of water so high she couldn't sense the top. From madmen and metal, blood-soaked cuffs. And from something else....

Again, such a faint and delicate thing deep in her chest. It rose and fell with each breath she took, strengthening itself. But not yet strong enough.

The unicorn had stopped running and was patting the ground with one stark white hoof. Though the more she saw of it the more it wasn't a hoof at all. It was changing, morphing into something different. Something new.

What hit the ground next wasn't a hoof but a thick, black paw, enveloped by flecks of green. If Ren could only reach out, perhaps she could touch it. Perhaps she should try.

She might have succeeded were it not for a sound, far away from the paw, ripping at her shallow realm of consciousness.

It rang out again, clearer than before. And Ren, at least, knew what it meant now.

A third time, louder still.

"Renée."

She woke with a steady ebb of nausea, the stench of dankness, like wet socks, and a dull pain ricocheting around her head.

"Renée?" A whoosh of buzzing erupted both from, and into, her chest.

My name is Umber.

Lance's face, full of uncertainty and fear, burned against her still closed eyelids.

"Call for Gideon."

I've come to bring you to the Council.

The light dimmed. The buzzing surged. Footsteps, faint, then loud.

If you take her to the Council...

Ren heard herself groan. There was an indistinguishable murmuring, and a flurry of movement she couldn't place.

...you'll never see her again.

Through several blinks and a watery squinting, Ren made out two things: a series of black splodges on a dingy ceiling of grey stone above, and a man.

"Hello, Renée." His gaze pierced hers beneath a pair of dark, prominent brows. "My name is Gideon." His mouth was framed by a manicured goatee. One half of his face was smooth, the other was less so, coated with a pinkish discolouration of aged scar tissue. When he smiled, the edge of his mouth on the scarred side moved less. He possessed no taio. "Welcome to the Council Chambers."

Ren had wondered, at various points, what the man who had instructed her return to Caerisle was like, and what the opportunity to demand the answers he, and his Council, owed her, would bring. But when presented with the chance to question him, Ren had only one. And she spat it at him with as much venom as her voice allowed, which wasn't as much as she'd have liked.

If her indignant demeanour bothered him, he hid it well.

Gideon held both his hands up, palms facing her. "Mr Allardyce has been detained, as per my order."

Ren glared. "Why?"

"Everything will be explained soon." Taking a step back from her bed, Gideon signalled to someone Ren couldn't see. "We've taken the liberty of providing you with clean clothes." These footsteps were softer. "You can wash through *there*, then Krisha here will bring you to one of our meeting rooms. Room A," he added, looking away from Ren for the first time.

Ren didn't allow herself to look away from him. In her chest, the buzzing had been rising steadily.

He turned back to a still scowling Ren, his eyes resting briefly above her head, his expression unreadable. "I'll see you in a short while." He turned, cloak of black satin fluttering outwards at the movement, and left. His steps echoed down what sounded to be a long corridor.

Ren took several deep breaths. Woozy and confused, she searched for the only thing she had left: the buzzing. Her fingertips grazed the centre of her chest.

Krisha cleared her throat. "I can prepare a bath." Krisha swallowed audibly. "Or whatever you'd like…" She trailed off.

Ren almost laughed. What she'd *like* was to leave.

The room was stuffy and smelt vaguely of vinegar. Besides hers, there were a further five beds. Her head, swimming with questions she was certain she didn't want to hear answers to, was still fuzzy. Even as she focused on Krisha's face, the other girl appeared to spin in Ren's vision. She failed to sit up, managing only with Krisha's assistance.

"Th-thanks."

Krisha offered a hint of a smile. "You're welcome."

With help – more than she would have liked – from Krisha, Ren exited the room cleaner than she'd been when she entered it. Gideon's employee, or whatever she was, was tall and slim, and decidedly pretty beneath the haunted half-moon circles beneath her large, brown eyes. She moved carefully, deliberately, as though she were a fawn learning to walk.

She'd handed Ren the clothes. The Council had provided her with a kind of black tracksuit. Ren had stripped herself of all her previous garments, each filthy, all except the knife they thankfully hadn't found. She slotted it back in place. With Ren still nauseous, and with everything around her still spinning, they made their way from the empty ward into the corridor beyond. Krisha, providing an arm to keep Ren in a straight line, led them down three hallways, each as dismal as the last.

The place was decrepit, more so than the fortress Brennett had held her in. Piles of rubble littered each corner, while deep grooves and cracks lined almost every wall. Parts of the floor were uneven; more than once Ren found herself grasping Krisha's forearm to stop herself plunging face first into a pile of dilapidated stone.

"*This* is the Council?" Ren's words sounded funny, even to her own ears. Slurred somewhat. Another wave of nausea rose within her stomach.

Krisha didn't answer as she brought Ren to a door with a shiny metal *A* nailed to it. The letter looked like the newest thing Ren had seen since waking. Krisha offered Ren a sideways not quite smile, and knocked three times.

The door opened with a creak.

"Ah." It was Gideon. Ren and Krisha stepped into the room, which was only marginally less dilapidated than the rest of the building Ren had seen. In the centre sat a large, dark wood table, surrounded by at least eight chairs. Two were occupied.

"Renée, you look better."

Ren didn't reply. She didn't feel better, and doubted she looked so.

Krisha led her to the closest chair.

"Please," Gideon said, gesturing, "take a seat."

She wanted to say no, and tell Gideon where he could shove his seat, but the wooziness was worsening. Reluctantly, she sat, the buzzing pulsing within her like a silent alarm.

Gideon was positioned next to a woman. She regarded Ren with the sternness of a school teacher.

Through her still blurry vision, Ren took in the sight of her. With her scrunched face and very little neck, she had the likeness of a bulldog. A taio of identical tiny white specks sat above her head, like Shae's.

"Ah, Renée." Gideon gestured to the woman. "This is Rosa."

The woman, Rosa, inclined her head.

Ren didn't return the gesture. Instead, she crossed her arms across her stomach, focusing on both the buzzing and her desire not to vomit.

"Renée," Rosa said, shuffling from side to side in her seat, "we owe you the greatest of apologies."

Ren whole-heartedly agreed.

Rosa continued. "It was a vast oversight on our part to have you Collected by Mr. Ambroise and Mr. Allardyce."

Ren opened her mouth, only to close it again as Krisha reappeared by her side, placing a small tray on the scratched surface of the wood. A blue and white cup with three separate chips around the rim was sitting upon it. It held something steaming and purple.

"This is yakai tea," Rosa informed her. "It is a common beverage here in Glendale."

Ren eyed it as the word 'Glendale' settled itself into a mild understanding. So she had left Axilion and been taken to the southernmost part of Caerisle, their England. Surely that only meant she was further away from Lance.

She hoped, more than ever, that Shae had evaded similar capture.

Wanting nothing more than to throw the yakai tea across the table into Gideon and Rosa's faces, Ren bit her lip. How long had it been since she had eaten? Enticing hints of liquorice and almond and something else emanated from the liquid. Ren brought the cup to her lips as Krisha placed two more in front of both Gideon and Rosa. The liquid swirled within the china. Maybe they were planning to poison her.

No, they needed her...didn't they?

Ren took a sip, then another. She hated herself for enjoying it.

Across the table, as Ren finished her tea, Rosa leant forward. "Your mother made me promise me a long time ago I'd bring you home."

Ren looked to Rosa. Her nausea was subsiding and the woman was clearer now. "You knew my mother?"

"No." Rosa took a sip. "I *know* your mother. And in three days' time, you will again, too."

Ren became acutely aware of her own heartbeat.

"Wh-where is she?"

Rosa offered a soft smile. "She has been awaiting you in Loreleith, for almost two weeks now."

Loreleith was in Caeracre, and was the place Shae had called the *home of magic*. They had arrived near the outskirts. Why would her mother have been waiting there? "Why?"

Rosa sucked in a breath, shooting Gideon a sideways glance. "That is where Ambroise and Allardyce were instructed to take you."

At her words, a high-pitched continuous ringing sound in Ren's ears.

"What?"

"We managed to track your location thanks to signs of increased *NáDarra* observed by civilians," Gideon said. "You should never have entered Ververos, let alone been so far south."

Despite the tea, Ren's mouth was very dry. "But...I was to go to Elder-something, Ember maybe."

Rosa pressed a palm into her chest with a sharp intake of breath. "I hope you don't mean Endermarch."

Ren only nodded. In her chest, the buzzing had settled low and steady. Her eyes flickered around the room, to each of the three others in turn. Her thoughts were plentiful but nonsensical.

It was Gideon who spoke, and he did so slowly, as though Ren were stupid. "Endermarch is a prison."

There was a hollow in her chest. "I know, but it's not in use, or—"

"Renée," Gideon said, his oversized brows pulled together. "Endermarch prison is a well-known, and rather problematic, location for gang activity. It certainly isn't anywhere we would conduct Council business."

His words didn't make Lance and Shae liars; no more did theirs make Gideon and Rosa liars. But she'd been through a lot more with the former two. The buzzing swelled.

"I have no reason," Ren began, praying her quickening breathing wasn't as obvious as it felt, "to believe you."

"No," Gideon replied, "you don't."

Ren sucked in a breath of surprise as he reached down, to something below the table Ren couldn't see.

He pulled several items upwards, placing each delicately on the surface. Two were papers of some kind, both folded and crumpled. Ren had seen one before, in St. Andrews, before it had been snatched out of her sight. Next, he placed Lance's knives, each identical to the one sitting against Ren's calf, and his sword. It took all she had not to let out a sob at the sight; a punch would have hurt less.

"This was everything taken when Mr Allardyce was searched." Gideon ignored the sword, and the knives, and reached for the first piece of paper, the one she knew.

Her hands shook as she reached for the water-stained dossier.

The job description, outlining her Collection, wasn't as packed with information as Ren would have thought. An address, with *Council Chambers* written before it, was near the top of the page. Was that where she was now? Did Lance come to work in this very building?

Below, she read both his and Shae's full names.

Any middle names?

Two, neither of which I have any interest in telling you.

A week ago she would have relished the information; now she didn't want it.

Not like this.

There was also information about her. *Subject for collection: Renée Arlene.* No surname. Its absence felt hollow. Ren forced herself to keep reading, scanning the page to the end.

Blinking back tears, she read the final instruction.

Delivery Point: Acquisitions Office; NáDarra'n Academy; Wylain; Loreleith; Caeracre (North).

It happened in a split second. Both Rosa and Krisha screamed, retreating to the rear of the room. Gideon stood. His mouth was hanging open. The flecks of purple Lightning magic ricocheted around the room, bouncing off walls and now splintered pieces of table before each one found its way back into Ren's taio. Only Ren remained still. Outwardly, she might have appeared calm.

Ren wasn't calm.

For a long moment, nobody spoke.

"Renée," it was Gideon, "I appreciate this must come as a rather large shock." Ignoring the strong breeze making its way through the modest room, he held her gaze with his. "But I wish to be honest." He took a breath, the slight waver in his gaze for a second his only sign of hesitancy. "We believe Allardyce – perhaps Ambroise, too – had struck a deal." Ren steeled herself. "Involving you."

A deal.

Involving you.

The words played over and over in her mind like a scratched CD.

When she didn't speak, Gideon continued. "We have discovered the same deal was offered to Brennett Graves."

Ren's eyes locked, once again, to each of the three in turn.

Rosa's expression was unreadable.

Krisha looked uncomfortable at best, downright terrified at worst, at the mention of Brennett.

Gideon's mouth held the ghost of something like a smirk.

Ren sucked in a breath. "You have Brennett Graves?"

Gideon nodded once. "We do."

"Where? A-and when?"

For the first time since Ren's accidental-on-purpose bolt of Lightning had struck the room, Rosa spoke. "Around an hour before you were tracked down. Just outside Shin."

It didn't seem very likely *that* was coincidence.

"From what we have gathered," Rosa was saying, "the deal was to take place somewhere – Endermarch we can now assume – but was changed to somewhere within the Hidden City."

Ren looked down.

"The Hidden City," said Gideon, "is virtually impossible to enter without contacts – criminal ones at that. There are usually coordinates involved."

Ren clenched her hands together, wishing the table was still in place.

"Then, for such deals to take place, an *abairt* is also needed." He sat then, regarding her across the broken remains of the table. "We hadn't recent coordinates, let alone either a location or a phrase. Had you entered, it would have been nigh on impossible to track you down."

The buzzing was lying, low and dormant. Ren said nothing, each piece of Gideon and Rosa's nausea-inducing puzzle repeating within her mind. Many things didn't make sense.

Some did.

Ren didn't want to think about those.

The Hidden City had been *her* decision, hadn't it?

The *abairt* hadn't come from her, but her mother. Could her mother have been betrayed for the phrase?

At some point, she had let go of the dossier and, during the Lightning bolt, the remainder of Lance's possessions had been scattered around the room. A small corner of pale yellow lay near Krisha.

Ren nodded at it. "What's that?"

Krisha brought the paper forward, handing it to Ren.

Unlike the dossier, the second piece of paper contained significantly less information. Five words were scrawled upon it. Ren's heart pounded so hard it hurt. Gideon produced a third piece of paper.

He handed it over. "This one was taken when Graves was searched."

Everything, from the words to the penmanship, was identical. Ren crumpled the indistinguishable notes in her palm. This time, no Lightning struck, nor were any winds blown. A heavy nothing had befallen her. All there was, in the hollow that had once contained her chest, was the buzzing.

Five words on one note, and duplicated on the other, written by an unknown, faceless threat. Ren's chest hollowed. One given to Brennett and the other...to Lance?

The weaver for the Hull.

Krisha led her to a bedroom; a blue, windowless square within which a single bed, desk, and sink had been crammed. Her clothes – the ones Brielle had styled her in what felt like months ago – lay folded on the desk. Her eyes burned to look at them.

Ren took a shaky step towards the bed. An oil painting had been hung above in a failed attempt to cover a wide crack in the wall behind. A golden beach beneath a cloudless, vast azure. The kind of picture hung in hospitals and therapists' offices. The kind meant to promote calm.

Ren couldn't have been less calm.

The wooziness she had experienced heading to meeting room A had gone; in its place was a hole of anguished uncertainty. The nausea remained, though it was different. It rose in time with the buzzing, as though it wasn't hers. Occasionally, the sensations would dip and Ren's breath would catch silently. Then she'd be overcome with an inane wish to make the crack in the wall bigger still.

Years before, in the months after her mother's disappearance, once well-meaning neighbours no longer appeared with sausage casseroles and apple crumbles and pointless well wishes of hope, Ren had found a box, and in her mind created another. The first – the real one – used to contain shoes; the other, she suspected, happiness.

In the first she carefully placed three things: a razor, a lighter, and a tiny screwdriver she had won the Christmas just past in a cracker. In the other she forced what having a mother felt like. They worked in tandem, the boxes. One real and one not. The contents of the first kept the second from staying open too long.

Having left at some point – not that Ren noticed – Krisha returned, this time clutching a tray of food. Ren stared at the tray, and then Krisha, her expression blank. "You should eat."

Ren didn't know whether to scoff, or laugh, or punch something, so did nothing.

"You're going to need strength," Krisha pressed, placing the tray on the desk by the clothes. Then she turned and crossed the small room in a few short steps. Her hand was already clasping the handle when she faced Ren again, adding, "Whatever happens."

She left Ren alone then.

Ren wished she had cared enough to ask what the words meant, as she sat, hours later in the dark with throbbing knuckles.

Her box would have made the task easier. Would have made forgetting the way his arms enveloped her easier. And try as she might, Ren's newest, imaginary box, the one she desperately tried to push any semblance of Lance Allardyce into, wouldn't close. Not for the first time, she pressed a balled fist against the centre of her chest as pain, not her own, racked her body. Only when it subsided, hours later, did Ren lie down, the buzzing and nausea pulsing with her heartbeat.

Krisha returned the following morning. Ren's throat was hoarse and her hand was bruised and aching. There were several black scorch marks on three of the walls that hadn't been there the previous evening. Krisha examined each one with a wary eye and placed a new tray in the same position she had put the one from the previous night. Ren only watched as Krisha then busied herself gathering the pieces of broken crockery and splattered food. As she stretched, the hem of her top rode up her back an inch or so, revealing both part of a tattoo, and a jagged, purple scar. Ren blinked at the sight. The ink was in the shape of a poker chip.

Finishing cleaning Ren's almighty mess, Krisha faced the

bed. "You have to eat."

Ren's empty stomach lurched. She ignored it, flexing her fingers. Not broken at least.

"I'm not very hungry."

"That's not a good enough reason to starve yourself, I'm afraid."

Ren's stomach, hellbent on betraying her, emitted a loud growl. She rolled her eyes at Krisha's smirk. "Fine," she spat, holding her hands out for the tray. Whatever the food was, it held no flavour and crumbled into a tasteless dust on her tongue.

"Once you're finished, I have to take you to them."

Ren swallowed. "Gideon, and that woman?"

"Rosa, yeah."

"Oh." Ren picked at some kind of bland lettuce. "Why?"

"I don't know."

By the time they left Ren's room, Ren felt both cleaner, having washed, and clearer. Even if she had wanted to ignore Lance's existence, which she was almost certain she didn't, the buzzing prevented that. He was there every time she so much as blinked. Every time she took a breath.

Perhaps there were explanations.

Perhaps there weren't.

Bitterness bubbled deep in her gut at the prospect there wasn't.

Regardless, she had to at least speak to him. It would hardly do to live her life continually buzzing, with the words *Delivery Point: Acquisitions Office; NáDarra'n Academy* burning into her mind each second she had to spare.

Why the hell *was he taking me to a prison?* She thought for the hundredth, useless time. She had given up trying to close the box. Even without the buzzing, how could she do anything other than miss him?

"Do prisons have visiting times?" she asked Krisha.

It was, in Ren's opinion, a reasonable question. Prisons on Earth had visiting times, mail services, conjugal visits.... Ren bit her lip, then tasted blood.

Krisha, however, shot Ren a most alarmed glance.

"I just need," Ren began, dropping her voice to a whisper, "to *see* him, even once, because–"

"Renée–"

"Ren."

Krisha's brown doe eyes were wide. "Ren," she said, her words scarcely louder than her breathing, "you won't be able to see him."

"I know they th–"

But this time when Krisha shushed her it was curt and louder and accompanied by a single, direct nod ahead.

Ren took stock of her surroundings. The corridor wasn't familiar. The door Krisha stopped at had no letter or marking on it.

Krisha knocked three times.

The door swung ajar.

The effect was instantaneous, as sudden as a thunderclap. Every hair on Ren's body stood on end as something spread over her, in the way a chill would. But it wasn't a chill.

Every question she had for Gideon vanished.

It was a sense of something, and it dampened every other thought and sensation her body held, more potent than the restless anger. It was an anxious wrongness, though from what or where, Ren didn't know.

"Ah, come in, Renée."

Ren didn't want to, but stepped across the threshold anyway.

Gideon stood in the centre of the room, Rosa by his side.

Ren barely saw them. What she did see stood behind them, and Ren realised where the sensation had originated from. She took half a step back.

The room was larger than the meeting room, but not by much. It was as run down as the rest of the Council seemed to be, with numerous cracks in the ceiling and walls. One of the corners was caved in, though the stone was now smooth, as though it had been blown up long ago.

A floor, and three of the walls, were crafted from the same grey stone as the rest of the place.

The fourth wasn't.

It was a pure darkness she had seen only once before, creating the monstrous body of the thing Shae had called a bodach and Ren had called a nightmare.

Every speck of awakened magic within her was on edge.

Gideon cleared his throat. "You needn't look so alarmed." Ren failed to see how she could look anything other than alarmed when faced with a solid wall of dead magic. "This," Gideon continued, gesturing behind him, "is a magical preserve."

What?

Ren must have looked even more alarmed.

"It is used," he said, voice emanating calm, "as a place for someone, usually a weaver, to store any surplus magic they may possess, for a short time. They can be extremely helpful. The, ah, *host*, will store your magic."

For the very little Ren knew about magic, and the far less she knew of dead magic, she did know one thing: this *host* would kill her magic.

She shot Krisha a brief glance, a sense of foreboding growing and prickling across her shoulders. Krisha was silent. The wall of dead magic, so dark it didn't seem real, loomed ahead. A senseless void of colour and of life.

Rosa was gesturing to the space in front of her. "Now, Renée, if you'll just come forward, into the centre here." Her tone was sweeter than Ren remembered from the previous evening, but the sound wasn't pleasant. Rosa's voice was high-pitched and somewhat thin. She watched Ren through a pair of red glasses and wore a smile that was stretched a little too wide. The same way Gill always wore hers.

Unlike Gideon, Rosa didn't wear robes. Instead, she donned a kind of navy trouser suit. Intricate silver buttons ran down the side of each trouser leg, and up the front of the jacket. If it weren't for the taio marking her as an arcanist she wouldn't have looked out of place on Earth.

Rosa was standing further forward than Gideon. Which made sense, considering Gideon didn't possess any magic.

Whether it was simply her anxiety at the presence of the wall, or not, something was wrong. More wrong than every-thing else. Ren was panting before she worked out why. It was harder to breathe in the room. As though the air were heavier somehow.

Rosa was watching Ren with an expectant gaze. Her arms were still spread in front.

Gideon took several steps in a semi-circle, arriving just shy of the back of Ren's shoulder. His presence there was perhaps the most unsettling of all.

Ren hadn't moved, but flinched as a sharpness stung the centre of her back. She turned but saw nothing, not even Gide-on, now somehow a few steps away, as the pain disappeared.

"Come on, Renée," Rosa pressed, but her tone was different; lower this time. Her words took a second to make sense. By the time they did, Ren had taken a shaky step forwards she didn't remember instructing her legs to make.

Rosa was grinning wildly. "That's it," she cooed, as though Ren were a toddler walking for the first time.

"Now, Renée." It was Gideon. Like Rosa's, his voice sounded strange, somehow far away. Ren's eyes had clamped shut.

She heard herself emit a soft grunt. A desire to crouch was overcoming her, an invisible weight pressing down upon her, driving her downwards. Ren ignored it – or so she thought until her knees hit against the cold stone of the floor.

She heard Gideon's voice but saw nothing. "Bring forth your Fire."

Ren felt herself sway, and her shoulders were grabbed, steadying her.

"Bring forth your Fire," Gideon repeated, his voice still distorted, but louder. There was something else present in his tone, something she could scarcely acknowledge but fought to recognise. A hint of success.

Ren sought them, her Fire, though didn't know why. In the darkness of the part of her where her magic lay, she saw them. They weren't sparking upwards.

They were shaking.

Several vanished from her mind's eye and manifested, she knew, by her hand.

"Good, Renée."

Ren didn't feel good. It hurt to breathe; each part of her shook.

"Now guide them forward."

Ren did, in spite of everything, magical or otherwise, telling her not to.

"That's it," she heard Gideon exclaim.

"N–" Ren began. The specks that remained in her mind – the only ones Ren could *see* – were quivering, *trembling*. Ren heard herself let out a stifled sob as she led the others against her will. Why couldn't she stop? They were nearing the wall, they had to be.

The grip on her shoulders tightened. "That's *it*, Renée."

But it wasn't.

With a cry that startled even herself, she wrenched her will from him, falling forwards. Her palms scraped rough ground and Ren, finally able to open her eyes, did so in time to see Fire specks – a hundred at least – dissipate from a whirling ball of red. They whizzed and sparked and looped and shot their way back towards Ren's taio. She felt them enter, then felt their slight ease.

Then she faced Gideon.

Though his face, hard and set, had softened under her stare, his eyes stayed dark, flickering between Ren and the wall of dead magic.

"Renée, I admit I am a little confused."

For the first time, though it shamed her to admit it, Ren saw it then. When nothing in the room with its hard-to-breathe air and wall of literal death was clear, something finally was. A truth that only presented her with more questions.

No ally would attempt to force her into killing her own magic. She knew something else then too: it would do little good to antagonise the man. Not while he held her there. Not while he held Lance. And while Shae was...wherever he was.

Ren didn't look away. "I'm s-sorry," she began. "I'm not sure what happened. Everything's a bit fuzzy and–"

Gideon inclined his head. "Not to worry, you can try again." She didn't miss the way he flexed his fist.

Ren clamped a hand over her forehead. "Ow!"

"Renée?"

"My head," Ren lied, "I think I need to lie down." She forced a smile she hoped didn't resemble a grimace too much. "Is that okay?"

It wasn't; that much was obvious from the way his mouth warped itself into a narrow line.

"Of course." He spoke as though the words tasted wrong on his tongue. "Krisha will accompany you back to your room."

Ren nodded, keeping her hand firmly in place over the right side of her forehead.

Krisha appeared by her side and together the pair turned away from Gideon, and Rosa, and the imposing wall of death.

As they reached the door, Ren faced him again. His expression was a stone cold mask.

"There are two days left," Ren began, "until my mum arrives?"

Gideon blinked, then nodded once. "Yes."

"Thanks," Ren replied, though she didn't know why. Krisha led her from the room. Ren's mind whirred. She hadn't asked about possibly seeing Lance, though perhaps that was best. The buzzing was low in her gut, though she suspected it would have been giving him some grief during her torment with the dead magic. Two days. She could hold out that long. Or, her makeshift migraine could.

As they exited the room the air was more breathable again, her thoughts clearer. Ren breathed a sigh. It had no visibly similar effect on Krisha, Gideon, or Rosa. Whatever it was, it had been Ren's burden alone to bear.

Gideon's voice was distant and cold, his words trailing behind them along the corridor. "I do hope you feel better, Renée."

24

Ren lay on her back, several hours later, staring first at nothing, then at what had to be at least several hundred separate things.

They still looked like fireflies.

It was dark in her room. What little Light magic there had been in the air had long been replaced by Dark. There was no light source of note, except her taio, and the...others. The specks of Dark, much like the Air ones, were acting weirdly. Ren swallowed, hard, looking this way and that. She had already tried the door, but found it locked. An ominous discovery.

The first night she had been too angry to notice them, and she'd spent a long time since in a similar vein. She was still angry, if the painful grooves in her palm her fingernails were causing were anything to go by, but she had experienced a shift, brought on by a sickening, crushing wave of a rise in the buzzing. For a minute or two, or twenty, the anger subsided, giving way only to fear. For him. Her stomach lurched as she thought of the dossier, then more as she remembered how his fingertips felt as they grazed her skin, soft, and rough. The way his arms held her.

The way it felt to kiss him.

Like home. His words.

Ren clamped her eyes shut, willing away tears. Were her hand throbbing less she might have punched the wall by the window again. Spots of blood were littered there from the previous evening.

It was then she noticed them.

Ren hadn't been around much *NeòNach*. For all the ones Shae had summoned in her presence, it hadn't been all that many, yet she had felt their influence on her own, usually a mere soft prickling, a brief annoyance.

Here they loomed, in the gaps and cracks, of which there were plenty, in the stone walls. Several gathered, hovering eerily, below the still splintered pieces of what was the desk. There was a similar, just visible, glow emanating from below her bed.

Thousands of specks of *NeòNach*. Surrounding her. Whether only in her room, or in the entire place, Ren didn't know. What she *did* know, however, was that they had been put there. Directed to stay there. With Ren.

Several of her own specks, red ones, appeared by Ren's clenched fist, and sparked upwards. They returned to her taio almost instantly. Far sooner than they normally would. Like the Dark and Air magic present naturally in the room, they were acting oddly. What she had been too preoccupied to notice before now made sense. Ren sighed. The *NáDarra* was surrounded and outnumbered by the *NeòNach* and it wasn't coping.

Neither was Ren.

Both the Dark and Air specks hung close to her, almost unmoving, unlike their usual behaviour. They knew, Ren supposed, they couldn't join her taio. Her best guess was that her own stores of both Dark and Air were full. She trailed her gaze to each one as she threw silent apologies into the air. It didn't seem fair.

A soft rapping at the door jolted her senses from the conflicting magic.

Krisha's silhouette emerged, lit from behind by the corridor outside.

Her voice was tentative. "Um, Ren?"

"Yeah?"

"I'm supposed to take you back."

"What, *now*?"

Krisha nodded.

Several of the Dark and Air specks floated past Krisha, away from the magical disarray of Ren's room. Ren let out a sigh for them.

"Tell them I still have a headache."

Shifting from one foot to the other, Krisha offered a soft half smile. "Gideon said he could help your head."

It hadn't been much of a plan to begin with, but staying out of his way was foiled. Ren swore aloud. Though she hadn't managed to twist enough so she could see it, her back was hurting from whatever he had done to her the previous day. "I-Krisha, I *can't!*"

Krisha's voice was low and rushed. "Listen to me." Her dark eyes bored into Ren's. "For now, you have to."

Ren's own voice was a laboured whisper. "He wants to *kill* my magic."

"I know." Her gaze darted around the room. "But right now-"

"What if they...?" Ren trailed off, not quite knowing how the question ended. *Take it,* she supposed was the most apt.

"You're a weaver." Krisha took a step closer.

Ren's face was hot. "I barely know what that means." She wasn't whispering anymore. "I don't understand enough to protect it."

"Only you can give your magic up." Krisha's pace had slowed as they approached a door, as unremarkable as all the others. "And they know that. I don't think Gideon expected you to resist yesterday."

"But what if-?" Ren found herself accompanying the other woman.

"Ren," Krisha pressed, her fingernails digging into Ren's forearm, her voice lower now they were walking, "If you leave now, while he's expecting you, Gideon will ensure you never see Lance again."

"Why? Can't we find someone else? There must be other Council people or..."

They were poised only a few steps from the door. Maybe she could leave, find somewhere to walk out, or someone else, another Council official. One less deranged. She had seen no others but she knew they existed thanks to Lance and Shae. They passed a particularly large crevice in the wall. How did Shae cope with entering this building on a regular basis? Perhaps that's why he was a Collector, so he didn't have to be around such disarray.

"Ren," Krisha whispered eventually, the words barely audible. "You aren't in the Council."

Ren gaped as they entered another corridor. Her mind was humming with too many questions and uncertainties. Did her mother really have anything to do with these people? What else had they lied about? The buzzing pulsed as Ren clenched her fist. All around her, on every piece of cracked and dilapidated stone, the image of Lance stared back at hers. Beside him stood the image of Shae.

What she would give to be able to break down.

She recognised little of the place, but two voices rose, coming from the other side of a nearby wooden door. The voices were heated, Gideon's more so.

"Push harder." It was Gideon.

"Graves *won't* give up anything."

Ren's mouth fell open, her head burling around to Krisha.

Krisha didn't return the gaze. Instead, her expression was set, her mouth a straight line, a mask of nonchalance. Only her eyes conveyed anything different. There was fear there...and something else.

"And the *other*? Any news?"

Rosa didn't answer right away. The apprehension was obvious. "No."

Ren didn't know who or what the *other* was, nor did she

have any inclination to dwell on it, but her mind, for the first time, blazed with a realisation that wasn't shrouded in hopelessness.

Brennett Graves was here, too.

What a bizarre thought, for *that* to be anything close to a comfort.

Mimicking Krisha's deadpan expression, Ren followed her towards the door.

She just had to get through whatever awaited her first.

"Ah, Renée," Gideon said as Ren appeared. He spoke her name in a way no one had in a long time. The way teachers had. Teachers who had usually wished to discuss why she had, yet again, been too sick to attend school. His words were measured, calm but not. "Have a seat." He nodded towards the table. The one Ren had sent a bolt of Lightning through had been replaced. This one looked older. Turning first to Rosa, whose trouser suit was a deep emerald, and next to Krisha, he said, "Leave us."

The door closed with a sharp thud.

Silence.

He was watching her with an air of scrutiny. "Sit."

Ren sat.

For a long moment, Gideon was silent. She wished he would seat himself opposite her. Instead, he stood, not two metres from her, looming tall and thin. His robes weren't thick, like Shae's cloak, they were sheer; Ren could see the small, silver buttons that lined the front of his shirt beneath. With each movement he made parts of the fabric flurried.

It was unsettling, his hovering. Ren swallowed dryly, facing ahead. She had felt them – or rather, her magic had – as she entered, she saw them. In corners, and in cracks. Thousands of them. Easy to miss, yet obvious now; brilliant white and ominous. Every speck of Ren's magic, nestled in place deep down in her mind, mirrored in her taio, was on edge. So was Ren.

She doubted he had any intention of offering her something for her feigned headache.

"Do you wonder," Gideon began, his words slow and careful, as though he valued each syllable, "why you were taken to another world?"

Something in his tone bristled her. Of course she had wondered. It was one of the things she had wondered about most since Shae had revealed the weighty truth. "Yes."

Closing the gap between himself and the table, Gideon placed his palms upon its top, interlacing his thin fingers. "Why you had to be *removed* from our society as an infant, hm?"

Removed. Ren felt cold, and then too hot. The *whoosh whoosh* of her pulse roared in her ears, yet she would have heard a pin drop. "Of course I do."

"Tell me, Renée, what is it you know of what you are?"

"Uh–"

"Provided you know anything, that is." Gideon's tone had soured; repulsion dripped from each word.

"I-I'm a weaver." Ren found her own voice far smaller than Gideon's. No longer did her eyes sweep the room; instead, they stared at Gideon's clasped hands. They were unscathed, flawless despite his years, save for the whiteness centred around each knuckle. A simple, silver band circled the fourth finger on his left hand.

She wondered whether she could strike this table down, too. Gideon's pointless questions, bitter as they were, would fare terribly against another bolt of Lightning. Though, would it be possible, with the sheer amount of *NeòNach* surrounding her? Ren remained motionless as she waited for him to respond. Inwardly, she readied a few purple Lightning flecks, before releasing her hold. Deep in her chest, the buzzing hummed. *He has Lance.*

"Weavers," Gideon said, "can control four elements." His voice was no longer calm and collected; emotion she couldn't place poured through each word. "You have six types of *NáDarra* within your taio."

For the first time, Ren's gaze ventured upwards. His face was a mask. Were his eyes not almost bulging, he might have appeared normal. "I know."

"Six, and still awakening."

It seemed fruitless to agree again. She looked at the table-top.

He droned on. "Even without *prior knowledge* we can assume you won't be fully awakened without all eight, can't we?"

It took her longer than it should have to acknowledge it was a question he was expecting to be answered. "Uh–"

"And therefore, Renée, it would be rather false to consider yourself a weaver."

Something about the way he spoke made her believe him. Believe the man she had only doubted this far. It wasn't a comforting thought.

"Oh."

Words, other ones, spoken by Shae what felt a long time ago, echoed in her mind: *It's...just very rare.* He hadn't looked at her when he'd said it.

"Are you aware, at all, of what happens when an element is awakened within you?"

Again, Ren swallowed, feeling both ignorant and confused. "I, well, I can *feel* it awakening, and–"

The snap in his tone was so sharp Ren flinched. "*Around* you, Renée. What happens *around you*?"

Ren's mouth opened and closed several times. "Th-the weather goes a bit funny," she replied meekly. Ren dared a glance upwards and wished she hadn't.

Gideon's expression was no longer composed, but wild and

staring, far darker than she had seen him.

The man looked livid.

And then, with a grimace that gave Ren the distinct impression it pained him to do so, their eyes met. When he spoke, his words were deep and slow. "I have known of your powers since before you were born."

Ren blinked. "Oh," she said again.

"Your mother was brought to me for assessment – a normal one, by all accounts. You see, Renée, all pregnant women who present signs of the child being gifted are assessed in the same way."

If he weren't talking as though she had outraged him for breathing, she might have found his words more interesting. Instead, Ren found herself barely taking the information in as her concentration centred on her chest, where her heart was pounding. Hard.

A creature caged behind the bars of her ribs, restless and fearful.

"This is a normal occurrence." He paused, surveying her through a dark and angry stare. "What wasn't normal was the results of your mother's assessment. All eight elements," he said. "There were three; three women. Three pregnancies. Three...*abominations*." The last word was whispered; it was worse than the loud disdain.

Ren barely heard it over the whoosh of her heartbeat. She wished she hadn't heard it at all.

"I, alone, knew the risks, presented the findings, and offered the...*solution*."

She dared herself to look at him. The darkness was no longer concentrated in his eyes. A not quite smile – a look so joyless could never be described as such – ghosted across his thin lips. "I was called mad," he informed her. "And cruel. Inhumane. The descriptors were numerous. But copious defiance lends us no truth. They were to be disastrous, the births. *Your* birth." Several of his long fingers twitched.

Ren's own were clasped together in her lap. It was the only thing that stopped them shaking. Deep inside, her magic was similarly tense.

"It wasn't disastrous." His whole expression blazed, with more than anger. "It was cataclysmic."

A heavy silence followed his words.

She waited for him to speak again. When he didn't, she looked down.

When she could bear the quiet no longer, Ren opened her mouth. She had to know, though she didn't want to. Shae hadn't known, and neither had Lance. "What do you mean?"

"I wasn't there at your birth," Gideon began, "I arrived after. To disaster." A lump had formed in Ren's throat, making swallowing difficult. "As you came into this world, *thousands* left it. All because your selfish mother took no heed of the warnings – *my* warnings." He was raving, his earlier composure entirely vanished. *Thousands.*

"I-I didn't–"

"Would you like to know the estimated death count from that day? Not many are privy to such information."

She wouldn't, but nodded as a single tear tracked its way down her cheek.

"Two hundred thousand."

What?

"In Caeracre alone."

Because of her? But, Ren hadn't...Ren was only a baby. She sucked in a shaky breath as she tried to picture two hundred thousand people. She couldn't.

"Tell me, Renée, the world you were fortunate enough to grow up in, is it thriving?"

Depends on who you ask, Ren thought.

"Are crops capable of growing without being wiped out by

earthquake after earthquake? The sunlight able to shine without risk of wildfires, rain without floods?"

Her mind drifted momentarily to the parts of Caeracre countryside she had witnessed. Each a barren wasteland.

"For the most part," she replied, voice small.

His voice was low and dangerous once again. "And, do you think we have such luxuries here?"

Swallowing, Ren shook her head, saying nothing.

"Do you know why?"

She could take a guess – an educated one – but didn't. Ren shook her head again.

"Because of you."

Gideon led her through several empty corridors, each as decrepit as the last.

Ren wished he would take her to her room; at least there she could attempt to gather some thoughts. As she walked, trailing just behind him like a miserable shadow, they were anything but gathered. Instead, strewn into every corner and crevice her mind possessed, fitful at best, screaming at worst.

Neither Krisha nor Rosa were anywhere to be found. She missed Krisha. She even hoped for Rosa, not that she felt much for the woman. Being alone with Gideon had shown something else, something dangerous. An inherent madness, festering in every glare he shot her, each stride he took. And it stemmed from a hatred he had held onto Ren's entire life.

Twenty years was a long time to cling to such contempt.

Perhaps Rosa grounded him somewhat.

More than once, Ren contemplated running, but in such a labyrinth, what chance had she of escaping? And if she managed to pull off what slim chance there was at making it outside, she was certain Gideon would manage to give an order, somehow, to have Lance hurt...or worse.

They pressed on.

"There are those who think you are powerful," he informed her.

Ren said nothing.

"It's ironic, really, that one can wield so much power, and yet still be killed by a fall, or a bite...or a blade."

Ren swallowed. Were his words a threat? Probably.

"Do you know, Renée, why it was imperative I had you brought here?"

"No."

"You cannot guess, even with the damage your mere awakenings have been capable of?"

"Th-they haven't caused any damage." The garden fence notwithstanding...

"The earthquake, which I assume accompanied your Ground awakening, was felt three miles from your location." If she could see his face, she was certain his eyes were bulging again. "At *least* fifty buildings were left in need of repair."

"Oh." Though, really, had her Ground not awakened there and then they would have been a nice snack for the pack of angry cat-sìth.

"You're lucky no one was killed."

No one else, Ren thought sadly.

"The Shimmering Vale is still flooded."

The what? Then she remembered. The series of rivers they'd had to cross after entering Ververos. She had nearly died there, though said nothing. She doubted Gideon would feel anything other than regret that she had survived.

"You're only two elements away from being fully awakened. Do you know what will happen when your final element awakens?"

"No," Ren said again. They were passing a wall into which several strokes had been carved. Dozens of identical, vertical lines, each around an inch long. They were separated, in places, by several indecipherable dark stains. Every few feet there was a door, each looking the same as the last. A small, rectangular window criss-crossed with metal bars. Ren swallowed.

As they travelled, Ren caught sight of yet more white specks of *NeòNach*. Always hidden, in cracks and gaps, as though lurking. Every so often she checked on her own magic. It still shook. The longer they walked, the more Ren felt the same sense of suppression bearing down on her, as though the concentration of *NeòNach* was increasing.

"An immense surge of *NáDarra'n* energy will occur, Renée. Far greater than those during single awakenings." He led them down yet another, identical hallway. "The like of which you have experienced once before, though you won't remember." He said it as though he was making a great but hollow joke that Ren failed to grasp. "I do, though."

Ren barely heard him as she surveyed the doors. They could only be cells. Ren opened her mouth – to ask what, she wasn't sure – when Gideon stopped so abruptly Ren nearly walked into his back.

They were in front of a door unlike the others. There was no window, and no bars. Its perimeter was littered with yet more *NeòNach*.

"I ensured you were brought here," he began, "so that were your final awakening to go ahead, it wouldn't cause the same destruction as your birth."

"You ensured I was brought...here."

Ren, you aren't in the Council.

*But...*Ren frowned as several pieces of information she had accumulated from various sources all fought for dominance within her mind.

The only place there would reasonably be cells would be a prison. Ren sucked in a breath.

She was in Endermarch.

He placed one bony finger on the door's surface. "I had to." Silently, it swung open.

"But you said..." The dossier flashed in front of her mind's eye. "Loreleith. That Lance had..."

Inside, there appeared to be a vast, empty chamber.

For the first time in all the time she had spent in his company, Gideon laughed. It was a faithless sound. "Very astute, Renée. How out of character." He nodded ahead, to the chamber. "After you."

Her heartbeat pounded in her ears as she took a half step backwards, away from him. "Why?" In her chest, the buzzing lurched, then quelled. Nausea crept up Ren's throat. It had looked so real, the dossier. And a part of her had believed him, Gideon. Believed that Lance, that Shae....

Ren hated him. Hated herself more.

"It is simple enough, and I shall explain once you step inside here—"

Again, the buzzing momentarily rose.

"No." Ren took another step. "Why did you lie?"

Gideon regarded her coolly. "I believed the emotional distress would be enough to provoke another awakening."

"But why would y–?"

"Apparently, I was mistaken. Now, Renée, if you would." He gestured once more towards the doorway sounding, if anything, bored.

"Was anything you told me true? Did my birth r–?"

"Everything you have learnt today is true."

Two hundred thousand. Surely that should have been the lie. Ren's heart ached for such a wrong to right itself, her soul aching alongside it. The buzzing pounded wildly with her pulse.

Her gaze rose to his. A steely grey, so distant she wondered if he saw her at all.

Something flip flopped from her chest into her gut. "Is my mother really coming?"

The thread of Gideon's patience snapped. His hand gripped her arm, below her shoulder.

She was shoved towards the door. Ren shouted, her body twisting, with no success. She was already thrust through before she remembered the knife. As he let her go, her body slamming into the stone floor, Ren felt her way to her ankle.

The door was closing before she got as far as lifting her trouser leg.

Before the thud of the door left her in silence and loneliness came Gideon's final words. "I have no idea where your mother is."

She didn't have time to process his words, and though they weren't surprising, they stung. Or they would have, if at that moment a jet stream of fire hadn't charged towards her, narrowly missing her head.

"Agh!" Ren ducked, scanning the chamber before she was forced, stumbling, sideways. A boulder the size of a basketball exploded against the wall by the door into dozens of small pieces of what looked like dirt.

What the–?

Boom.

It echoed from the other end of whatever the hell this torture chamber was. It was followed by several smaller bangs.

Oh good, Ren thought, hissing as a falling rock bounced off the top of her head. *The room is capsizing.* She backed up, shrinking herself against the wall, surveying the scene. The grey chamber now looked like it had given home to an apocalypse. Fire roared, pouring from unseen sources, and boulders, some as small as marbles, others the size of Ren's old car, crashed down from who knew where. She dropped to a crouch as something hit her leg. She didn't feel it. From nowhere, and also everywhere, a deep rumbling encased the chamber as rocks began to pelt from above. Ren, still crouching, took off, skirting the walls, past fire and steam and blinding flashes of brilliant light. The deafening sounds of crashing rocks blocked out all cohesive thoughts but one: *Stay alive.*

The most alarming part wasn't the falling boulders, the debris of which Ren had to dodge at a rate that far exceeded her fitness level; it was the noise. The crashes each boulder made upon contact with the floor, or wall, were deafening. They split into smaller pieces on impact, all of which shattered randomly, which only gave Ren more to run from. The space was around the size of two tennis courts side by side. Ren sprinted from one end to the other.

Her skin was slick with sweat, hair clinging to her face and neck. Pushing a few stray strands from her eyes, Ren deliberated. She had found her way to the corner furthest from the door and was backed up as much as possible against the smooth, hot stone. As she panted, the falling rocks seemed to have subsided for the moment. Then they gave way for the fire jets to pelt at full force. Angry flames were pouring into the room.

Her brain, as much as she willed it to clear and present her with the answers to her survival, was fogged, her thoughts either too fast, too slow, and too muddled all at once.

Stay alive.

Ren panted, hard and fast, as the flames hastened to cover the room. One stream was to her right, elbow height. Ren watched the flames cut harsh shapes and unnatural angles through the smoke and air. She lowered herself further down and blinked. At first, she ran. Ran for her damn life with little more than adrenaline to guide her.

That had been dumb. Ren, through a gulp of nausea, scolded herself.

You're an elemental.

NáDarra flowed through her, *in* her. When it was around her, she knew.

And yet, through panic or ignorance, she hadn't known.

A what? The memory was hazy as she gulped smoke that felt only like hot air. Her eyes roamed over the nearby flames.

Someone that can control NáDarra.

Deep inside, through panic and nausea, a part of her stirred.

A part both new and familiar. The part that would save her.

Ren blinked at the chaos, at the fire and the flashes and the boulders, but didn't see them. Instead, she saw fireflies. And then she swallowed. Because the fireflies were wrong.

The magic was wrong.

Each remnant from each boulder, every flash and flame, was shrouded in tiny specks of white, smaller than any fleck of *NáDarra*.

Ren hadn't sensed them because this fire hadn't been created with *NáDarra*.

Technically, it can also mimic NáDarra, in a sense, but it's weak, and can be overpowered by its natural form very easily.

Ren swallowed again, and readied herself. As though of their own volition, specks of red had begun to appear by both of her palms. They weren't sparking; they were shaking still, a heavy weight of reluctance surrounding them.

But they were there, for Ren. More and more each second. Until a soft tug somewhere deep inside, which Ren knew was on her taio, meant she was approaching the point when she couldn't bring forth any more.

Still though, she had hundreds. She guided them forward, towards the imitation. They didn't hurry, and Ren didn't hurry them. Around such high levels of *NeòNach*, her specks were fearful.

As she watched them, something broke through the panic and fear: pride. A pride others would never understand but one she always would.

The first of Ren's specks had reached the pretend Fire. Their shaking had intensified as they'd travelled, and on contact they began to reverberate wildly. Ren would have felt it had she not seen. Something, somewhere within herself, reverberated, too.

One by one, speck by speck, they started to not only vibrate but swirl, circling the *NeòNach* over and over, dampening its effects and, eventually, overpowering it. As Ren's magic worked against the other, the flecks of brilliant white began to leave the fire, floating away as their purpose was taken. They dissipated, floating away in different directions. A smell like burning rubber hit her as the last of the first jet stream was lost in a blurry haze of Ren's specks. Set into the wall, through which the *NeòNach* was evidently fed, was a pipe, an inch or two wide, and still open.

Ren searched for something, a piece of debris that might fit. Unless...

There were still at least four fires, but she could spare other specks.

She decided to bring forth several specks of Water magic and guided them towards the pipe opening. They slotted in tightly. For the first time since entering the chamber – and perhaps since she had left Shin – the hint of a smile ghosted Ren's lips. It was gone as quickly as it had come, but it meant something. Ren turned, eyeing the next fire and readying her own. They weren't shaking as hard; neither was she.

It meant she could beat this.

The second stream was extinguished quicker than the first. Ren continued down the chamber, the hiss of the remaining fires a stark contrast to her dull footsteps and thumping heartbeat. Nearing the third stream, Ren lifted her hands to direct her specks when a familiar boom echoed around the room.

She screamed as the boulders started. As before, they crashed against walls and floor, erupting into dirt. One cascaded into the back of her shoulder with a painful blow, the force throwing her downwards. With barely time to cough, a sinister whistling of something hurtling through the air towards her forced her up, and running, to a wall, any wall. Not that they provided any shelter. She would have to return to her corner, dodging the boulders, waiting...

No.

Earth exploded around her, so close that clumps of it were caught in her hair, bouncing off her legs, surrounded by tiny specks of white.

This was no more Ground magic than the fires were Fire magic.

Ren's green Ground specks left her taio easily, and though they shook, they yielded, hurtling towards an oncoming boulder. They met it in mid-air and Ren watched, half fearful, half fascinated, as fireworks of white and green swirled and battered against each other. It was Ren's Ground specks that won, though, and the *NeòNach* floated away, joining its counterparts that had made up the false fire.

She didn't have time to dwell on their whereabouts – not with the barrage of further boulders her magic had to contend with. Some, the smaller ones, were almost easy. But the larger ones needed more Ground magic to collapse. Ren felt the struggle, and produced as many specks as she could, careful not to push too hard. Some had to stay within her taio.

Before long, each step she took, along with each attack her magic pushed on a new boulder, was arduous. Exhaustion gripped her, slowing her limbs. She felt each assault her magic made within herself. Even when she directed her Fire specks to join the Ground, which did very little to help the situation, there was no solace from each small victory. With every boulder, at least five more appeared. Ren searched upwards, but there was no obvious answer this time; no pipes for her to block.

She was hit again and again. Eventually she felt none at all, not understanding why her knees buckled. She only understood that neither she nor her magic could continue for long. But the rate of boulders, she thought, perhaps wrongly, did seem to be slowing. Ren's Ground specks flew at a sphere the size of a large dog. The altercation took a long time, and Ren took a bashing from several smaller boulders as her magic worked, and eventually decimated the imitation Ground, separating it into pieces that rained down upon her.

There were fewer. She could do it. *They* could do it. Ren stayed on the ground, panting and directing her magic. She felt neither pain nor nausea, only grit.

They were near the end. There were three, only three. Ren grasped a sliver of hope. If she could finish off the remaining boulders, she would have three jet streams of fire left. She could manage that.

And then there were two. The bigger of the two she shot her magic at, but the smaller, she had little choice but to cover her head and duck. She felt nothing of it, but was hurled against a nearby wall.

Silence.

Maybe...she'd won? Through bleary eyes she saw specks, hers, both red and green, surround her.

And then what feeling there was in her body turned cold, as a boom – louder than any that had come from the boulders – rang out, followed by a flash.

Lightning.

She would have to fight false *NeòNach* lightning.

Get up, Ren thought, but it was useless. A second boom reverberated around her, forcing her eyes closed. She struggled, attempting to force them open again, but it felt hopeless to try. She couldn't. She tried to move her arm. Couldn't.

Another flash met her closed lids.

Only then did she feel pain.

And then nothing.

A loud groan broke through an expanse of darkness, followed by a sharp pain that coursed through the side of her head, then another down the right side of her ribs. A further groan.

Ren's groan.

As she slowly came to, so did various jolts of pain. They were impossible to distinguish between, her body a solid wall of ache. As hard as it was to concentrate on anything other than the multitude of sores, she sought out the buzzing. The only tangible thing that still tied her to Lance. *Still there*, Ren told herself. *I miss you.* It pulsed, steady and defiant, beside her probably broken ribs. *I doubted you.* The realisation was worse than any pain. *I'm so sorry.*

Through her own laboured breathing, a set of soft footsteps met her ears. She couldn't see Gideon, not now. Not after....

Each detail of what had occurred since she had last met him hit her, one by one, each assaulting her in painful detail. Lies and truths. And torture. The chamber with its unrelenting barrage of attacks stayed at the forefront of her mind, the memory unyielding. Gideon's voice, ever present, echoed close by.

Two hundred thousand.

Something burned in her chest. And her throat. Somewhere, that wasn't in the past, a door squeaked open.

Because of you.

She barely had the chance to turn onto her side – a complicated manoeuvre given the state of her – before vomit, hot and awful, sprayed from her mouth.

"Oh." More footsteps, much closer this time. "Oh no." The

voice, at least, was female.

Ren found herself blinking at Krisha.

"Ren," she said quietly. Her shoulders were slumped, her skin splotchy, eyes red. She looked as though she hadn't slept in days.

Ren swallowed, willing the taste of sick away. "Hi," she croaked, turning, with difficulty, onto her back once more, hoping something might hurt less. Nothing did.

New guilt seeped over Ren as Krisha busied herself cleaning the vomit from the cracked stone floor. She looked at what she could see of the room. She had been placed in the same ward as before, on a bed too hard and too cold, even to Ren. Ren wrinkled her nose, then immediately regretted it, adding the front of her face to her long list of pained body parts.

As before, only Ren's bed was occupied. The room was lit by a few meagre torches. The small window opposite was all that broke up the cracked grey of the walls. Beyond the pane, Air magic danced across a dark sky. Inside, there were far fewer Air, and even less Dark. The ones inside didn't dance.

She turned her head back towards Krisha. "I'm sorry, for..." Ren trailed off.

Krisha was on her knees, her forehead bobbing into Ren's line of sight every few seconds as she cleaned. "Don't be sorry."

Ren still felt it, for many reasons. Namely, two hundred thousand of them.

"He lied," Ren said. She'd intended the words to be a question, but they felt no more than a statement. A flat one Ren should have known the truth of it sooner than she had. The realisation burned all over again.

Krisha rose, offered Ren a small smile that was shrouded in hopelessness, then sighed. "He did."

Ren took a deep breath that caused several pangs of pain. "So did you."

She blinked. "I-I don't–"

"Your tattoo. I saw it the first night."

She paled. "Ah."

"Lance has the same one."

She only nodded.

"Do you think he was going to sell me?"

For a split second, she looked to the centre of Ren's chest. It was all the clarification Ren needed. Silently, the other woman shook her head.

"You can sense bonds," Ren said.

Also not a question, but Krisha nodded anyway.

"You know, your face when Rosa mentioned Brennett, it was–" Ren stopped, almost amused at the way the other woman's eyes grew large, "exactly like it is now, Priya."

"That...it's complicated."

"Yeah. I imagine having an affair with your boyfriend's best friend, then letting said boyfriend believe you were dead for years would make things complicated."

Priya opened her mouth, then closed it again. When she spoke her words were slow, measured. Glancing over her shoulder, Priya swallowed. "I didn't know about the deal. I didn't know he'd been arrested until I returned. Which I shouldn't have."

"So, why not leave?"

"I–" Priya swallowed. "I'm not here by choice. When I came back, I was arrested. There'd been a warrant. Thanks, Lance," she added dryly.

...and instead of locking me up, offered me a job in exchange for anything I could give them on Brennett Graves and anyone we'd associated with.

"Anyway," Priya continued, "I was in the Council chambers and Gideon appeared and brought me here. He had all my identification, and details of every member of my family. One year of service – that's what he said – and I was free to leave. That was over two years ago."

"He knows your real name?"

Priya sucked in a breath. "Technically, Krisha *is* my real name. I hate it," she added bitterly.

"But, did you ever think of going back to the real Council? Telling them."

"Ren, Gideon is still High Councillor."

"But you said–"

"We're not *in* the Council, no, but Gideon is High Councillor. He *is* the Council. And I'm still wanted. Here, it's been... safer, in a sense. Then another prison might've been."

"But the rest of the Council can't know," Ren glanced around, "about this or me, or..."

Priya shook her head. "They don't. Endermarch isn't supposed to be in operation."

For the first time since realising Brennett was in the same building, Ren felt something stir, something akin to hope. "Then we can tell them, we can–"

"Ren, I don't know everything." Priya's words were lower than before, and she spoke them with a soft hiss. "But I do know he murdered every other Council member who knew of your existence – at least twenty, maybe more."

"But, why–?"

"I don't know. But getting you here has consumed him."

"But surely the Council should know, and maybe there's another way for my magic to fully awaken, one that won't involve...it won't be...like it was when I was born."

"There might be," she acknowledged. "He told you?"

"He told me I killed two hundred thousand people."

Priya's mouth was a set line. "Two of them were his wife and daughter."

Ren felt a sudden urge to vomit again. "His wife, and..."

Nodding, Priya took a shaky breath. "It's never been about anything else, not for Gideon."

Ren had known, at some point during her last conversation with him, that something had turned. She knew it now to be a truth she would never wish to acknowledge.

It was about revenge.

"Priya," Ren breathed, "what do I do?"

Priya's eyes darted at first over her shoulder, to the door, and then to the window opposite, before she dug in her pockets and pulled out two items, the first a small vial of gold liquid. "You take this." She reached forward, allowing Ren to pull herself, with much grimacing and grunting, so she was sitting. She held up the second item. It was smaller than Shae's had been, and had, if Ren remembered right, different markings upon its smooth surface. "And if we can get out of here before sunrise, which is when he's expecting you to wake, we leave." Priya placed the scrystone back into her pocket.

"We leave," Ren repeated. The hope-like something stirred again, as though sniffing the first air of spring after a long winter. She took a shaky breath. "But your identification, your family?" Ren wondered what the word meant here. Did people from Caerisle use passports? Once – *if* – they escaped, she would ask.

Priya nodded once, she looked sad, but determined. She looked past Ren. "I think this might be more important for everyone. But we must get you to the Council, Ren." Her words were rushed yet she stressed each syllable. "Because I don't think he's wrong about what will happen when your eighth element awakens. He wanted it to happen in the chamber."

Ren's throat was dry. "He...*wanted* my last elements to awaken?"

Priya nodded again. "He had the chamber specially made; he thinks it will contain your last awakening. And weaken you."

"But why?"

"I think, after you're fully awakened, he intends to extract your elements. In *this* state," she gestured down Ren's torso ,"he thinks you're more likely to give them up willingly."

"Why?"

Priya swallowed. "Th-there's more. Ren, after extracting your magic, he intends to kill you."

Her pulse whooshed wildly in her ears.

"Kill–"

Priya nodded. "And," she paused to take a long breath, "tomorrow morning he's planning to do what he did before, with the other Council members, ones who know about you."

"But there aren't any other Council members who know about me."

"Ren, I don't just mean *Councillors*, I mean–"

It hit her with the force of a hurricane.

Ren's voice was both hoarse and squeaky. "Collectors." Ren took a breath as she tried to twist her torso. The pain tore through her. "If you're found helping me..."

Priya regarded her for a few seconds in silence. "I left Lance to deal with Brennett's almighty mess alone. It feels like the least I can do is make sure the one he's bound to gets out of here before..."

"I need to find him. *Free* him, I–" Once again, guilt flooded her, the words *believed Gideon* hung in the air between them.

"I know where he's being held, but it's not like here. To break him out would be almost impossible."

"Unless..." Ren reached for the vial. She probably should have hesitated, once upon a time would have. Instead, she downed the liquid in one.

Priya's voice was small. "I don't think you'll have much of a chance of–"

"*I* won't, no." Ren's mind was whirring as a warmth spread

from her throat to each of her extremities. Deep inside, in the place she connected with her taio, every speck of magic she possessed shifted. Possibly due to Priya's potion. Possibly something else. Fire began to spark once more. Green Ground specks wove, this way and that. Water arched and Lightning crashed. Determination and hope rose in her chest. The buzzing rose, too. "But someone with a really, really good criminal mind might."

Priya's mouth fell open. "You cannot mean what I think you mean." Her voice squeaked.

"Do you know where he is?"

For a second, Priya only blinked, then sighed. "If he murders me," she said, allowing her eyes to close for a second as she paused, "my death will be on your conscience."

"Noted."

Priya's slim frame was deceptively strong. A relief, considering Ren had relied on the woman not only to help her dress and shimmy herself off the bed, but to get through Endermarch prison.

They walked, Ren leaning almost her entire weight against Priya, through a labyrinth of corridors, all as decrepit as the rest of the place, their way lit by streams of moonlight through the few windows they came across.

"This," Ren began, her words strained through her pain, "is...brave of you. Thank you."

"Don't thank me yet; we still might get caught."

"That's...why...I'm thanking you now," Ren spluttered, feeling a crushing pressure in her chest with each cough. It was only partly true, but somehow 'and also I might die in the next ten minutes' might put more of a dampener on their already mad plan.

Priya inclined her head towards a nearby stairwell. "The

cells are down there." And then to a heavy-set concrete door to their left. "And that's a way out. An unguarded one," she added. "Which is a rarity."

Ren looked towards the single door, but didn't see it. Instead, she saw Gideon, with his desperate madness, seeking her. If her throbbing, weakened body told her anything, it was that she couldn't face the chamber again. Maybe that was his plan all along: to weaken her will to the point that, after her final awakening, she would hand her magic over to whatever end he needed it for. Ren couldn't put herself in a position where she was presented with the choice; she didn't know if she was brave enough to make the right one. Her dad would have. So would Luke. *So would Lance.* The door swam into view. She could run through it and leave this place of pain and horror.

"R-Ren?"

How long had she stood there, staring at the exit? Long enough to dwell on not one, but two, imaginary boxes: one, Lance's, which simply refused to shut, and one closed so tight it would have taken several power tools to unlock were it a real, tangible thing.

It hurt, more so than her ribs, her face, her legs, but Ren allowed the thought to sweep across her mind. Two separate embraces, one maternal and the other...everything. Things both from long ago, and not, of scenes and sayings and tears and laughter, filled her all at once. Ren allowed herself to do the one thing she swore she wouldn't.

...and that's how we'll always find each other.

Ren let herself remember. Not only the bad. But the good.

And there had been so much good.

She turned to Priya. And then to the stairs. No words passed between the two as they made their way towards the first step.

At the bottom step, Ren clutched both palms to her right

side, fighting the constant urge to cry out..

They had emerged in another corridor, this one danker than the ones above. More cracks littered the walls, along with a powerful stink of mould. There were, however, far fewer specks of *NeòNach*. Perhaps Gideon had only ensured they stayed where Ren was. Perhaps due to their absence, or the sheer adrenaline keeping her upright, there was a slight lifting in the air around her. Deep within, her own stock of magic wove and danced. It strengthened her somehow. If they weren't shaking, then Ren didn't need to.

"Here." Priya placed a black pellet, around the size of Ren's thumbnail, into Ren's palm. "I took this from Gideon's lab."

"He has a *lab* here?"

"He has three," She nodded. "He's obsessed with the study of *NáDarra* – or, he was. Now he just seems to be obsessed with you. I don't think anything he's developed in it is legal."

Ren examined the pellet. "And this…"

"If the notes are right, if it's squeezed, it should produce a gas: a huge burst of oxygen and Air magic, I think. Only someone gifted in Air could breathe it without fainting."

The other woman's eyes bored into Ren's, her gaze set, ready. An understanding passed between them. Since they had left the ward, Ren had regarded Priya as her out, without considering that she might also be Priya's.

"So, I just have to…squeeze it?"

"Yes. But all the guards will need to be in the same place. The gas isn't supposed to have much spread."

Ren tried not to think too hard about the task at hand. The pellet sat, nestled within her sweat-slicked palm. It looked a small, innocent thing.

Taking as deep a breath as her painful ribcage allowed, Ren nodded. "Okay, how do we get them in the same place?"

"We get them in the control room."

"And where's that?"

"Through there." Priya nodded ahead to where a single door stood. Beyond, Ren heard nothing. "All the blocks are set out the same way. There will be two doors: straight ahead leads to the block and the one on the right leads to the control room. It looks out into the block. You'll have to take the keys off one of their belts – they should all have a set. There's a window where you can throw them out."

"To you?"

Priya nodded. "If I head back up the stairs, and out the other door, I can reach the outside of the cell block and attempt to open the other main door into the block. It won't open, of course, but it should be enough to set the alarm off. Then I'll wait outside the control room window."

"All right, Butch Cassidy."

"Who?"

"Doesn't matter. So, I wait 'til I hear the alarm?"

Priya nodded. "They'll head to the control room. Wait maybe half a minute, then release the gas into the room after them. Once they're unconscious and you've thrown the keys, I'll get in the main door and find Brennett, and hope he doesn't crush my head into the wall." It was the part she sounded the least sure of. "You'll either need to climb out the window after the keys, though." She paused. "Perhaps you'd better just walk through to the end of the block – that's where the door is. And where we will be."

Where you should *be,* a small voice in Ren's mind said. Far too many parts of Priya's plan depended on what ifs. What if Priya didn't manage to set the alarm off? What if the guards didn't head to the control room? What if either of them were seen? What if Brennett did crush Priya's head into the wall?

And yet, as Ren watched the other woman, it was there again. In the way Priya carried herself that little bit straighter. And her eyes, even in the dim light, shone a little brighter. *That was over two years ago.* It held her, in barely noticeable ways: hope.

The strongest thing either woman possessed.

It also offered a small look into the type of woman who falls for Brennett Graves.

"And then," Priya was saying, "we leave."

Ren took a breath. What absolute absurdity. If her father could see her now, he'd need a long sit down and a beer, maybe a gin. Then, Ren realised, he would tell her to *hot foot back up those stairs, Renée,* and he'd *mean it.* Or, Ren, still holding her side, readying herself, perhaps he would pat her on the shoulder, with a sparkle in his eye not unlike the one in Priya's, and tell Ren as he chuckled in the way he always did how you could *examine the engine 'til you're blue in the face, but sometimes you just gotta get in an' turn the damn key.* The door, old and grey, loomed ahead.

"Turn the damn key."

Priya blinked "What?"

"Nothing, I–" Their eyes met. Ren nodded. "Then we leave."

With Priya by her side, it had been far easier to grasp at a false sense of bravado. As Priya's footsteps disappeared to the floor above, Ren was far too aware of her solitude. *It's for Lance*, Ren told herself. *It's for mum.*

Doing her best to ignore her aching everything, Ren approached the door. *This is insane*, she told herself. In her mind, she sought the place that connected her with her taio. If nothing else, she should probably have some specks on standby. Like an elemental would. When – she tried hard not to think *if* – she saw Shae again, he'd be proud.

She waited, lump in throat. For now, it all rested on Priya.

And then it would all rest on Ren.

Knowing very little of the building's layout, she had no way to know how long Priya was supposed to take. Not that it mattered, she supposed, for time might as well have stopped.

After a while, she counted her own heartbeats.

Just as she was wondering what her course of action should be were the alarm never to sound – around heartbeat one hundred and fifty two – a siren began to wail through the walls of the quiet prison. Though Ren had been expecting it, *hoping* for it, the noise cut through her. Each note of it started low but grew in intensity to a huge, wailing boom, ringing out, then starting again.

A heavy squeak, alongside several sets of muffled steps, met her ears. The guards.

Ren swallowed, waiting. At least three – no, four – sets of footsteps and several exclamations. Ren heard a door bang shut. She pushed the first door open.

It was far heavier than Ren's weakened body was prepared for, though it swung inwards soundlessly. She emerged, puffing, in a smallish grey square, and was met with the sight of two further doors. The first, opposite the one she had entered through, was heavier than the second. Faded letters were plastered across the front. *No Unauthorised Entry.* A sign reading *Guards Only* was below. To one side there was a keyhole and three separate bolts, though none were drawn. At least she didn't have to worry about that one; not yet anyway. She turned to the other. There were neither warning signs nor heavy bolts, just a simple handle. And the sound of different voices.

Push it under the door, Priya had instructed. The pellet was lodged between the pads of her thumb and middle finger. Ren swallowed, then pushed them together. It flattened. At first there was nothing unusual. Ren, frowning as her heart pounded harder still, examined the thing. It happened quietly, a gentle hiss before a slight rush of cold met the inside of her palm. As if from nowhere, a steady stream of white Air specks began to emerge. Ren gasped. As quickly as she could, given the state of her ribs, she bent double, wincing, placed the pellet on the ground, and flicked it through.

Ren waited.

Two definite thuds. One rather loud *what the fuck.* One boom. One scream. And a vast array of Air magic zooming back from under the door. Ren took as long a breath as she dared, and reached for the handle.

The room was small. She could make out the line where the ceiling met the wall, and not much else. Ren's mouth opened in surprise. How had such a concentration of Air magic been encased in that tiny pellet? The specks were chaotic, not content with their usual gentle blustery movements, but instead opting to rave. Visibility was poor and the small area had developed its own wind pattern. Pieces of paper blew into Ren's face. She ducked to the side, a new wave of pain radiating from her side as she nearly tripped over something soft, which turned out to be a leg.

Okay, Ren thought, *get keys.* Simple enough.

She crouched, a groan escaping her, and began to fumble her way, crudely, around the leg. The alarm stopped then, as abruptly as it had begun. Her ears rang with a high continuous note as staggered shouts rang out from her left – the block. Confused prisoners, no doubt. How many people did Gideon hold here, and why?

Ren snaked her hand inside the pockets of the man on the ground. She felt no pride in it. His pockets held a bar of chocolate, a small ornament she couldn't make out, and a heavy ring of keys. Though she returned the ornament, she pocketed the chocolate. Not many things outweighed her guilt, but chocolate was, undoubtedly, one of them. Attached to his belt she found what looked like a maroon baton. She heard very little – no ringing or distant cries – as she took it. *Just in case,* she told herself.

Ren stood, hoisting herself upright with a nearby table. All she had to do was reach the window. Across an ocean of white specks and the miniature gale, she could make out a rectangular outline.

She could make it. She *was* making it. The window appeared like a mirage. The briefest of smiles ghosted her lips as she approached, her hand outstretched for the handle. She'd made it. The window swung inwards. Several white flecks darted past her into the night beyond, and a voice rang through the whirl of Ren's pain and relief.

Only, it wasn't coming from outside.

Nor was it Priya's.

"What the fuck is this?"

Ren froze, gripping the keys. She threw them hastily out the open window, not checking to see if they made contact with Priya, or even if Priya was there. She whirled around. If Priya acknowledged them, Ren didn't hear it. Her attention was demanded by the string of expletives being thrown across the heavy blanket of Air magic. Visibility was still limited, though after a second or two, or ten, Ren made out a silhouette, and ducked.

It hurt. A lot. She concealed her hiss of pain only by clamping her teeth together so tightly it was a miracle they didn't shatter.

An uncomfortable tingle rose across the tops of her arms, spreading down into her chest. The man, whoever he was, was walking forwards. Each step he took seemed to echo. Ren shimmied to the side, sliding her boots along the concrete floor as quietly as her injuries allowed. She found herself beneath a nearby table. The man, having reached the window only a second or two after Ren, was grunting throatily.

She should have followed the keys out the window.

Only someone gifted in Air magic could breathe it without fainting. That was all well and good, until one booted and angry guard, who just happened to be an Air bearer, was mere inches from Ren's bent knee. He'd settled in front of the window, the route that should have been hers.

He swore. Under her breath, Ren did the same. Her hair whipped around her face, half covering her eyes and sticking to her lips. The wind was growing stronger, along with, Ren suspected, this man's contempt. He grunted again.

Ren could hardly blame him for being angry, though as one of the boots slammed down again, missing her by a mere inch or two, she wished he were more amenable. Above her, a roar was barely audible over the room's weather. Enough clarification that *amenable* was the last thing he was.

Beneath her table, Ren began to move. She could skirt to the side of him, then head back towards the door, now her only chance of escape.

She could see little but the zooming specks of white; felt nothing but pain and the sting of freezing wind.

As she approached the end of the table that would give her a clearish path to the door, Ren twisted, readying herself. The action, though slight, caused yet more pain. Ren gasped, stumbling enough for her shoulder to jolt the table leg. A scraping, barely audible over the wind, filled the room.

As much as her body screamed to cry out, Ren managed to clamp a palm to her mouth. But it was too late. The boots turned in her direction, and a pair of knees appeared. This time, her gasp wasn't stifled.

She had barely a second to pull together a cohesive thought. In her hand, the baton she'd stolen shook. *No,* something told her. Once again, Shae's words filled her.

Think like an elemental.

There was Air: Ren had Air and wind in abundance. But so did he. A flash of wonder sparked deep down, close to the place she held the magic of her taio.

She couldn't use Air.

And with the excess oxygen released within the pellet, adding Fire into the mix would likely kill every guard in the place; maybe make the building explode.

Water. No, any amount of Water combined with *that* much wind would create a tsunami.

Think like an elemental.

She didn't need something that would exacerbate the already present Air.

Dark? Maybe. Lightning? Too temperamental.

No.

A half-concealed face appeared, his eyes two beady orbs glinting through a mass of white.

Before he so much as blinked, Ren sent forth a stream of specks. Green ones. *Ground* ones. Heading to the point where his boots met the floor.

It happened in a cry and a crunch so loud it swallowed the deafening roar from the wind. Below his soles, the concrete shifted. The grains of sand, dirt and gravel in the flooring started to move and drift apart, breaking the very floor.

He seemed to fall in slow motion.

Ren held her breath as his shoulder hit the ground. She sent a further stream of Ground specks. Through his yells and the still crashing gusts of Air, Ren stood.

Blindly, nearly stumbling over two bodies, Ren made her way towards the door. From behind, she heard more yells, but didn't stop, the oblong outline was within her sights.

Deep inside, lower than where her magic danced, lower than the buzzing, right in her gut, something rose. Grit.

The handle was cool and smooth. Ren hardly dared breathe as she pulled. It swung inwards. Around her, what had to be thousands of specks of white whizzed past.

She clocked something hanging on the wall, only a few feet from her position at the door.

She had seen it once before, though she'd be able to recognise it until the day she died. In any other circumstance, she would hesitate. Any qualms about riskiness were for other times. Ren reached up, hissing in pain, and unhooked both Brennett's crossbow and the small pouch of bolts hanging behind. Then she sent a further flurry of Ground specks over her shoulder and, not waiting to listen for signs they'd hit their mark, hotfooted it from the control room and took a sharp right.

The door into the block was heavier. It was a strain to pull it, but it was, thanks to Priya, unlocked. She relayed Priya's words: *straight through*. Ren went as fast as her broken body allowed, past blurry prisoners behind blurrier bars. She sought out their faces. Men and women alike; above each was a cluster of specks.

They were all older than Ren, and everyone had a taio with more than one type of magic within it. Some had all four, others three, or two.

Were they awakening, like her? They all looked too old.

Her breath seemed to halt within her.

...for the past few years almost every weaver has gone missing.

Ren ignored every shout and holler. She reached the end of the block. A soft *psst* to her right, in a smaller corridor in front of a set of downwards stairs, stood two figures.

Priya, clutching a knife and looking as though she'd seen the ghosts of a thousand men, ran to embrace her. Brennett looked mildly amused.

"I thought something had happened," Priya squeaked. "We were about to come find you."

Not quite knowing how to address the man she wasn't sure they should have freed, Ren passed him his crossbow. His only good eye, blue and searching, met hers. The other was covered with a makeshift black eye patch, crudely fashioned from a length of satin-looking fabric.

She held onto the baton.

"It did," Ren replied, turning back to Priya, "one of the guards is an Air bearer."

Priya clamped a hand to her mouth as she beckoned Ren forwards.

"You got the keys?"

Priya held the ring aloft.

Ren's gaze darted between Priya and Brennett, and the way she had come from. "How long would it take," she asked, the words uncertain but steady, "to free them?"

Priya's hands shook on Ren's arm. "Ren, we don't have–"

But Ren was turning. Though the largest part of her heart lay beyond the door ahead, so close she could make out the details in its lock, another part of it existed here.

With each weaver Gideon had locked up.

The solid mass of dead magic Gideon had forced her in front of swum in Ren's mind. There was a reason some didn't possess all their elements anymore.

Just as he had tried to take Ren's, Gideon had taken them. Killed them.

"Brennett," Ren said, taking a step back into the block. "Keep watch."

Ren led Priya to the nearest cell. As they approached, the same oppressive unease befell Ren. And then she saw them, just as those Gideon had placed around her room. *NeòNach.* Coating the cell. Ren swallowed as she examined its inhabitant. A man, around her father's age, an unkempt salt and pepper beard cascading down his chin. His taio danced above. Ren took stock of each speck as Priya tried first one key, then another. Fire. Water. Ground.

"I–"

But Ren cut him off. "Do you know how to get to the Council?"

The man stepped free for the first time in who knew how long. "I do, but–"

But Priya and Ren were already moving to the next cell, where a woman sat, her eyes large and round, watching them silently. "You need to get a message to any senior Councillor you can," Priya was saying, "to head to Longwretch."

"Long–"

"Go!" Priya said, both to him and the now released woman. Her clothes, much like the man's, were dirty. So was her skin. Her hair looked like it hadn't been brushed in a year. Her taio contained Dark and Lightning.

313

A shout echoed from somewhere.

Ren sucked in a breath. They still had eight cells to open, and no time. Ren's fist was balled, clasped to her chest. *I'm coming*, she breathed.

From behind, Brennett's voice rang out. "Uh, you two do know–"

"Not now, Brennett," Priya snapped, her hands fumbling, the keys shaking within her grasp.

"Sure, but *this* opens them all."

Both Ren and Priya turned in time to see him push a large, hard-to-miss red button. There was a scraping as cell doors opened around them. At least ten prisoners in this block were freed. Ren could have hugged him.

They headed back to the corridor and the stairs. Not one prisoner spoke, their silence all too palpable. Had they endured what Ren had? By the looks of them, they'd endured worse. And for how long? Ren's lungs burned with every step, mind too full and anxious to wonder too much.

Priya thrust the largest of the keys into the exit door's keyhole, and turned it. Together, Brennett and Priya pushed the door.

And the three, and then the others, stepped outside, to a still dark sky, the scent of the sea and the sound of waves. And freedom in a burst of *NáDarra* that drove outwards alongside them.

The sky, lit with the magic of a few thousand specks at least. Every type of *NáDarra* created a rainbow firework display across the still night. Ren felt it. Each speck's freedom. How much *NeòNach* had Gideon had placed within the prison to subdue them, and her?

She had no time to dwell. Not only were the specks zooming and darting and dancing, but along with them was rain, and thunder, and gusts of wind so strong it was a wonder they all remained upright. Flames from nowhere danced in the corner of her vision.

They moved over to the left towards a steep grassy embankment. Ren was once more clutching her ribs.

She was nauseous, dizzy and exhausted. Adrenaline had enabled her to make her way through the block and find them, free the others, but it was leaving her. Each small movement caused shocks through her entire body; every fibre of her wished to scream.

And then even the non-existent scream was snatched from her at a flash of green by Brennett's leg. Ren dropped to her knees, barely hissing at the way they burned with the impact. "Brogan," she breathed, ignoring Brennett's exclamation.

The cù-sìth stepped forward with a low moo-like howl and nuzzled her outstretched palm. Ren, with the smallest sob – the only kind she would allow herself – buried her face in Brogan's shaggy neck. "We're going to get him," she whispered into the emerald-tinted fur. "I promise."

They took off first at a crawl, and then a slow walk, Ren's far slower than the others. Brogan remained by her side, his giant head low. Several of the freed prisoners attempted to speak to her. Each time she shook her head, grimacing against the agony roaming her body. Their way was a dirt path flanked on one side by sea and on the other by trees. After what was probably mere minutes, though to Ren could have been hours, Brennett called from ahead. Ren and Priya found him at the entrance to a cave. Ren's back slammed against slimy, rough rock. She exhaled shakily as she sat. Beneath her, sand shifted a little.

Brennett let out a low whistle. "This, I did not expect."

Gritting her teeth as she pushed into the side where her ribs burned the most, Ren replied, "Join the club."

Priya had stood, turning to the prisoners and paying neither Ren nor Brennett any mind as she pulled out a small, silvery stone. Then mumbled something to neither of them about a line of *NáDarra*. Then, as Shae had done weeks ago in the clearing by Culloden, began to create the portal in a burst of bright purple light.

"After we've gone," she said to the first man, the one with

the beard. "Get to the Council." Ren looked at each of them in turn. A sorry lot, each barefooted and too skinny, dressed in not much more than rags. Two women to Ren's right were clutching each other. The rest stood mutely.

"Where–?"

"*That's* Endermarch. We're on an Air line," she said. "Long-wretch, remember."

The man only nodded, taking the scrystone from Priya's shaking hand as the portal, now a door-like, touchable thing, took shape. The rest were soundless, regarding the trio with wild looks and dazed expressions.

"All right," Priya said, her attention turning to Ren, then Brennett, then the cù-sìth, a hairy statue beside Ren. "Let's go save Lance."

End of Part Four

Part Five

28

Ren emerged, coughing and grasping the side of her torso. It felt ready to fall off. She would know, wouldn't she, if something was really wrong? Were she bleeding somewhere internally, she doubted she'd still be standing. She hoped. She swayed on the spot, centring herself as she searched deep down for her magic, certain it was the only part of her not in pain.

They were standing on the edge of a large flat plain. Behind them, trees loomed above. Otherwise, nothing but grass met Ren's gaze in almost every direction. Close to the ground, green specks were hovering, dancing in the beginnings of the sunrise. Above them, Air whooshed, the opposite of how they'd behaved in the prison. These ones were free and wild.

At least something was.

There were equal parts Dark and Light specks. The sight, which only occurred twice a day, sung a song in a hidden part of her. There was an intrinsic harmony, despite the frightening and the bleak. Despite Gideon's truths and the fact she needed to find someone on this damn island who could help her not blow two hundred thousand more people up before her last two elements awakened.

The thought pained her far more than her injuries, and she grabbed at the mane of fur at the back of Brogan's neck to keep her hands from shaking.

To their right, Brennett was casting his eyes over their surroundings. "You said he was in Longwretch." His voice was a reluctant monotone.

"He is." Priya looked, if possible, more exhausted than Ren felt. "But we can hardly barge in, can we?"

"I don't see why not."

There was a snap in her tone. "Because we'd all end up behind bars."

He didn't reply, and for a long moment none of the three spoke. Brennett didn't look away from Priya. His jaw twitched and a dozen horizontal lines crossed his forehead like rivers.

It was his eyes that betrayed him. Priya held them with her own. Her expression, much like his, was somehow both hard and soft. A thousand unspoken words must have been passing between the two. Ren turned away, examining a nearby fir in the light of the barely risen sun. A small rise in the buzzing brought her fist to the centre of her chest.

When he did speak, Brennett's voice was a low growl. "Alright." Ren turned back, in time to see his bow rise, level with Priya's throat. Though his gaze still burned with something that looked an awful lot like pain, his aim was steady. "Time for some fucking answers."

If the action alarmed her, Priya didn't show it. Instead, she sighed. "Brennett."

"Don't you *Brennett* me. After six years you think you can just–"

"Free you from prison?"

A snarl accompanied his reply. "Walk back into my life like nothing happened."

Ren, wishing she was almost anywhere else, looked off across the plain, tracking a nearby speck of Dark. Beside her was a soft whine.

"I am aware of everything that happened."

The wobble in Brennett's voice was unmissable. "You and Lance."

If Ren hadn't felt awkward before, that did it. Losing track of the Dark speck, she blinked several times, then frowned as something, also dark but far larger, flickered in the corner of her vision.

It was shrouded in green Ground specks.

"That was a mistake."

Whatever it was, it was only slightly smaller than the large canine by her side. Ren frowned. It appeared to be hiding, without much success, behind a tree. She glanced at Brogan, who barked softly, then back at the creature.

"That you kept on making."

Priya spoke through a yawn. "Brennett, that was a long time ago."

"I'd have been more than willing to have this conversation then, only you fucked off on some boat."

"You were in *prison*. We couldn't have had anything. You–"

The words roared from his mouth like a thunder crack. "I would have at least known you were alive." Ren looked away from the mysterious mass of black and green. "You let me think you *died*, Priya." The crossbow wobbled.

"I know." The words were barely louder than a whisper, the opposite to his own. At some point, Priya had dropped her gaze, her stare fixed on the grass below Brennett's boots. "I-I am sorry."

He made a noise somewhere between a snort and a *har-*

rumph, and dropped his bow.

"Once this is done," he said, enunciating each word, "I never want to see your face again."

She didn't know if Priya believed him, but Ren certainly didn't.

When she looked back, the dark shape in the swirl of green specks had vanished. In its place, a little further to the side, she saw a strange hint of purple light. It was not like her purple Lightning; more like the scrystone portal they'd stepped through only a few minutes prior. Ren squinted but saw no more. If it wasn't for the low growl coming from her side, she might have believed it was some trick of the light.

"Brennett–"

"Where are we?" He spoke as though the words tasted bad. "You said he was in Longwretch and we don't have long, so why the hell have you brought us to the back end of fucking nowhere?"

"Longwretch is only a quarter of a mile from here." The sentence was quiet and rushed, strung together in a breathy whisper.

Brennett's wasn't. He spat each syllable in an angry stacca-to. "In what direction?"

A few tears were tracking their way down Priya's cheeks. "I..." she began, opening and closing her mouth several times. "Through the woods, but...Brennett–"

Brennett didn't seem to hear the crunch Ren heard. He didn't whirl around like she did, scanning the dim tree line. She really wasn't sure; there had to be animals close by, perhaps–

Snap.

"What?"

"I-I'm sorry." Priya was openly crying now.

A further snap. Another crunch. A cloud of tiny, white specks. Identical to Shae's.

Several more crunches.

Ren took a step closer to Brennett, certain now. She wasn't the only one. Brennett's bow, which had been hanging, lax, by his side, was once again poised. The bolt was level with Ren's eye line and she followed its point to a narrow gap in the trees.

Brennett took two steps, positioning himself between Ren and whatever, whoever, was approaching.

Brogan's growl was louder this time.

From behind, a further, "Brennett," rang out.

Neither Brennett nor Ren moved.

"Nicely done, Priya," an unfamiliar voice said.

Somewhere between her chest and stomach, Ren's breath caught. Something deep within, deeper than either her magic or the buzzing, told her to run, as fast and far as her legs would carry her, and then further still.

She didn't move.

A burly figure was emerging, the last of the night's moonlight bouncing off his bald head.

"Ah," the stranger said again. His voice was slick, like oily water. He had a hulking frame, easily surpassing six feet. His arcanist taio hovered half a foot above his head, unmoving. Ren swallowed. "I didn't expect to be handed you as well, Graves."

Brennett snorted, bow poised towards the newcomer's chest.

The man looked unfazed. He turned to Priya. "You've surpassed yourself."

Fear gripped Ren. She was running out of time. As rapidly as the sun was rising, so was her chance to get to Lance before Gideon knew she was gone.

Priya didn't reply. Despite her tall frame, she looked somehow shrunken.

Ren looked between the three others. Running seemed a wise idea again, but she was as rooted to the spot as if the ground itself had bound her to it. Swallowing, she watched the stranger, whoever he was, who had come for her. To take her, plucking her from her rescue mission like a cow for slaughter. Like Gideon had. Like Brennett had.

Brennett's voice rang through a haze of realisation. "You can't have her."

Have her?

Ren stared at the man, hard. Both her hands shook. This man, who had the audacity to stand before them, before Ren, and...stare. The latest in a who-knew-how long list, who saw her as either a bargaining chip or a tool. To take from her or take from others using her. As she stared at him, resentment coursing through her veins, she hated him, perhaps more than she hated any other.

The stranger, still regarding them in silence, took several long breaths.

Brennett, clearly done listening to the sound, fired a bolt into his thigh. He didn't flinch. A burgundy stain began to spread over the light brown fabric of his loose trousers.

"That isn't your decision, Graves." His eyes hadn't left Ren's face, and though Ren stared back, it wasn't him she saw. Inside, she searched, finding them as poised as she. There was less green, no doubt still depleted from the prison, but the rest were full. Looping and swirling and sparking and crashing. Waiting.

Eager.

"I'm making it my decision," Brennett said.

The man inclined his head. "Your girlfriend has ensured otherwise." He was gazing at Ren's taio. "Haven't you, Priya?"

Brennett shot another bolt, this time into the man's shoulder. This one earned a groan. "You're done, Zed."

Zed wants her alive?

Her blood went cold. *Zed*. The name circled round in her mind. This man had arranged for Brennett to kidnap her.

Probably so he can kill her himself.

Of course. Her fists shook harder. This man didn't want to lock her up or even use her powers; he wanted her dead. Fabulous. Once again, she checked on her magic. They were readied, hovering, waiting for Ren to tell them where to go.

Zed was having difficulty pulling the second bolt out, if his huffing was anything to go by. Good. It granted Ren time to force the nuts and bolts of her vague idea to tighten.

Brennett fired a third bolt into the man's stomach. Despite his obvious discomfort, Zed didn't cry out as his knees hit the ground.

"Get down," Ren muttered. Anxiousness niggled at her.

Brogan obeyed, lowering himself onto his belly.

"How many...of those...have you got?" His words were barely audible through his clamped-together teeth.

"Enough," Brennett replied with a snort.

"You'll never kill Z–" The word was snatched from him as his life was.

"Is that so?" Brennett asked, smirking.

"Yes." Another, stranger, voice rang out from behind them. They turned. A large woman, albeit smaller than Zed, stood not five metres from them.

Ren's chest was hollow. They hadn't heard her approach.

"That is so." She wasn't alone, Ren realised with a further jolt of horror. "Because Zed isn't one man." The grin she shot them was wide and twisted. Throwing her arms in the air, the woman glanced over each shoulder, where at least twenty other men and women stood flanking her. Around half had taios. "Zed is all of us."

Ren let out a shaky breath as she tried and failed to count each person.

To the woman's left, a hooded man unsheathed a sword. Brennett swore.

She was speaking again, the newcomer, though Ren barely heard her. The words were there but jumbled together.

Brennett shuffled, manoeuvring his body between Ren and the sea of Zeds.

The woman, and several of her companions, laughed. The sound of it, of them, sparked something deep within, further than both her magic and the buzzing. An instinctual understanding.

And some don't want that trust in the Council fixed. They want it broken.

They want chaos.

Ren's eyes, which had been drifting from each one of the Zeds, snapped back to the woman, who was waffling about nobody getting hurt while failing to keep the laughter from her voice. Whatever *this* was, it was shrouded in wrongness.

She hadn't been in control since the day Shae had arrived in her life, haloed by fireflies. She hadn't been in control for any single event that had befallen her since she'd travelled to this cursed excuse for a world. The only parts worth saving lay in wherever Shae had run to, and a prison called Longwretch.

And, she supposed as a snout nuzzled her ankle, by her side.

She felt them before she saw them. They were sparse in numbers, but enough to cause a smallish spark to erupt from her fingertips. It was joined by a tiny fork of Lightning, and a fist-sized cloud of pure darkness, distorted by an ever-so-slight gust of wind. When she called the green ones to her, small clumps of earth fell to the grass. Ren raised her head, straightening her spine in the way her dad always told her to. *Gives off a good impression,* he'd say, *powerful people have straight backs.* Behind her was a snap, like the one made by the first Zed. Only this one wasn't caused by a madman.

She'd known, really, since they'd arrived not ten minutes before. A swirl of green specks looming through the trees.

A part of her had known when her own Ground specks had awakened.

The woman took a step, her pale yellow Light taio barely visible in the growing dawn. A bearer. Her eyes, as Ren's had, zoned in on a flurry of green. Something brushed against the side of Ren's knee. It took all of a second for the bravado to leave the woman's demeanour. "Is that–?"

Ren spoke for the first time. "Yeah." The growl was low and seemed to confirm her words. Her own eyes blinked downwards, long enough to lock with two pale yellow orbs, and enough Ground magic to cause several earthquakes.

Brogan rose, almost to her shoulder.

"That's a cù-sìth. And this…" Her eyes met the woman's. She wouldn't be their chaos. "Is a cat-sìth." She'd be her own chaos.

Brennett, whose crossbow was once again raised and aiming at first one Zed, then another, in no discernible order, shot Ren a look of confusion over his shoulder, followed by a wide-eyed stare as his gaze landed upon the large feline.

The woman, cockiness somewhat diminished, held both her hands upright as though surrendering. "Now," she said, "Renée."

Ren snorted but said nothing. A low hiss emanated from the cat-sìth.

"There's no need for anyone to act rashly."

Perhaps she was right. But really, was Ren acting rashly? Ren was following through on a very thought-out plan she had begun to conjure back when Zed meant no more than one bald, beefy idiot. She hadn't had enough Ground magic then, not while hers was still depleted from the prison.

And now, thanks to the cat-sìth that had come for her, sought her out when she had needed the help most, she did.

It began with a rumble.

"When I give the signal, get your head down and run into

the trees," Ren whispered.

"What?" Brennett hissed. "What bloody signal?"

The first tremor came. A soft vibration through the soles of her boots. A smile ghosted across Ren's lips. "You'll know."

It took the smallest flick of her fingertips for Ren's specks to fly outwards. They spread out, meeting almost every Zed bar one, right at the back. A tall, robed figure. Ren frowned, but had little time to dwell as the woman spoke again, her voice high and shrill. She was no longer looking at Ren. "You were told to bring her once she had a shikkane fitted."

Ren allowed herself a moment to glance back at Priya.

Priya shrugged. "I guess I forgot that part."

It was all Ren needed. For once, control was hers.

"Now!"

Brennett ran past her, making for the trees, head bowed. Colourful specks, coming from both Ren and the Zeds, flew above them.

"Go with Brennett," Ren instructed the canine.

With a low howl, he relented. The cat-sìth stayed by her side.

Ren focused first on Fire, hurling clusters of red towards them. Then she crashed Lightning, quickly learning she'd never fully direct it; it came down where it felt like coming down, forked and angry, forcing various Zeds to duck and dodge. A barrage of Water narrowly missed her from a nearby Water bearer and a mass of *NeòNach* specks whirled overhead. She felt their effects straight away, the dampening of her own the closer they got. She drove as much Dark forward as she was able, disorientating the Zeds enough for Ren, clutching the cat-sìth for support as the pain in her ribs rose, to hasten backwards.

"We got this," she told it, and knew it was understood. "Now," she whispered, guiding it forwards with a trail of green.

The feline took off, Ground magic surrounding its claws

and gleaming in its jaws. It was as sleek as gossamer, silent as the air at midnight.

A further rumble, this one louder, then another. The lulls between them were filled with shrieks and screams. Another stream of Water. This one made contact but was so weak she ended up with no more than a damp arm.

It was then that Ren's pain made way for something else. Something powerful. She rose in time with the last roar. Flexing her fingers again, Ren watched the cat-sìth down three of the Zeds as a tremor so loud it threatened to break the world in two forced those remaining to their knees.

"Stop!" one shouted – not the woman. "Stop. We...give– Stop!"

And she did. With a further few flicks, Ren's magic had dispersed, leaving the plain and the Zeds, until only groans and her own panting remained. The cat-sìth, having returned to Ren's side in a jaunty trot, was purring.

Gazing over the scene, her face was hot. At least seven bodies lay motionless. She swallowed hard at the realisation of what that meant. Three more were kneeling. One was bloody – the cat-sìth's doing? The rest had vanished. Only one was standing, immobile and somehow passive, face covered by a low hood. Her heart pounded at the sight.

"Leave," she said, surprised by the command present in her own voice. The three stood, the nearest to her shaking as he did. In the morning sun, now fully risen, she could see him for what he was. A gangly redhead, face full of teenage acne. He blinked at Ren as he staggered to his feet and, without a word, turned, marching across the grassy plain. The other two followed suit.

The robed figure hadn't moved. He only did once Ren turned her attention back to him. A sob escaped her as she made her way towards him. A pair of dark hands removed his hood as he, in turn, strode towards her.

It was all she had to slam her broken body against him. Ren didn't quite reach his shoulder and so cried into his chest. Behind her, a joyous *a-rooo,* rang out.

"Y-you're...you were...a Zed?" The question sounded ludicrous enough without her laborious breaths.

"Not quite."

Ren only cried harder. "I thought...I didn't– I don't..."

"I know."

"Lance..." It hit her like a punch to the gut, a truth too brutal and cruel she never wanted to acknowledge it. Around them, evidence of morning, of daytime, of the fact Gideon would know by now, was too much to bear. "He's in prison..." It couldn't end here, and yet, how could it not? He would take Lance, as Ren's birth had taken his family. "Too late," she mumbled, her breaths coming fast and uneasy. How long would it take them to travel a quarter of a mile? "We'll be too late." Any second the buzzing would cease. The thought forced hot bile to her throat. "We're too late."

"No," Shae replied, squeezing her shoulders. "Look at me." She did, and his eyes sparkled with infinite hues of brown. "We're not too late."

Having Shae back by her side had an inherent *rightness* to it, despite her fears. Elation filled her, but it was fleeting. A rim of dark was hovering around the edges of her vision. Ren blinked, then, as pain, great and all-encompassing, pierced what felt like every inch of her body, she screamed. Had Shae not had the foresight to first grab and then lower her to the spongy grass below, she would have collapsed.

She was somehow Fire, and Ice, and Lightning, and Dark, all at once. And not in the endearing way she had come to think of the elements. Each caused its own agony, and through her they coursed, surge after surge. It was everything she endured for all those years on Earth, all the aches and pains and ways her body failed her multiplied by a thousand and rolled into one.

Tears blurred what little vision she had.

"Shae," she screamed, clutching his forearms. "Shae, what's happe–?" She only screamed more.

Through the gaps in her shrieking, she heard Shae's voice, the only calm in the storm raging through her. "Listen!" But she couldn't. For all she heard were yet more of her wracked sobs, broken only by her screams. "You're...ag...pass."

The broken words meant nothing. All Ren had was to anchor herself against him as her body tried to adjust to the hellish circumstance. Shae knelt, allowing her to grip his arms so tightly they'd probably be bruised for days, reassuring her of things she couldn't hear. Ren didn't know how long it took for the pain to subside enough for her to sit, praying for some respite to the spasms gripping her muscles. Eventually she was quiet enough to hear his voice and register his words.

He spoke with a soothing calm only he could. "Can you

hear me?"

Ren swallowed, nodding as she allowed her shoulders to drop, for they, along with everything, had tensed so much it had rendered her momentarily immobile.

"It's called a *lag*. When an elemental uses their powers, they lose certain sensations – pain being one of them."

She remembered the stream of water she'd barely felt. Looking at the place it had hit, the skin was red raw. And she hadn't felt it.

"Rationality being another," Shae added. His tone, for once, wasn't pointed. Perhaps it should have been.

Ren searched their surroundings. It was littered with bodies. "I killed them," Ren said flatly. "I–"

Magic is like a drug. The voice, which wasn't there, but spoken from the top of a giant mushroom, echoed in her mind. *And you don't want to overdose.*

Against her arm, the one red and raw, was a brush of black fur. Ren turned her head to it. "Hi." She offered the creature a soft smile as she patted its head, easily the size of a football. The creature purred again.

"As if you weren't enough," Shae mumbled, running deft fingers through the fur by Brogan's ears. A gigantic green tail began to waft from side to side.

"Well." A series of gruff coughs rang through the mostly quiet plain. "That was interesting."

Ren, with Shae's help, rose. "You remember Brennett?"

The arcanist looked the other man up and down. "Vaguely." He looked between the two several times. "Is there a reason you're with *him*, or...?"

Brennett was watching the cat-sìth's tail swish from side to side, a more elegant movement than the whooshing of Brogan's. "Charming."

"Shut up, Brennett," Ren hissed as she rubbed her arm. It was tender. "It's a long story." She yawned. A way off, between a few trees and grossly out of place, stood Priya. "Why were you with the crazy Zeds?"

"Ah," Shae replied, "that's a *grand* story. I'll tell you on the way."

The buzzing in her chest was rising, as was a mounting determination. She hadn't come this far, evading whatever crazy torture Gideon had had planned next, along with the plethora of lunatics, to lose him now. She hoped Shae was right.

"To the prison?" Ren asked.

Shae, who had, in such a typical Shae fashion, begun to stride ahead, replied, "Yes, and no."

"What do you mean '*and no*?'"

Shae ignored her question. "Lance will be fine." He pointed a long finger towards Priya, who appeared to be looting a nearby body.

After pulling something from the main woman, the one who had spoken, Priya stood.

"Is she with you?"

Brennett scoffed. "Absolutely not."

For a moment, Shae almost showed some semblance of surprise. "Oh."

"She *was*," Ren corrected. She kept her voice low. "That's Priya, she's..." She trailed off. How did she begin to explain Priya, who had helped, but apparently also tried to hinder her in equal measure?

"Oh," Shae said again. "That, I wasn't expecting."

"Neither was I," Brennett said darkly.

Priya watched the three – five including the two large animals – in silence. Fresh tear tracks were shining down both her cheeks. Her bloodshot eyes never left Ren. "Ren," she began, "I-I'm sorry."

Ren couldn't remember a more painful confrontation. "You

didn't bring us here to save Lance."

Only then did Priya look away.

"Did you?"

"Longwretch *is* a quarter of a mile away." She glanced away, to the trees. "That was true."

"But the rest?"

When Priya said nothing, Shae interjected. "You were their informant." Priya only nodded. "You've been selling Gideon out, for..."

"Months," she admitted.

A memory of jumping out a window, and running, and reading a note she didn't understand. They'd only been in Caeracre a day. "The village," she said to no one, before turning to Shae, then Priya. "That's how they knew where to look."

Shae was nodding. "She must have given them a general area."

Priya was staring at the ground, but nodded.

"Gideon suspected where you'd emerge, but not when. But no one else was supposed to know. He believed you'd get Ren to Endermarch easily. I thought...it was best," she finished meekly. Her answer annoyed Ren almost more than Priya's actions angered her. The Zeds, as far as Ren knew, had wanted the same thing Gideon had: Ren dead. There was never a *best*, not for Ren.

"For who?" Ren demanded.

It was Brennett who answered. "For her."

Priya didn't dispute his words, and when she looked up, she stared at the point past Ren. "It was a way out. I-I'm sorry, but it was the second chance I never would have got by staying with Gideon. The Zenthian promised they'd keep my family safe, and that I...I'd be free. I'm sorry," she said again. "I'm so sorry, Ren." In her hand, Priya still grasped the thing she'd taken from the woman's body. A wad of papers.

The Zeds had her identification.

And it had been, to Priya, worth Ren's life.

Ren turned her newly-formed tears away. In the centre of her chest the buzzing was pulsing in the same nauseating way it had over the past few days. She took a few breaths.

The sun was higher now. Gideon would know that Ren, and his trusty assistant Krisha, were gone. In her mind's eye she saw him marching through the crumbly corridors, Rosa hot on his heels, to fetch a scrystone. Which could probably take him directly into this Longwretch. Prisons, she imagined, were built on wey lines, making transportation between them easier. It was a quarter of a mile away for them, but for him it could be mere seconds. She cursed Priya's betrayal all over again.

Ren forced the wobble from her voice as she faced Shae. "You said he was safe?"

Shae inclined his head. "I said he will be safe."

"Shae?"

"Yes."

"I need to get to him." The *please* remained unsaid. Many things felt like an almost boiling pot. Anything else and it would boil over, the contents splashing over the rim.

Of that, she was sure.

Shae had already started to walk. "Then let's get you to him."

Priya didn't move. Ren regarded her for a few seconds, then the papers, shaking in her grasp.

"Go," Ren said.

Priya's mouth opened, then closed.

"Go." Her mind was already far from Priya and her papers.

Ren didn't wait for a reply. The breeze nipped at her damp cheeks and every twist and small movement she made caused more pain to radiate around her as she followed Shae. The cat-sìth padded silently by her side.

Brennett, after a few seconds of deliberation, matched Ren's stride. "You are aware she tried to *sell* you?"

Ren halted, and a fork of purple Lightning crashed into a nearby tree, leaving it a towering mass of green and red and purple. And the wind, which had been a slight, pleasant breeze, hit against Brennett with a force that stole any further words from his mouth. A few seconds later he was surrounded by thousands of white Air specks, whipping his shaggy chin-length hair and thin tunic around him.

"So did you!" Ren screamed, then turned on the ball of her foot with such ferocity she felt the ground swivel beneath her. She marched away, hearing nothing but the whooshing of her own racing heart. The tree she had struck by lightning was still on fire. Ren ignored it as she stormed away, only turning after the fifth time Shae cried her name.

"What?!"

His voice, infuriatingly, exuded calm. "Put it out."

"No." It was the only thing there that felt real. That felt how she did. Ren looked at it. The fire was no longer centred to the trunk; several patches of grass and twigs beside it were flaming. Everything was bright with Fire and Air and Light. She swallowed.

"Ren." Somewhere, in the depths of the white inferno that had taken over not just the tree's vicinity, but her mind, was Shae's voice again. "Put it out."

Reluctantly, she did.

Then she called the Air specks that were still zooming around Brennett to her, stilling the air around him. His cheeks were glowing red and he was gasping like a goldfish. He looked as though he had many things to say, but he remained silent, if glaring. The only sound that broke through the small group was a vibrating hum as the cat-sìth once again began to purr.

Despite putting the fire out, everything around her was still bright. From the sky to the ground, the light blazed, paying no mind to the shadows of the trees around. Ren's fingers twitched, the way they did when she called specks forwards. And then a Light so brilliant it had to come directly from the sun itself blocked out everything else.

Shae and Brennett disappeared.

The cat-sìth vanished. So did the cù-sìth.

The burnt tree with its blackened branches and piles of scorched leaves by its base; all gone.

In their place, sunlight was hitting against a thousand diamonds in the warmth of the first sign of spring. Life, both old and new, was coming to and also leaving the world. Summer nights and crisp winter mornings and endless days. Flowers and every hue of yellow. Laughter and love, and heat. It spread through her, to each of her extremities, down every strand of her hair.

As it dissipated, she was surrounded by dancing flecks of pale yellow.

Light.

For a few long seconds, no one spoke, though the realisation of what it meant screamed, echoing around her mind. Until Light – her seventh element, she had had the smallest blessing in that there were still two to go. At least one before her eighth and final element awoke...and very likely caused an explosion capable of killing a further few hundred thousand people. In truth, she had hoped time would wait for her, at least until Lance was free. Then she would approach the Council, the *real* Council, and have the time for them, at least, to formulate some notion of what the hell to do with her. Perhaps there was somewhere isolated, some desolate rock in the middle of the sea, that she could be left on.

Something.

Time, though, was no longer a luxury Ren possessed.

Shae watched her in silence.

"All right," Brennett said eventually, his voice purposefully even. He didn't appear to have noticed her latest awakening. "I *might have* nearly handed you over to that crazy lot, but you just trapped me in a tornado. I'd say we're even."

Ren snorted as they once again set off through birdsong she didn't recognise and oaks larger than skyscrapers, away from the heady scent of burning wood, and death, and towards Longwretch prison.

Towards Lance.

"We're not even close to being even."

It took only five minutes of walking to emerge, blinking, on the opposite tree line. The further they walked, the more her pain worsened, not as bad as during what Shae had called the *lag*, but enough for her to pant, hobbling and limping, and wincing. The awakening had dulled it enough for her to make good speed, but with each step she slowed. Shae had vehemently ignored her hissed worries of her own, possibly imminent, detonation, telling her to *cease fretting*.

Ren huffed, for really, if there ever was a time to fret, this was it. She fell silent.

They dropped, one after the other, looking down into a clearing. The cat-sìth followed suit, stooping low on its front paws. The area was smaller than the one they'd left the dead Zeds in. A square building, surrounded by metal fencing and what appeared to be several guards, loomed ahead. It was bleak and grey. The bars on each window were visible from the woods. Though her stomach sank at the sight, the buzzing rose. It was the closest she had been to him since Shin. Did he know, somehow, she was there? Close enough that, were she to start running now, she would reach the building – and probably every guard – in a minute or less? Was his breathing also the tiniest bit harder than it had been a few minutes ago?

Did he know in those precious past few moments that she had become a ticking time bomb?

She realised then that Brennett was speaking.

"...two entrances." His voice was low, calculating. "Probably at least one more we can't see. Those two posts," he pointed to first one, a tall antenna-like pole Ren hadn't noticed, then another, "are alarms. See the boxes near the bottom, the yellow ones?" Ren could. "Any of the guards hit one of those, we're done. Probably on a wey line that leads to that nutter Gideon."

For the first time, Ren saw something in Brennett she'd known was there, buried, but assumed forgotten. She watched him, the way his eyes darted this way and that. The words he spoke held no trace of sarcasm or malice. It took her a moment to realise she felt, among myriad other, scarier things, grateful.

"Two floors, probably a basement, too. Seven windows; they're definitely cells. Assuming there's at least a few rec rooms, control and staff rooms, probably two offices, we can assume this place can hold at least fifty prisoners. *If* it were full, and *if* it were operating under Caerisle law, they'd need *at least* twenty-eight guards."

Ren's stomach sank all over again.

"It's neither," Shae interjected.

Brennett nodded curtly. "Didn't think so. Though, going in is still going to be risky, even with Ren able to set them all on fire. It's those alarms. Ren, could you–?"

Shae held up a hand to silence him. "We have something we need to do, before we go marching down this hill."

Brennett blinked at him. So did Ren.

Nodding over to the side, where nothing but a small shrub stood, Shae said, "Over there."

"What?" Ren said, harsher than she meant. She was only more confused when Brennett breathed a long, slow *oh*, as though the shrub meant anything at all.

They approached it, still crouched.

Ren honed in on the shrub. It vaguely resembled a rose bush, only instead of roses its spiky flowers were coloured such a dark blue they looked black, dotted with white. Its thorns were more prominent, too, as dark as the flowers. Otherwise, it seemed unremarkable.

Brennett was regarding it with far greater enthusiasm. "We used to have a bloke grow these." He rubbed a leaf between his thumb and forefinger. "It wasn't a bad little business."

Up close, what she had believed to be white spots, Ren realised were actually specks of *NeòNach*. She frowned at the sight. The situation couldn't have been more different than in the prison, but still she wished the tiny white specks weren't there. They made her feel closed in, somehow suffocated, in a way *NeòNach* hadn't before Gideon had trapped her in with so much of it.

Shae was searching in his many pockets, his face, as it so often was, an unreadable mask. Both the cù-sìth and the cat-sìth were lying on their bellies, watching Brennett with a twitch in their tails. Brennett was busying himself punching the ground.

He stopped after several seconds, rubbing his knuckles. "You still got that baton?"

Ren pulled it from the waist of her trousers and handed it over.

Brennett began, once again, to pound the dirt. "Ah ha!" he exclaimed as a whirring, almost mechanical, sound rang out beneath their feet.

Both Ren and the cat-sìth jumped.

Below the bush, something strange was occurring. Ren watched in alarm, mouth gaping, as a patch of dirt, around two foot in diameter, simply fell away, revealing a hole, through which several hundred specks of *NeòNach* zoomed out, and darkness.

"How the–?" But her question was cut short by Shae, now holding a scrystone to his mouth.

"Cassidy?"

Who?

It took whoever Cassidy was less than a second to answer. "Shae? Everything go okay?"

"Yes."

"She's there?"

Whoever this Cassidy was, he knew of Ren. A prickling of unease crept over her shoulders.

The first time Ren had seen a scrystone was an eerily similar moment. She willed both the memory and the sudden rush of tears away.

I look better in person; less stone-like.

"She is," Shae replied. "And Lance is-"

"With me, yes." Another sharp gust of wind. Ren heard herself gasp. He was there, with this Cassidy. Every inch of her skin was suddenly buzzing acutely. "Did you find the dig spot?"

"Yes."

Gasping, Ren threw a fist to her chest as the buzzing soared within her like a great bird aching for freedom. Something, within Lance, had shifted. An understanding? Possibly.

"Has she been briefed?"

"No."

"Well, don't take all day about it. First floor, second window, you-"

"I remember."

"Does five minutes work for you?"

"It does."

"All right." Whoever this Cassidy was, he paused. "Shae?"

"Yes?"

"Good luck."

"And you." Once again there was a rush in the buzzing, though it wasn't like what she had felt at the prison. That had held dark undertones, notes of despair, and pain, and longing. And nausea. These didn't. While the longing was still there, so was something else.

Something that told her she would see him soon.

Ren exchanged glances with Brennett. He looked as in the dark as she felt. Shae, in no apparent hurry to enlighten them, deposited the scrystone in a concealed pocket.

Brogan whined.

Ren wished she could, too. "Who is Cassidy?" she asked Shae.

"The Zeds aren't the only ones with infiltrators," he said cryptically as his gaze flicked between Brennett and his crossbow. "How good are you with that?"

"Very."

"Good enough to hit one of those alarms you pointed to?"

Brennett's jaw twitched. "Yes."

Shae nodded. "That solves one problem." He turned to Ren. "When you were both being, ah, accosted, in Shin, I took the coordinates. I was able to enter the Hidden City. Then, it took a further day and a half of searching, but I was able to trade some information, using your abairt."

"*Còmhla mar aon*?" Ren whispered.

Shae nodded. "I imagine I'd have had success sooner had I been saying it correctly. Anyway," he continued, ignoring Brennett's snort, "that led me to a group." For a second, his eyes left hers, to look upwards, at the cloud of what she'd once thought of as fireflies. "Led by Cassidy, and your mother."

"My–"

He nodded again. *And that's how we'll always find each other.* "I don't know what Gideon told you, nor do we have the time to fill in the blanks. And for that I apologise." A strange rumbling met Ren's ears, which seemed to come from the very ground they knelt upon. "In a few minutes, Brennett is going to set off one of the alarms." Ren swallowed hard, knowing the words before they came. "Gideon will arrive, then so will you."

"I don't–"

Sometimes, the way Shae talked, with barely any emotion, was a help, and sometimes it was a hindrance. Right then, she wasn't sure which it was. "You're going to offer him a deal."

The rumbling was louder now, and easier to interpret. Someone, or rather, someone*s*, were climbing up the hole Brennett had found by the shrub.

"But I–" *can't face him again.* She was shaking.

"Ren, listen to me. Gideon didn't just have Lance brought here." It was only then she saw the brief slip in his facade. "He had him poisoned."

The shrub was suddenly blown with such a gust of wind every flower on its branches was scattered into the air.

"Gideon is the only one with the antidote." The sky was suddenly no longer blue and breezy, but dark. Thunder rolled overhead. Brogan's whine was higher this time.

The sharp pulses she had felt in their shared buzzing, and the nausea that came with them, all made sense.

"Shae, wh–"

"He probably knew it would come to this, somehow." A deep hopelessness had buried itself in her gut. Alongside it lay hate. Ren had felt it before, the unfairness. On Earth, her whole life had felt unfair. But this...it was cruel. Why had he put her through it, all of it, if all he'd had to tell her was that he'd poisoned the man her soul couldn't live without? *Because,* a very small voice told her, *you killed his family.* Gideon didn't see Ren; he never had. He saw the reason why he had lost everything. "Though," Shae was saying, "I imagine he attempted to perform an extraction himself, anyway." Ren nodded numbly. "Men like Gideon like contingencies."

"I..." Ren stifled a sob, "offer him a deal?"

Shae was gripping her forearms. "The only thing he wants more..." *than seeing Ren suffer.*

What twist of fate had allowed her to escape him, damn near killing her in the process, for nothing? Perhaps, in some crueller twist of irony, this was why she had only known her magic for a few weeks. Would that mean she'd miss it less? When she spoke, the words tasted sour. "I need to offer to give up my magic."

"Yes, and no," Shae said. A smidgen of hope graced her. "You need to make him *think* you'll give it up."

30

Before she could grill him further, a collection of shimmery, ever-changing specks popped out of the shrub hole. A mop of messy, black curls covered his head, and he wore a grin that was, in Ren's opinion, far greater than the situation called for.

The faedra greeted them with a cheery, "Hello," as he hauled himself out of the hole, blinking in the sunlight.

"Ren, this is Lowell," Shae said. Lowell's wiry form came fully into view.

Before Shae could say any more, Lowell had already shaken Ren's hand with such gusto she felt the strain in her shoulder, and turned to Brennett. "Who's this, then?" he asked. "A stray you picked up?" No one laughed except Lowell himself.

"That's Brennett. He's an old...*acquaintance* of Lance's."

That was one way of putting it.

"Hello," Lowell said again, peering curiously at Brennett's crossbow.

Brennett, who was looking, if anything, alarmed by Lowell's presence, was saved from the need to reply by the appearance of a second taio, this one blue. Ren wondered if it was her mother's. A twinge of nervousness tugged in her belly as the top of a head followed the specks. Its owner was bald and large, and male. Definitely not.

"This is Ruff," Shae informed them as the man hoisted himself upwards. What looked like a shotgun hung from his shoulder. Ren blinked at it. She'd seen nothing of Earth-like weaponry on Caerisle.

"Ren," Shae said, nodding towards her, "and Brennett."

Ruff regarded her, then her taio, for several seconds. "So it's true." He whistled. "Seven elements?" he added.

She nodded. "I don't know when the last will awaken, but–"

"Don't worry," Ruff said. Then he smiled a smile that revealed at least two missing teeth. The skin on his face and head was weather-beaten. Stubble coated the bottom of his face and both sides of his neck were covered in barely legible tattoos.

Ren took a deep breath.

Despite Ruff's rough aesthetic, there was something calming about his gap-filled grin. "We have a plan for that."

"We do?"

"As soon as we can get the information from that loon Gideon."

Despite everything looming, his words coaxed a small smile to Ren's lips. Ren turned to Shae, who was holding the scrystone to his mouth once again. The sight opened a hollow in her chest. "Shae," she said, her voice hardly more than a whisper.

"No." His eyebrows shot up at the gust that whipped the edge of his cloak. "And don't look at me like that; I'm immune to guilt."

"But–"

"You're far too unstable."

"To *talk* to him?"

"You've been smoking since you learnt he was with the other stone."

Ren tightened her fist, unaware Shae had noticed. "Well, that's hardly the point," she muttered.

"A word of advice," Shae said, this time addressing the rest of the group, "you don't want to be standing anywhere near Ren when she sees Lance." She didn't miss the hint of a smile that tugged at his mouth; she scowled as he continued. "She has an alarmingly small amount of control. Over anything," he added.

She didn't answer, not while the others chuckled, and begrudged the single roll of thunder overhead that only strengthened his point.

"Let's go," Ren mumbled.

They moved back to the spot from which Ren, Shae, and Brennett had examined the prison.

"Okay," Shae said, "Brennett, send a bolt into one of the alarms. As far as we know, that'll lock every cell in the place, and will bring every guard into that courtyard there. While you do that, I'm going to remove the window pane from the infirmary."

First floor, second window, Ren remembered.

"Then I'll push the fence, enough for you, Ren, to walk over. You're going to approach from the front. Once they see you, do whatever you can to keep their eyes on you. They won't hurt you; you're too valuable."

Ren swallowed, wishing she was anything but valuable.

"Position yourself near the empty windowpane. Ruff and Lowell will approach from that side." Shae pointed over to their left, where a few measly bushes stood between the trees and the prison. "Brennett, since you're here, you can do the same to the right. You'll have about fifteen seconds before Gideon arrives. Take the guards down."

Both Ruff and Brennett nodded.

Lowell didn't; he was looking rather pale.

"When he does, Ren, demand the antidote. Say whatever you need to say."

"Okay." Ren's voice was small. "I don't have to go with him, or–"

"No," Shae said, "but you're going to need to convince him to explain part of the process of extraction."

"Wh-wait, what do you–?"

"Ren," Ruff said. Her eyes darted to him, suddenly frightened. Extraction was what Gideon had tried to do when he'd put her in front of the wall of death. Absolutely not.

Ren had *felt* her own magic shaking with fear.

"Do you know what happened when you were born?"

"Yes," she snapped, "but I can't send my magic to die, I-I can't, I-" it sounded absurd, and monumentally selfish. Ren knew others wouldn't regard her magic in the same vein as people, and neither probably, should she. But she had felt their fear and their pain. "I can't send them to *death*!" She was shouting now. If she carried on they wouldn't need Brennett's bolt, but she didn't care. It was raining on them all. Great, thick droplets bounced off her. Ren swallowed hard.

"Ren," Ruff said again, "what if there was somewhere else some of them could go, some*one* else?"

"Some–" She blinked at him. "Is that possible?"

"Without another whose power matches yours, no. But lucky for us, we have one."

Could that be true? Another whose power…. Ren opened her mouth to ask who, only to realise Ruff was still speaking.

"…will have given you something, a relaxant of sorts, before he tried, so you were susceptible to extracting them."

This time it was Ren who nodded, remembering the sudden wooziness that had befallen her, how willing she became to adhering to his instruction.

"That's all we need," Ruff informed her. "Then we can *safely* extract your magic. Not *all* of it," he added, "but you will need to lose some elements."

Ren swallowed hard at that.

"But without the relaxant – and no legal ones are known to work on weavers – the strain would most likely kill you."

She tried not to focus on his last words. "The relaxant."

Ruff nodded. "You get him to explain what that is, and this

can be over."

The thought of losing any of her elements wasn't pleasant, but the prospect of not blowing up the population of a large town was. Did she have a choice? Not really.

Could it really be over?

Lance. Poison. Gideon. Antidote. The possibility of blowing up every individual within a hundred metres of her. Extraction. Her mother. The dead Zeds. Each one circled to the forefront of her mind. It would be too much for anyone, let alone Ren, who had so often in her life found the prospect of preparing dinner too much to cope with. Her breaths threatened to come out too fast, then not at all.

Think, Ren told herself. She asked the only thing she ever had when anything was too much: *what would Dad do?*

She knew then. Knew what he'd do, what he'd say. He'd make her write a list, because lists make lots of things less scary. Ren's rain and thunder dampened somewhat as her panic was replaced, a little, by determination. "Okay," she said, glancing at each of them, cycling through the list in her mind. All she had to do first was reach the prison. "Let's do it."

Brennett's faith in his aim was well founded. No sooner had Shae informed Cassidy and Lance in the scrystone that they were 'ready,' the bolt was flying, quicker than Ren could keep up with it towards the small yellow box. It hit it square centre. At first nothing happened. Ren let out a breath as she glanced at each of the others. Had something gone wrong?

But then, in a single note that rose from nothing to a deafening finale, only for it to begin all over again, an alarm roared across the land, like the one Priya had let off at Endermarch. In a rush of fear and dread and focus, Ren stood. She took a step, paying no mind to Ruff and Lowell skirting away to her left, or Brennett doing the same to her right. The cat-sìth, having stayed close and low, made to follow Brogan just behind.

"No." She shot them an apologetic look and offered each

furry head a pat. "Wait here. Until we need you."

They dropped back down silently.

Ren looked ahead, down the slope to the square, featureless building, and felt it, stronger than she had since he'd been taken from her. No longer was the buzzing low, pulsing against the centre of her chest, nor was it sweeping over her skin. Ren took a step, then another. With each one it grew. No longer a hum or a whisper deep within, but a writhing and roaring thing, reverberating everywhere. The fear was there still, but it was reserved just for him. *Her* him. Her Lance. Who *he*, another he, had had poisoned. The truth of the extent to which Gideon was willing to go, how much he had lied, to hurt her, and take from her, hit her over and over.

There were several guards mulling around the courtyard.

As she approached the compound, a whoosh rose above her. She felt their presence before she saw them. Shae's specks. More than she'd seen him conjure before. Each one attached itself to the fence.

Beyond it, the guards had begun to gather, watching her. One stepped forward and opened his mouth. Whatever he began to say was drowned out by a violent combination of crunching and metallic grinding.

The fence was crafted from huge silver squares, each at least eight foot tall. Barbed wire lined the top, enhanced with thousands of specks of *NeòNach*. The square closest to Ren fell forwards, crashing to the ground. Several shouts sounded. The barbed wire hung, still swaying, at either side of the still erect fence, leaving Ren's opening.

As a guard ahead raised something that looked alarmingly like a pistol, a familiar whistling rang through the air. A bolt shot clean through his neck. The man fell forwards with an odd gurgling sound and exclamations from other guards, then silence.

It was short-lived, however, as bodies began to drop. In addition to Brennett's bolts, only one of which missed, there were streams, far stronger than any Ren was sure she could create. If it weren't for the blue specks surrounding them she wouldn't have known they were water; they were no more than great, grey blurs. It took a few seconds for the ground to be soaked, blue specks dancing lazily above, while bodies – how many, she didn't know – lay motionless within the red-tinged liquid. Ren, her boots soaking through with each step, manoeuvred herself towards the only window without a pane. She willed herself to see him, staring at the empty rectangle. The buzzing flared. Did he know? He must. It was stronger still, yet her chest was an aching cavity.

"And here I was thinking my hospitality was exemplary."

A tingling, separate from the buzzing, crept over Ren's shoulders as she turned. She shouldn't fear him, not here. Not with Shae and Ruff, even Lowell – *even Brennett*, nearby, yet she did.

She hadn't heard him approach.

"Renée."

"You bastard."

He regarded her with something akin to amusement.

Bastard, she thought again.

"I beg your pardon."

"You poisoned him."

His face didn't shift. "I'm afraid I don't–"

A roll of thunder, louder than any her unruly emotions had created thus far, drowned out the rest of his words.

"Lance!" Ren screamed.

The water that had originated from Ruff's jet was no longer motionless. Instead, as gusts of wind were beginning to form, so were waves. Both Gideon and Ren were soaked from the waist down.

"Ah, yes," he cried. It was barely audible over another thunderous roar. "Mr. Allardyce."

"Give me the antidote."

Gideon said nothing, and though it couldn't be later than mid-morning, the sun all but disappeared, encasing the two in a stormy dark.

"Give. Me. The. Antidote."

She knew he spoke, for his mouth moved, but she heard only wind, and rain.

"The antidote!" This time she screamed it. "Or, I swear–" She realised she was crying.

Gideon took a step closer, the base of his robes sloshing in the freezing water. "Renée," he cried, gesturing around them, "can't you see now?"

"Y-you need..." Whether through her cries, or more thunder, or something equally as loud yet unknown, she couldn't continue. She was numb, and Gideon's face, now devoid of humour, was contorted in what could have been pain.

"Look, Renée!"

And she did.

The sight that met her wasn't dark nor wet. Past a radius of no more than a few metres, circling Ren and Gideon, there was Light, blazing Light, and smoke. It had created yet another perimeter, this one not made of Water, or Dark, or thunder, but Fire. She saw Ruff and Lowell, then Brennett. Lastly, she saw Shae, poised and watching, trapped by flames she had neither memory nor knowledge of creating. The breath she emitted came out in shudders as, past the wall of Fire, great flashes of purple Lightning forked downwards. Several trees were engulfed in flames.

But Ren hadn't caused this. She couldn't. The scene was unbridled chaos.

"Renée," Gideon repeated, his voice a heavy boom. "You must allow me to end this."

End this.

Once more, she sought out Shae. The deal.

"I-I will, for the antidote!"

"You will?"

"I'll give up my magic," Ren cried, "to save him."

Gideon didn't reply. Reaching into an inner pocket of his robes, he brought forth a small vial. He tossed it forwards, to Ren.

She caught it as a voice called from above; it was somehow familiar.

"Up here."

Lining up the shot, Ren threw the vial upwards, holding her breath until it was nestled in the palm of a stranger: Cassidy. He disappeared. The buzzing rose as she turned back to Gideon and the elemental anarchy raging around them.

"I have upheld my end." Outstretching his arms, Gideon took a further step towards her, the way a parent might.

Ren didn't move. "I need...before. I-I want to know what you did to me. B-before last time." In her peripheral vision, the small black blob she knew to be Shae seemed to be moving. "Y-you did something to me. It made me feel weird."

Gideon opened his mouth, though the words he was no doubt preparing to say were replaced by a sharp cry, as a deep sound, separate from the thunder, rumbled from below. Green specks that hadn't been there a moment ago were bouncing and whizzing around them. It was only when she raised her hand to push her sodden hair from her eyes that she saw their origin: her.

Flecks of green and blue and purple and red and black and white and yellow were cascading from her at breakneck speed. And Ren hadn't known. "Stop!" Ren searched inside, for the place she connected with her taio. But, as though someone had built a roadblock, she couldn't see it. "STOP!" she screamed.

"You're out of control, Renée."

"I know!"

"You must come with me; we can perform the extraction–"

"Tell me what you did!"

In any other scenario, he might have looked comical, robes

dripping, clinging to his soaking frame. He took another step closer, though still had to shout to make himself heard. "You were injected with enough magical anaesthesia to knock out a fully grown crodh-mara, through a shikkane needle into your spine. Now, let's–"

It happened in a sploshy thud, and a small wave that sent icy water up the side of her leg, and five words Ren barely heard.

"She's going nowhere with you."

How Ren stayed on her feet, between the sight of him and the rise in the buzzing, so powerful it momentarily blocked out all other sensation, she didn't know.

Everything about Lance looked wrong, from his ragged, faded clothes, to the way his hair, matted and bloody, whipped around his head. There were angry welts on his arms and blotched bruises, ranging from a deep purple to an ugly yel-low, covering what little of his skin was visible. The sword he clutched was a rusty thing that looked older than him. It was pointed at Gideon's chest.

Ren stifled a sob no one heard. But he was there, beside her.

That, at least, was right.

A flash of Lightning, larger than any she'd created before, hit the ground behind Gideon, erupting in what sounded like a flurry of gunfire. It left a continuous note ringing in Ren's ears.

"Hi, beautiful," Lance cried, "think you can work on calm-ing this lovely storm down a bit?"

"I–" A thousand things she wished to say, and each one failed her. She glanced down at her palms, each with a steady stream of coloured specks hurtling from them. "I-I tried, but–"

"I know, it's okay." Though he was shouting, his words were soothing. "Just keep trying." He took several steps forwards, placing himself at Ren's side, just in front. A second sploosh, and accompanying small wave, emanated to their left. There, holding his hands upwards, was Cassidy. He was short and stocky, his shoulder-length hair a deep red. A jagged scar ran from his forehead to his jaw line. Purple specks were flying towards him, entering his palms in a small burst of light, then disappearing.

"...ardyce, you must see it is in Renée's best inter–"

"No." The rage in his voice, contradicting the way his fingertips gently stroked across her shoulder, was a raw, concrete thing. "You don't get to say what's in her *best interests.*"

Gideon's gaze flitted between Lance and Ren, then off, past Ren, as she worked on demolishing the blockade keeping her from control over her magic. It was impossible. She knew where to look, where to feel, but she was met with a locked door she'd never encountered. "Very well. I can perform the procedure here."

"If you think you're getting near her again, you're deluded." She was closer, she had to be. For the first time since Gideon's arrival, Ren felt the familiar presence of her magic within herself.

"Renée was never put in harm's way."

At his words, a gust so strong it prompted Lance to clutch her to him raged against them.

She couldn't open the door, but she could knock on it. She could try.

"I don't know what the fuck you did to her," Lance yelled, "but I felt every damn thing, you son of a bitch."

She focused, not on Gideon, but on Lance's hand. On Cassidy's pained expression as he fought to contain a fraction of Ren's magic. And on the fact she was putting not only Shae, but others, a few who didn't even know her, but had come to her, in danger. On the fact it somehow bothered her she was putting Brennett in danger. When that didn't work, she closed her eyes, clutching Lance. She had to control it, for she could control nothing else. Because Ren had *never* had control over anything else. Not her health, not her mother leaving. Not who she loved and not being sent away at birth to a world that made her sick.

Because of him.

Her eyes opened, snapping to Gideon's face, to his lies and trickery. To false pretences that were little more than a misplaced desire for revenge.

The door lay shattered and in pieces. Her magic was accessible. Ren looked past Gideon to the dark sky, to the Air and the Lightning and the Fire beyond. To four figures, each stood a small way apart, waiting. Then her hands. No longer were specks flying from them.

It started slowly. The wind was the first to dampen, then the Lightning, after which Cassidy let out a long breath. The rain lessened and so did the Fire. She saw Ruff point his jet streams towards the nearest. And she saw it begin to go out.

"Well done," Lance said, voice lower. Then, as Gideon went to speak, he interjected, "If you want to keep breathing, shut up." She wished for nothing more than for them to be someplace, anyplace else, where neither their scars nor the threat she posed were real. He frowned. "Is that...Brennett?"

The others, minus Ruff, who was still extinguishing fires, were walking towards Ren, Lance, Gideon and Cassidy.

"Y-yeah," Ren said, her gaze following his. "Priya and I sort of broke him out of prison."

He shot her a look of utter bemusement. "Priya, as in..."

"She only did it to sell me to the crazy Zeds." Ren shivered, the edges of her vision beginning to darken.

"The–" But he halted as the others approached, dropping his sword by his side for the first time to throw himself into Shae's, rather reluctant, hug.

"Ugh! Lance, you're filthy!"

"I missed you, too." He hugged Brennett next, though Ren didn't see it.

Hearing a groan, which she then realised had come from herself, Ren's body, with little input from her brain, began to crumple.

"Lance," she heard Shae's voice, though it sounded far away, and staticky, like a wrongly tuned radio, "she's going to lag again." Then the pain, the kind she had only experienced after fighting the Zeds, returned.

It racked her for a second time, waves of agony and ice, nausea and fire. It struck and gnawed at her, prickling like needles and squeezing like a giant vice. The only difference was this time she screamed against Lance instead of Shae.

She didn't know how long it lasted, only that it went on for far, far too long. When it stopped, it felt like waking up suddenly from a deep sleep, woozy and uncoordinated, only able to move in slow motion. She was shaking, and there was an indecipherable low chatter between the others. She breathed in blood and earth and smoke and rain. They were soaked, him sitting, her pulled against his chest, enclosed in his arms. His fingers were weaving through her hair, though stopping every few seconds as he came across a new knot or tangle.

"Um," Lance murmured. "Hello."

Something warm and furry was nudging Ren's elbow. "This is my...new pet," she mumbled into his chest. "I...think."

The cat-sìth emitted a low chirp-like noise. A second large shape joined them.

"Brogan," she breathed as Lance ran his fingers through the cù-sìth's wet fur.

"All right," she heard from above, "if Ren can get there, we should think about heading off. The sooner we perform the extraction, the sooner–" His words were halted by the clearing of a throat.

Ren groaned again. She'd almost forgotten about Gideon. Almost.

"Renée is going nowhere."

Low enough that only Ren, and possibly the cat-sìth – and cù-sìth – could hear, Lance hissed.

Whatever it was, Ren felt it, too, the deep nausea. The same kind she'd felt for days. She said nothing, though, and gripped him tighter.

"And you're planning on stopping her, are you?" Brennett said.

"Yes," Gideon replied simply.

Brennett only snorted. "Is that so?"

"Yes, Mr. Graves."

Ren, with her face still pressed against Lance, didn't see, but heard enough.

Ruff swore.

Someone else – she suspected Lowell – seemed to whimper, and Brennett muttered, "I've got to stop saying that."

Peeling herself from the sanctity of Lance's grasp, she followed the gaze of the others. She and Lance gasped together, clutching each other as the nausea grew.

"Whatever happens," Lance whispered, his lips pressed to her ear. He was shaking, they both were. "Know my soul is yours. *Anam.*"

Standing not twenty feet from the small group were at least thirty others. All but one was wearing the same Dragon Corps uniform Umber had worn when he'd taken Ren to Endermarch prison. The last was Rosa.

Ren looked at each in turn. Some had taios, though most didn't. Not that it mattered. Her magic was depleted. Her body broken. She held onto Lance not just because her heart had to, but because she was certain she'd never hold herself upright. Every part of her ached. Exhaustion held her, iron clad and unwavering. Shae had called it a lag, but it was so much more. So much worse.

Gideon's minions were closer now. Ren could make out Rosa's pearl brooch.

"I think it's time, Renée," Rosa said, smiling sweetly, "we take you back."

She snaked one arm tighter still around Lance's waist, fighting the urge to vomit. One glance and she knew he was struggling with the same. She breathed Brielle's words as quietly as she could. It felt like a lifetime ago. *The one with whom your soul is shared.* "My...co-anam."

31

Utter bedlam ensued.

The group of Dragon Corps drove forwards. Some had pulled swords as if from nowhere. The ones with taios brought forth specks, readied between their raised palms. One man, a full head shorter and quite a few years younger than the rest, was wielding an axe nearly as big as himself. Ren scanned the crowd of them, heart thundering somewhere between her throat and her ears. There weren't *that* many of them, not really. But she and her friends were outnumbered. More so thanks to the fact Ren was less use than a spare part, broken and inept.

Lance, sword raised, had forced her behind him, backing them up towards the prison wall. His blade met two sprinting bodies, halting their run, mid step, one in the neck and the other in the thigh, then the eye. Brogan had dived at a third, his great body sloshing in the water.

Ren stopped looking then.

Specks, both white and coloured, were once again littering the air. A way off, jets of Water, presumably from Ruff's Water gun, were being blasted from one end of the courtyard to the other.

Lance ducked, dragging Ren with him, switching the rusty sword he'd been wielding for one of the downed Dragon Corps' ones. "It'll do," he mumbled, testing its weight. "We're near the door," he continued, pulling Ren sideways, around bodies and spells and blades. "Get inside."

"Wh-no."

"Ren!"

They were in front of the door now. "I'm not leaving you."

"I'll find you af–"

Something small and painful grazed Ren's arm. "Agh!" An arrow was lying on the ground by the wall. It had missed, mostly, but blood still oozed from the cut, mingling with water as it trickled down her arm.

Lance growled. "Inside."

"Bu–"

"I'm not spending–" he was hauling her into the doorway, "any more time not knowing if you're about to die." The door swung open as Lance wrenched at it and a wave of nausea rose. "You," he ordered at somebody Ren couldn't see, "get in there with her."

Then, despite her protests, which were feeble at best, he pushed her, stumbling, into darkness. The door slammed shut as she fell – the cat-sith's tail narrowly missed being squashed – and a fiery pain exploded in her ribcage as she hit the floor.

She realised then, as the door shut, how loud the fight had been. In the small square hallway they now occupied, the sounds were muffled, quieter than her own heartbeat and ragged breathing. A few rogue specks of Dark magic, and some white Air ones, lingered above. Several rushed to her, joining her depleted stores. Nowhere near enough. The clouds of green circling the cat-sith's claws and fangs cast the eerie glow in the small room.

The giant feline positioned itself against her side as she pushed herself, with difficulty, to sit. By the time she was done, it hurt to breathe. Ren leant into its fur.

A deep boom echoed from outside.

"I should be out there," Ren said. Her mind sought out her magic. Thanks to the cat-sith, she had plenty of Ground, though what use was it? All she knew was how to create earth-quakes, which would affect everybody. She had some Air again, which only provided the same problem. She had enough Light, but what use was Light in a fight?

Ren didn't know.

When it came to her magic, Ren didn't know all that much. And, some small part of her informed her, that was what made her little more than a liability. Yet, the guilt remained, as prominent as the pain.

When she spoke next, it was whispered. "This is because of me."

What strange twist of fate had it been, that Ren, who knew little else than how to change a barrel of lager, had been thrust into such a different life?

A different world.

Though, really, she contemplated, watching several specks of white dancing by the cat-sìth's snout, which world was the *different* one?

She knew so much more than she had on Earth, yet no longer knew what day, or month, it was. How long had it been since she'd taken Lance's hand and stepped through a scrystone for the first time, after a mass of dead magic had trawled the streets of St. Andrews searching for her? Since Culloden? What had happened to them, the bodachs, after they had left? Ren hoped they'd stayed miles from Ainhill.

Was her dad hunched over the engine of a Fiat 500, or laid on a creeper board, working out why the brakes of a Mini Cooper weren't working? Was it Saturday? Was Luke playing rugby? Had his university offers come through yet? Did he know, for certain, that he'd become a medical student?

Would her dad be okay when Luke did just that?

Ren swallowed, then groaned. She'd always assumed she'd be there after Luke left. Where else would she have been? They had discussed it once, her and Luke, and with more sick days than worked ones to her name, no qualifications or prospects, it had seemed inevitable. It hadn't bothered her, not really. Not enough to ever admit.

Until....

The door didn't open in the same way it had when Lance had wrenched it ajar. This time the act was tentative, careful, with sodden robes and deft hands and a look that coated her in a cold wash of vulnerability. One that said *got you.*

And he was right, even if the cat-sith's low growls suggested otherwise. She had nothing left. Certainly not strength. Barely any will. Reason she had, but each was outside, fighting for and without her. Because Ren couldn't fight anymore.

And if his expression taught her one thing, it was that Gideon knew it, too.

He took a step towards her in time with the door clicking shut, and retrieved something from his robes. Ren braced herself for a weapon, but instead was greeted with a jar, no larger than a pint glass. It was filled with a glowing white liquid.

"Do you know what is in here, Renée?"

Of all the things she hated about the man, the way he said her name might have been what she hated most.

"No."

Gideon replied as he began to unscrew the lid. "Did you know that, given the chance, *NeòNach* will vie for freedom." He took a step closer. "It is one of the reasons arcanists must learn such stringent control from a young age. While *NáDarra* has, in many ways, barriers, each is bound to a specific purpose." The jar lid squeaked with every revolution. "Once *NeòNach* has been utilised by the arcanist who conjured it, it has no such purpose." His long fingers stopped turning. "Did you know, Renée, that once it has fulfilled that purpose it can travel for millions of miles before dying?"

Ren watched what she could see of the jar's contents. She could make them out now. Hundreds of thousands of specks of *NeòNach*. They lit up Gideon's silhouetted frame.

"And if captured and released, they will spread. With enough *NeòNach* you can cover rather large surfaces. It makes for fascinating study." He pulled off the lid; the jar was empty in less than a second.

Ren groaned as she felt their effect once again.

They'd spread, as Gideon had predicted, to every surface, leaving only two small perimeters on the floor, one where

Gideon stood, and the other where Ren and the cat-sìth lay.

From outside, she heard shouts, and a high-pitched scream. She swallowed hard.

The cat-sìth whimpered, its head bowed in between its two front paws.

"I know," Ren told it, "it's okay."

The nausea in the buzzing was worse, as was the pain. Her magic was quivering, not coping with being so vastly outnumbered by the *NeòNach* Gideon had caged them in with.

The shouting was louder now, none of it familiar.

Ren, huddled with the cat-sìth, wondered if it was really that bad to be without magic.

And then what it was to be without pain. She'd known, for a while, what that meant. And, while fighting the Zeds, had known what it meant to be powerful. But it had cost her something, both wondrous and entirely unmanageable.

Something dangerous, that had hurt and destroyed. And killed. An overdose. Of magic.

Gideon, she realised, as a bang and a muted shout echoed through the room, was speaking again.

"–have studied *NàDarra* in more detail than anyone else." Replacing the empty jar back within his robes, he pulled out something quite different. Something long and very thin, no more than a foot in length.

Ren couldn't hope to recognise its purpose. It was coated, she realised through eyes threatening to close, in specks she'd only seen once before, hovering above the strange apothecary owner. Grey and almost translucent.

It was the only element that hadn't awakened. The one that, were it to awaken, could cause what happened when she was born to happen again. Ren eyed the thing wearily.

"Do you know what this is?" Gideon asked, taking a further step, almost closing the gap between them.

"Aether." Ren coughed, then heaved. The feeling was growing stronger; she really might be sick. Perhaps if she had any food to throw up, she would have been.

"I don't mean the element," Gideon replied, his tone impatient.

"Then...no." She was shivering again, and the buzzing was rising, not in the way it did when she saw him, or when she kissed him. In the way it did when he was hurt. "You said that was the antidote."

"You can feel it, can't you? Mr. Allardyce's...affliction?" Gideon smiled then. "So could I, when my wife was crushed to death beneath a collapsed building."

"Y-you were bound."

"*Are*, Renée. *Are* bound. Death means little to such magic." Gideon knelt, his face inches from hers. She was no longer leaning against the cat-sìth; the back of her head was pressed hard against the floor, like the rest of her. "And now you will feel Mr. Allardyce die, too, as I did. And you'll know as he dies," he was whispering, "an antidote isn't what will save him, but you. Or, rather, your *NáDarra*."

"Wha–?"

"Did you know when you inject an ungifted person's blood with NáDarra, only someone gifted in those specific elements can extract them? A potion infused with them, much like the one I gave you, can dampen it, enough that a weaver wouldn't sense them." He smiled again then. "For a short while, anyway, and by the looks of you," – Ren was heaving again – "that time is over. The elements – now, Renée, no need to look at me like that, it was only the primaries – they're currently whirling around Mr. Allardyce's bloodstream, and soon he'll be dead, like Cora. And you'll know you could have saved him. Like me," he added, all trace of anything but malice gone.

"N-No–" Beside her, the cat-sìth let out a solitary, low *mow*. "I was a baby." Ren began to scramble, forcing what meagre strength she could muster to get to the door, to him.

Gideon's face appeared above her. "So was my daughter."

She saw it then, the specific madness he kept hidden beneath the surface. A *darkness*.

"Do you know how *she* died, Renée?"

"I-I'm sorry, I–"

Gideon raised the hand containing the long, Aether-covered instrument. "She was impaled."

White hot pain, unlike any that had been inflicted on her thus far, pierced her bicep, so intense she heard little of her own screams or the door being blown apart.

Gideon was no longer looming over her, not that it mattered.

Her right arm was spread outwards, the thin, Aether-clad instrument protruding from it. When she tried to move it, more pain erupted. The thing, whatever it was, was lodged, not just in her arm, but out the other side, into the floor.

"Move that arm," Gideon's voice rang from somewhere, "and your last element will awaken. And you will kill us all." He fell quiet then, though the silence was laced with his victorious presence.

"N-no." She moaned as Shae's face appeared above her. The buzzing, which had been low and painful, jolted, and then there was less of it. No. "L-Lance?"

Shae shot her a grave look.

"Go to him." If she couldn't, Shae should.

"Brennett's with him," Shae informed her, the calm in his voice barely there. His words shook in a way they never did. "He told me to come here bef–"

"Before what?"

His hand took hers, and squeezed, as he had on the beach as they ran for their lives. So much had changed. Ren let out a sob, then another, as a single tear tracked down Shae's cheek. The buzzing was weakening, fading with each second. He didn't want to finish his sentence, she knew he didn't, but she pleaded silently. "Before he lost consciousness."

"No."

She didn't know long she lay there, with Shae on one side, the cat-sìth on the other. The dampening that came with the excess *NeòNach* had gone, not that it mattered. Instead, she felt a huge pulse of something she both did and didn't recognise. The Aether. The specks surrounding whatever the thin, piercing instrument embedded in her arm were a strange sort. Their energy was both slow and fast, contained and wild; not quite alive and not quite not. In any other situation they'd have fascinated her.

But she didn't care about the Aether. She no longer cared about Gideon. Or the pain or the weakness or her personal death toll or the cruel twist of fate that had been her life. She used to. Until mere minutes before she had. And it had caused untold chaos. Now there was no chaos left to cause. And she knew then she couldn't lose control because there was nothing left to lose. What there was lay only metres from her, and Shae's hand in hers was the only thing keeping her from wrenching her arm, to hell with consequences, to reach him.

Other than hopelessness, Ren felt nothing.

A shout rang from somewhere. Ren didn't bother to decipher it. Why should she? Shae's hand shook in hers before he pulled it away. When she glanced upwards, he was frowning, then he stood.

And then instead of fading, the buzzing began to rise. Ren looked back to Shae's face. "Shae, he's–"

But Shae was already hotfooting his way from the room, casting a huge bunch of specks towards the corner where Ren realised Gideon stood, fencing him in place, to various shouts and cries, and one, lowly *woo*. As Lance, somehow, came back to her.

"Ground." Alone the word made little sense, and wasn't spoken by any voice she recognised. "I still need Ground."

"Could Ren–?"

Shae's voice was closer than the others. "No, he's stuck a *snathad* in her."

"He's...*what*?"

"Shit."

"Ground," Ren whispered. Before she could say more, as though the creature knew her very thoughts, it sprang to its paws and took off, hissing at Gideon as it passed.

It took no more than a few seconds, though to Ren it might have been a year, before the buzzing rose further. Her body was still numb, her thoughts a jumbled, confused mess. Until then, she felt very little.

Then she heard his voice, and she felt everything.

Despite the several warnings Ren heard various others giving him about moving too quickly, Lance appeared in the partially lit entranceway. He knelt, and neither of his hands, not the one he held hers with, nor the one he placed at the side of her face, felt real. A part of her didn't believe he was. Perhaps she'd died, too.

It wasn't until he leant down further still and pressed his lips to hers that she did know. The buzzing roared, more power-fully than it ever had, and nothing else mattered. Not Gideon or the *snathad* in her arm or what would happen were she to move it. Using what very well could be the last of her energy, she wrapped her free arm up around his neck. Ren would have stayed there all day. It wasn't until a voice, one she'd heard outside, said, "Um, excuse me?"

Lance's hands didn't move as they both looked up. Standing in the doorway, looking rather bemused, was a familiar, freck-led face. *No way.*

Ren frowned, her eyes darting above his head.

A room far from where they were, before she and Brielle had hid in a cupboard, at the time she'd believed Brennett her greatest adversary.

He – the *other* weaver – had been taken away, and she'd all but forgotten about him.

"Mind if we come in?" the stranger asked. He was looking between Ren, Ren's taio, Lance and Gideon, still silent and entombed by Shae's specks in the corner. His hair was longer, and he was no longer wearing what Ren had come to think of as Earth clothes. Now, he wore sapphire blue robes.

"Of course," Lance said. "Thanks, by the way."

"Don't mention it." His accent, unlike her own, which had never been that broad, was prominent and seemed out of place. He must have hailed from Manchester. "Just glad I got to you in time." His own taio, so much like Ren's, was missing only two elements – Ground and Dark. He stepped into the room. "I'm Grey."

"Lance."

"Ren."

His gaze lingered on Ren's taio, as hers did on his. "Seems we've got something in common."

She only nodded as a second silhouette momentarily blocked the doorway, their only real light source. She expected Shae, or Brennett.

Instead, every part of her numbed all over again.

A blazing taio, full of sparking red specks, hovered above the head of an achingly familiar figure. She stepped across the threshold, rendering all else a dull, blurry nothing. If Ren could have moved, she'd have been frozen.

A sharp intake of breath. "I was afraid it wouldn't really be you."

When Ren spoke, it was in little more than a breathy whisper. "M-mum?"

"Hi, darling."

Any chance of a sentimental reunion was gone the second her ocean blue eyes, so similar to Ren's own, clocked the Aether-shrouded *snathad*. Ren's mother whipped around, black robes and auburn hair whooshing upwards, and closed on Gideon.

Ren could no longer see her mother's eyes, but would have bet a lot of money – if such a thing existed on Caerisle – that they were blazing.

"You." Though her voice was steady, there was something else there, something low. Something dangerous.

If Gideon was intimidated, he hid it well. "Murryn."

At least that much was true, Ren thought, using what little reason she had that wasn't clouded in the pain radiating from her right bicep. Her lower arm lay useless, bent awkwardly upwards. She tried to bend each finger in turn. None moved. With her left hand she gripped Lance's. The tiny shred of whatever was keeping her from screaming again and again until her voice was cracked and as useless as the rest of her might sever entirely if he let go.

Murryn didn't reply. She turned, first to them, once again taking in the sight of her daughter sprawled on the floor, before marching towards the door.

"You," she said again, to someone Ren couldn't see. She spoke with barely less venom than she had when she addressed Gideon. "Come here."

Ren had to angle her head up to see the door.

Shae's face, once again nonplussed, appeared.

Murryn stretched one arm towards Gideon. "That *NeòNach*

is yours?"

"It is."

"Remove it."

"I'm not–"

"Remove it."

In the smallest of movements, only visible by the slightest twitch of his sleeve, Shae guided the specks he had imprisoned Gideon with towards the door, releasing them.

Murryn inclined her head forward. "Thank you," she said, before advancing again on Gideon. No one spoke. With four silent observers, Murryn threw her elbow backwards, and the sleeve of her robes flew up, revealing a tattooed pattern of what looked like vines Ren had never seen before. For a short second, she didn't move, poised and waiting. Murryn was taller than Ren, scarcely shorter than Gideon himself. Ren didn't know what passed between the two in that moment, and readied herself to see a flurry of red and a swirling of flame. None appeared. Murryn drove her fist forward, into Gideon's nose. An unpleasant crunch sounded as Gideon's head flew backwards. He let out a soft groan as the back of it hit the stone behind.

"Nice." It was Grey.

"I was going to do that," Lance muttered.

Murryn's breathing was heavy. "You still can."

Gideon, dabbing the back of his hand to his nose, said, "This is hardly necessary."

"Many, many things," Murryn replied, "weren't *necessary*. This isn't one of them." When she looked back at Ren, the hardened expression she wore dissipated, then reappeared as she once again took in the sight of the *snathad.* "How much Aether is attached?"

"Two hundred," Gideon replied, his voice having taken on a nasal quality.

"How *long*?"

"An hour; ninety minutes at the very most. But now, well I couldn't possibly guess. Forty minutes, perhaps."

Ren's eyes met Lance's. He said nothing, but squeezed her hand tighter still. At some point the cat-sìth had returned to her other side. Its fur was cool and damp against her arm. A part of her wanted to shout and scream again. Forty minutes. She didn't need to ask what happened in forty minutes. She felt it, felt them by her arm, some of them *in* her arm, in her. Of the seven awakenings Ren had experienced, she'd been aware of none until they happened. One – Water - she hadn't even known was happening at all. This time, though, she was so very aware of the specks attached to the *snathad.* They were unlike any she had known before. There, and yet not, like a shadow or a daydream. Two hundred distant memories, none of which she recognised or remembered. Because these specks weren't hers, not ones she was supposed to have anyway. Not yet.

And yet there they were, forcing their way in. Knocking on another door, one Ren couldn't open. One that wasn't supposed to open until it was ready.

And it wasn't.

Of all the things he had taken from her, her final awakening, a thing so intrinsically *hers*, was one of the worst. It was invasive, an unwanted presence he'd thrust upon her.

"The Council is coming," Murryn informed them, not taking her eyes off Gideon.

"In less than forty minutes?" Ren saw it then, a flash in his face she had seen once before, before she stopped offering her specks to his wall of dead magic. Triumph. "They'll struggle to, with no scrystones."

"You always did think of everything."

His eyes, for the smallest of moments, met Ren's. "When it comes to this, yes."

The glance wasn't lost on Murryn, and for the first time, her tone changed. Softened. "You know she did nothing."

"Often there is a fine line," Gideon replied, "between nothing, and everything."

"She was an infant."

"Yes." This time, when he stared at Ren, he refused to look away. "She was."

"Cora wouldn't have wanted this."

At her words, a twitch began by Gideon's temple. "You have no idea what Cora would have wanted, Murryn. And neither do I."

"Then hate *me* if you have to," Murryn said, a plea in her voice. "Punish *me.*"

Grey, taking advantage of the fact Gideon had paid him little attention, moved just behind Ren. He crouched by her head. Specks of his taio danced at the very top of her vision.

Gideon looked between mother and daughter. "In a way, I suppose I am." He placed a hand inside his robes, to an unseen pocket, and brought forth a vial and a cube, no more than half a foot in both height and depth, and a long needle, not unlike the *snathad*. Placing his hand around an edge of the cube, he loosened one side, and took a step forward, ignoring both Murryn, who stiffened, and Lance, who, letting go of Ren for the first time, rose in one fluid movement. One more rummage, and Gideon brought forth a tote. In the dim light, it looked like black velvet.

Lance's words were little more than a low growl. "Get the fuck back."

"Now, Renée," Gideon said, ignoring Lance. "We've been here before." He pulled at the loosened edge, opening the cube. The tote hung from his forearm.

The effect was instantaneous.

Ren, Grey and Murryn all took in short, sharp intakes of breath. By the door, Shae took a step backwards as several specks – far more than the cube should have held – flew outwards, and then into Gideon's raised palm, where they disappeared.

They reappeared floating above his head, in a taio Ren hadn't known he could possess.

A taio she hadn't known *anyone* could possess.

A taio of pure black. Not *Dark*, like the ones present in hers, that glimmered in moonlight and began to dance at dusk, but a pure, soulless black.

Death.

Every speck of magic Ren possessed was shaking.

"I have studied *NáDarra* more than any other," Gideon was saying. Tossing the cube to the floor, where it bounced against the stone, he focused his attention on the tote bag. Ren barely heard his words. "Gone further than anyone else was willing to."

"Gideon." Murryn had taken several short steps backwards, placing herself beside Lance, shielding Ren. "This...you can't... you know what they'll *do.*"

Gideon continued as if she hadn't spoken. "It has always been known that *NáDarra* works as one, each element coexisting. Each paired to another, and, as a whole, they meant one thing: life. That's all it is. The opposite of death." He began, his movements careful, tentative, to pull several small items from the tote.

Ren heard the gasp, not realising it came from her own mouth. What she had thought of only as *the door*, the one she'd desperately fought mentally to keep closed, without having the faintest clue how to do so, was opening. Her heartbeat boomed as a hollow *something* started to open in the place deep inside. A space for her eighth and final element.

The time she'd prayed for was gone. Aether was getting ready to awaken.

Gideon placed each on the floor, not two metres from Ren's face. Past both Lance, and her mother's legs, lay shards of what looked like light grey rock.

"You're close, aren't you?" The words were low, hurried.

Ren blinked up into Grey's freckled face, and nodded.

"If I take that," he inclined his head the tiniest amount to the *snathad,* "I'll draw all the Aether." Concealed by Lance and Murryn, Gideon hadn't noticed their whispered conversation. "It's already awakened in me. And then...." He swallowed.

And then Ren knew. There was a reason they had both ended up there, plucked from the magicless world they had been cast away to. Had he, too, lived a life of pain, and ailments, plagued by hospital trips and a constant stream of misdiagnosis?

What if there was somewhere else they could go. Ren stared up at him. "*Someone else?*"

He was staring at her, brow furrowed.. "But, we don't have the relaxant, or someone to–"

She knew then. "I don't think we need one."

"But–"

However much he'd studied *NáDarra,* and however little time she'd spent with it, there were pieces he didn't understand, couldn't. *NáDarra* wasn't some clinical thing, nor was it simply the *opposite of death.* It was everything, but more than that. It was *hers,* and Ren knew, if she told them, they'd go to Grey. They'd understand in a way Gideon never could. "He didn't give me it because I couldn't give up the elements," Ren hissed as she looked at Gideon's shards.

He finished lining them up, and stood.

Ren's mouth was dryer still as she realised they weren't rocks, but bones.

"Gideon." Murryn's voice was strangled, as though the sight pained her. "You can't do this."

Ren turned back to Grey. "He gave me it because he wanted me to give them up *to die.*"

"It is a beautiful thing, Murryn," Gideon said, "Renée has the required *life,* and I have..."

She didn't know if he finished, for a jolt, deep inside, of

something unnatural and relentless, demanded all her attention. For the first time, she sensed them, the strange, grey specks. Her eyes snapped back to Grey. "Do it now."

"I–"

"Now!" She was no longer whispering.

As Grey reached forward, his fingers curling around the *snathad*, Ren felt them falter, hesitate for a moment, trying to understand. Then Grey wrenched the device upwards, Ren's screams echoing around them as he did.

"Ren!" Both Lance and Murryn had ducked to her side.

Gideon let out a howl of rage. "You've killed us all."

"No," Grey said, "I haven't." And Ren felt Grey's unspoken call to the Aether that had almost been hers. His hand grasped her own and she felt them leave as she told them silently it was okay. "Hold him off," he said, not to her, and she felt Lance shift beside her as he stood again.

It's okay, she thought. *It's okay.*

There was no time for a discussion, both navigating the hurried negotiation through no more than instinct.

"Lightning," Ren groaned. "I need your–"

"Do it, give me your Light."

She did. And it was painful, and awful. An overwhelming sadness befell her as she bode goodbye to Water, though it was her Air specks that put up the most fight. By the end she was pleading forgiveness as she pushed them, the first ones that had ever awoken. The ones that had blown over her dad's fence and called Shae to her. They left in a shroud of what she was certain was betrayal. Ren hated herself.

Deep inside, in the place she'd known Air, and Water, and Light, and almost Aether, four types of coloured specks danced. No longer was her arm forced in place. Instead, as Grey helped her to her feet, it hung uselessly, no matter how much she tried to move it.

Gideon was staring, watching Ren and Grey as the pure

373

black specks of his taio loomed. "Do you believe, Renée, this little display of yours will stop me? None of you can touch me. Any magic you throw at me will die."

"I know," Ren said. The pain that had plagued her arm had all but vanished; in its place a heavy nothing. She took a step, positioning herself on the left side of Lance.

Just behind, Grey followed suit.

"But if you taught me anything," Ren said, "it's that one can wield so much power, and yet still be killed by a meagre fall, or a bite." Leaning as close to Lance as she was able, Ren whispered two words: "Left ankle." She addressed Gideon again. "Or blade."

It happened quicker than she was prepared for, quicker, perhaps, than it should have. Lance found the knife deftly, and threw it with the precision of a hunter, of a fighter.

Of an expert.

It hit just left of the centre of Gideon's chest, and he fell both in, and surrounded by, death. His final moment was a dull thud on the floor. In the silence that came after, Ren sought his face. It might have been handsome once. It must have been, to Cora if no one else. Upon it was a mixture, a fleeting combination of shock...and something else.

It might have been relief.

Whether she had grown used to the dark entranceway, or whether death seemed more fitting to night-time, it seemed wrong to emerge into the late morning sunlight. It was present, the wrongness, in the birdsong and the breeze. Nobody spoke as they shuffled out. Gideon's body, along with the various instruments he had brought, remained, littered across the hard floor, beside the collection...of bones.

She felt like a giant bruise. No part of her wasn't throbbing or aching in some way. The only part that wasn't was her arm, which still felt nothing at all, even when she prodded it. She said nothing of it, as though suddenly losing the use of her dominant arm was of little importance. Instead, she half walked, and half allowed herself to be dragged beside Lance.

The first thing she saw were the bodies.

Several others were lingering; only Ruff and Brennett were among those Ren recognised. Lowell was nowhere to be seen.

"You've got to be kidding me," Murryn muttered from Ren's other side. "Let me guess," she said, loud enough for everybody present to hear, "you just got here."

A small, aged man, barely taller than Ren, broke free of the small crowd. His purple robes hung loosely over his spindly frame, the edges of them a darker mauve thanks to the still wet ground. He peered first at Ren, and then at Grey, paying more mind to their taios than their faces, craning a long, thin neck that made him appear somewhat turtle-like. "Why, yes," he replied, frowning. "Not two minutes ago."

"Fabulous," Murryn snapped, "that's very useful."

The man peered at her. "Murryn?"

Something in her mother seemed to crack. When Ren looked, her eyes held a glassiness. "Yes, Odo."

Two others, a man and woman, joined Odo. The woman wore similar robes, though hers were a light grey.

"Lance," the man acknowledged.

Lance's tone was curt. "Wade."

"So, it's true," Wade said, "two weavers."

The woman was examining their taios, as Odo had. "But," she said, glancing behind, at the small group that included Brennett and Ruff, "we were told they had the Power of the Eight. Where's Gideon? What's–?"

Inside Ren, something snapped. The company of these strange Council officials was like a grabbing of her windpipe.

"Ren?"

She didn't know her eyes had closed, but when she opened them she was looking at her mother. There were a few more lines around her eyes and mouth, her reddish hair was longer than Ren remembered, but she was there.

It was everything she'd wished for since the night at Culloden.

Murryn grasped Ren's shoulders in her hands, before turning to Lance. "You're bound to my daughter, aren't you?"

"Yes, ma'am."

Murryn looked over her shoulder, towards Odo and Wade and the woman, and then at Ren. "You don't need this," she said, "not today."

Lance's fingertips brushed gentle patterns up and down her shoulder. "I," Ren began, "I can't deal with...n-not now, not–"

Murryn only nodded. Ren turned then, away from them all and, with difficulty, and a lot of help from Lance, began to hobble away. The cat-sìth followed suit, trotting ahead, tail swishing. It was joined, seconds later, by Brogan. Ren didn't know where she, they, were heading. Anywhere that wasn't

Longwretch prison would do.

"Now, hang on!" Wade called, ignoring Murryn's shouts.

Lance didn't bother to turn his head to call a decisive, "Not now."

Another voice, this one further away, cried something.

Ren wondered if he'd found Gideon's body. She couldn't be there to see it again.

Two sets of heavy, sloshy footsteps ran up behind them. On one side of them, Wade appeared.

Ren wished she had the energy to tell him to piss off.

Shae appeared on the other, followed by Murryn.

"Look, Lance," Wade began, his gaze flicking between them, "I understand that some shit has happened." At Ren's glare, he continued, "A *lot* of shit. But the Senior Councillor is dead, and you lot were the only ones on the scene, you," he nodded at Ren, "don't exist on any records, but are apparently the reason the *NáDarra'n* Office has been doing nothing but clean-up for weeks. Even more than usual. There was a bloody earthquake on one side of Caeracre three weeks ago that they felt five miles away."

Shae, after clearing his throat, said, "I am very much in favour of an official investigation taking place. My – ah – *our* report will be very thorough."

Lance snorted. "Nothing new there, then."

Ignoring him, Shae continued, "It would be beneficial for Ren to have some time – a night at least, to recover. She experienced two considerable lags this morning alone." Wade was staring at Ren's taio. "This was while she had seven awakened elements."

Wade was frowning. "I don't–" Then he sighed, running a hand through his hair. It was nearly as long as Lance's, and a deep black, streaked with white. He reminded Ren of an overgrown badger. His gaze settled on Ren's face. For how awful she felt, she must look worse, though that might work in

377

her favour. "That true?" Wade asked.

Ren nodded.

He sighed again, and pinched the bridge of his nose. "Look, I don't know what's going on but I can't stall them investigating you for longer than, say, a day, if that."

"A day," Ren replied. Her voice sounded strange, weak. "You'd give us until tomorrow?"

Wade nodded, his expression grim. "If it wasn't you," he said, holding his hand out to Lance, who took it. "You know I wouldn't."

"I know."

He buried a large hand in a pocket, and pulled forth a scrystone.

Wade handed it to Lance. "Take the Ground line to outside Steerpike, ten turns," he added. "Be at the Council at midday tomorrow, CC Meeting Rooms." He regarded both of them with the air of a disapproving teacher. "If you're not–"

"We will be," Lance said. "Appreciate it."

"Go now." Wade nodded back towards the prison. "Odo's coming and I doubt he'll be best pleased."

Murryn scoffed at his words as she stepped in front of Ren. Many, many things passed between the two women. When she spoke, Ren's mother's words were hushed, her tone strained. "I will explain it all."

Ren said nothing, knowing if she did there was every chance she would break down entirely.

Murryn looked as though she were fighting similar impulses. "Five years."

Lance must have handed the stone to Shae, who had set the scrystone portal just in time for Odo to approach.

"I…" Ren began, her eyes refusing to leave her mother's face.

"Go." Murryn gave a series of small nods, as though it was herself she was convincing. "Rest now. You look like you're ready to collapse." Ren felt worse than that. "I'll see you tomorrow."

Ren's reply was whispered. "Tomorrow."

Neither she nor Lance bothered to look over as Odo began to protest, stepping through, away from everything they'd seen and faced not only that day but every day since he'd been taken from her in Shin.

Her eyes were closed when they emerged wherever they were, and closed they remained. Ren knew only that the light was dim, the air cool and that she could both hear and smell the sea. He lifted her, one arm beneath the crook of her knees, the other across her shoulders, and carried her over what sounded like bare floorboards – several squeaked under his step. He lowered her onto a bed. Placing one hand to the back of her head, he pressed his lips first to hers, then her forehead. Ren blinked. The building was little more than a wooden shack. Lance was pulling his blood-smeared shirt over his head. There was a scattering of new scars and bruises across his torso.

At first, they said nothing. Lance offered the softest hint of a smile as he sank down beside her, hissing as he did. It was accompanied by a sharp buzz-like pain in Ren's chest. She didn't want to think of what he'd endured not only from his own injuries, which looked numerous, but from all the pain she'd been put through. His words echoed around her muddled mind: *I felt every damn thing.*

"I have never," Lance began, rolling over, nestling her against his bare chest, "been so fucking happy to lie down."

And there it was: solitude. And the knowledge that, for now, they were safe, and together.

The beating not only of her own heart, but his.

And for that moment, at least, it was enough.

R en woke with a start. She was alone, save for the cat-sìth and Brogan, who had both taken to snoozing at the bottom of the bed, and in the process had ended up taking up around two-thirds of the mattress. She was shrouded in both aches and nausea. Not too far away, she heard waves crashing.

"Ren?" Lance's head appeared around one of the two doors in the shack. "Hey," he said as she blinked at him, grimacing at a throb by her ribs.

The only part of her without a dull, aching pain was her right arm, where she still felt a defiant nothingness. It wouldn't move.

"Hi," she croaked.

Lance, who had stripped himself down to only a thin pair of shorts, crossed the small, bare room and sank down beside her.

She allowed him to help her become somewhat more up-right. "What time is it?"

"Four-ish."

"In the morning?"

"Mm." That gave them hours before they were due in whatever the CC Meeting Rooms were. "How are you?" Lance asked.

Ren, beginning to peel off her black cotton prison attire to examine her arm, said, "Stiff, and sore." Each memory of the previous day cycled round her mind. "Sad." Pulling the top over her head and noting the way it caught on what had to be several large knots in her hair, Ren reached her left hand forward, placing it on the centre of Lance's chest. "And happy."

Lance didn't appear to be listening. He was frowning.

Ren followed his gaze to her upper arm, her eyes widening at the sight. "Holy–"

The point of impact was obvious, for it was at the centre of an intricate and disturbing pattern. It looked like several bloody, already scabbing tentacles, and ran not only down her arm, but up, over her shoulder and, Lance confirmed, across part of her back.

"You'll need to have a specialist healer look at it."

Ren wrinkled her nose, as she tried again, unsuccessfully, to move her arm. "Great." *More doctors.* "It's so ugly."

Lance chuckled, placing a soft kiss to her forehead. "No part of you could ever be ugly."

Her nose was wrinkled as she examined what she could see of her bicep's strange new scarring. "You know if we weren't bound, you'd turn and walk out that door."

"Ren, please." He raised both eyebrows. "If we weren't bound I'd have sold you to those nutters weeks ago." He rose, stretching his arms, dodging her feeble attempt at a slap. "I bet I'd get a ton of horses, or something."

"Well, that's just insulting." She scoffed, gaze trailing his bare form. "I'm worth a few unicorns, surely." His bruising looked nastier than it had the previous day.

"Ha, I wish." He began to walk back through the only other door. "Unicorns are useful."

Ren, dismayed she had nothing within her good arm's reach to throw at him, began to shimmy herself off the bed.

"Want a bath? There's a few clothes in that cupboard."

"Nah," she called back, running a hand through the mess that was her hair. "Thought I'd stay like this." She stood, and though various pains, both new and old, appeared with each movement, she managed to cross the room, which functioned as a bedroom, living room and kitchen.

"Ugh. Well, you can forget unicorns." He was bent over a

wooden *bath* that was little more than a barrel. It barely looked large enough for one fully grown adult, let alone two. "I'd be lucky to get a stray dog for you like tha– Ah!" Her slap hit his lower back. "That's just rude."

She looked up at him, relishing the way the buzzing steadily rose as he pressed his front against hers. "I'm not rude." She placed her good arm around his waist, pressing herself into him, breathing in the – now rather pungent – scent of him. "You smell," she mumbled, her voice distorted against his skin.

"Oh, no." Using one hand, he rubbed the pad of his thumb up and down her temple. The other he trailed down her back. "You're a real delight."

The barrel masquerading as a bath didn't take long to fill, and there was far from the amount of toiletries she'd need to feel close to human again, but the small bar of plain soap Lance found did, at least, lather a little. Finding anything close to a comfortable position in which to even begin washing, proved tricky. It was Lance, ever the problem solver, who managed to manoeuvre her, planting her in his lap, their fronts flush together.

"Ah, yes," Ren remarked, "what an optimal washing position."

He only smiled and pressed his lips to the side of her jaw, before, with only the meagre soap and a pitcher from the kitchen, began to work through all the knots in her hair. Reaching as best she could with her one good arm, Ren did the same, running as much soap as she could through his long curls; they were far more tangled than hers. It was a lengthy job – made lengthier still by Ren only having one working arm. They spent it sharing everything that had happened from the moment they were separated.

"I don't really remember," Lance was saying. "I'd punched two of the guards, head-butted another. Something was happening with you; this," he gestured above the point where their chests were pressed together, "was going crazy. Think they sedated me or something, they must have injected it then."

"The first night?" she asked, guilt flooding her.

"Mm. I thought..." He didn't continue.

Ren forced herself to look at him, hating herself all over again at the sight of his tears. As he blinked, two broke free, tracking down his cheeks. She watched them, then gently brushed them away. "I wasn't being hurt then," she told him. "Not physically anyway."

He said nothing.

"Gideon had...I don't know, a copy of something...of the *dossier*," she said the word with disdain, "for *Collecting* me. It was to try to force another awakening, he told me a few days after."

"What was?"

"Making me think you were going to sell me."

"Wh–"

"It had the *delivery point*, or whatever, as the *NáDarra'n* Academy, and he said that Endermarch was used by gangs, and there was a note – one identical to one they'd found on Brennett that he said you'd had on you that said *The weaver for the Hull,* and I just, I didn't know what to think." His brows were drawn together in a way she didn't like. "I didn't *believe* it, not really. And not for long. I just...I'm sorry." It didn't sound enough.

"Not *really*?"

Oh, shit. "But then I broke Brennett out of prison to come rescue you." He looked as though he was going to open his mouth, when Ren hastily continued. "After he – Gideon, I mean – put me in front of a big wall of dead magic and then made a room collapse on top of me."

"A what?"

"And about ten crazy Zeds tried to kill me, or kidnap me or something, thanks to Priya," she added, the words bitter.

"I'm still hazy on that. How was she...?"

She told him everything Priya had told her.

"Then Brennett said he never wanted to see her face again. I don't think he meant it, though."

"Probably not."

For a long while neither spoke, each simply continuing with the task of washing the other. But she was acutely aware of the tension between them. The buzzing prickled.

She squeezed the top of his shoulder. "Please don't be mad."

He sighed, running a hand through his considerably cleaner hair. "I'm not mad. I'm just...I'm fine. With everything that happened, it's nothing, and you still came for me."

His eyes stared into hers, deeper than they ever had before.

"Of course I did," she whispered. "Remember when you came to get me from Brennett's weird fortress?"

He nodded.

"I think it's...what we do." He placed one hand on the nape of her neck, drawing her closer. "We come for each other." His breath was warm on her cheek; the buzzing returned to something close to normal. When she looked, his mouth had twisted into something of a smirk.

"Is it now?"

She had no time to reply, as much as a hasty *you know that's not what I meant* had begun to form in her mind as soon as the words had left her mouth. His grip on her neck tightened, just enough to guide her head forwards, her mouth to his.

How he managed it, given the state of him, she didn't know, nor did she care to ask. His mouth didn't leave hers as he lifted not just himself, but her, from the barrel bath. Locking her legs together at the ankle, behind Lance's back, Ren anchored herself to him. Their fronts still flush together, and together they stayed as Lance somehow expertly manoeuvred them, still soaking, still kissing, towards the bed.

He laid her down with a tenderness Ren had no memory of ever receiving before. As though she were a piece of old, valuable china already littered with hairline cracks.

Swallowing audibly, he stared down at her. His eyes were glassy, so dark in the dim light of the early morning that barely penetrated the window hangings they looked black. His expression was both soft and pained as he reached forward and ran the pad of his thumb down the side of her jaw.

His body dipped downwards, though his weight remained upon his elbows, each propped on either side of her shoulders. When he kissed her, it was hurried and rough, as though any second they'd be separated. Again.

"I thought I'd never see you again," he whispered against her lips.

Ren snaked her only working arm up, around his neck. The buzzing was roaming across every centimetre of skin that met his. In her chest, it was positively erupting. "I know." A tear trickled from the corner of her eye down her temple. "When I was inside... and you were..." The words hurt, far more than her numerous injuries did. "I felt you..." *die.*

He cut her off with a kiss, this one neither hurried, nor rough. "Don't."

So, she didn't. Instead, she kissed him more, and focused her energies into pulling his torso further against her own, something Lance was adamantly determined not to do.

"I'm not going to risk hurting you more." There was finality in his tone despite the ragged breath he released as Ren bucked her hips upwards.

She wanted to huff, but try as she might, she couldn't hide the hiss of pain as she lowered herself back against the covers. "I'm...fine."

He chuckled quietly, though the sound was hollow. "You are not fine." He pressed a line of kisses from her lips, down the side of her neck, her chest, each of her breasts. Not once did he allow himself to properly lie on her as he lowered himself further down her bruised frame. "But you will be." She barely heard him as his tongue swept gently across the centre of her stomach. "I'll make sure of that."

All she managed was a sigh as her hand roamed his still wet curls. For a second, he halted the ministrations between his mouth and Ren's abdomen – much to her disapproval - to interlace his fingers with hers. "For now," he said, placing a single, achingly soft brush of his lips to her wrist, "I'll do what I can to help you forget the pain...for a while."

A shiver crept down her spine.

"*Anam*," he whispered.

His head dipped back to her stomach, lower this time, then lower still. His hand remained clasped within her own; she clutched it hard as his tongue explored her, each caress tantalisingly slow.

Her skin, coated in goosebumps and encased in buzzing, was both hot and cold as Lance teased her hips, the tops of her thighs...the inside of her thighs.

And, as his mouth settled itself against her gently squirming frame, she did forget the pain. Forgot how much she had needed this, needed him.

She forgot, for a while, how close he, her *co-anam,* had been to leaving her.

How close his soul, his *anam,* had been to leaving hers.

By the time half past ten rolled by, they were even more rested after an impromptu nap, washed, almost dressed, and fed. Lance had located some oatcakes and sheets of pasta, and a small gas hob. Ren lit it, though she felt several pangs of regret as she called the red specks forwards. The place inside, while full again, felt half empty. She hadn't known her specks long, not any of them, but she'd known Air the longest and it hurt, in a way she couldn't hope to explain, to know they wouldn't be back.

"Do you think Grey will look after them?" she asked, then felt foolish.

Lance, to his credit, didn't laugh. "Yeah." He pulled on a shirt, which resembled a large cotton potato sack, then placed a brief kiss to her cheek. "He saved your life."

"And yours," she pointed out.

"I think we can safely assume he's an all right bloke."

They had made the decision to head into Steerpike, where the Council headquarters were located, and only ten minutes away from their shack.

"You ready?" Lance asked, flapping the hem of his shapeless shirt a bit.

Ren's was no better, fitting worse than Lance's. With her boots mostly dry from the previous day, she opted to not bother with the trousers, and instead used a line of twine she'd come across in a drawer, fashioned into a belt.

"Or are you planning to pout into that window some more?"

She turned away from what little of her reflection she could see in the pane and, scowling, joined him by the door. "I do not pout."

"You bloody do."

The cat-sìth chirped as it stepped outside ahead of them.

"See, he agrees."

They blinked against the morning light. Out in the sun, the bruising on Lance's face and arms was far more visible.

Ren looked down, examining her arm. While bathing had got rid of a lot of dried blood and grime, the marks were still raised and angry. Lance planned on taking her to some healing centre, though could they help? Was it a usual occurrence, for a weaver to be stabbed with whatever a *snathad* was? Ren didn't know. Nor did Lance.

They walked for several minutes in silence. At some point,

his hand had found hers, and their fingers laced. With no current threats, that they knew of anyway, the journey could have been relaxed, were Ren not quite so anxious.

To their left lay the sea, its still expanse dotted with a myriad of boats.

"I've never seen that sea so still," Lance noted as he looked down towards the bay. There was a beach, and further up a small marina.

Up ahead, sprawling to their right, was the beginnings of a city, and more people than Ren had seen thus far in Caerisle put together. Steerpike was made of mismatched cobbles and winding streets. They entered the city beneath a giant metal arch made of what looked like cogs and were greeted by a nearby artist painting a mural on the front of a store. While the shop hadn't opened yet, in the large window Ren saw hats and scarves, and jewellery made from stones she couldn't place. Across the street several stalls stood, their wares ranging from bread to slippers, fabric to meat. A little further up a man in a white cloak was admiring his own hog roast. For a few of Ren's Fire specks, he presented them with filled to bursting bacon sandwiches, even throwing a few fatty end pieces to the cat-sìth and cù-sìth.

The sky, for once, was calm. No flashes of lightning, nor scent of burning, lingered in the air. The few gusts of wind were caused by their proximity to the sea, and not by Ren.

She was only half paying attention as she finished the last of her sandwich.

"You want to talk about it?" Lance asked.

Ren took a breath. It was something she had never faced before in any past relationship – not that there had been many, that lying about her feelings was a fruitless endeavour. "I..." She leant into the arm he'd wrapped around her shoulders, finding herself hissing in pain every few steps. The city's steep and hilly layout was doing little to help. They had climbed for around twenty minutes before the trajectory began to even. Their pace slowed the further they walked, and Ren had to rely on Lance to steer her ahead, the aching in her ribs having returned with a vengeance. But it wasn't the pain, or the shops and stalls, alleyways and cafes that made up the streets around her that Ren's mind focused on.

"I found my mum...or, she found me."

"Yeah, she did." He nodded ahead. "That's the Council up there."

The building was huge. It was crafted from what looked like pale sandstone, adorned with white marble pillars, each towering at least thirty feet high. Near the top of each there was a black symbol carved into each pillar, all different.

"What do they mean?" Ren asked, nodding ahead, looking to each in turn.

Lance pointed at the furthest left first. "Department of Acquisitions – that's where Shae and I work." He moved his finger to the next, which seemed to feature a pair of wings and a paw print. "Department of Creatures, Beasts, Non-human Beings."

"That sounds ominous."

"Wade, who you saw yesterday, with the moustache, runs it."

The next symbol she was certain she had seen elsewhere. "Dragon Corps." *On the uniforms,* she thought, *of the men working for Gideon.* The Justice Division's symbol came next, then the Department of Societal Upkeep. "The last two are for *NáDarra* and *NeòNach.*" Ren looked at the *NáDarra'n* one. It was the most complex, featuring eight conjoining circles. She shouldn't have, but felt a pang at the sight of all eight together.

Four of them existed within her. She could sense them so much easier now. Though she hated to admit it, even to herself, more easily than she had the day before. Perhaps it had been a little crowded.

Lance didn't lead her to the Council Chambers; he veered sideways, to a low, white building. Its exterior was far less impressive. "You two," he told the two creatures, "wait here and stay out of trouble."

The cat-sìth plonked itself down exactly where it stood,

spreadeagled, Brogan mimicked the action. Between them, they took up over half the path, ensuring passers-by had to dodge to pass.

Keeping his arm around her shoulders, Lance led Ren inside the white building. She didn't have to know anything of Caerisle, or Steerpike, or the Council, to know he'd brought her to the Healing Centre. It was almost identical to hospitals on Earth: cool and clinical.

They walked, Ren trying not to groan out loud, towards a wide reception desk. A woman with a taio composed of yellow Light specks watched them approach from above a clipboard. She offered Ren a look of bewilderment, and Lance a wide smile.

"Hi, Lance."

"Hey, Tia. Any chance of seeing a healer?"

"Of course." Everything about the woman, from the large sunflower she wore in her hair, to the silvery notes present in her voice, was chipper. "Magical, or...?"

Lance nodded. "*NáDarra*, Aether specialist if possible."

Tia nodded, handing Lance a clipboard. "Take a seat; fill this out."

Their wait time was impressively short, especially considering the number of long hours Ren had spent in hospital waiting rooms on Earth. They had filled out Ren's form as best they could, but with no home that wasn't through a very specific and rare – and probably illegal to obtain – scrystone, no occupation or sensical medical history, most of it was left blank. In the box that asked her to *describe the problem*, Ren found herself staring sadly at the page.

"Well," a somewhat familiar voice rang behind her, "this is a surprise." It belonged to the woman they'd seen the previous day, clothed in grey robes, who'd stood perplexed, along with Odo and Wade. Her hair, a bright ginger, was tied loosely. A smattering of freckles coated a pale face and a taio Ren hadn't noticed hovered above her, filled with slow-moving grey specks. "I don't think we met properly," she said. "I'm Kaiya."

"Ren."

"Oh, I'm aware." Kaiya gestured towards a nearby hallway. "You've caused quite a hubbub." The healer led them to a consultation room and instructed her to lay on a bed. She was glad of the chance to lie down. Kaiya began to poke and prod her sensationless arm.

"There *are* a few residual specks of Aether," Kaiya said, searching in some drawers beside the bed. "I can remove them through a small incision, though whether the movement will return, I cannot say."

"Through a–"

Kaiya had already obtained a scalpel. "Hold still, Renée."

They left the Healing Centre around twenty minutes later, Ren sporting a heavily bandaged arm and Lance a canvas tote full of potions that if Ren didn't take *exactly* as instructed, Kaiya would *take delight in administering a second, larger incision.*

"She was far scarier than any tiny woman should be," Lance noted as they stepped back into the street. Brogan trotted over obediently, while the cat-sìth, for whom Ren really ought to pick a name for, stayed put. It appeared to have attracted quite the crowd as it juggled two balls of yarn – obtained from who knew where – between its front paws and back. Every so often, an onlooker would throw it a treat and the *show* would start over. Impressive, really. Ren had never known such a resourceful animal.

Lance, clearly, didn't agree. "He's eaten better than we have."

"He's so clever."

Lance snorted. "Ready?"

She nodded, and they headed, the cat-sìth trotting behind, carrying both balls of yarn in its mouth, towards huge doors, full of several streams of people coming and going.

Inside was a hall so vast it was impossible to take everything in. The ceiling was a huge dome, decorated with a gargantuan mosaic. A clock hung from the ceiling, its circumference easily six foot. They had fifteen minutes before meeting Wade and Odo.

Magic, a mixture of Light, Air and Aether, as well as *NeòNach*, was present above. The place was lit by huge, hovering clusters of Light magic. Doorways, more than she could count, lined each wall. People were coming and going from each one, giving the place the feel of a giant anthill. Ren hadn't seen close to this many people since arriving. Faces and taios alike merged into one.

Lance dropped his arm, taking her hand; the buzzing centred there. He led her across the colossal floor. "The meeting rooms are up those stairs." He nodded ahead. "Will you be okay?"

Ren groaned. Didn't these people appreciate flat ground? "Just."

"I'll carry you, if you–"

She rolled her eyes. "Shut up." Though, by the time they had reached the top of what had been enough stairs to cover at least three floors, she was regretting declining the offer.

They turned down a hallway and were greeted by an excitable, "Aha!" A small man, wearing both a gold monocle and a lime green cape, was almost dancing at the sight of them. "Everyone's terribly excited."

Ren doubted that.

"Head into the first room on the right, *there.*"

They filed through, Lance first. He hadn't let go of her hand and she hoped he wouldn't. Inside, sitting around a large table, were a number of people, most of whom she recognised.

"Ah," Odo said. "You found us then."

Ren nodded as she took one of the two remaining vacant chairs.

"You look better," Murryn whispered, wrapping her in a brief hug. "Do you feel it?"

"I don't know." Her gaze swept the room.

Grey sat on the other side of Murryn. She smiled at him, feeling another pang as she glanced at his taio. The expression was mirrored as his eyes travelled to hers.

Ruff and Lowell sat beside Grey, and Brennett beside them, oddly subdued and looking down at the table, his expression dark. Perhaps they were planning to arrest him again. Perhaps they already had.

On the other side of Lance sat Shae and beside him was Cassidy, the red-headed Lightning bearer who had been with Lance in the prison infirmary.

On Cassidy's other side and as badger-like as he had appeared the day before, was Wade. Next to him was the young boy, no more than sixteen, with his red hair and acne; the only thing missing were his Zed robes. His eyes refused to meet Ren's scowl.

Beside him, and no doubt the reason for Brennett's mood, was Priya. With a start, Ren realised both the boy and Priya were wearing handcuffs.

Ren shot a sideways glance at Lance, wondering if he shared Brennett's obvious disdain, or whether there would be something else there at the sight of Priya, but he wasn't so much as glancing at the other woman.

Two more Council officials, one wearing red robes and the other in green, hovered in the background.

Odo, with no apparent seat, cleared his throat over the light buzz of conversation that had developed.

"As you're all aware," Odo began, gesturing to his fellow Council members, "we, as the Council of Officials for the land of Caerisle, are faced with a rather obscure and difficult situation. With the arrival of yourself, Renée, and you, ah, Grey, that nobody knew of – except for Councillors Gideon Adair, who is, ah, no longer with us," Lance's leg shifted against Ren's, "and Rosa Vreen, who appears to be, ah, missing." *Missing*.

That was news to Ren. She thought of Rosa, with her trouser suits and immaculate hair and false sweetness, and wondered where she was now, and why she had followed Gideon with such loyalty.

"We're hoping," Odo was saying, "that between you, we can piece together, ah, well, as much as we can."

Odo invited Shae to talk first. The arcanist stood and began explaining how he and Lance had been summoned, given two scrystones, and a dossier.

At the mention of that, it was Ren's turn to squirm, though Lance's hand on her thigh didn't falter.

Shae spoke as though the words were rehearsed; it wouldn't have shocked her if they were.

At the mention of the bodach, Wade's eyes bulged.

"This is outrageous!" Wade began to rave, looking less like a badger and more like a flustered walrus. "Gideon sent, what, *several* bodachs there, to this *Earth*?" He spoke the word as if it personally offended him. She hadn't cared enough to really look at him the previous day, but saw now he was large, in everything from his stature to his voice, which boomed through the meeting room like a foghorn. His robes were all holes and patches. The tidiest thing about the man was his handlebar moustache.

Odo inclined his head with a sigh. "It would certainly seem that way. It looks as though his Plan A, shall we, ah, say, was that neither Renée nor Grey made it here, for only a bodach could have extracted even unawakened elements." A shiver slithered down her spine. "The Collectors, I believe, were merely there to lead the bodachs to their targets."

"Charming," Lance muttered.

Wade's face was an interesting shade of red. "But where did he *get* them? He couldn't have bred them at Endermarch bloody prison, could he?"

"Considering," Odo replied monotonously, "you are head of that particular department, I'd say it was your job to find such things out."

Silence followed, the kind that hung thickly in the air.

Ren didn't know whether to gasp or laugh.

Lance had opted for the latter, and was silently shaking.

"Um," it was Priya. A collective shock hung through the air as she spoke. "Gideon never sent any bodachs. The Zenthion did."

Zenthion. The collective name for the crazy Zeds.

Wade emitted a noise that was more a snarl than anything else.

"Ah." Odo merely blinked. "Thank you, Miss. Continue, Mr. Ambroise."

Shae did, recounting everything they'd encountered from the bodachs to the note from the Zeds, the *Zenthion*, to Ren and Lance both being taken at Shin. Then he recounted the piece of the puzzle Ren hadn't known. How he'd found his way to the Hidden City, attempting, without much luck, to find anyone who knew of the phrase *Còmhla mar aon ,* only to realise he'd been saying it wrong for two days. How he had found his way to Murryn, and Grey, who'd been rescued from the Zeds by Ruff and several others Murryn had assembled to her cause. How he had gone himself to the Zenthion with just enough information about Ren that they trusted him, and how they'd known of Ren's escape thanks to Priya.

"But what, exactly, did these *Zeds* want?" a woman, one of the other Council officials, asked. "If, as you say, the weavers held the Power of the Eight, and were both more than a little unstable, what could they possibly have achieved?"

Shae's tone was cool. "One is positioned over there." He inclined his head towards the cuffed teenage boy, who was looking a tad green. "Why don't you ask him?"

"Excellent idea, Mr. Ambroise," Odo said. "You there, Mr, ah..."

"Fairley," the boy squeaked. "Anders Fairley."

It was Wade who answered him. "Moira's boy?"

Anders Fairley nodded.

"That's no good, son, getting mixed up in all this."

Anders only nodded again.

Odo addressed the boy. "Mr. Fairley, you may be able to provide a great insight into this, if you would."

Anders, much like Brennett, looked nowhere but the surface of the table. "At first, we – ah..." - sheer terror crossed his features at the faux pas - "*they* wanted the weavers dead. Then, once they learnt the bodachs had failed, the plan changed." He took several long, deep breaths, the way someone on the cusp of an asthma attack might. "They wanted to extract their elements, a-and use them–"

Odo looked as confused as Ren felt. "*Use* their powers?"

Anders swallowed, and continued. "I don't know how. They n-never trusted me enough..."

"I can't imagine why," Lance whispered, and Ren had to feign a coughing fit to hide her misplaced laugh.

Again, Priya cleared her throat and, refusing to look at either Ren, Lance, or Brennett, said, "Gideon had created a way to make a *snathad* work either way."

The woman Councillor's mouth fell open. "That can't be possible. A *snathad* can be used to distribute elements, to *elementals,* but not extract them; that's such a specialist discipline, the training lasts years, he couldn't have–"

"He did." Ren realised it was her own voice that had spoken. She didn't look at any Councillor, or Priya, but Grey, who was nodding. "Grey took my Aether using it."

"So," the woman was saying, "say it was possible, and Gideon was successful; he had Renée captured for days, why not extract them then."

"The host," Ren said, "the recipient of the element needs to already possess it. Or, have the person you're extracting from willing to kill them. He drugged me, to try to get me to force them into a wall of dead magic."

The woman blinked. "A wall – why did he have a *wall* of

dead magic? Only a *dannsair marbh* could–"

Beside Ren, Murryn was nodding.

The woman blanched. "No." She stared between Murryn, Odo and Ren. "A...I mean, he had been looking pale whenever he bothered to show up to meetings lately, but I thought it was a lack of sunlight. He was always so engrossed in his research, I never..."

Odo placed a wrinkled hand on the woman's shoulder, before addressing the rest of the room. "The *snathad* he used on Renée has already been taken in for testing. It was found with what appears to be human bone, though it is unclear why."

And then everything made sense.

She knew she had to speak, but it took the words a long moment to come. When they did, her voice was small. "He saw NáDarra as life. And that's what he wanted: life. Because he'd already mastered death."

The woman looked as confused as ever. "That doesn't make sense. How did Gideon not have life?"

"*He* did," Ren said. If any of them looked at her eyes, they would see the threatening tears that had gathered. She swallowed, hard. The bones. At least two had been long, sturdy things. Several had been tiny. "The bones belonged to his wife, C-Cora, and his daughter. I don't know what her name was, though. I wish I did."

She was answered by three echoes, one from her mother, one from Odo, and one from the Council woman. "June."

"Her name was June."

For a long while, no one spoke. And it was the woman who eventually broke the silence. "If he really had created a two-way *snathad*, why not use bearers to gather enough elements to...I-I don't know if what he wanted to do was possible."

"He tried," Priya said. "He stopped experimenting with bearers; he only wanted weavers." She swallowed. "And then, once he'd gathered all except Aether, he wanted Ren. At first he said he couldn't have what happened when Ren was born happening to another world..." Her voice was smaller then. "But I don't think it was *really* about that. He wanted to finish his work with Ren's Aether. It ruined quite a lot of his plans when he realised Aether was one of the few that hadn't awakened yet."

"But..." Odo was frowning, beady stare fixed to Ren. "Why? Why Renée?"

Several faces turned to her.

"For the same reason he sent me away in the first place," Ren replied, her throat dry. "Because me being born...was the reason they died."

They dispersed soon after.

Grey, who had spent the entire meeting in silence, looked rather shocked when invited to speak. He had been Collected by another team of Collectors, named Errol and Reah. From what Grey said, they sounded grossly unpleasant, having all but kidnapped him from the bank he'd been working in – at this he had had to explain what a bank, and indeed money, was – and took him to a mirror point outside of Manchester. They had emerged in Ververos, where Grey became very unwell, and had been handed over to Brennett, who didn't look nearly guilty enough, and, eventually, the Zenthion.

He'd escaped thanks to Murryn, who had believed the captured weaver to be Ren, at the same moment the Zeds were facing off against Ren and Brennett.

He rushed through the tale, tripping over several words.

And then he described what it meant to know Ren.

"Like someone gets it, you know?" She offered him a soft smile. She did get it. What only the two of them ever would. "It's not just the magic, which is great and all, it's being ill your whole life and never knowing why. Never feeling too hot or cold – which sounds great, but I've caused others to get second-degree burns because I didn't know when bathwater was too hot, or people have taken my advice on the weather and got the flu, because how the hell do I know whether or not to wear a bobble hat?"

Every pair of eyes was on him, each person listening.

"It's being seen as a bloody freak your whole life because you can't go swimming without nearly drowning some other kid, or nearly causing a church, of all places, to set on fire when you're handed a candle in a stupid nativity play. It's waking up to have the tree your foster mum planted the week before fifty feet high outside your window like you're Jack and you've sold a bloody cow for some beans." Ren didn't know whether to laugh at the blank faces that surrounded them at his words, or hug him.

Grey put a voice to everything she needed to say and more. He understood her in a way none of them ever would.

"You were taken to this, ah, Earth," Odo said, "as an infant, like Renée? We have no records of either of your births, or..." he trailed off, looking rather lost.

Grey looked down then. "Not *exactly* like Ren, no." He swallowed. "I was found by a farmer." When no one spoke, he continued. "The police searched for her, whoever had left the baby in the field, wrapped in a grey blanket."

Grey.

A deep sadness opened in Ren's chest as he spoke. She had, at least for fifteen years, not been abandoned entirely. She'd had a mother. And a father and brother.

He'd had no one.

It was Murryn who pieced several more parts of the mystery together. During her pregnancy, Gideon had been the one to conduct some routine tests every pregnant woman undergoes. He had been the one to detect the anomaly. Eight elements.

Murryn's voice shook as she relayed the way he demanded she terminate the pregnancy, then of how he was admonished by the Council when he'd tried to enforce it. When she told of the night Ren was born, when she stood, shrouded in death, and was given a choice: leave, or give up her daughter.

She hadn't realised leaving would involve travelling quite so far.

"There were three," Odo began, "magical accidents, for that's all we've known them as. Two decades ago. It was never known what caused the devastation." Ren wished to disappear as Odo relayed the numbers. From the Glendale explosion – Grey's birth, they presumed – the death count was a little over two thousand, and from the one reported in Axilion, seven hundred – the Axilion birth had fewer answers, and no twenty-year-old to speak of.

In Loreleith, there were two hundred thousand casualties. The only ones with answers Gideon himself, and those he had killed.

Until then.

Ren wanted nothing more than for the meeting to end. And though she'd spent weeks working out exactly what she'd say once given the chance to confront the Council about the unwarranted and unfair path her life had been forced onto, when gifted the opportunity, she felt very little desire to say much at all. She thought of her list, still in Lance's room in the Lira Village. There was little point to demanding justice for her various ailments, not now. She answered when prompted, explained what she could of everything she had learnt and been told of Gideon's plans.

"Thank you, Miss, ah," he glanced at Murryn, "Lennox."

It stung more than it ought to. "Kincaid," she corrected. Her father's name. *Her* name.

"Of course."

Odo decided then that statements would be gathered from each individual who had been involved in any way with either Gideon, Ren, or Grey.

Both Priya and Anders would face a trial.

No one could quite work out what to do with Brennett. Freed from prison by a Zed, he'd played an integral role in their ploy, only for him to play an equally integral one in thwarting it.

It was Wade, having been regarding Brennett in silence, who offered something of a solution. "If Miss, ah, Kincaid, would vouch for you," he told Brennett, "and what Shae said was right about your aim with that bow, why don't we put that skill of yours to some good?"

Brennett blinked. "Uh."

"I could use someone with that kind of aim."

"You mean like a job?"

"Exactly like a job, Mr. Graves."

Even Lance, Odo decided, would face no repercussions for his part in Gideon's death, given the *extenuating circumstances.* Ren breathed a sigh.

"As for you two." Odo regarded first Grey, then Ren. "As Caerisle law dictates, and has since the day such laws were declared and signed by the first Council of Elects, anyone born on Caerisle soil has, and always will have, the rights of any other Caerisle citizen. This extends to yourselves, regardless of how soon after birth you left.

"As the law of our land dictates, you are entitled to bide here, on our land. You are entitled to sustenance and shelter. And you are entitled to formal, and proper, education – not only of our ways and means, but of how to use, and control, the powers that already exist within you. You have, as any Caerisle citizen has, the right to lead a lawful, and worthwhile, life." Odo paused to draw breath, the room around him so silent Ren would have heard a feather fall. "However, due to the, ah, unusual circumstances surrounding your, ah, infancy, you have every right, should you wish it, to return to the world I have no doubts you both still see it as your home.

"But heed this." He paused, and Ren was certain it was for dramatic effect. "The type of scrystone needed to sustain a pathway to Earth, or any other world, is large and rare, and, thanks to Gideon, now in noticeably short supply. You may go back. But you would never be able to return. One scrystone, one journey. This is all the Council can offer."

Ren suddenly felt very sick. She didn't hear Odo wrap the meeting up, only realising it was over when Lance stood. She followed suit, feeling a great number of things, and yet none, all at once.

Murryn introduced the other Council woman as Phillipa.

Ren tried to speak but found no words and merely nodded at the woman.

She walked with a cane, the handle of which was carved into the head of a python, and she wore a hardened expression that reminded Ren of her old headteacher. She was also, it turned out, Shae and Lance's boss. "Do you know how much of a headache I've had trying to find you two?"

"Aw, Phillipa," Lance said, the corners of his mouth twitching. "We didn't know you cared so much."

The woman was an inch or two shorter than Ren and she blinked up at Lance, her mouth a thin line. "I don't care about *you*, boy." Phillipa jabbed him in the chest twice.

Ren felt each one with a short, buzzing surge.

Lance's eyebrows shot up as he lost the battle to conceal his smile.

"I care about your job being done. A job the pair of you have been absent from for nearly *two months*, may I add."

"You may," Lance replied, then dodged as Phillipa's cane rose. "Agh! Calm down, we're back now."

"Humph." Then, for barely a second, Phillipa almost smiled. It took years off her. "I expect you back at your desks." She turned on her heel and strode towards the door, her purple robes lifting behind her as she did.

"When?" Shae asked.

Phillipa didn't turn back. "Right away."

Lance looked disgusted. "What, *now*?"

"Oh goodness, Mr. Allardyce, imagine being expected to do your job."

She left without a further word.

"Couldn't agree more," Lance muttered, turning to the small gathering made up of Ren, Murryn, Grey, and Brennett. The latter was looming in the background casting a series of dark glances at Odo.

Lance's eyes didn't leave hers. "I don't have to, if you're..."

Ren linked her good arm through his. "I think you do." She managed a small smile. "I'll be fine." Glancing back, to her mother, knowing *that* was a conversation she both ached for and was scared to start, to Brennett, now scowling at nothing, to Grey, positioned on Lance's other side.

His hand clapped Lance's shoulder. "We'll look after her."

Murryn beamed. "Absolutely."

"Well," Brennett said drolly, "they will. I probably won't."

They descended the staircase to the main hall in silence, and there they said goodbye to Shae and Lance. He held her to him as though it were the last time he ever would.

"There's a pub," Shae was saying. "Across the road from the guesthouse you're both staying in, owned by the same woman, called the Everwyn Arms. Just down the main street, on the right. We'll meet you there when we're done."

"*If* we're ever done," Lance said, so low only Ren heard. Then he let go. "Oh, don't be like that," he whispered.

She knew his buzzing was low and pulsing sporadically, like hers. "You're feeling the same thing," she pointed out.

He placed his hand to the back of her head and guided her closer forwards. His lips met her forehead. "*Anam.*"

Behind him, Shae was addressing Grey. "Order whatever you want, say I'll do a few sets this weekend."

"*Co-anam,*" Ren said sadly. It felt wrong, the day after getting him back, that she had to say goodbye. If only for a few hours.

She exited the Council with Grey and Brennett, Murryn, and Ruff, who Ren hadn't noticed had joined them and who, she realised with a start, had placed an arm around her mother's shoulders. The sight jolted her. It had been years, she knew. And it wasn't as though her dad hadn't...there had been weird Amanda, who smelt of fish, and Jen, who owned the Rhino Cafe and had sold Ren her first car. She'd always come to their house armed with raspberry and white chocolate cheesecake, Ren and Luke's favourite.

Ren swallowed, trailing at the rear of their odd group. Perhaps a part of her had always wondered, hoped, that maybe she would see her mother and father together again.

An absurd, unrealistic fantasy, of course.

Outside, the sun was high, the sky cloudless. The specks of white Air magic were hard to spot. She glanced at Grey and hoped he loved it, the sight of them dancing and looping and twirling across the sky, as she had.

Almost the entirety of the winding, sprawling city of Steerpike was visible from the top of the hill the Council sat upon. It was colourful, even from this angle, and bustling beneath the midday sun. Down to their right lay the sea, and the beach.

Murryn, breaking away from Ruff, took Ren's arm in her own. "I know, darling," she said simply. "I know."

They started down the cobbled path, past passers-by, and carts led by horses. The cat-sìth, who'd sat obediently below Ren's chair for the entire meeting, trotted ahead, still carrying its two balls of yarn. Brogan, she assumed, had gone with Lance.

Her dad was a big believer in following your heart over your head, and Luke – lovely, logical Luke – had been the exact opposite. *He might have made a good arcanist*, she thought sadly. Ren had never known which side she favoured. Not that it mattered. This wasn't a case of her heart *or* her head. This was one side of her heart pitched so cruelly against the other the very notion of such a choice ought to be criminal.

"I think I always knew." Ren kept her voice low. "That it would come to this."

"It was inevitable, really," Murryn agreed.

"What will you do?" Ren asked, watching the streak of grey that cascaded through Ruff's hair.

Murryn squeezed Ren's arm. "I didn't spend all these years

trying to get you back to lose you again."

"But–"

"He knows." Their pace remained leisurely as they continued their descent. "And he understands. Whatever you do, Ren, you'll have me."

Ren tried to hide the few tears that escaped her, though failed.

Murryn sniffed. "I've missed so much."

"Yes...and no. Nothing much happened, really." It wasn't much of a lie. "Th-that night, I never... Mum, I don't remember."

"He was there," Murryn said. "Or, he had some of his crooked Dragon Corps there, waiting. They attacked as we stepped through. I had suspected something would happen; that's why I created the *abairt*." The flash of light. The darkness. The marks. "I pushed you back through, thinking I could take them. I was wrong. I'd spent so long dampening my magic I was weakened."

The words hung, hard and heavy, between them. "He'd put a warrant on my name, my face. As high Councillor, he could have me thrown in any prison in Caerisle without a trial. I couldn't reopen the portal," Murryn said, the bitterness in her voice real and raw, "and I couldn't beat them. So, I ran. They chased me for nearly three years.

"And I spent the time, and the two years after, finding those who would help me. Then, thanks to the Zenthion and a contact I'd made, I learned of his plan to Collect the weavers. So, I waited." Murryn swallowed. "But what a price, to be without you. Without you, when I alone knew you needed to be here, where you could have been taught how to manage the symptoms."

Ren said nothing. Maybe it didn't matter how much she'd endured. For it had given her the time with her dad and Luke. "I finished school. Then all my friends left except me. I worked at the pub when I was well enough – which wasn't that often, to be honest. And I got ill. A lot."

"And y-your dad? And Luke?"

"One is still running the garage and butchering power ballads, and the other has an unhealthy obsession with rugby, and still wants to be a doctor."

"He always did."

The tears that this time graced her mother's pale cheeks hadn't come as a surprise. Her mother's face was starkly like her own, then. Ren had never seen what so many others had always claimed to, but she did in that moment. It had always been that way. Ren was like their mum and Luke like their dad. She supposed she had to ask, and yet it seemed crueller still.

"Mum?"

"Hm?"

The words didn't come easily, fought her with vengeance. "Dad..." She lost the fight.

"When I arrived in Scotland, I had nothing, only you. I'd wrapped you in your shawl, the one that used to be mine, and left. Gideon wanted to kill us both," she added bitterly. "Your dad found me at the side of the road; he'd been picking up some tyres. Thought I was a mad woman – he told me that several times." They passed shops and cafes; across the street stood a store packed with so many books they were sprawling from its doorway. "He wanted to take me to hospital but I wouldn't let him. You know, it never occurred to me to lie to him about where we were from."

"And he just believed you?" It had become difficult to swallow.

"Not initially. But after I lit the wood burner with my bare hands he began to come around." Murryn sighed. "Then we learnt some ex-girlfriend was carrying his baby. He was *so* scared whenever he spoke of it. Not to be a dad – because he was doing that already, with you...but because of her. I think she was on every drug imaginable. What John had *ever* seen in the woman will forever be a mystery to me. She didn't want the baby, or maybe she did. She absolutely wasn't equipped to care for him though. She appeared, in a similar way to how I had, now I think about it, with this tiny bundle. And then left."

"Luke."

Murryn nodded. "The number of comments I got because there were barely ten months between the two of you."

"Luke never knew."

"No," Murryn admitted. "Neither of you did." They were approaching the Everwyn Arms, with Brennett, Grey, and Ruff all exclaiming how in need they were of a beer. "Maybe that was wrong. But by then we'd already forged two birth certificates thanks to your dad's friend Alan."

"Dodgy Alan?"

"No, straight-laced Alan," Murryn replied dryly, earning her a brief jab in the ribs. "I miss that boy every day."

"I'm sure dodgy Alan misses you, too."

Murryn returned the elbow jab as they crossed the threshold. The place resembled some kind of bric-a-brac stall. Tables – some actual tables, others barrels. Some were old crates, littered randomly around the room. The chairs were just as varied. "Anyway, darling, my point – which I've really gone a long way to make – is that while no, John Kincaid is not your biological father, he was there for every appointment, every parents' evening, every bedtime story, every time you demanded to paint his nails, every trip to the caravan…oh, I…you…you know."

She did, and only nodded. Perhaps she should ask. The question pushed its way to rest upon her tongue more than once. She should know, she supposed, who her…she couldn't bring herself to think the words *real father*. She didn't ask. Maybe she would later.

Murryn wiped Ren's tears, and Ren wiped Murryn's, and they joined the others at a nearby table that wasn't a table at all but a large tree stump.

Brennett and Ruff were listening to Grey describing the intricacies behind a rocket-propelled grenade.

Ren sank into a squashy sofa beside him.

"Aha!" A woman, short and plump, with a kindly smile and a taio of lazy, yellow Light specks, greeted them. "I was told to expect two wayward weavers." She looked between Ren and Grey, her eyes crinkling at the sides like Lance's. "Cassidy called in, explained your situation. You both have rooms across the road, for as long as you need. I'm Eve," she added.

Ren felt a lump in her throat as they thanked the woman.

"Now," Eve said, "what can I get you all?"

Each of them settled on beer, and any food Eve was kind enough to grace them with. Which turned out to be a lot.

As the afternoon wore on, her head grew fuzzier. It was welcome. At some point Murryn and Ruff had opted to head for a *wander*, leaving Ren as part of the most unlikely trio she had ever drank with, considering how one had played a part in kidnapping both others.

And yet, they were somehow comfortable. Brennett was happy to relay a constant stream of anecdotes from his and Lance's childhood, most of which had Ren and Grey half on the floor in helpless hysterics. He was telling his latest, which involved Lance's head being stuck in an iron railing for the better part of two days, when Lance himself, flanked by Shae and a woman she didn't recognise, appeared. At the sight of him the three erupted in yet more, alcohol-laced giggles.

"The railing," Grey all but wheezed.

Ren barely caught her own breath enough to reply, "The horse," before Lance, sporting a bemused expression, joined them. He squashed Ren into the centre of the small couch.

"Oh, hello, Lance, it's nice to see you," he said tartly, spreading an arm over Ren's shoulders.

Ren hiccoughed, then laughed harder.

"So," Ren heard Lance say, not that she could see him, her eyes too full of tears. "This is Ren, the girl I'm starting to regret telling you about, that's Grey, and I have no idea who that is, ignore him. And no, I have no idea what drugs they've taken *or* how to get any."

They did, eventually, manage to compose themselves, long enough to say *hi*, and properly meet Rowen.

"Well, Ren," she said, "I've heard so much about you I feel like I know you already."

"And you still *chose* to meet her?" Brennett said, taking a sip of the pint Shae placed in front of him.

"Shut up, Brennett."

Grey snorted.

Ren turned back to Rowen. "You're a Collector, too?"

"Mhmm." She nodded. "The best they've got, really."

Lance scoffed. "Wouldn't quite go that far."

"Oh, I have no doubt you're better than him," Ren replied, deciding she rather liked Rowen. "Where's Brogan?" she asked Lance. The cat-sith had been snoozing by her feet for most of the afternoon.

Lance took a large swig of his own drink. "He's in my room."

"Where's that?"

"Honestly, Ren, you need some self-control. We're having a nice drink with friends; it's hardly the time–"

She elbowed him and brushed a rogue curl away from his eye. He smiled then, and in the dingy light of the pub, his face lit up...

...because of her.

The buzzing was a strong, steadfast thing.

From across the table, Rowen let out a long, "Woah."

"Believe me," Shae said, "it gets tiresome."

As the sun set, the little Everwyn Arms came to life. The pub, with its mismatched furniture and likable landlady, was a bustling hub of noise. Their tree stump table was covered with empty glasses and plates and surrounded by laughter – though Ren had little idea what any of the others were speaking about anymore. At some point she had ended up plonked in Lance's lap, and the pair had spent the better half of the last hour ignoring everyone else present.

"Okay," she heard Brennett say, "as unlike me as this is, and I beg you all don't judge me for it, I'm ready to turn in."

"Where? You don't have a room," Grey pointed out.

"Fuck."

They erupted into yet more laughter as Lance dug in his pocket, producing a set of silver keys. "Shae can show you where to go," he said as they landed on the stump. "Feed my dog," he added.

"All right." Brennett swallowed the remainder of his current beer, then looked at Ren. "Lance says I've got to feed you, so..."

She had to shout over the others' laughter to make her stream of insults heard.

They followed Brennett's lead and headed out into the evening Steerpike air. They watched Shae head uphill, Rowen and Brennett in tow, and bade Grey goodnight. The cat-sìth slunk away, alone, into the balmy night. Then they found Ren's room, a feat made trickier by their continued falling over.

"Fuck." Lance's eyes were roaming her face, even if he was swaying like a leaf in a breeze. Behind them, the door clicked shut. "I really...don't..." He trailed off.

The buzzing surged in the palm she placed at the side of his face. The first time she'd seen his face it had been coated in little more than stubble. Now he sported a full beard, as dark as the hair on his head.

"I know," she whispered.

"Shae says I shouldn't ask you to stay." He blinked and a single tear fell. "He says it's," – he hiccupped – "not fair and it has to be your decision. And I...I know that...so I won't." He looked crestfallen. Lost. A part of her felt the same.

She scanned the room, noting the small desk, on top of which lay what she needed. "Come here." She took his hand. Again, they nearly tumbled over. "I need to show you something."

36

Cassidy was far quicker than Shae when it came to setting scrystones. He whizzed his fingers around the small sphere like the Lightning zig-zagging around his taio. Around him, several glyphs shone. "You sure, Ren?" he asked.

They stood by the marina, where Cassidy had informed them lay several wey lines. The one they wanted was a Fire line. It would lead them directly into the centre of Ververos, to the same mirror point Grey had emerged through. Lance stood on her left, Murryn and Grey on her right. By their feet stood the cat-sith.

"Mhm," she replied, grimacing at the *eileamaid lag* potion she was trying not to spray all over the ground.

Grey was doing the same.

Murryn and Cassidy had swallowed theirs without so much as blinking.

"All right." He scanned the four of them. "There." With a final twitch of his index finger against one of the many symbols that covered the stone, and a flash of brilliant white light, a familiar doorway formed. "Who's first?"

They passed through one by one.

Entering Ververos was like coming back to a place she had known a long time ago. Once again, the sheer size of the gargantuan pines made her stop, her breath hitching somewhere between her chest and throat. With the strange, red hue of the air casting a pinkish tinge everywhere she looked, and specks of both various types of *NáDarra*, and faint ones she realised were *NeòNach,* her view wouldn't have looked out of place in a fairy tale.

Without her extra elements, the *eileamaid* had been the correct dose. She experienced no nausea or head pain, no forced elation. Instead, something akin to a consciousness grew, deep inside. Between the place she connected with her taio, and the forest itself.

When he'd first talked of the place to her, Shae had described Ververos as *inherently magical.* And it was.

It would have been nice, save for the gaping hole that had opened up in her gut.

"Over here." Cassidy guided them left, to a small, grassy clearing, much like the one they'd stopped in days ago. The magic was strong here; not only could she see it, with great swarms of specks hovering in the air around, but she felt something, similar to what she'd sometimes felt on Earth. A connection, between a part of her and something far greater than her. A knowledge she'd never fully grasp, but knew far more of than she once had.

Ren stepped towards him, as did Grey. She felt his hand rest gently on her shoulder as they watched Cassidy.

"All right. Need a few specks from each of your elements, Grey," Cassidy said, while Ren dug in her pocket for the small, wrapped parcel.

Grey held his palm outright, and produced several specks of each Air, Water, Light and Aether. Though the pang she felt at the sight of them was still there, it was less. Grey silently instructed his specks to hover in front of Cassidy.

"Now you, Ren. Don't worry about Lightning, though." He produced those himself with a slight flick of his fingers.

Ren passed the parcel to Lance and focused on her specks. They came with an almost eager air about them as they erupted from her palm.

Cassidy's eyes locked her own. "This is your only chance."

Lance had placed his free hand on the small of her back.

In her chest, the buzzing was unsettled, her heartbeat racing. Her cheeks felt hot; so did her eyes. "I know."

Cassidy inclined his head forward, and began setting another, bigger, scrystone.

You're going to the other world... She remembered the words as if her father had said them only five minutes before. Ren exhaled as the portal emerged. Both she and Grey gasped. It wasn't Scotland. The city lights beyond the sparse tree line belonged to Manchester. Grey's former home, not hers. And yet the scene in front was so close to the M6, Ren could have reached Ainhill in only four hours.

"Cars," Murryn said. "I nearly *died* when I saw one of those for the first time."

Earth.

Lance let out a small chuckle. "So did I."

Britain.

Grey was silent. Was a part of him pining, for a life that shouldn't have been his, theirs, and yet had been?

Ren turned to him. "You're sure someone will find it?"

"I can't promise," Grey replied, "but this is a popular spot. Plenty of cyclists, dog walkers... I'm sure someone will find it, yeah."

There wasn't enough blinking to quell her tears. Not anymore. They spilt down her cheeks in streams of longing, and loss. She stared down at the small parcel nestled within her palm, then up at Lance. And then back at Britain. No more than a few paces away.

"Goodbye." She threw her arm back. "It's been..." Clutching the parcel in a shaking fist, Ren launched it into the portal. "... an honour." It took all she had to continue. "I love you."

No one spoke, not Cassidy as he closed the portal, and not Lance, who held her as she sobbed against his chest.

It had taken Ren a long time to calm down. Cassidy had set the return stone back to the marina. Each of them stepped through wordlessly. Had she not still been suffering with the after effects of her numerous injuries, Ren would have sprinted back to Eve's guesthouse.

Once she'd trekked her way back to her room, not caring to join in with Lance and Murryn's brief small talk, she had remained there, entirely, for six full days.

Apart from the cat-sith, she allowed only Lance and Murryn in. And only once did she allow either Shae or Grey to join her. Ren had no idea why they still bothered, for she barely spoke. There was a tightness in her chest that hadn't left since they'd arrived back in Steerpike. Stomach cramps had plagued her, as had nausea, both helped and worsened by Lance forcing her to eat. Every part of her felt heavy, her heart most of all.

By early afternoon, exactly a week since Ren had given up ever seeing her father or Luke again, during one of the few times Lance had gone into work, a sharp rap on the door pushed images of her dad temporarily from her mind.

Running a hand through her, admittedly very greasy, hair, Ren padded across the small room. Each step felt like wading through treacle.

Three familiar faces greeted her. One squealed while another offered her an encouraging smile. The third informed her she looked like shit.

"Cheers," Ren mumbled, voice muffled against a mass of blonde waves, shooting Brennett as much of a glare as she could muster over Brielle's shoulder. Though really, where was the lie? Her room had a small mirror over on the far wall and Ren had been vehemently avoiding the sight of herself for days.

"Oh, Ren," Brielle said. Taking a half step back, she held Ren's shoulders at arm's length. She wore a dress made from a scarlet scarf, almost shade for shade with her eyes. They were sparkling, though darkened as she looked at Ren. Her hair was loose, though free from twigs. "You've looked better."

"I know."

Brennett let out a laugh. "Understatement of the year." Then, as she opened her mouth to argue, he held up a hand. "Get up. Get washed. Get out of this fucking room."

"No."

"Now, Ren." Brielle's brows knitted together. "You must."

"I–"

"We aren't asking," Brennett said.

"I agree," Grey said. "We all do. This isn't good for you. This wouldn't be good for anyone."

The statement was hard to argue with. As was the smell Ren was fairly certain was emanating from her. She gave them a small nod.

"We'll be across in the pub," Brennett informed her. "If you aren't there in half an hour, I will personally drag you out of here and throw you in the sea."

Gray looked mildly alarmed. "That seems a tad extreme."

"And," Brennett continued, "since you can't control Water now you'll probably drown and die, and then we'd be stuck with Lance moping around forever."

Ren blinked at him. "I can see how awful that would be for you."

"Good," he replied. "See you in half an hour."

Grey, at least, had the decency to throw her another brief smile. "See you."

Brielle, on the other hand, didn't follow, and instead, pushed her way into the room.

"Oh, you're staying?"

"Yes," Brielle replied, holding up a brown bag Ren hadn't noticed as her red eyes travelled up and down Ren's form. Her forehead wrinkled as she took in the sight of Lance's oversized shirt, the one Ren had taken to wearing throughout her entire isolation. "And it's a good job I'm here." From the bag, Brielle pulled first something squashy, and blue. Ren nearly burst into tears at the sight of Luke's jumper. "You're welcome," Brielle said, voice warm.

They entered the Everwyn Arms arm in arm forty minutes later. Ren had washed, and was dressed in another of Brielle's masterful scarf tops, this one black, laced through with a gold thread. A similarly coloured ribbon was braided through her hair. Brielle herself, wearing only her own red scarf and a little too smug grin, sat herself willingly beside Brennett.

Ren couldn't help glance between the pair as she took a seat opposite. At her feet, the cat-sìth stretched and yawned. It had been out prowling the Steerpike streets for the whole of the previous night. "So, you two are friends now, or–?"

Brennett shrugged. A perplexed look had settled on his face as Brielle began to sing some jaunty folk tune. Clearly the blonde, with her bare feet and intrinsic brightness, was an anomaly to him. "I have no idea. A month ago I'd have happily had all of you beaten and sold in exchange for several barrels of gold. Which I'd then have traded for something more useful."

Brielle wrinkled her nose. "Hush and drink your beer."

He did, then said, "I'm not sure what the fuck has happened to me these past few weeks."

He would be due to start work with Wade soon. Ren wondered for the first time what that would involve.

"Clearly," Grey was saying. "You're a changed man."

Brennett only grunted.

They were nursing their third round when Grey turned to her. "I found a name."

Her mouth dropped open. "Yours?"

He shook his head. "My mother's...maybe."

"That's huge, Grey."

418

"Yeah." He ran a hand through his hair. It was longer now. It sort of suited him. "Yeah, I suppose it is."

"Where?" Then she broke into a smile – the first since before they had travelled to the mirror point. Two figures entered the dimly lit room. Her stomach did a small flip flop at the sight of him. Tired, and dirty. Her favourite version of him.

"Her most recent details show Loreleith."

"We'll be there later in the year." Grey only nodded at her words as she shimmied over. Lance and Shae – and, she realised, Brogan, too – joined them. "Hi."

He planted a soft kiss on her temple. "You look..." his gaze trailed downwards, "good."

"So do you," she said, keeping her voice low. "Hi," she offered to Shae as Lance let out a series of small coughs.

"After this," Brielle proclaimed, taking a sip of something purple and fizzy, "we should go to the beach."

Her suggestion was met with a general murmur of agreement, and a realisation that Ren hadn't needed to construct a plan in what felt like a very long time.

Less than an hour later they made their way down various cobbled streets. None were the same. Neither were the buildings. Without any transportation, except for a few horse-drawn carts here and there, the roads were full of people. No one glanced twice at a man sitting cross-legged near the centre of the street, surrounded by paints and pallet knives and a canvas the size of a door, nor at the two old ladies perched in identical rocking chairs.

They ambled towards the bay, the afternoon sun hanging low in the sky. It didn't take long to arrive at the marina. Several boats were docked there. And though they had to keep *ssshhhh*ing Brennett, who kept proclaiming loudly how he'd go about stealing each one, the journey was peaceful, and calm, smelt like fish and sounded like wind and seagulls. Being by the sea, Ren decided as she looked out across the bay, held a certain appeal that was universal.

People, some robed, some not, some with taios, and others

without, couples, some in groups like theirs, milled around the seafront. Soft music was playing from what seemed like the very air around them.

The beach lay to the side of the marina. It was quiet; not many others were interested in a late afternoon trip to the sea. They settled around one of several metal fire pits that were dotted about the sand. Lance and Grey busied themselves finding wood, which Ren lit. And there they stayed, the six of them, eight including the cat-sith and Brogan. The latter was emitting a series of *a-roo*s every time the feline insisted on booping his snout, purring loudly with each hit.

In time, they broke off into pairs. Brennett disappeared with Shae in search of some form of sustenance, while Brielle explained faedrism to Grey.

Ren and Lance sat in almost complete silence, his arm flung round her neck, hers across his back. Her other one hung, still useless, by her side. The scent of saltwater was strong, though not everything was.

"I can't see them as clearly now," she admitted. "Water, and Air, and Light, I mean. Aether too, but I never really understood that one."

Lance twirled a few strands of her hair around a finger. "You've been so brave."

Ren didn't feel brave.

The sun dipped as the light of the day was replaced by the cool evening air, and Shae and Brennett returned, clutching several packets of something that smelled incredibly familiar.

"Holy shit," Grey said with a gasp. "I never thought I'd see fish and chips again."

And perhaps it was the fish and chips, or perhaps it was the way her neck buzzed against Lance's touch, or perhaps it was simply them, all of them, but for the first time, since long before she had sent her parcel and handwritten note that she prayed each day some kind soul had picked up and followed her carefully scrawled plea of sending north, Ren felt a small semblance of hope. Maybe things would be okay.

More than okay.

They were joined in different ways and by different things. By the several hundred thousand grains of sand beneath them. By good food and absurd anecdotes. By the sound the waves made against the shore. By partnership and by brotherhood. By understanding, and by, in many ways, what should have been impossible. By two souls bonded together as one, and by the knowledge that each of them had been there, *were* there, and would be again.

Through friendship.

No. Ren leant closer into Lance, resting her head into his chest. Not friendship.

"You told me once you believed family was something that can be forged, with anyone, from the darkest of places."

His breath was warm on her forehead. "I did."

She sought each of them in turn, lingering, last of all, on Lance. "Do you still believe that?"

"I do," he replied simply.

The fire crackled and popped, and specks of red rushed upwards, sparking above the flames.

Joined, each of them, by a number of things. But maybe most of all through something else. Something bigger and greater than each of them.

Family. Not one she had been handed at birth, nor one she'd chosen.

But one where each member had been thrust into her life with, in their own ways, an unparalleled fierceness.

And maybe that would be what kept them there, for as long as each of them would have her.

The End

Dear Dad

You told me once – no, actually, you told me several times – your happiness is one you'd trade, if it meant me finding mine. I hope that's still true. I hope it's still true enough for you to forgive me. Forgive me for staying here.

I think somehow you always knew I wasn't meant for our world – your world now, I suppose. You told me often enough I was meant for more.

Turns out you might have been right.

Even if a part of me wishes that wasn't trueI want you to know I did what you told me to. I found her. And she's okay.

We both are.

And I found something else. I'm sounding poetic and annoying here, aren't I? Anyway, I found happiness. He's called Lance and I think you'd get on.

I also found magic, though I had to give some of it away. Don't ask; it's a long and boring story.

It's incredible, really. A lot about this world is.

I miss you, though. And I'll never stop. Nor will I ever stop repeating the words to 'It's a Kind of Magic' over and over because – although it's oddly fitting now I think about it – it's how I remember you the most.

I miss you. I miss Luke. Tell him everything, if you haven't. And tell him to become the best damn doctor Scotland has ever seen.

Tank you for loving me as hard as you did, when you didn't ever have to.

Love, Ren

Pronunciation Guide

Còmhla mar aon	Coh-la mah roon
NáDarra	Nah-dah-rah
NeòNach	Nay-oh-nach
Bodach	Baw-duch
Crodh-mara	Crow-mah-reh
Caeracre	Care-acre
Caerisle	Care-isle
Eileamaid lag	Eel-ae-mah lag
Faren	Fah-rin
Cat-sìth	Cat Shee
Cù-sìth	Coo Shee
Fuath	Foo-ah
Anam	Ah-nam
Co-anam	Coh-ah-nam
Abairt	Ah-bursht
Dannsair marbh	Dan-sair mah-rab

Suzanne Rho

Acknowledgements

Thank you to Luca, it was your developmental feedback that took my plot hole-riddled hot mess of a manuscript and sent me on my way to crafting it into what I pray resembles, well, maybe not quite a diamond, but perhaps a rather nice garnet.

To Nick, my editor, thank you for your professionalism, hard work, and kind words. Your work took Ren's story and gave it the thorough polish it - and she - deserved.

To Kaitlyn, my proofreader, your service was invaluable, incredibly thorough, and so greatly appreciated.

To Franzi, my endlessly talented designer, thank you for the life and love you breathed into Power's cover.

There are some services you never really think you'll need in life. One of mine was a Gaelic expert - thank you Michael.

I began this journey years before *Power* was even a concept, by dabbling within a world I didn't create, and with characters who weren't my own. A necessary step, without which *The Power of the Eight* wouldn't exist. There are too many of you to mention, but to every person I forged a friendship with along the way, thank you. To *Fairest*, thank you for showing me what it was to feel worthwhile, and useful, and for teaching me it doesn't matter how small a thing may be, if it does a little bit of good, and makes one person feel a little less alone, it's worth doing.

To Jodie, and the friendship I didn't know I needed. Thank you for writing, and creating with me, for leaving one world and diving into another with me. For the madness that was the *101 Dalmations* retelling that cemented the fact that you're never leaving my life. For every step we've taken, and for every win. Thank you for being the reason I don't feel alone in the big, scary world of *real* books, and the even scarier world of real life.

To Cheyenne, I am endlessly grateful to the *Game of Thrones* discussion threads that forged what, quite frankly, might be the greatest dinosaur-centric friendship two people could ever have. Thank you for reading, and championing, everything I've ever written. You mean so much more than you know.

To Sami, thank you for over fifteen years of friendship, and for being the first person to ever tell me Ren's story meant something.

Thank you to my parents, and to the old, battered copy of *The Lord of the Rings* my father pretended to have read whilst courting my mother. Thank you for raising me to understand the meaning of community, to harness integrity and appreciate good music, good stories, and the understanding that, whether it takes the form of a stone wall, a power ballad, or a perfectly poured pint, that which brings us joy is no less important than what sustains our life.

And, finally, *some folks just have one, others they have none –* and how lucky am I, to have each of you? To Aria, Ronin, and Kaiya, you exist in these pages for a reason. However many stories I tell, and however many books I unleash into the wild, they will never truly be my legacy, for it is the three of you. Even when you're grown and carving your own place in this world, I hope, if you ever feel alone, you remember a part of you has a home within these pages. Thank you for showing me how hard I could love, how much I could laugh, and that magic really does exist once you learn where to look.

And to Ross, thank you for holding my hand through the best times, and loving me through the worst. To me, you hold many titles: husband, father of my children, sounding board, confidant, best friend, and the reason coffee percolators, and poker raises, could render me helpless with laughter even at the most inappropriate times. Thank you for making me laugh every day for over a third of my life. And thank you for telling me, far more than any rational adult should need told, that I could do this; even when I didn't believe you, you were right. I love you.

Writer and mother, wife & owner of two mad huskies and one sassy cat, Suzanne Rho is a lover of thunderstorms, music made a few decades before she was born & sentences crafted so beautifully they make the breath catch in your throat.

She fell in love with books around the age of six, with morally grey characters around sixteen and with telling stories in her early twenties. She's been enamoured ever since.

The Power of the Eight is her debut novel.

https://www.suzanne-rho.co.uk

Instagram: @rho.writes

Twitter: @WritesRho

Facebook: Suzanne Rho - Fantasy Author & Cartographer

Lightning Source UK Ltd.
Milton Keynes UK
UKHW012028271021
392940UK00001B/4